MICHAEL TOWNSEND'S

AMAZING GREEK MYTHS OF WONDER AND BLUNDERS

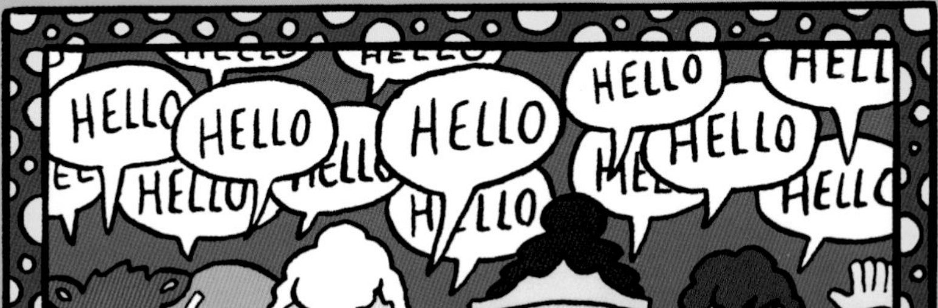
HELLO
HELLO
HELLO
HELLO
HELLO
HELLO

WELCOME TO THE WONDERFUL WORLD OF GREEK MYTHOLOGY

Dial Books for Young Readers
an imprint of Penguin Group (USA) Inc.

PLEASE ENJOY →

DIAL BOOKS FOR YOUNG READERS
A division of Penguin Young Readers Group
Published by The Penguin Group
Penguin Group (USA) Inc., 375 Hudson Street, New York, NY 10014, U.S.A.
Penguin Group (Canada), 90 Eglinton Avenue East, Suite 700, Toronto,
Ontario, Canada M4P 2Y3 (a division of Pearson Penguin Canada Inc.)
Penguin Books Ltd, 80 Strand, London WC2R 0RL, England
Penguin Ireland, 25 St. Stephen's Green, Dublin 2, Ireland (a division of Penguin Books Ltd)
Penguin Group (Australia), 250 Camberwell Road, Camberwell,
Victoria 3124, Australia (a division of Pearson Australia Group Pty Ltd)
Penguin Books India Pvt Ltd, 11 Community Centre, Panchsheel Park, New Delhi - 110 017, India
Penguin Group (NZ), 67 Apollo Drive, Rosedale, North Shore 0632, New Zealand (a division of Pearson New Zealand Ltd)
Penguin Books (South Africa) (Pty) Ltd, 24 Sturdee Avenue, Rosebank, Johannesburg 2196, South Africa
Penguin Books Ltd, Registered Offices: 80 Strand, London WC2R 0RL, England
Copyright © 2010 by Michael Townsend
All rights reserved
The publisher does not have any control over and does not assume any responsibility
for author or third-party websites or their content.
Designed by Jasmin Rubero
Typography by Mike Townsend
Manufactured in China
ISBN 978-0-8037-3308-4

1 3 5 7 9 10 8 6 4 2

TABLE OF CONTENTS

THE BOOK YOU ARE ABOUT TO READ CONTAINS NINE BIZARRE AND WACKY TALES THAT TAKE PLACE IN A GREEK-TASTIC MYTH-O-RIFIC WORLD!!! A WORLD THAT YOU, THE READER, MIGHT NOT BE FAMILIAR WITH. SO, LET'S BEGIN WITH A QUICK INTRODUCTION!!!

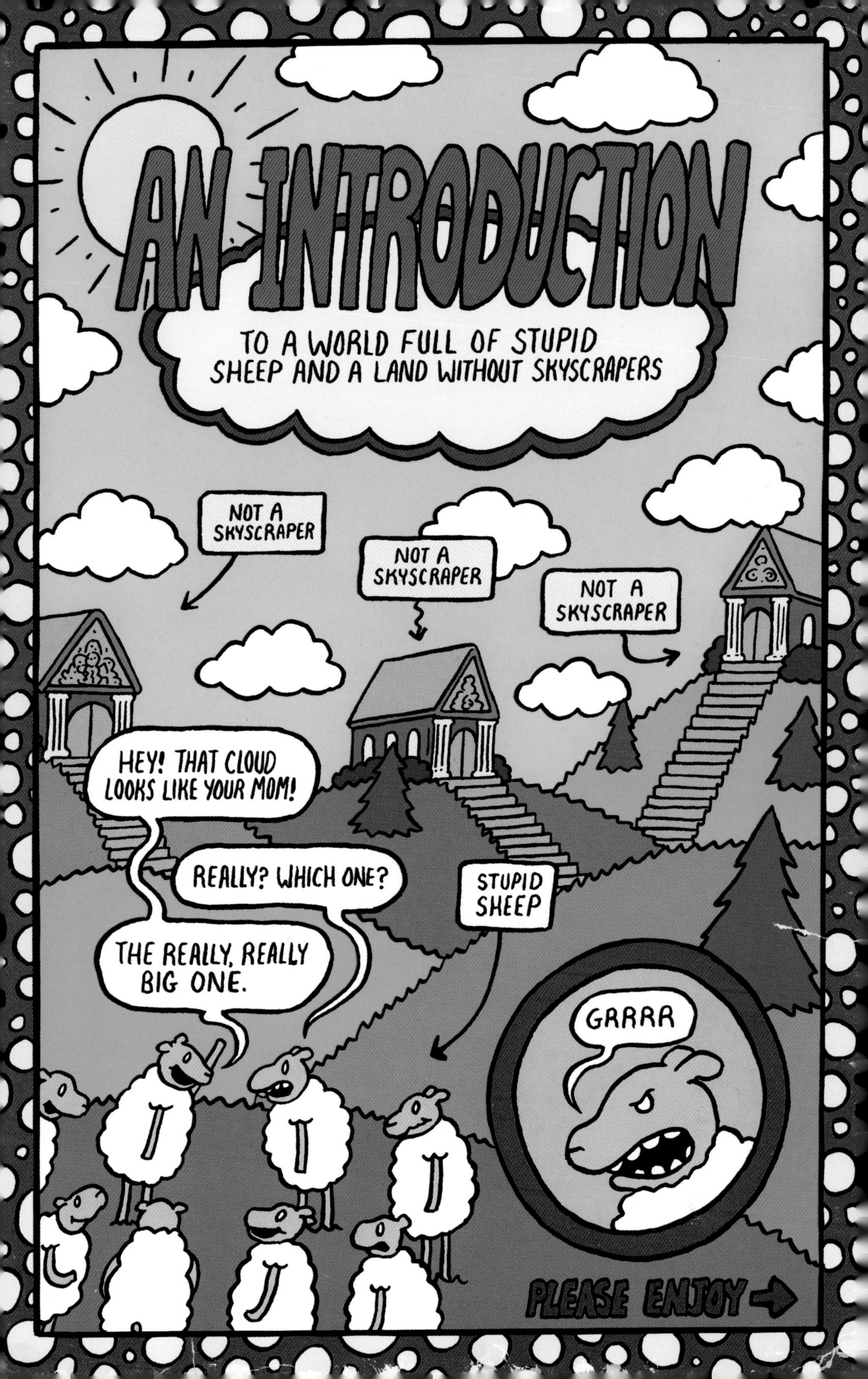

AN INTRODUCTION
TO A WORLD FULL OF STUPID SHEEP AND A LAND WITHOUT SKYSCRAPERS
NOT A SKYSCRAPER
NOT A SKYSCRAPER
NOT A SKYSCRAPER
HEY! THAT CLOUD LOOKS LIKE YOUR MOM!
REALLY? WHICH ONE?
THE REALLY, REALLY BIG ONE.
STUPID SHEEP
GRRRR
PLEASE ENJOY

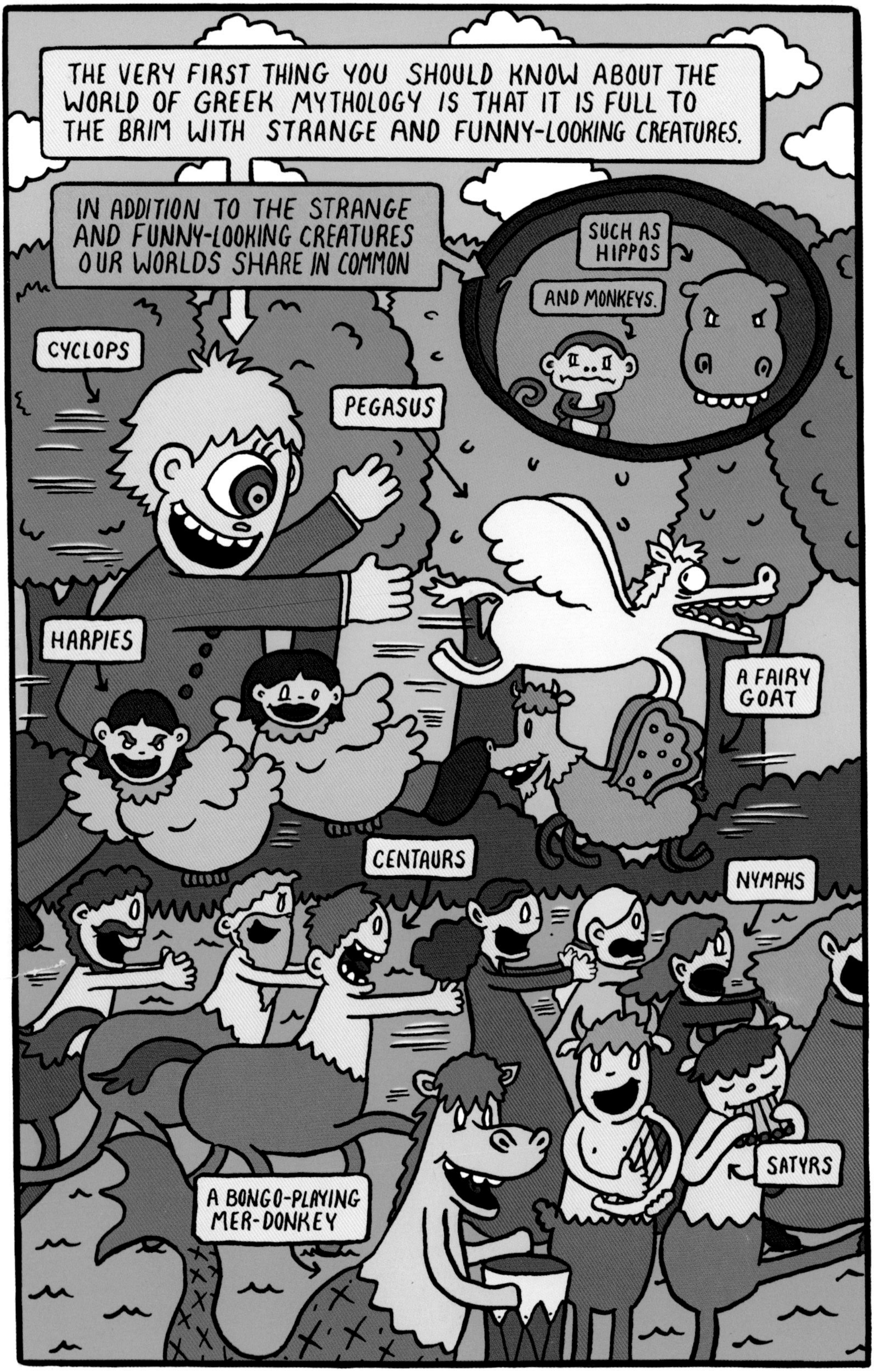
THE VERY FIRST THING YOU SHOULD KNOW ABOUT THE WORLD OF GREEK MYTHOLOGY IS THAT IT IS FULL TO THE BRIM WITH STRANGE AND FUNNY-LOOKING CREATURES.
IN ADDITION TO THE STRANGE AND FUNNY-LOOKING CREATURES OUR WORLDS SHARE IN COMMON
SUCH AS HIPPOS
AND MONKEYS.
CYCLOPS
PEGASUS
HARPIES
A FAIRY GOAT
CENTAURS
NYMPHS
SATYRS
A BONGO-PLAYING MER-DONKEY

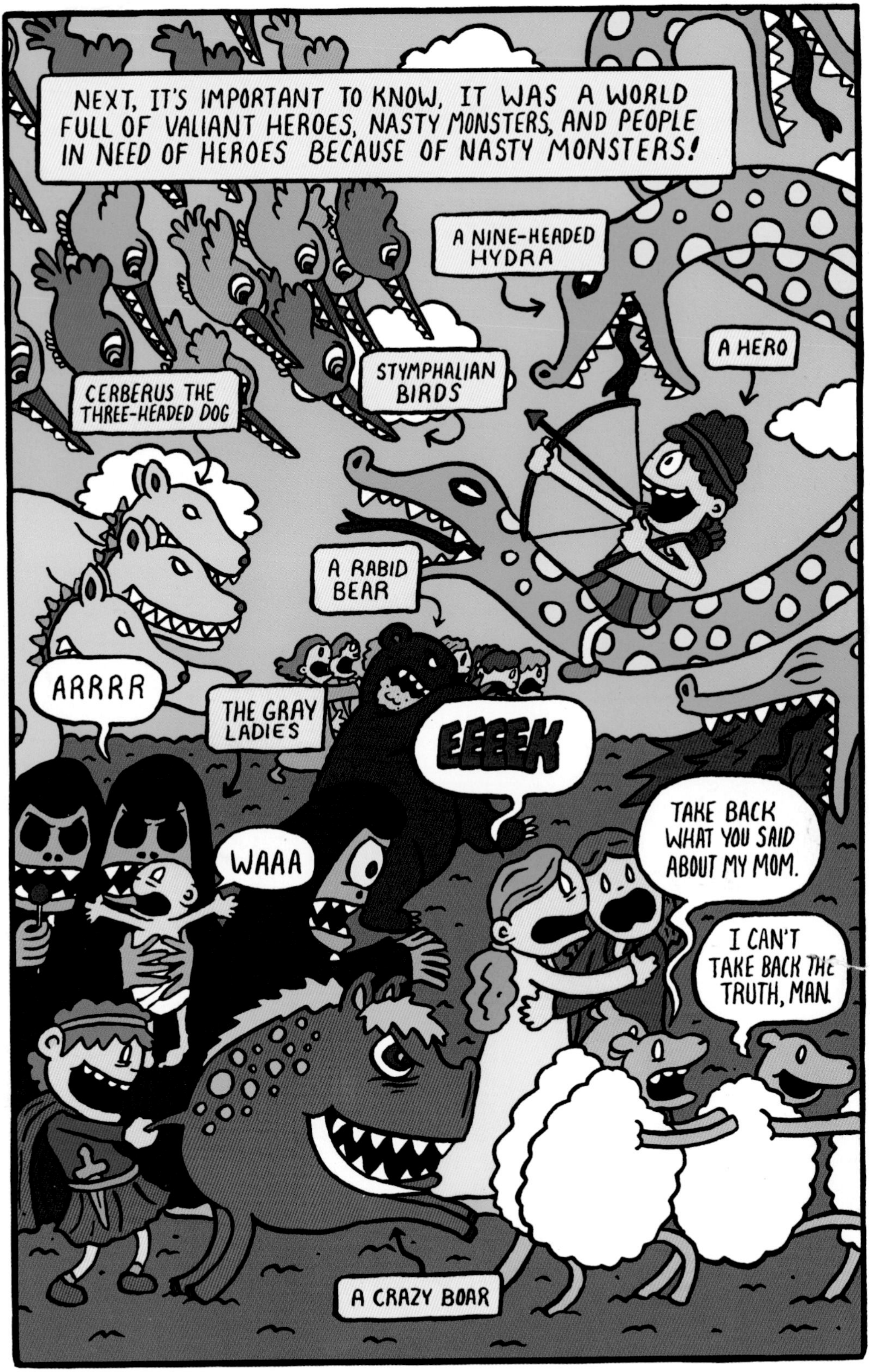
NEXT, IT'S IMPORTANT TO KNOW, IT WAS A WORLD FULL OF VALIANT HEROES, NASTY MONSTERS, AND PEOPLE IN NEED OF HEROES BECAUSE OF NASTY MONSTERS!
A NINE-HEADED HYDRA
A HERO
STYMPHALIAN BIRDS
CERBERUS THE THREE-HEADED DOG
A RABID BEAR
ARRRR
THE GRAY LADIES
EEEEK
TAKE BACK WHAT YOU SAID ABOUT MY MOM.
WAAA
I CAN'T TAKE BACK THE TRUTH, MAN.
A CRAZY BOAR

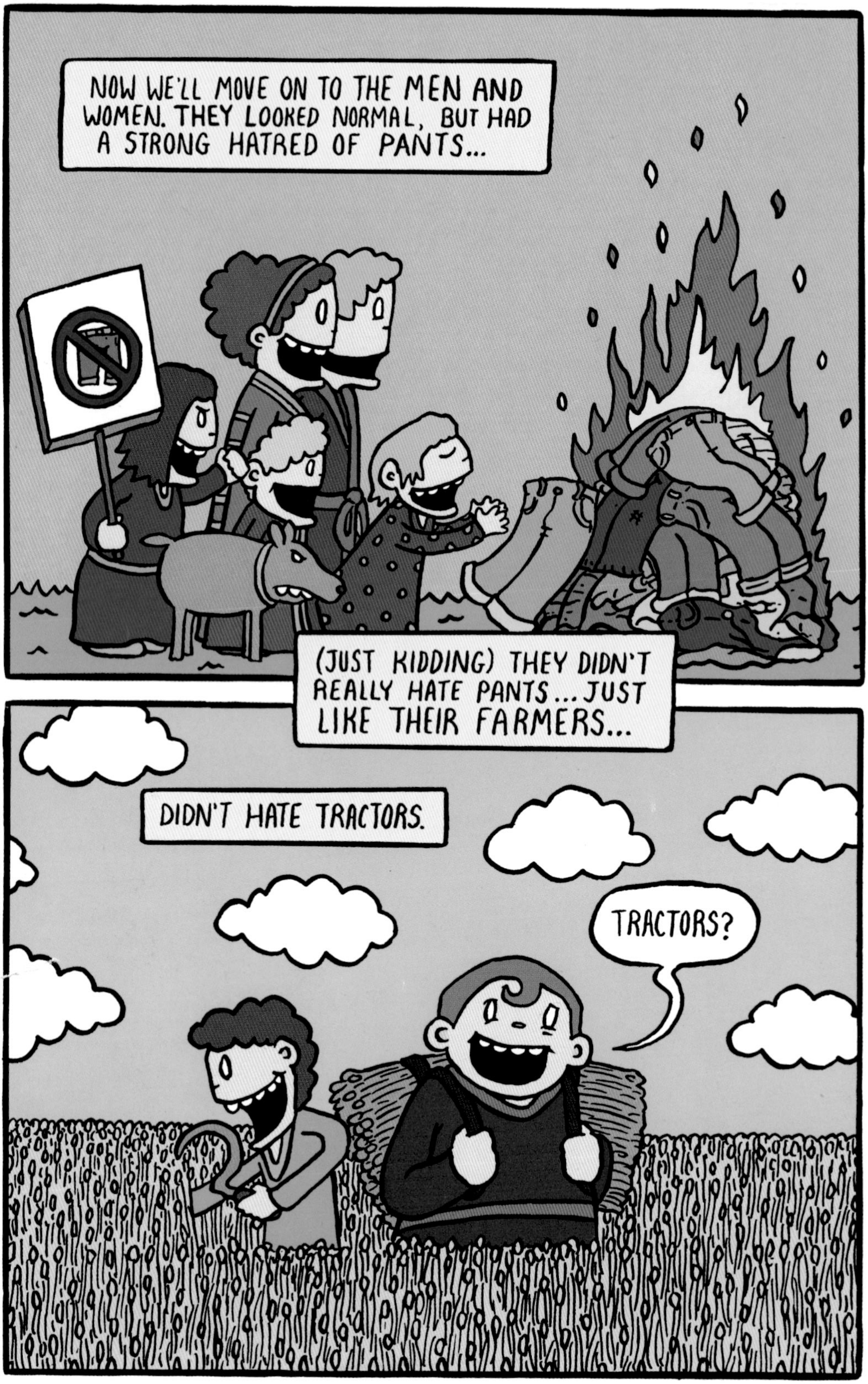

NOW WE'LL MOVE ON TO THE MEN AND WOMEN. THEY LOOKED NORMAL, BUT HAD A STRONG HATRED OF PANTS...
(JUST KIDDING) THEY DIDN'T REALLY HATE PANTS... JUST LIKE THEIR FARMERS...
DIDN'T HATE TRACTORS.
TRACTORS?

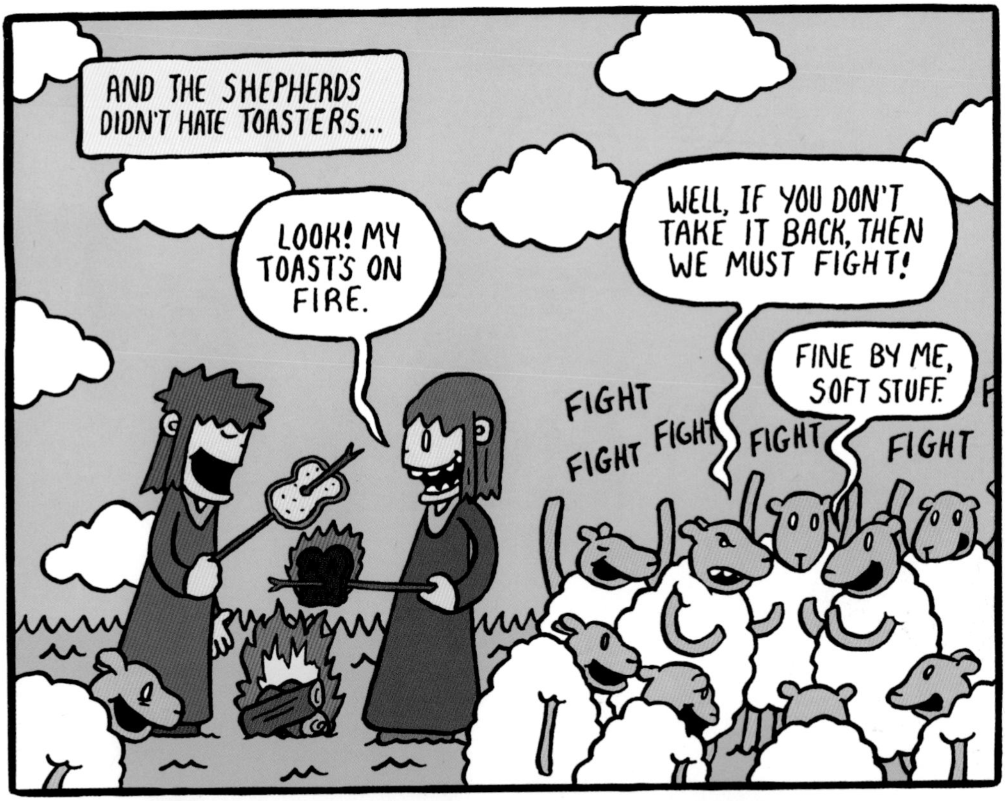
AND THE SHEPHERDS DIDN'T HATE TOASTERS...
LOOK! MY TOAST'S ON FIRE.
WELL, IF YOU DON'T TAKE IT BACK, THEN WE MUST FIGHT!
FINE BY ME, SOFT STUFF.
FIGHT
FIGHT FIGHT FIGHT
FIGHT

THESE THINGS JUST DIDN'T EXIST YET...

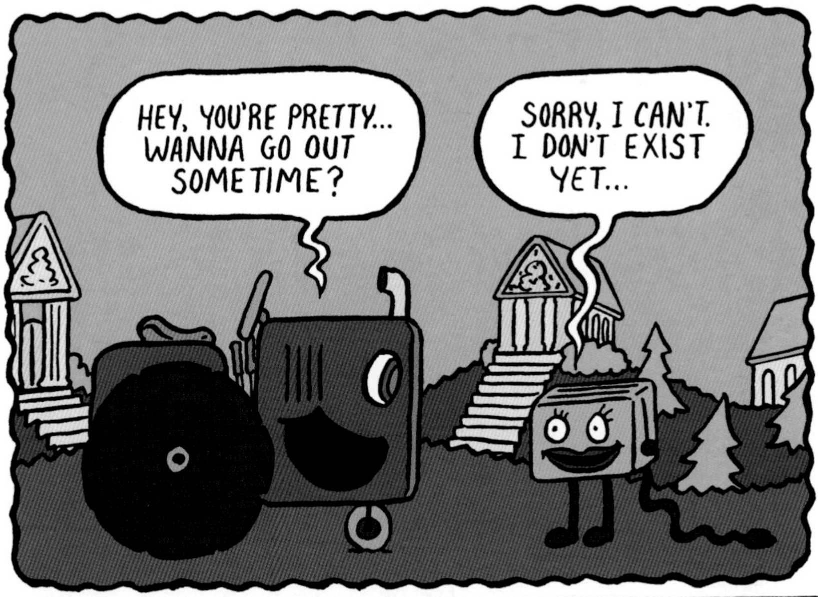
HEY, YOU'RE PRETTY... WANNA GO OUT SOMETIME?
SORRY, I CAN'T. I DON'T EXIST YET...

IN FACT, NO ELECTRONICS OR MODERN MACHINES EXISTED YET.

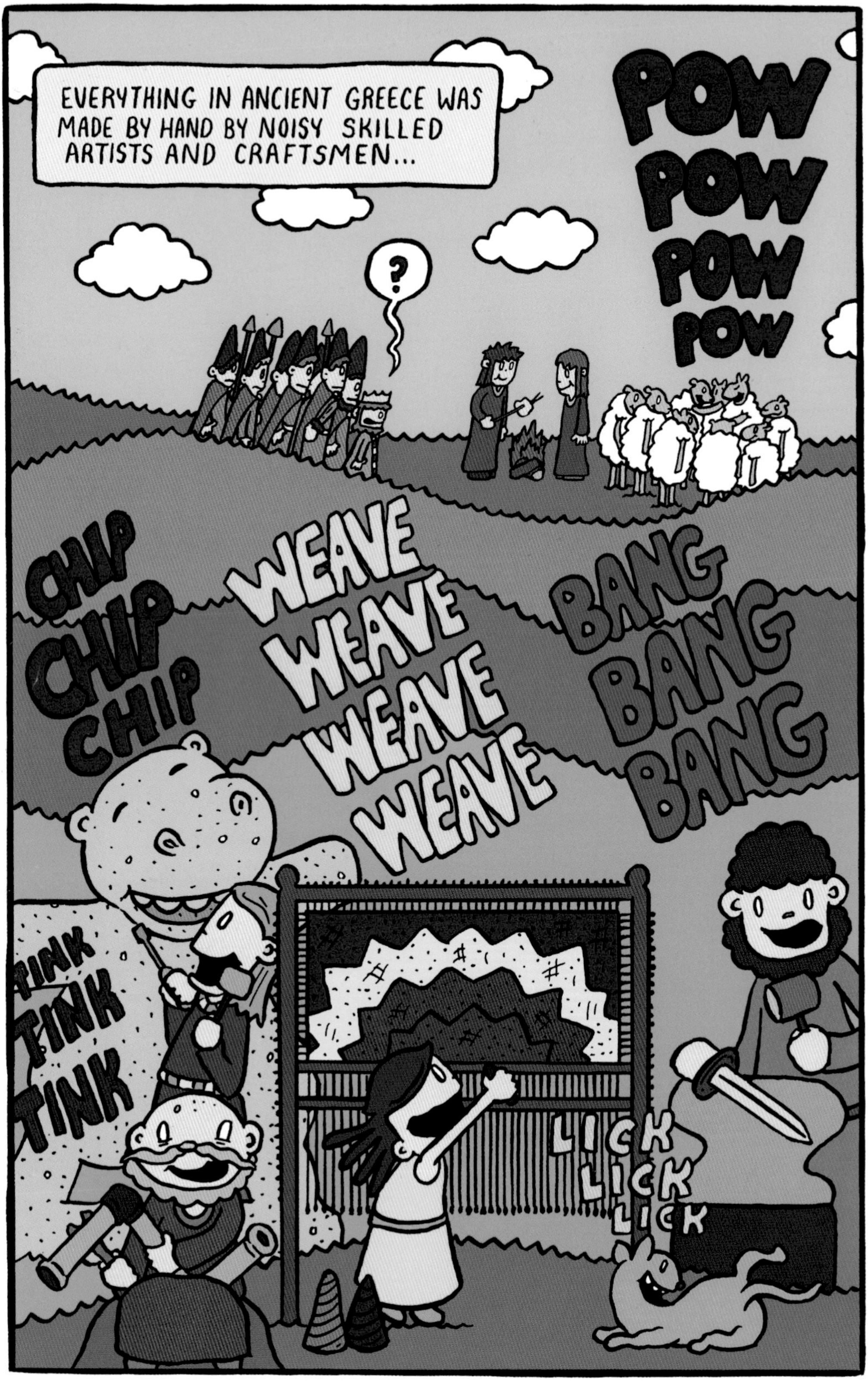
EVERYTHING IN ANCIENT GREECE WAS MADE BY HAND BY NOISY SKILLED ARTISTS AND CRAFTSMEN...
POW POW POW POW
?
CHIP CHIP CHIP
WEAVE WEAVE WEAVE WEAVE
BANG BANG BANG
TINK TINK TINK
LICK LICK LICK

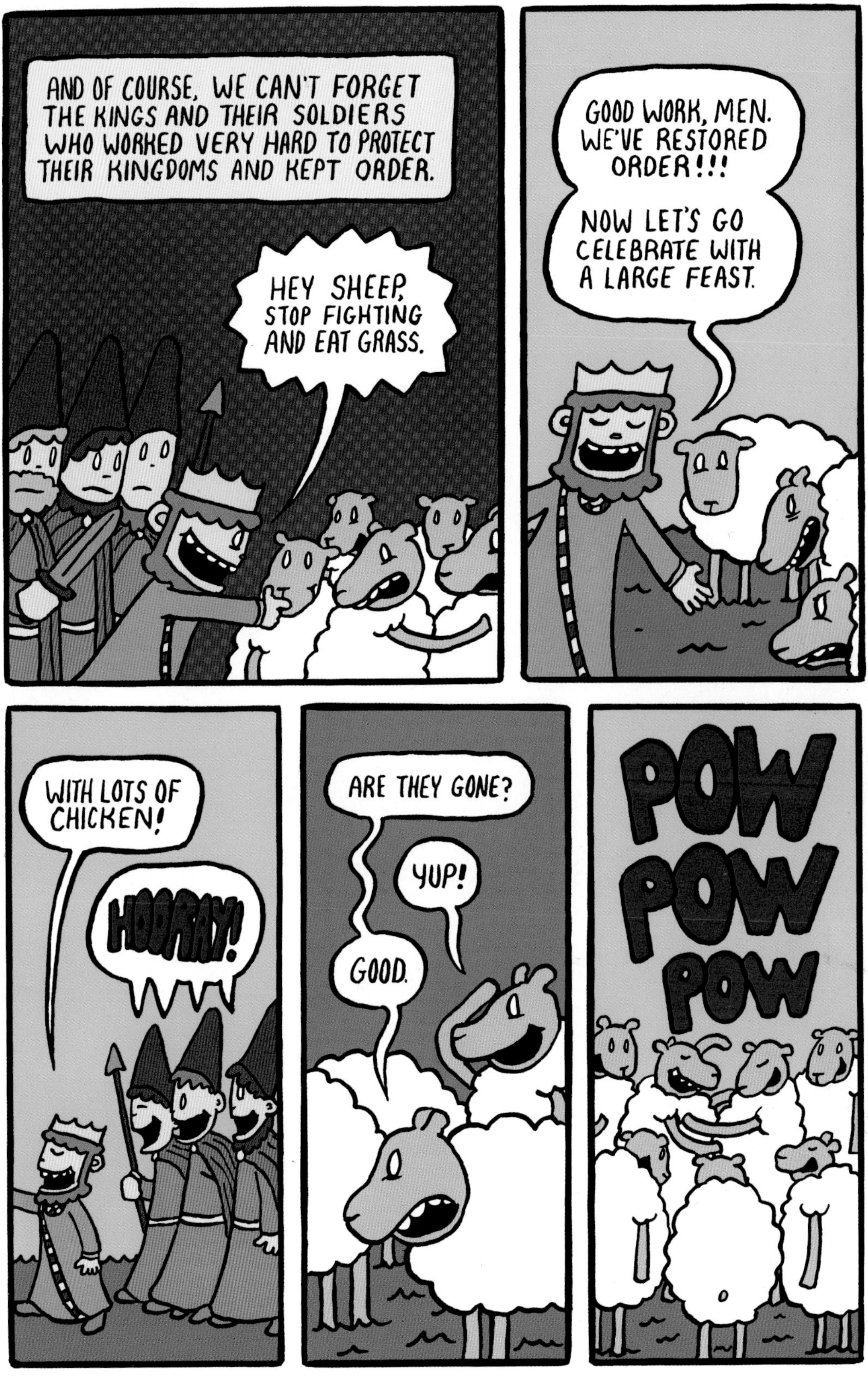

AND OF COURSE, WE CAN'T FORGET THE KINGS AND THEIR SOLDIERS WHO WORKED VERY HARD TO PROTECT THEIR KINGDOMS AND KEPT ORDER.
HEY SHEEP, STOP FIGHTING AND EAT GRASS.
GOOD WORK, MEN. WE'VE RESTORED ORDER!!!
NOW LET'S GO CELEBRATE WITH A LARGE FEAST.
WITH LOTS OF CHICKEN!
HOORAY!
ARE THEY GONE?
YUP!
GOOD.
POW
POW
POW

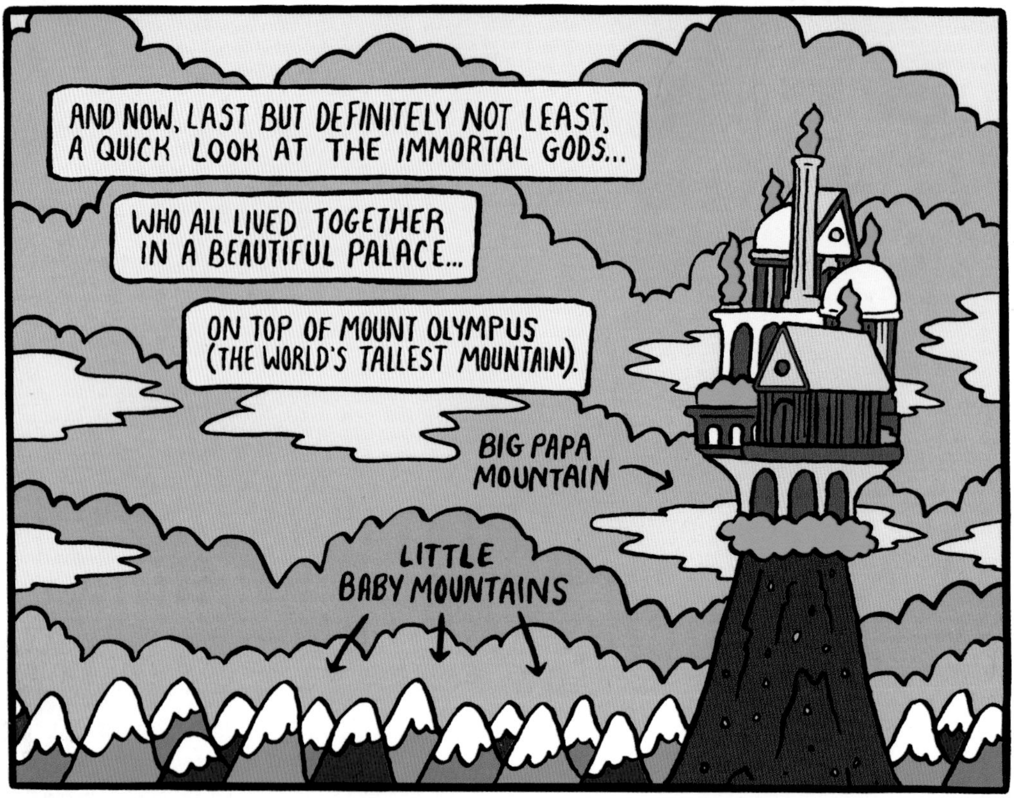
AND NOW, LAST BUT DEFINITELY NOT LEAST, A QUICK LOOK AT THE IMMORTAL GODS...
WHO ALL LIVED TOGETHER IN A BEAUTIFUL PALACE...
ON TOP OF MOUNT OLYMPUS (THE WORLD'S TALLEST MOUNTAIN).
BIG PAPA MOUNTAIN
LITTLE BABY MOUNTAINS

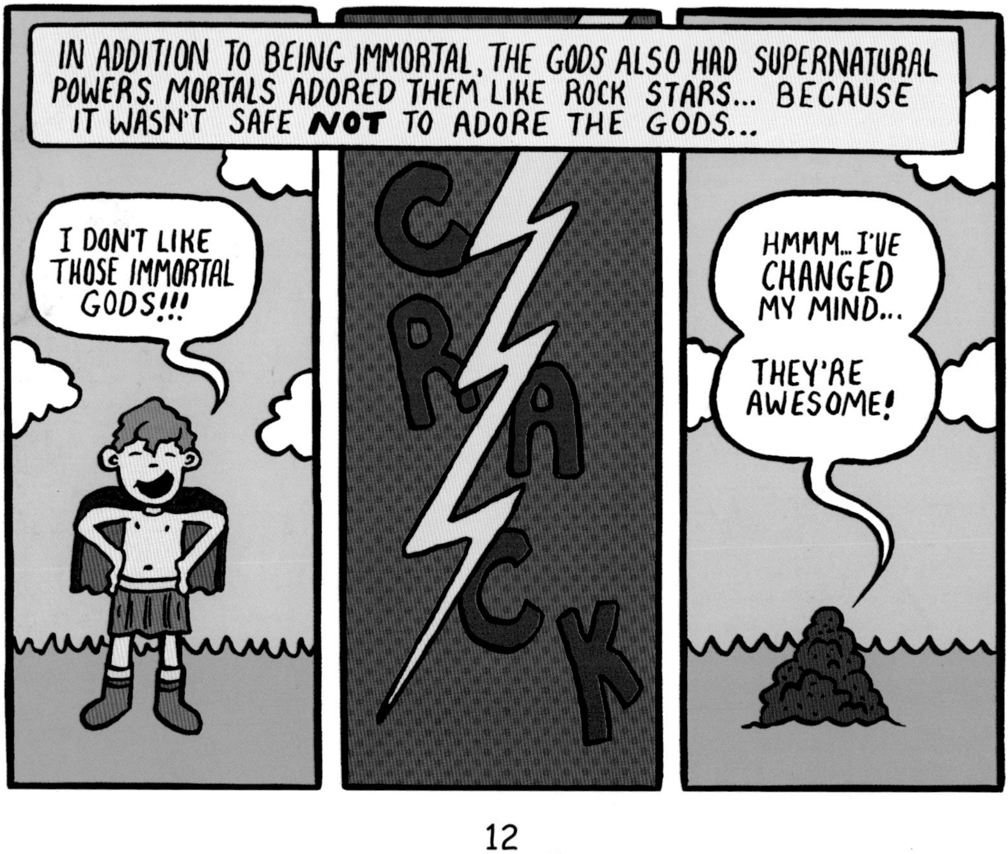
IN ADDITION TO BEING IMMORTAL, THE GODS ALSO HAD SUPERNATURAL POWERS. MORTALS ADORED THEM LIKE ROCK STARS... BECAUSE IT WASN'T SAFE **NOT** TO ADORE THE GODS...
I DON'T LIKE THOSE IMMORTAL GODS!!!
CRACK
HMMM... I'VE CHANGED MY MIND...
THEY'RE AWESOME!

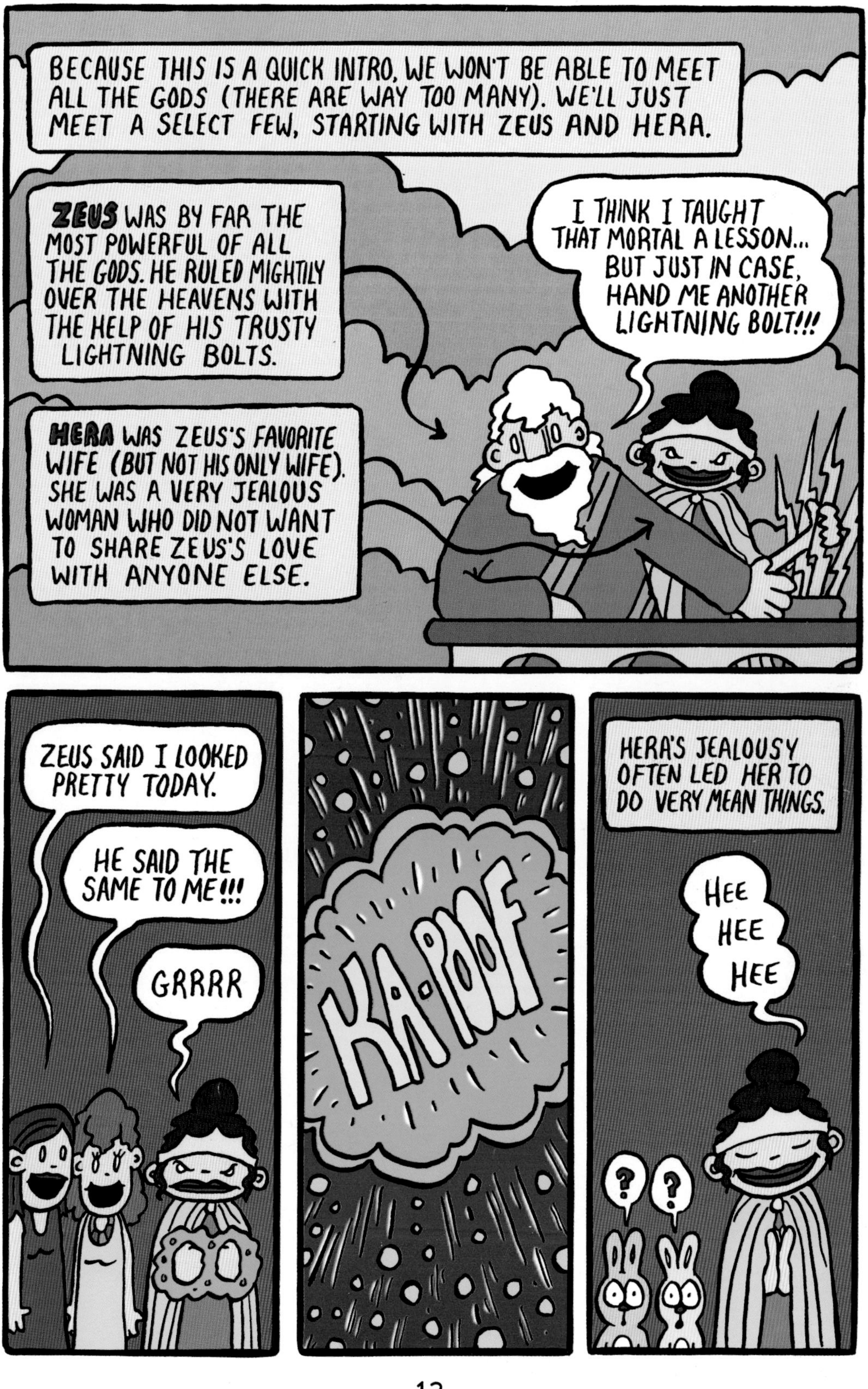
BECAUSE THIS IS A QUICK INTRO, WE WON'T BE ABLE TO MEET ALL THE GODS (THERE ARE WAY TOO MANY). WE'LL JUST MEET A SELECT FEW, STARTING WITH ZEUS AND HERA.
ZEUS WAS BY FAR THE MOST POWERFUL OF ALL THE GODS. HE RULED MIGHTILY OVER THE HEAVENS WITH THE HELP OF HIS TRUSTY LIGHTNING BOLTS.
HERA WAS ZEUS'S FAVORITE WIFE (BUT NOT HIS ONLY WIFE). SHE WAS A VERY JEALOUS WOMAN WHO DID NOT WANT TO SHARE ZEUS'S LOVE WITH ANYONE ELSE.
I THINK I TAUGHT THAT MORTAL A LESSON... BUT JUST IN CASE, HAND ME ANOTHER LIGHTNING BOLT!!!
ZEUS SAID I LOOKED PRETTY TODAY.
HE SAID THE SAME TO ME!!!
GRRRR
KA-POOF
HERA'S JEALOUSY OFTEN LED HER TO DO VERY MEAN THINGS.
HEE HEE HEE
?
?

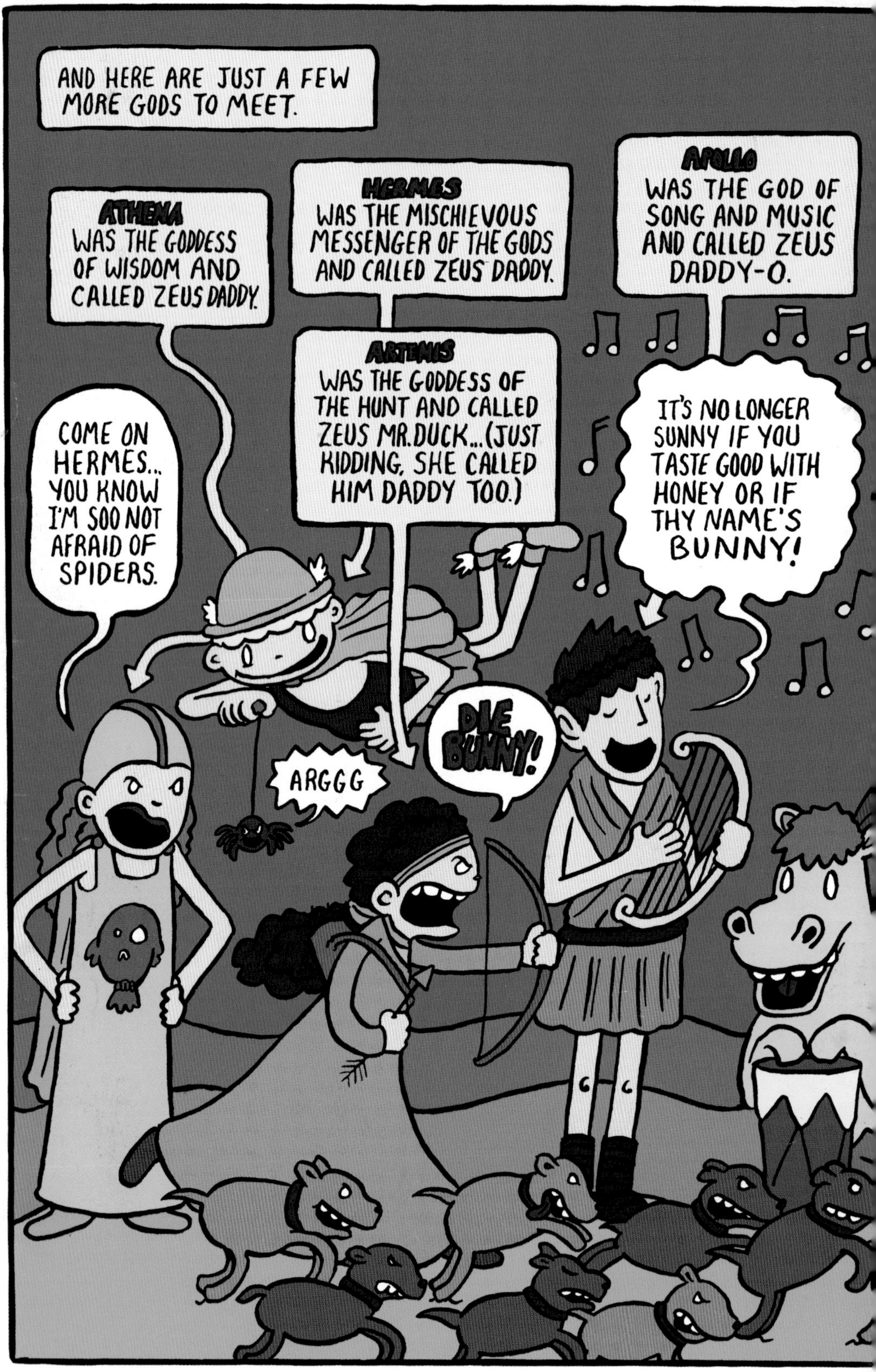

AND HERE ARE JUST A FEW MORE GODS TO MEET.
ATHENA WAS THE GODDESS OF WISDOM AND CALLED ZEUS DADDY.
HERMES WAS THE MISCHIEVOUS MESSENGER OF THE GODS AND CALLED ZEUS DADDY.
APOLLO WAS THE GOD OF SONG AND MUSIC AND CALLED ZEUS DADDY-O.
ARTEMIS WAS THE GODDESS OF THE HUNT AND CALLED ZEUS MR.DUCK...(JUST KIDDING, SHE CALLED HIM DADDY TOO.)
COME ON HERMES... YOU KNOW I'M SOO NOT AFRAID OF SPIDERS.
IT'S NO LONGER SUNNY IF YOU TASTE GOOD WITH HONEY OR IF THY NAME'S BUNNY!
ARGGG
DIE BUNNY!

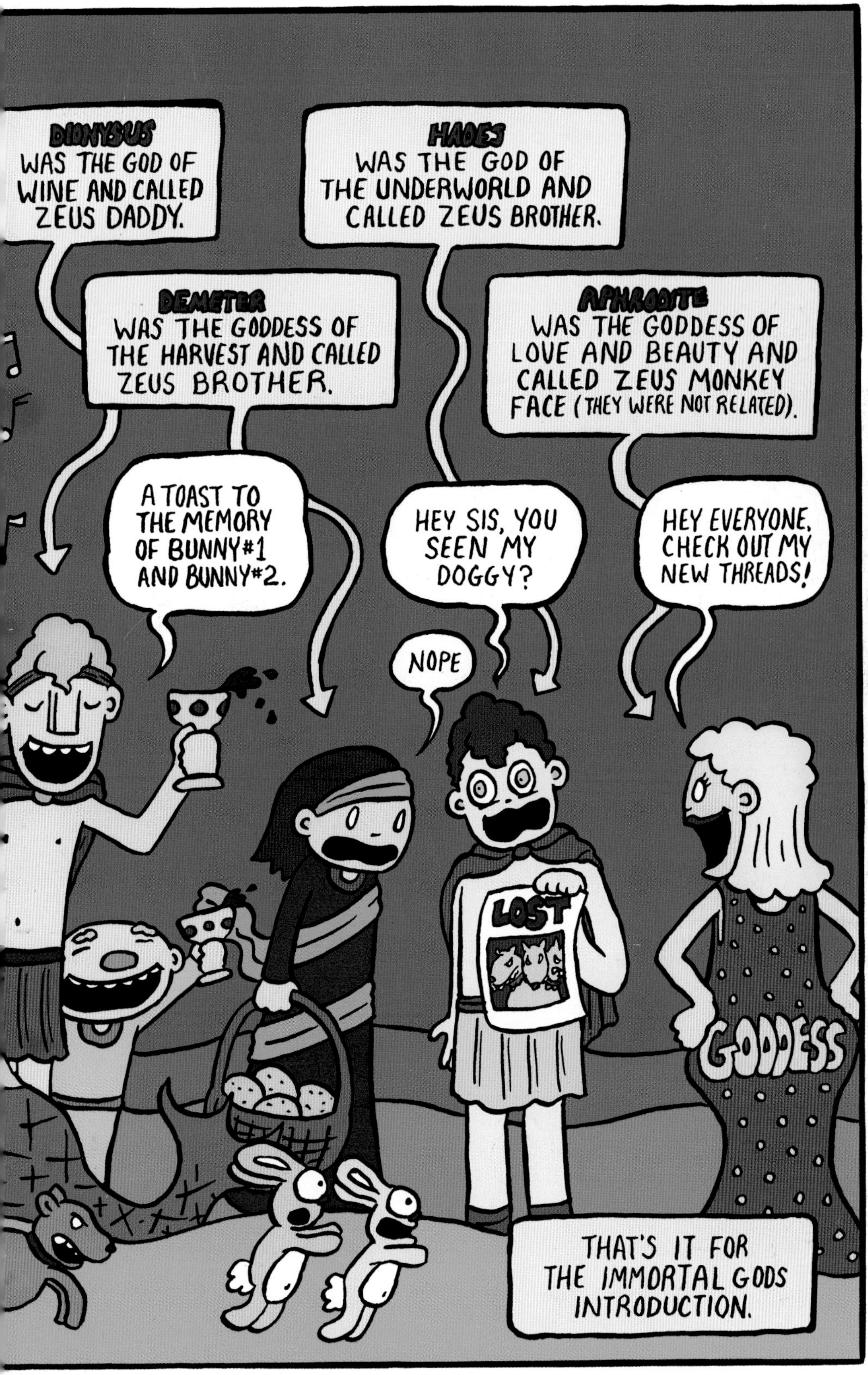
DIONYSUS
WAS THE GOD OF WINE AND CALLED ZEUS DADDY.
HADES
WAS THE GOD OF THE UNDERWORLD AND CALLED ZEUS BROTHER.
DEMETER
WAS THE GODDESS OF THE HARVEST AND CALLED ZEUS BROTHER.
APHRODITE
WAS THE GODDESS OF LOVE AND BEAUTY AND CALLED ZEUS MONKEY FACE (THEY WERE NOT RELATED).
A TOAST TO THE MEMORY OF BUNNY#1 AND BUNNY#2.
HEY SIS, YOU SEEN MY DOGGY?
HEY EVERYONE, CHECK OUT MY NEW THREADS!
NOPE
LOST
GODDESS
THAT'S IT FOR THE IMMORTAL GODS INTRODUCTION.

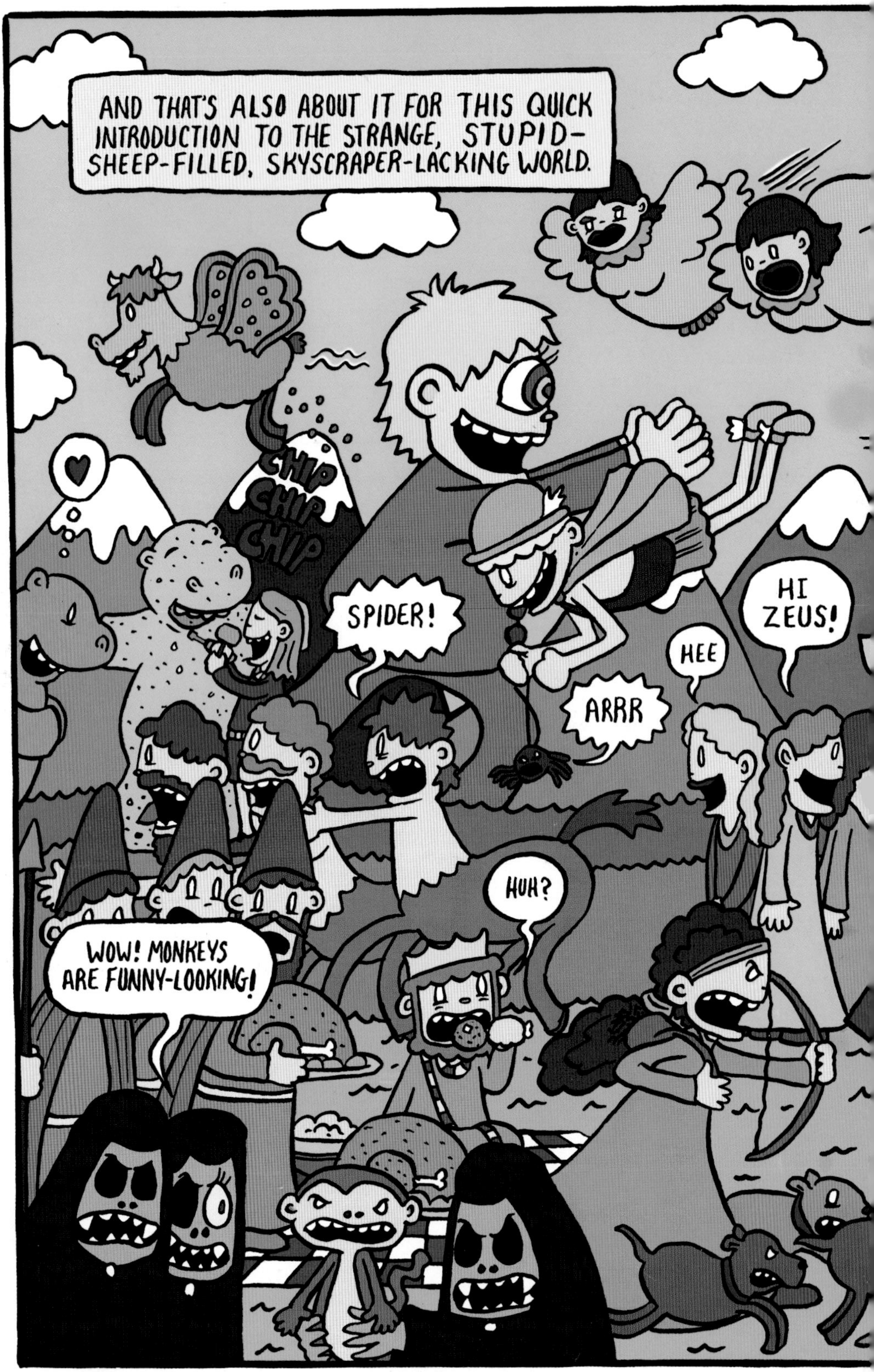
AND THAT'S ALSO ABOUT IT FOR THIS QUICK INTRODUCTION TO THE STRANGE, STUPID-SHEEP-FILLED, SKYSCRAPER-LACKING WORLD.
CHIP CHIP CHIP
SPIDER!
HI ZEUS!
HEE
ARRR
HUH?
WOW! MONKEYS ARE FUNNY-LOOKING!

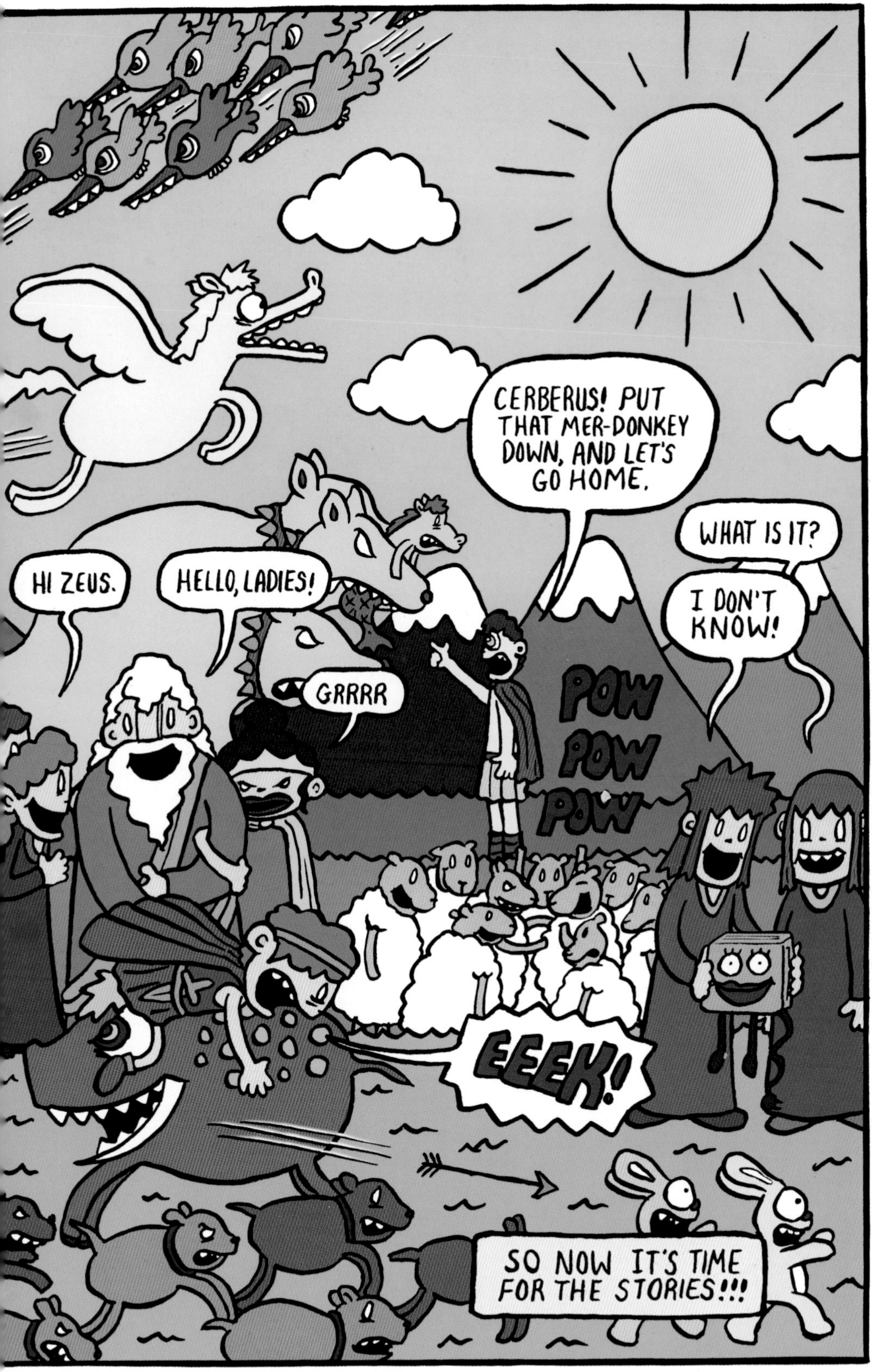
CERBERUS! PUT THAT MER-DONKEY DOWN, AND LET'S GO HOME.
HI ZEUS.
HELLO, LADIES!
GRRRR
WHAT IS IT?
I DON'T KNOW!
POW POW POW
EEEK!
SO NOW IT'S TIME FOR THE STORIES!!!

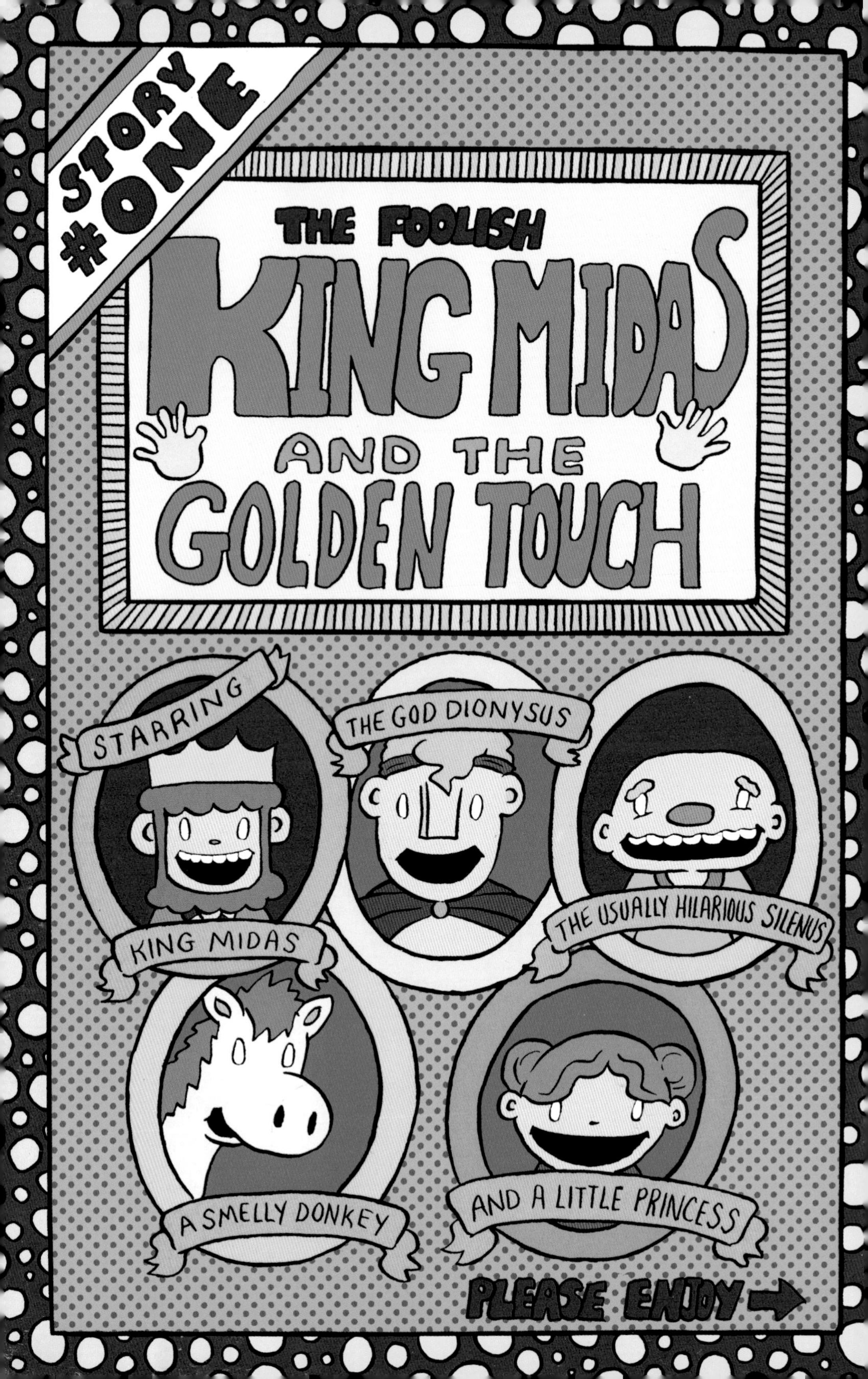
STORY #ONE
THE FOOLISH
KING MIDAS
AND THE
GOLDEN TOUCH
STARRING
KING MIDAS
THE GOD DIONYSUS
THE USUALLY HILARIOUS SILENUS
A SMELLY DONKEY
AND A LITTLE PRINCESS
PLEASE ENJOY

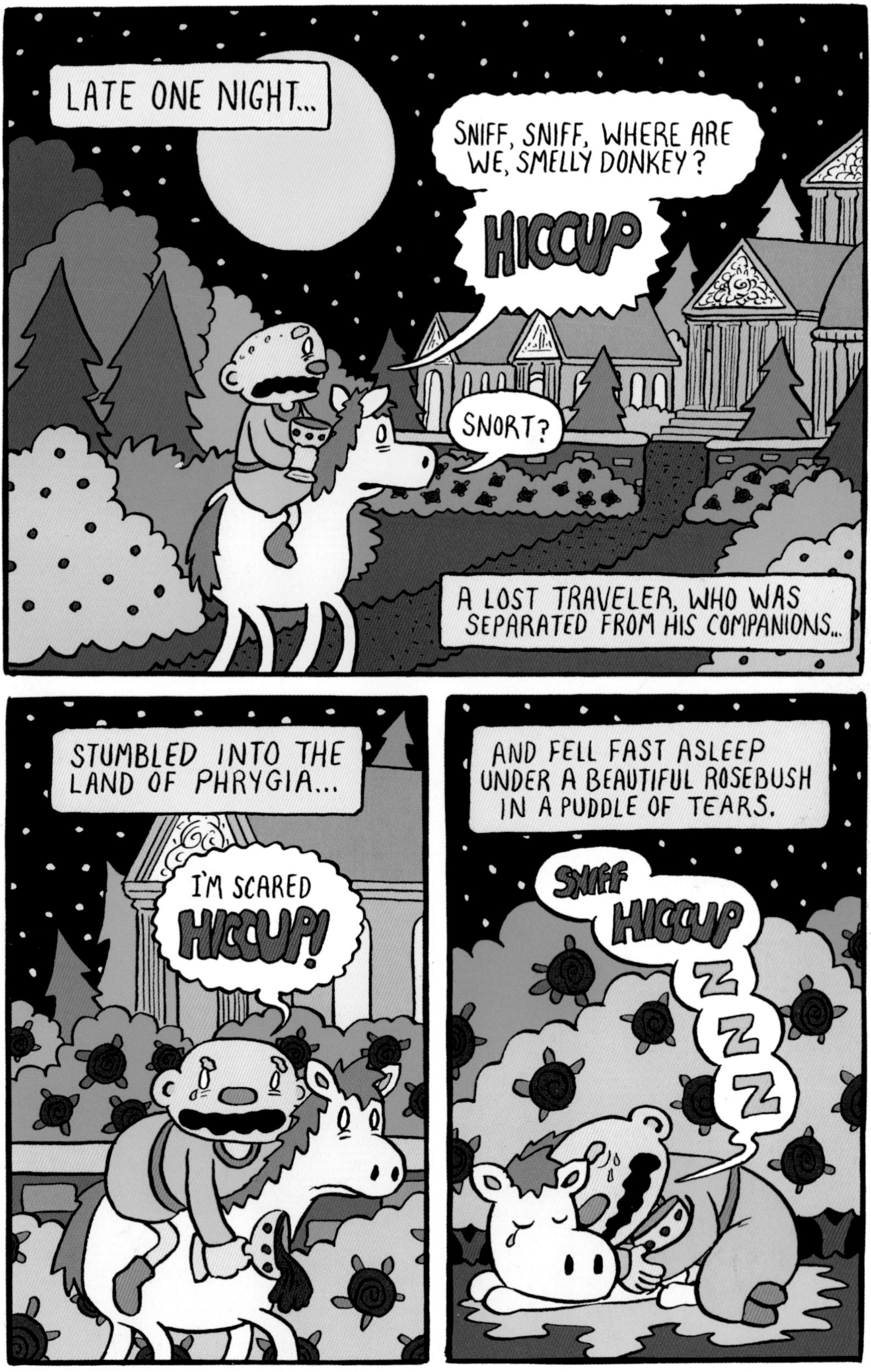
LATE ONE NIGHT...
SNIFF, SNIFF, WHERE ARE WE, SMELLY DONKEY?
HICCUP
SNORT?
A LOST TRAVELER, WHO WAS SEPARATED FROM HIS COMPANIONS...
STUMBLED INTO THE LAND OF PHRYGIA...
I'M SCARED
HICCUP!
AND FELL FAST ASLEEP UNDER A BEAUTIFUL ROSEBUSH IN A PUDDLE OF TEARS.
SNIFF
HICCUP
Z
Z
Z

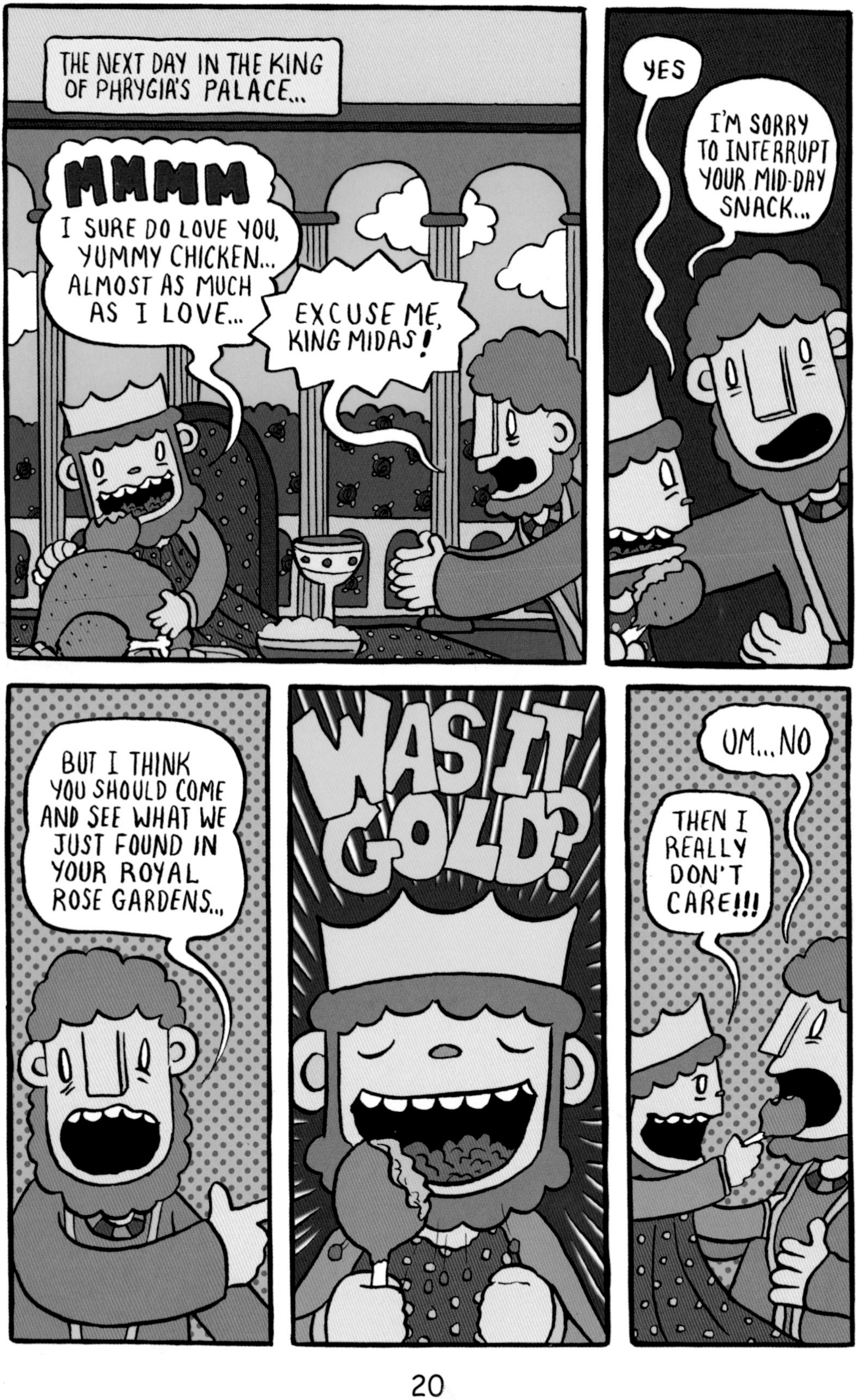
THE NEXT DAY IN THE KING OF PHRYGIA'S PALACE...
MMMM
I SURE DO LOVE YOU, YUMMY CHICKEN... ALMOST AS MUCH AS I LOVE...
EXCUSE ME, KING MIDAS!
YES
I'M SORRY TO INTERRUPT YOUR MID-DAY SNACK...
BUT I THINK YOU SHOULD COME AND SEE WHAT WE JUST FOUND IN YOUR ROYAL ROSE GARDENS...
WAS IT GOLD?
UM...NO
THEN I REALLY DON'T CARE!!!

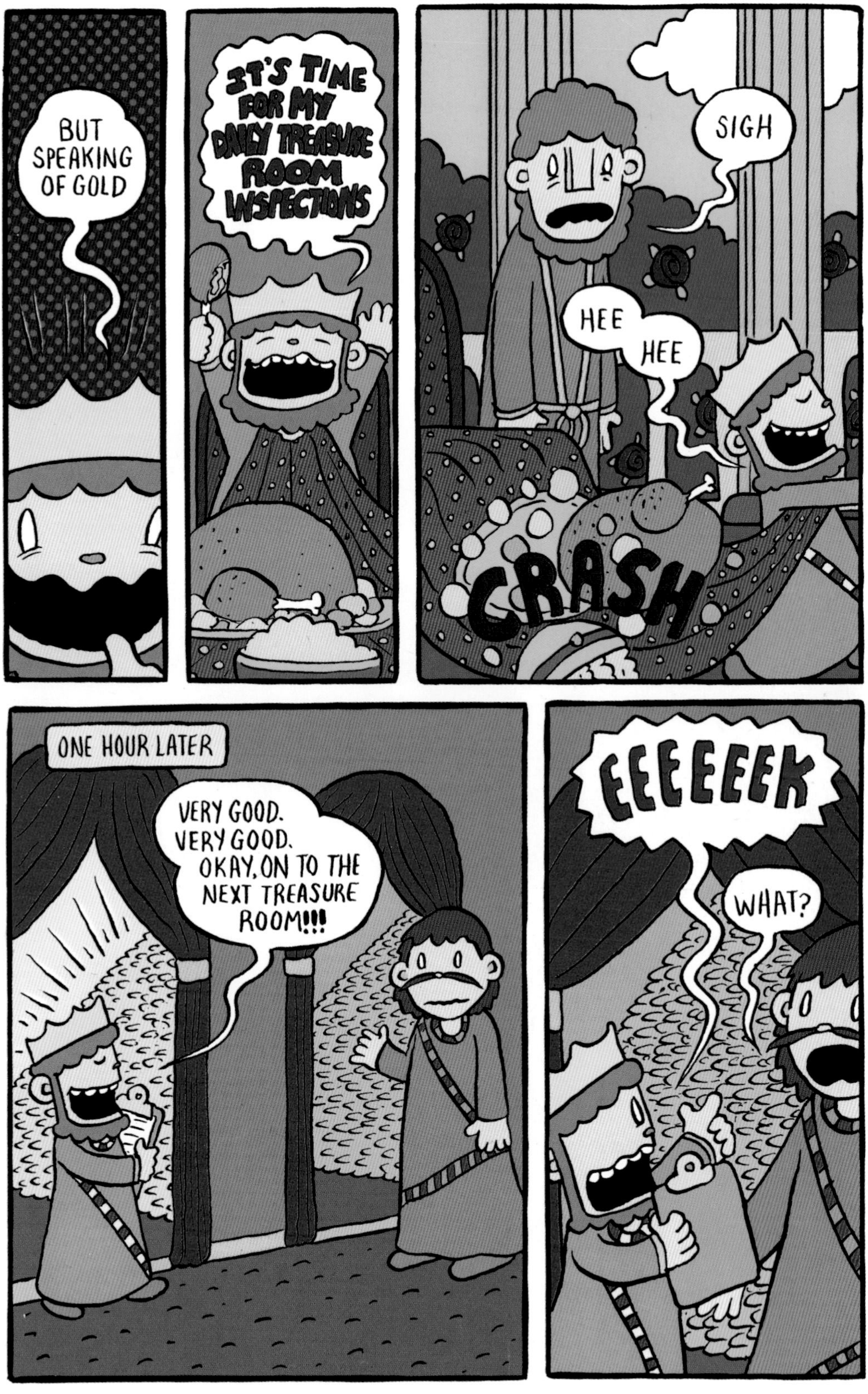
BUT SPEAKING OF GOLD
IT'S TIME FOR MY DAILY TREASURE ROOM INSPECTIONS
SIGH
HEE HEE
CRASH
ONE HOUR LATER
VERY GOOD. VERY GOOD. OKAY, ON TO THE NEXT TREASURE ROOM!!!
EEEEEEK
WHAT?

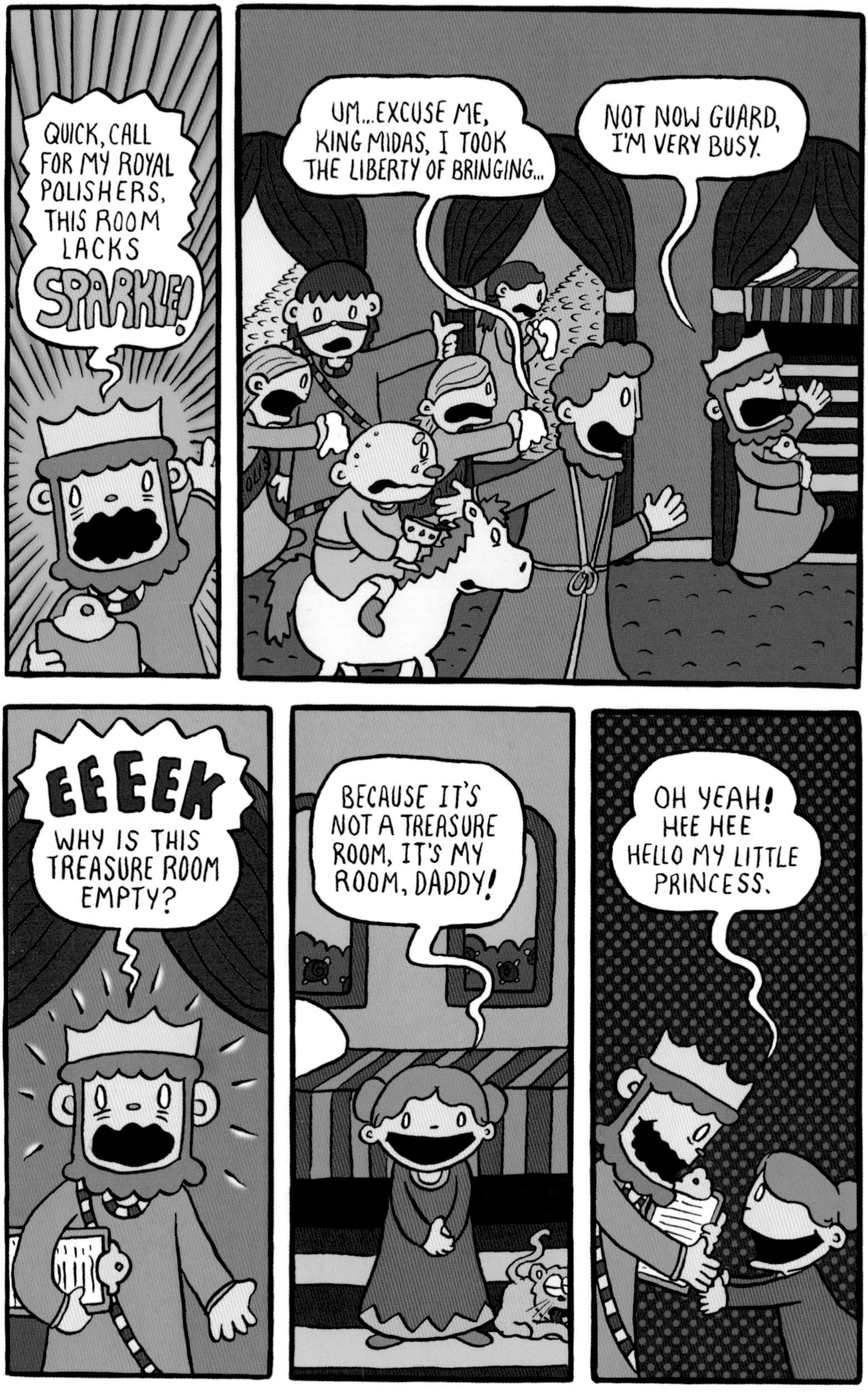
QUICK, CALL FOR MY ROYAL POLISHERS, THIS ROOM LACKS SPARKLE!
UM...EXCUSE ME, KING MIDAS, I TOOK THE LIBERTY OF BRINGING...
NOT NOW GUARD, I'M VERY BUSY.
EEEEK WHY IS THIS TREASURE ROOM EMPTY?
BECAUSE IT'S NOT A TREASURE ROOM, IT'S MY ROOM, DADDY!
OH YEAH! HEE HEE HELLO MY LITTLE PRINCESS.

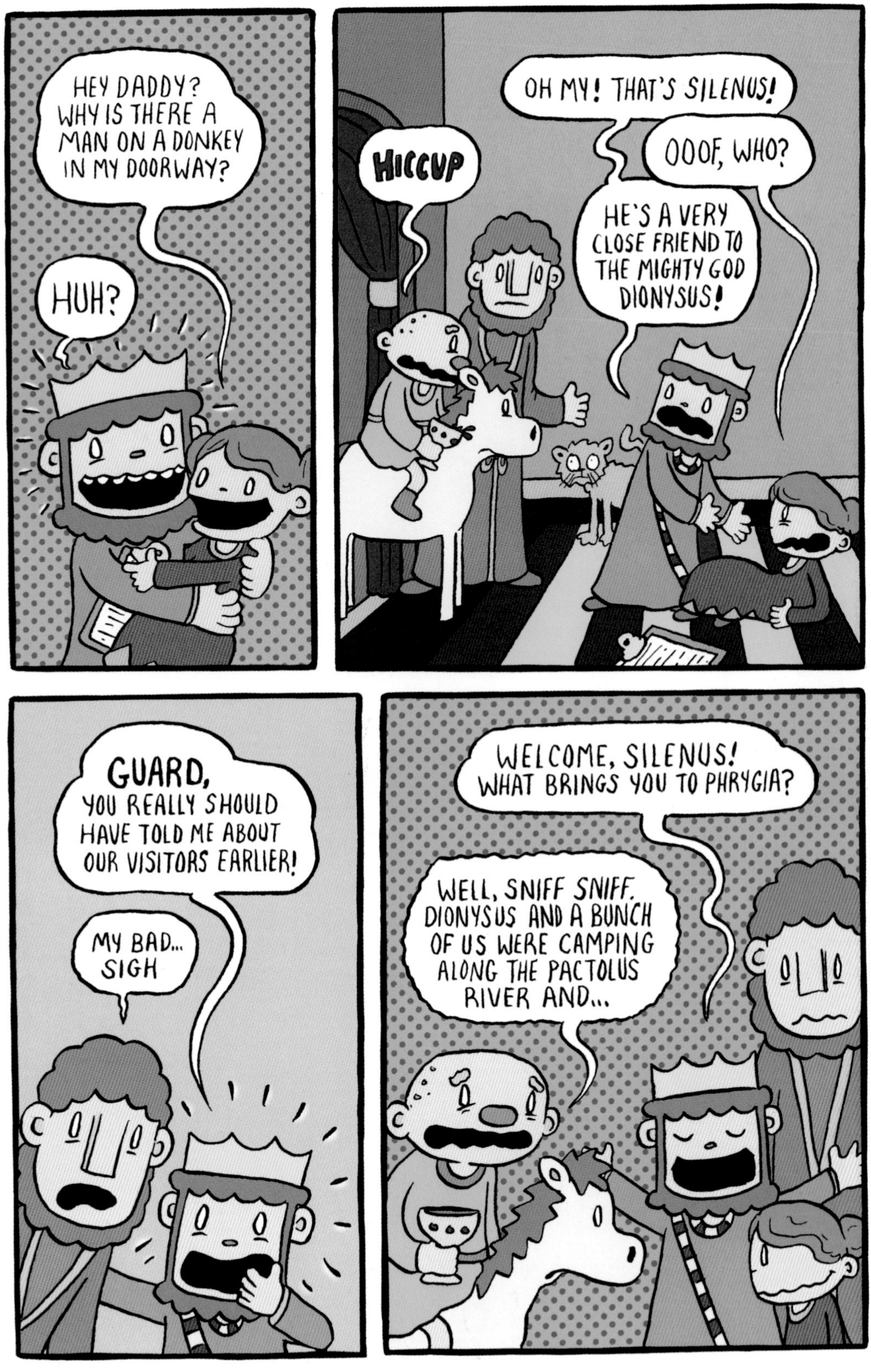
HEY DADDY? WHY IS THERE A MAN ON A DONKEY IN MY DOORWAY?
HUH?
OH MY! THAT'S SILENUS!
OOOF, WHO?
HICCUP
HE'S A VERY CLOSE FRIEND TO THE MIGHTY GOD DIONYSUS!
GUARD, YOU REALLY SHOULD HAVE TOLD ME ABOUT OUR VISITORS EARLIER!
MY BAD... SIGH
WELCOME, SILENUS! WHAT BRINGS YOU TO PHRYGIA?
WELL, SNIFF SNIFF. DIONYSUS AND A BUNCH OF US WERE CAMPING ALONG THE PACTOLUS RIVER AND...

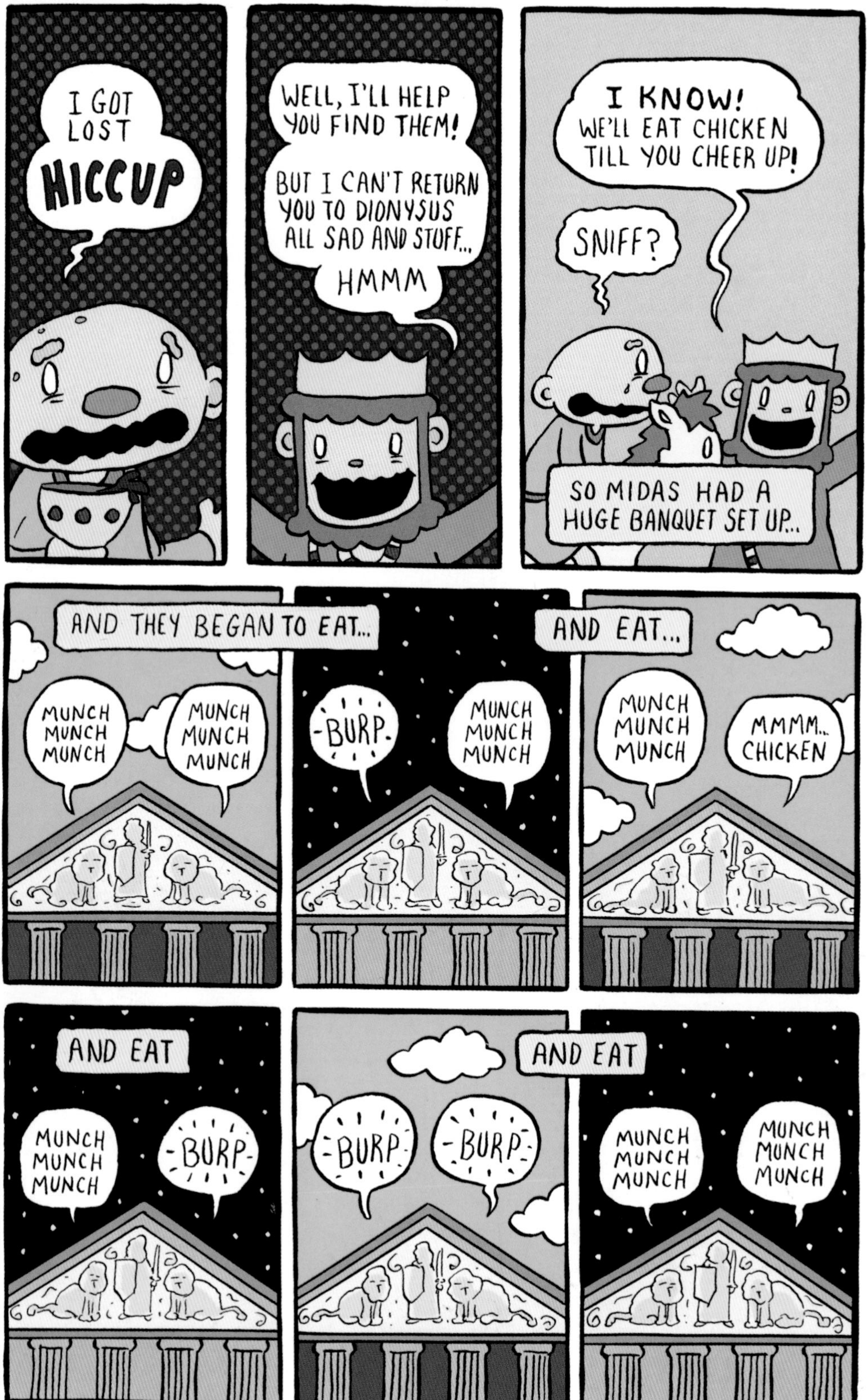
I GOT LOST
HICCUP
WELL, I'LL HELP YOU FIND THEM!
BUT I CAN'T RETURN YOU TO DIONYSUS ALL SAD AND STUFF...
HMMM
I KNOW! WE'LL EAT CHICKEN TILL YOU CHEER UP!
SNIFF?
SO MIDAS HAD A HUGE BANQUET SET UP...
AND THEY BEGAN TO EAT...
MUNCH MUNCH MUNCH
MUNCH MUNCH MUNCH
BURP
MUNCH MUNCH MUNCH
AND EAT...
MUNCH MUNCH MUNCH
MMMM... CHICKEN
AND EAT
MUNCH MUNCH MUNCH
BURP
AND EAT
BURP
BURP
MUNCH MUNCH MUNCH
MUNCH MUNCH MUNCH

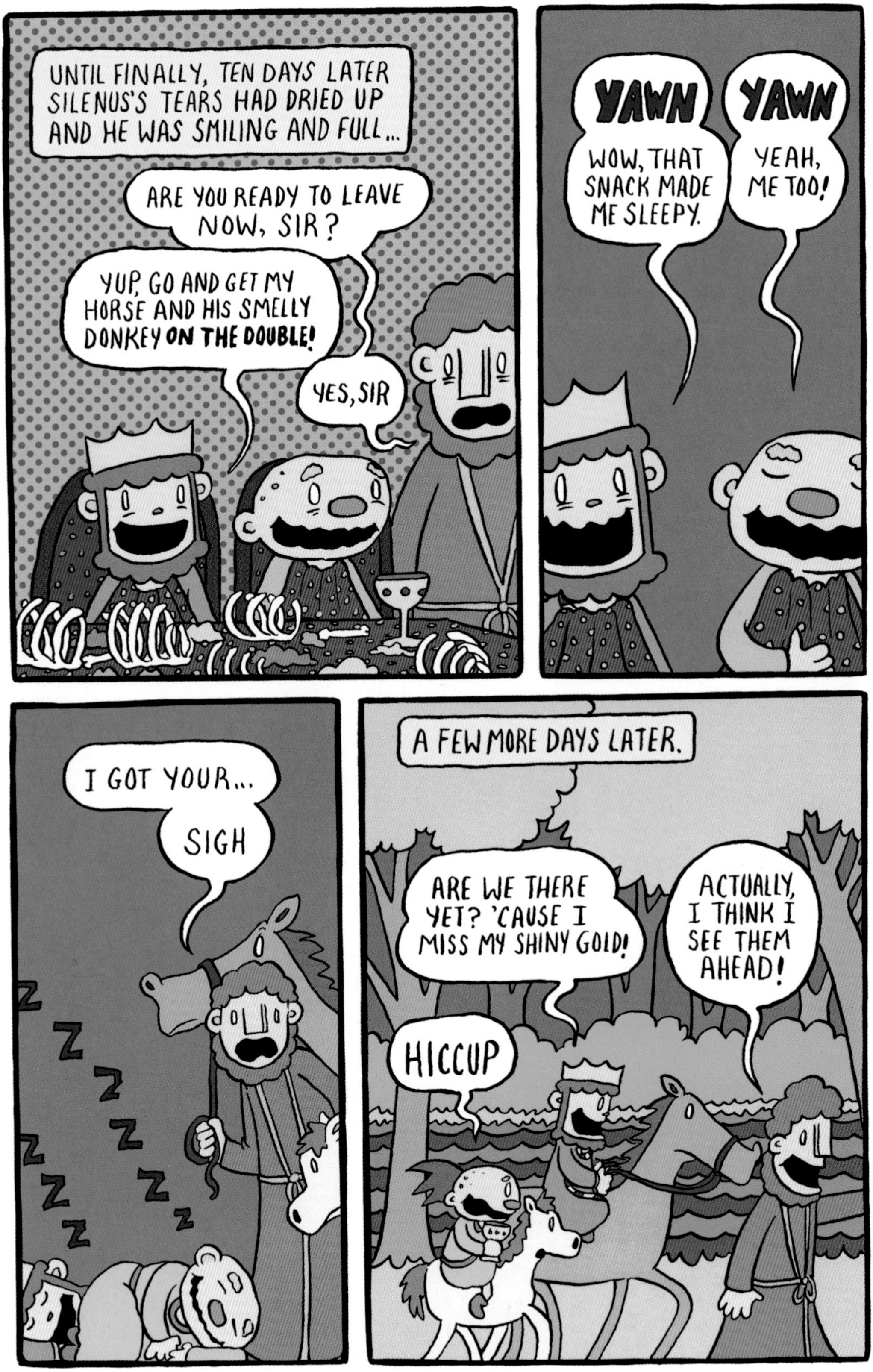
UNTIL FINALLY, TEN DAYS LATER SILENUS'S TEARS HAD DRIED UP AND HE WAS SMILING AND FULL...
ARE YOU READY TO LEAVE NOW, SIR?
YUP, GO AND GET MY HORSE AND HIS SMELLY DONKEY **ON THE DOUBLE!**
YES, SIR
YAWN
YAWN
WOW, THAT SNACK MADE ME SLEEPY.
YEAH, ME TOO!
I GOT YOUR...
SIGH
Z Z Z Z Z Z Z Z Z Z
A FEW MORE DAYS LATER.
ARE WE THERE YET? 'CAUSE I MISS MY SHINY GOLD!
ACTUALLY, I THINK I SEE THEM AHEAD!
HICCUP

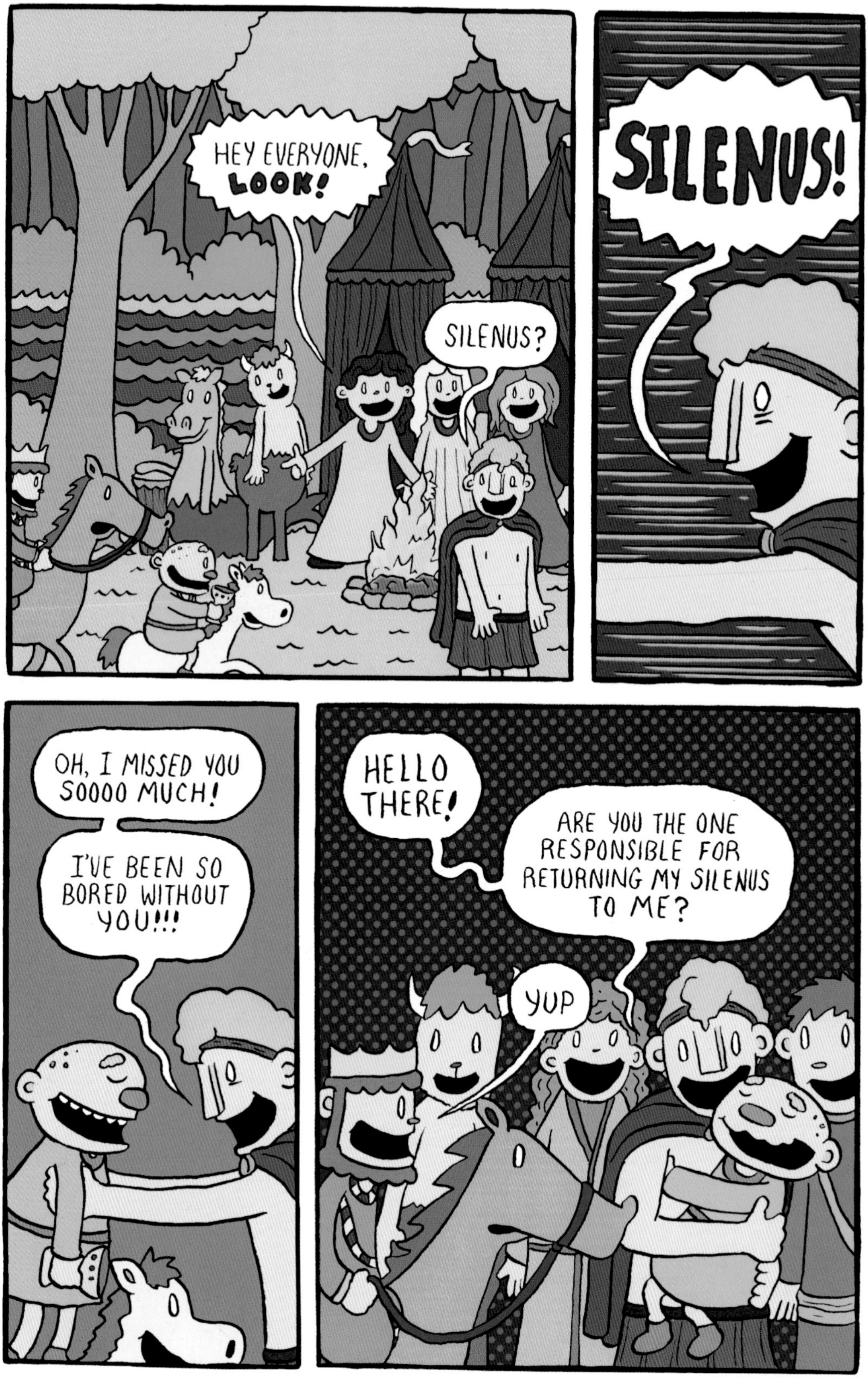
HEY EVERYONE, LOOK!
SILENUS?
SILENUS!
OH, I MISSED YOU SOOOO MUCH!
I'VE BEEN SO BORED WITHOUT YOU!!!
HELLO THERE!
ARE YOU THE ONE RESPONSIBLE FOR RETURNING MY SILENUS TO ME?
YUP

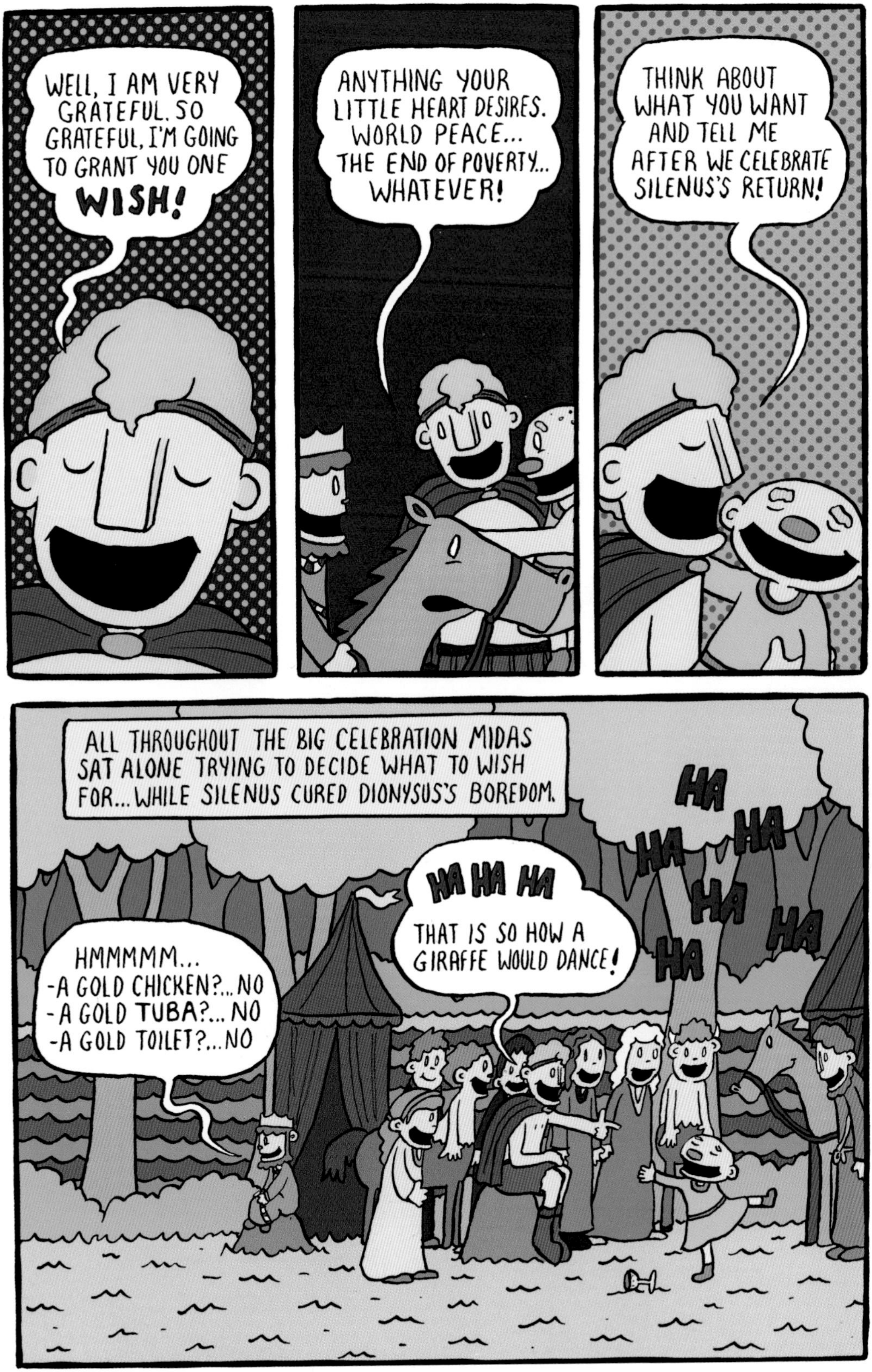
WELL, I AM VERY GRATEFUL. SO GRATEFUL, I'M GOING TO GRANT YOU ONE **WISH!**
ANYTHING YOUR LITTLE HEART DESIRES. WORLD PEACE... THE END OF POVERTY... WHATEVER!
THINK ABOUT WHAT YOU WANT AND TELL ME AFTER WE CELEBRATE SILENUS'S RETURN!
ALL THROUGHOUT THE BIG CELEBRATION MIDAS SAT ALONE TRYING TO DECIDE WHAT TO WISH FOR... WHILE SILENUS CURED DIONYSUS'S BOREDOM.
HA HA HA HA HA HA
HMMMMM... -A GOLD CHICKEN?... NO -A GOLD TUBA?... NO -A GOLD TOILET?... NO
HA HA HA THAT IS SO HOW A GIRAFFE WOULD DANCE!

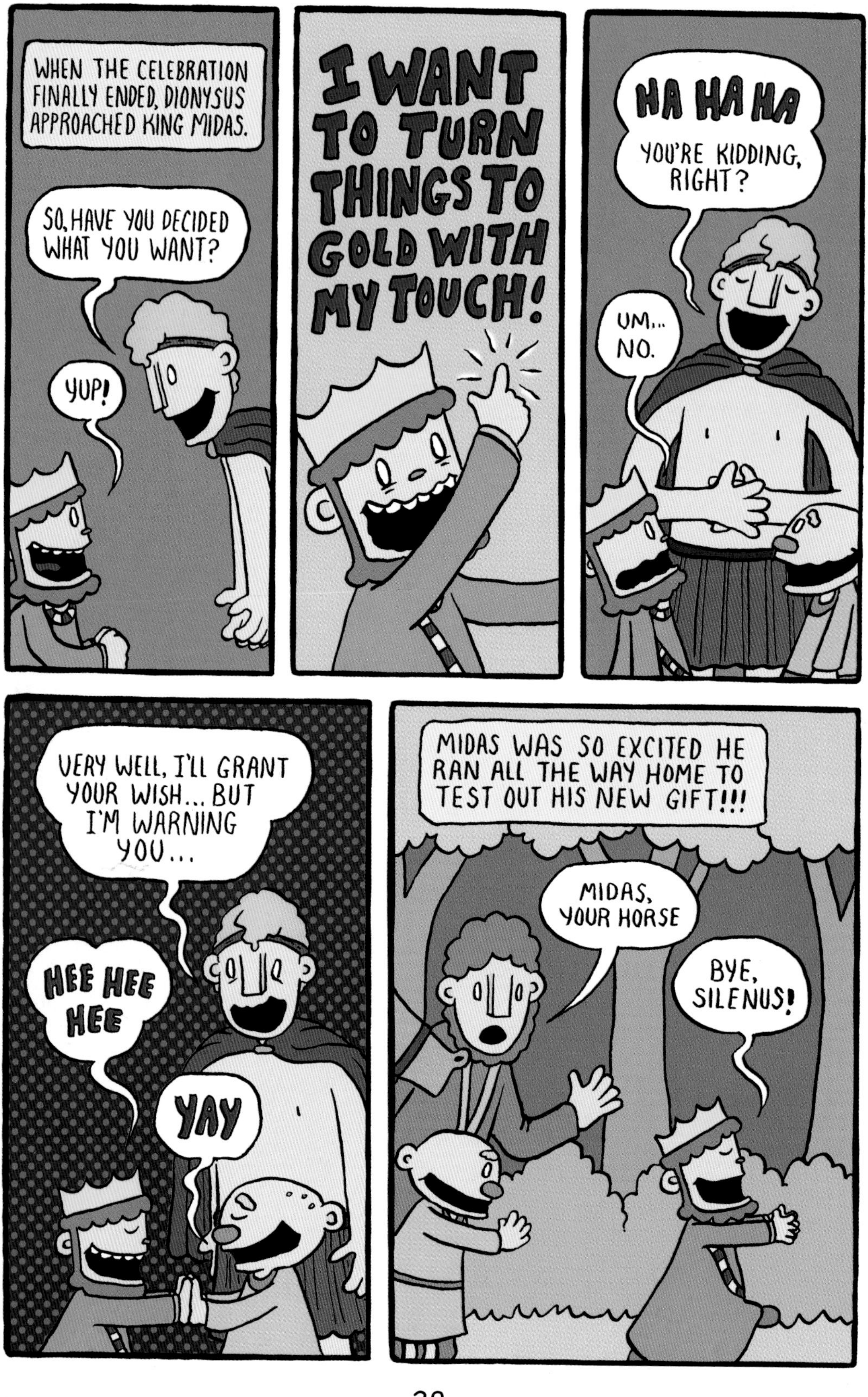

WHEN THE CELEBRATION FINALLY ENDED, DIONYSUS APPROACHED KING MIDAS.
SO, HAVE YOU DECIDED WHAT YOU WANT?
YUP!
I WANT TO TURN THINGS TO GOLD WITH MY TOUCH!
HA HA HA
YOU'RE KIDDING, RIGHT?
UM... NO.
VERY WELL, I'LL GRANT YOUR WISH... BUT I'M WARNING YOU...
HEE HEE HEE
YAY
MIDAS WAS SO EXCITED HE RAN ALL THE WAY HOME TO TEST OUT HIS NEW GIFT!!!
MIDAS, YOUR HORSE
BYE, SILENUS!

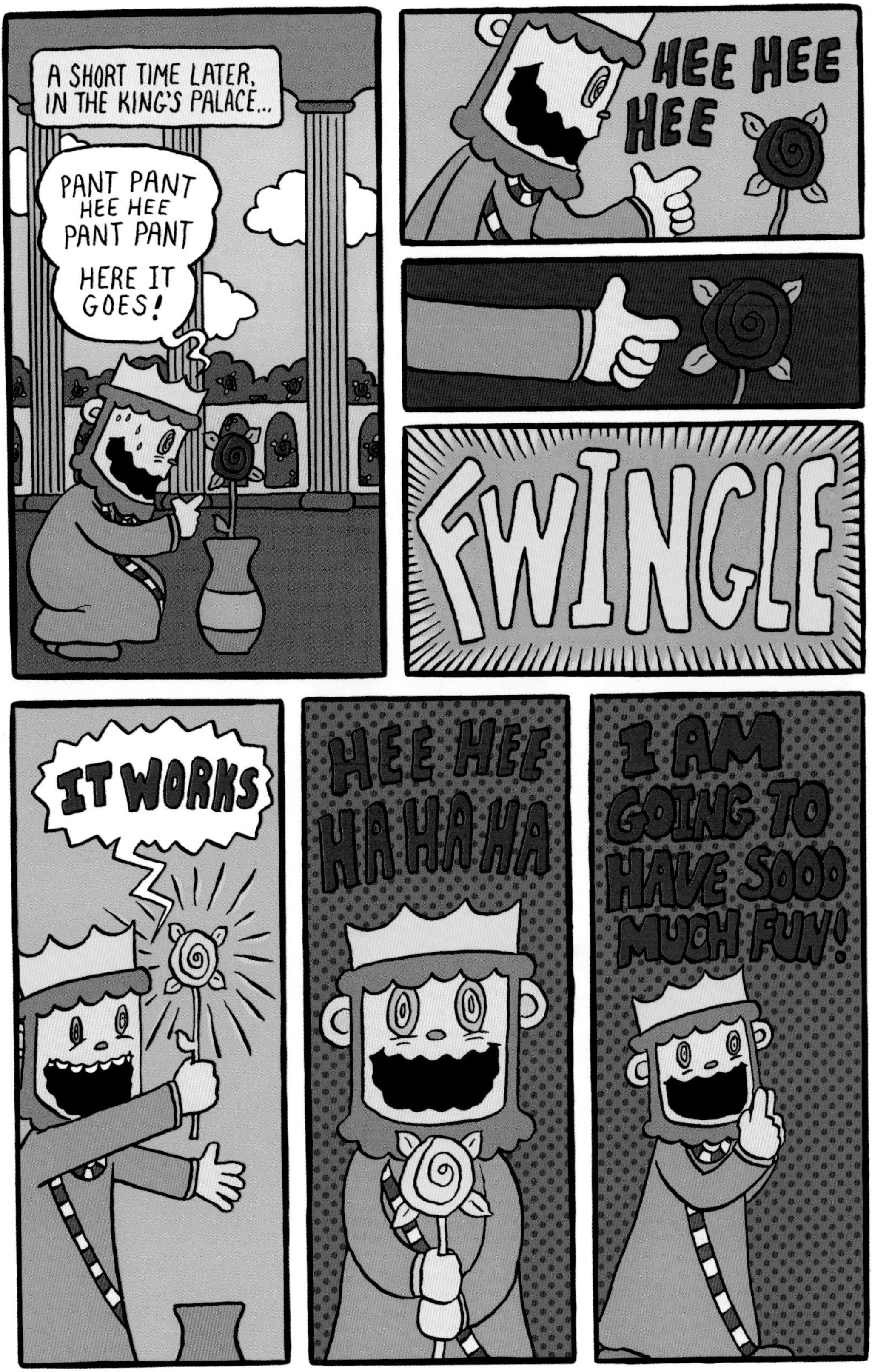
A SHORT TIME LATER, IN THE KING'S PALACE...
PANT PANT HEE HEE PANT PANT
HERE IT GOES!
HEE HEE HEE
FWINGLE
IT WORKS
HEE HEE HA HA HA HA
I AM GOING TO HAVE SOOO MUCH FUN!

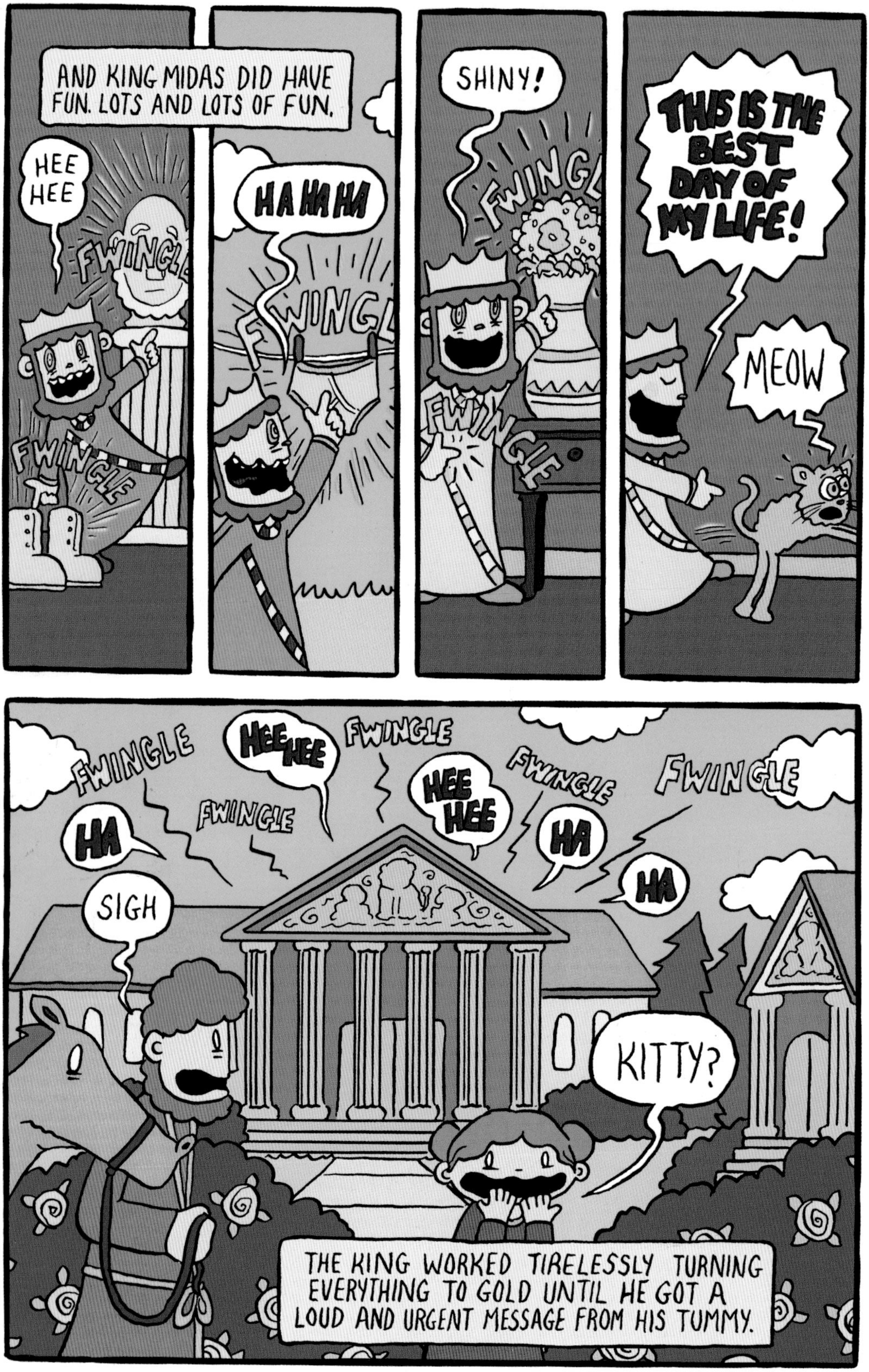
AND KING MIDAS DID HAVE FUN. LOTS AND LOTS OF FUN.
HEE HEE
FWINGLE
FWINGLE
HA HA HA
FWINGL
SHINY!
FWINGL
FWINGLE
FWINGLE
THIS IS THE BEST DAY OF MY LIFE!
MEOW
FWINGLE
HEE HEE
FWINGLE
FWINGLE
HEE HEE
FWINGLE
FWINGLE
HA
HA
HA
SIGH
KITTY?
THE KING WORKED TIRELESSLY TURNING EVERYTHING TO GOLD UNTIL HE GOT A LOUD AND URGENT MESSAGE FROM HIS TUMMY.

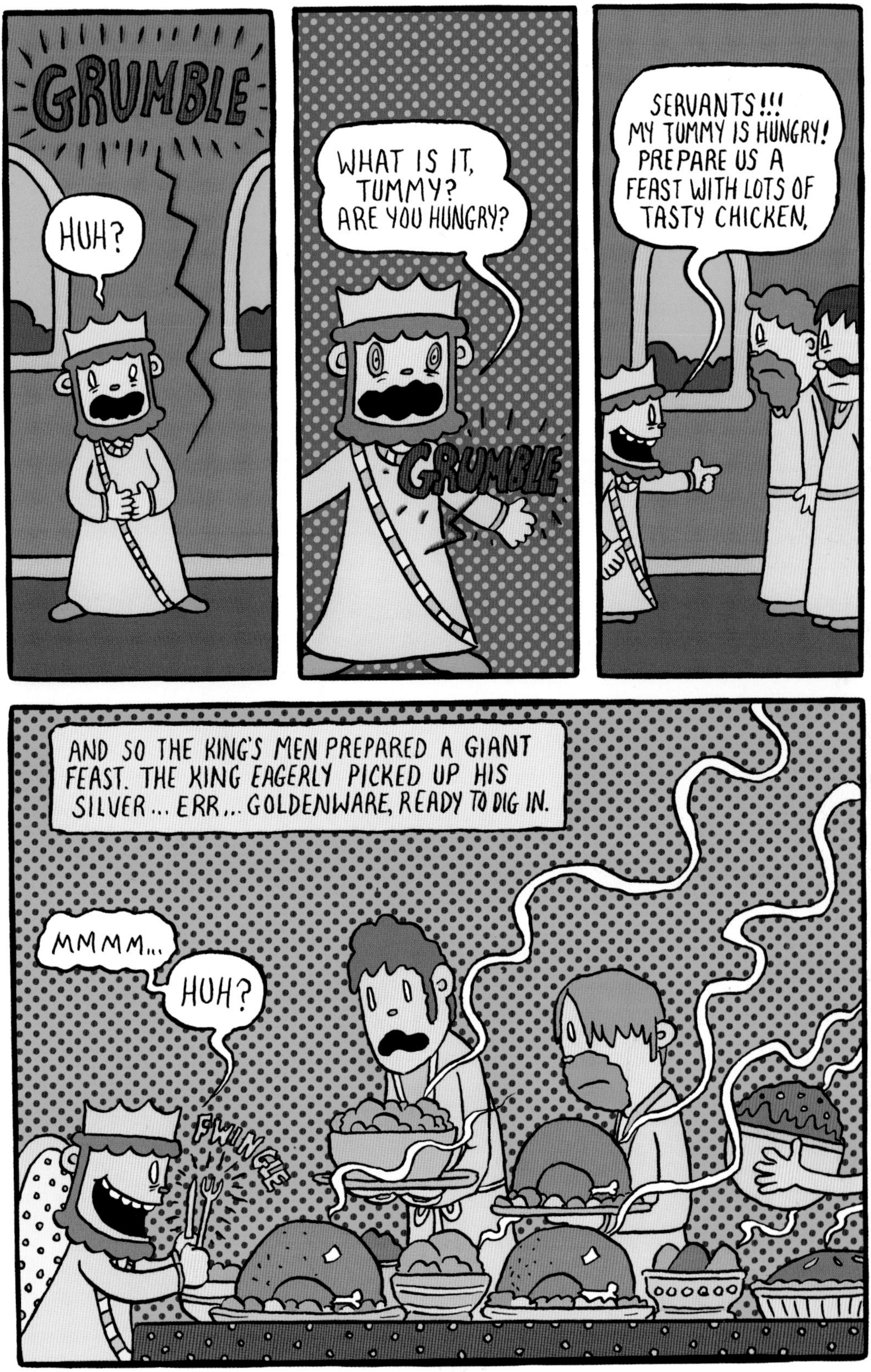
GRUMBLE
HUH?
WHAT IS IT, TUMMY? ARE YOU HUNGRY?
GRUMBLE
SERVANTS!!! MY TUMMY IS HUNGRY! PREPARE US A FEAST WITH LOTS OF TASTY CHICKEN.
AND SO THE KING'S MEN PREPARED A GIANT FEAST. THE KING EAGERLY PICKED UP HIS SILVER... ERR... GOLDENWARE, READY TO DIG IN.
MMMM...
HUH?
FWINGLE

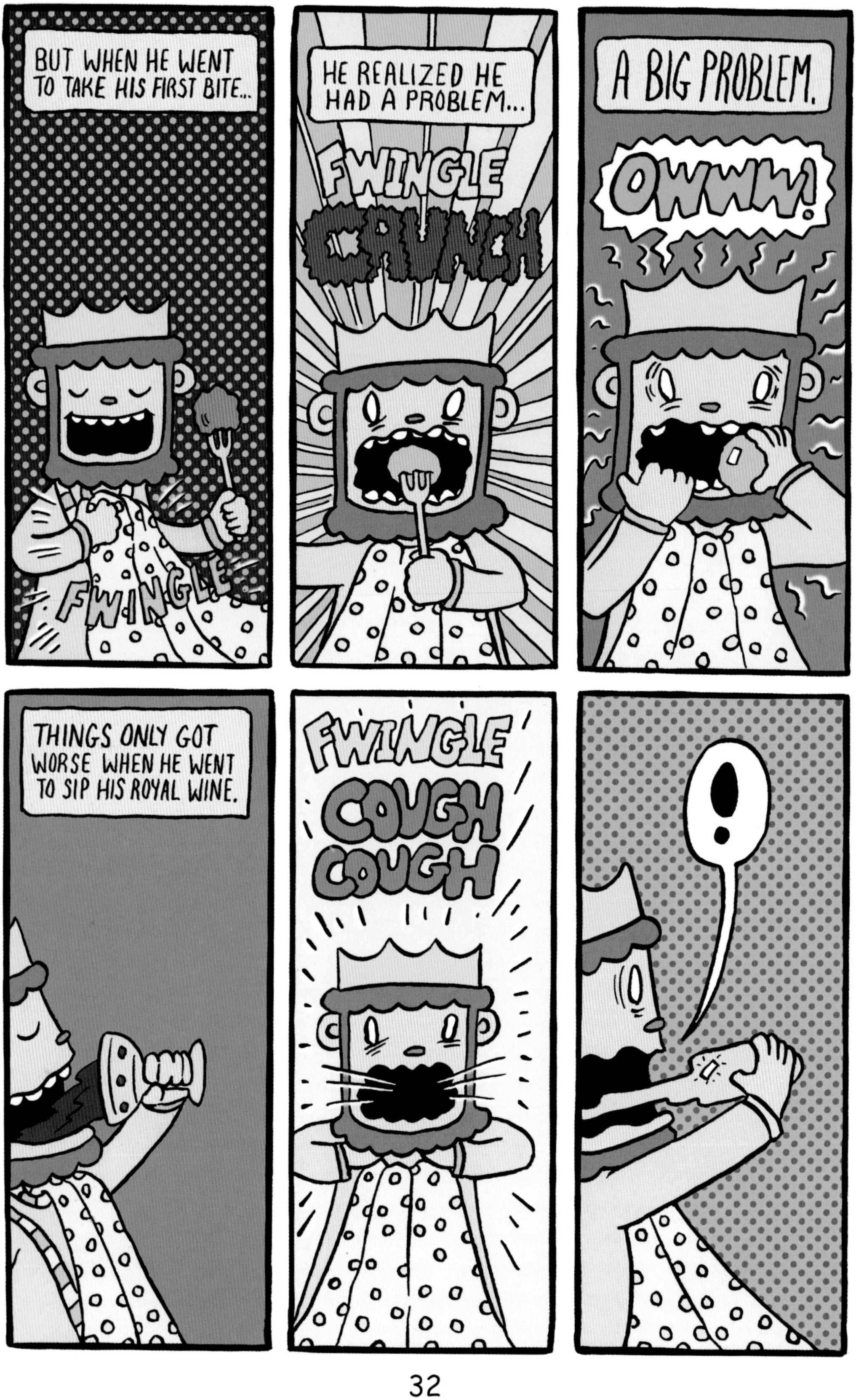
BUT WHEN HE WENT TO TAKE HIS FIRST BITE...
FWINGLE
HE REALIZED HE HAD A PROBLEM...
FWINGLE
CRUNCH
A BIG PROBLEM.
OWWW!
THINGS ONLY GOT WORSE WHEN HE WENT TO SIP HIS ROYAL WINE.
FWINGLE
COUGH
COUGH
!

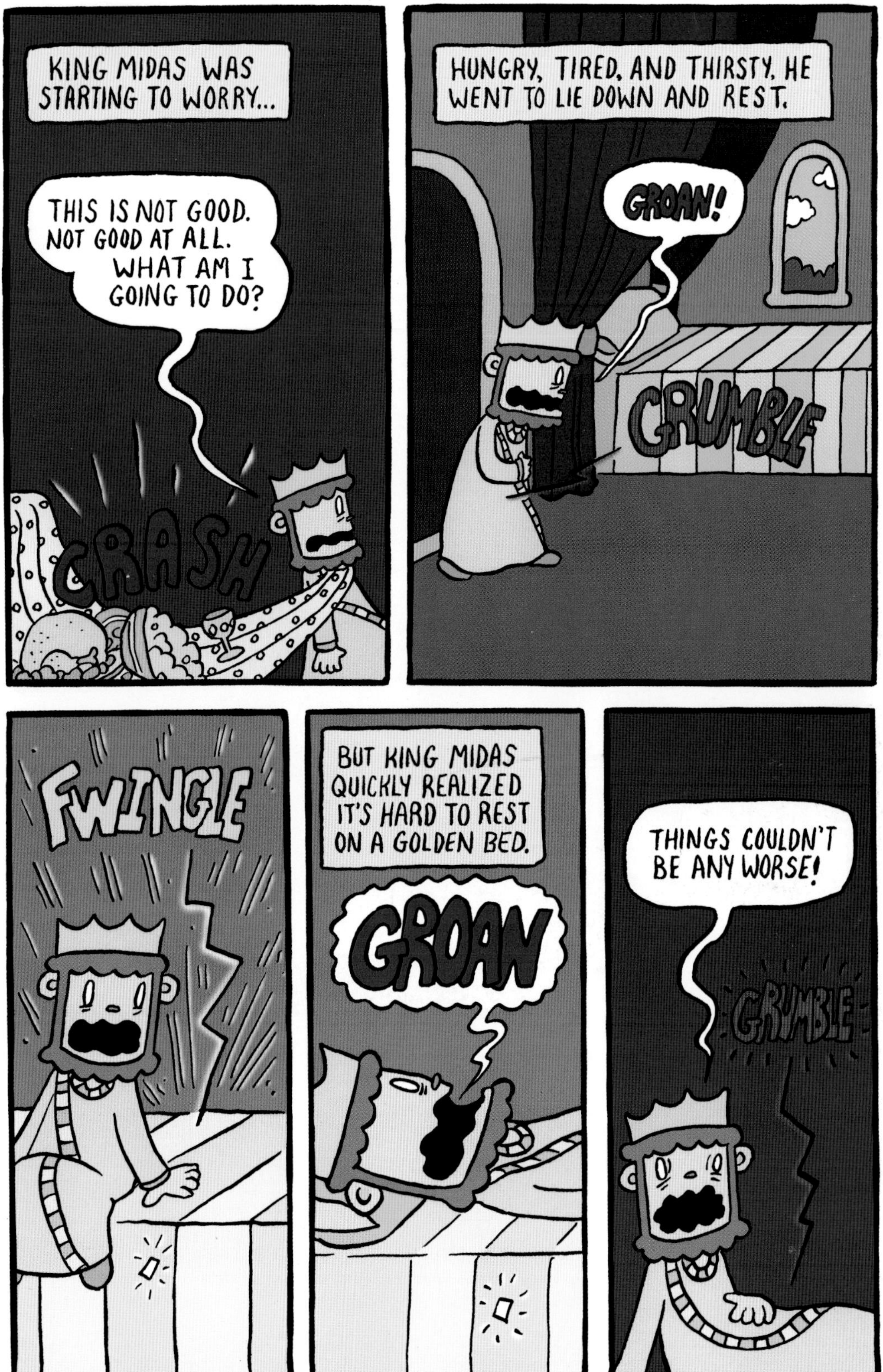
KING MIDAS WAS STARTING TO WORRY...
THIS IS NOT GOOD. NOT GOOD AT ALL. WHAT AM I GOING TO DO?
CRASH
HUNGRY, TIRED, AND THIRSTY, HE WENT TO LIE DOWN AND REST.
GROAN!
GRUMBLE
FWINGLE
BUT KING MIDAS QUICKLY REALIZED IT'S HARD TO REST ON A GOLDEN BED.
GROAN
THINGS COULDN'T BE ANY WORSE!
GRUMBLE

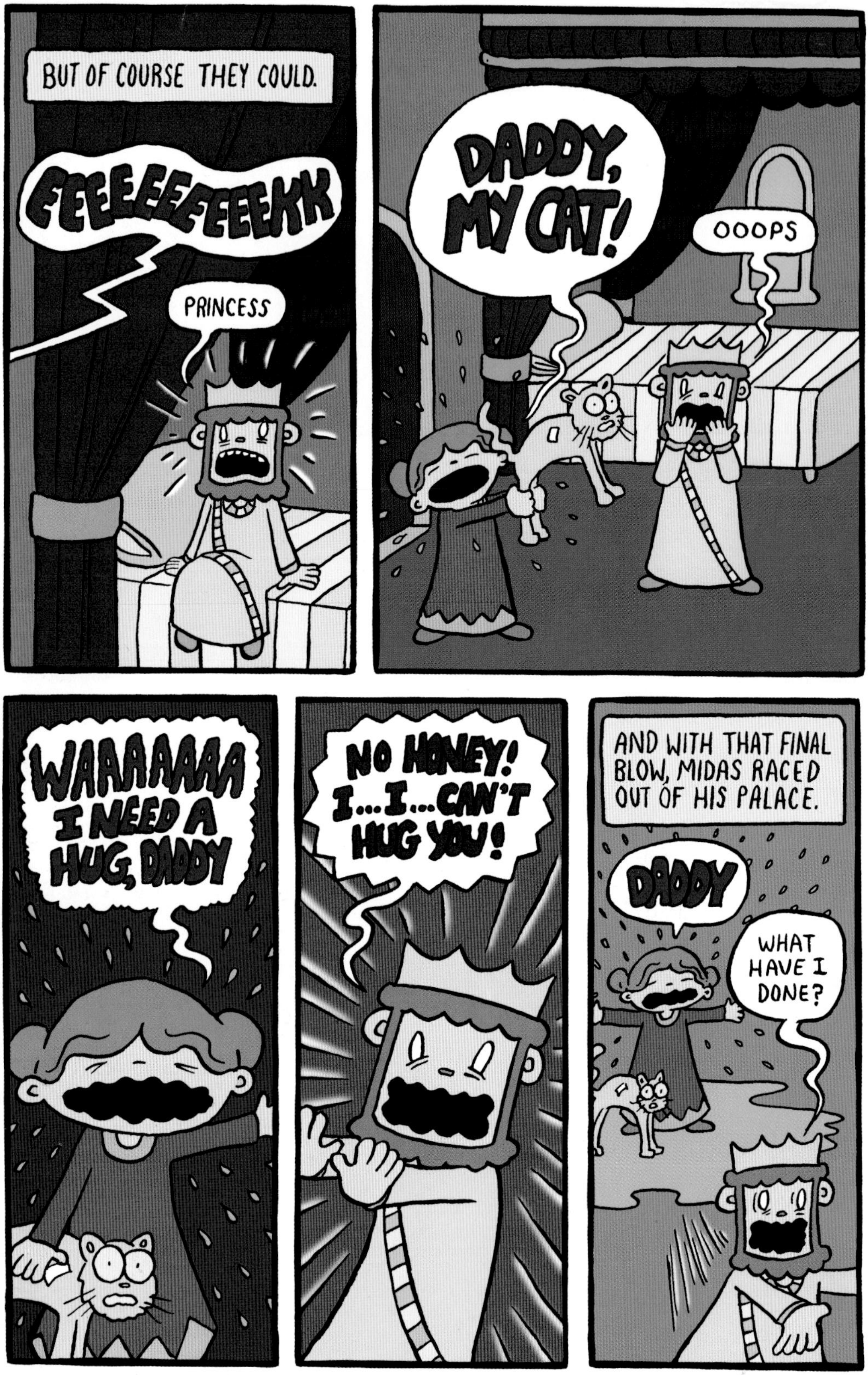
BUT OF COURSE THEY COULD.
EEEEEEEEEEEKK
PRINCESS
DADDY, MY CAT!
OOOPS
WAAAAAAA I NEED A HUG, DADDY
NO HONEY! I...I...CAN'T HUG YOU!
AND WITH THAT FINAL BLOW, MIDAS RACED OUT OF HIS PALACE.
DADDY
WHAT HAVE I DONE?

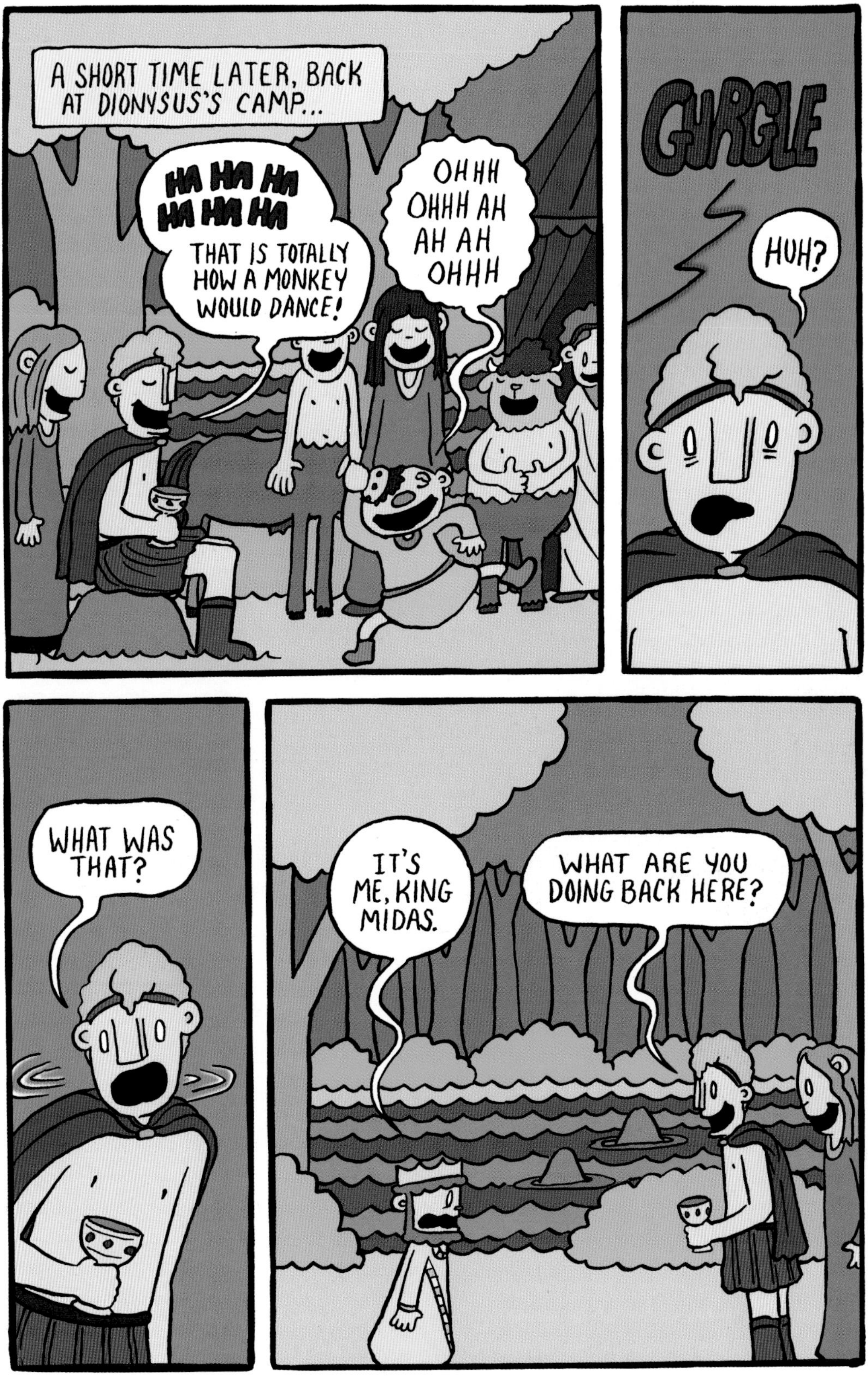
A SHORT TIME LATER, BACK AT DIONYSUS'S CAMP...
HA HA HA HA HA HA
THAT IS TOTALLY HOW A MONKEY WOULD DANCE!
OHHH OHHH AH AH AH OHHH
GURGLE
HUH?
WHAT WAS THAT?
IT'S ME, KING MIDAS.
WHAT ARE YOU DOING BACK HERE?

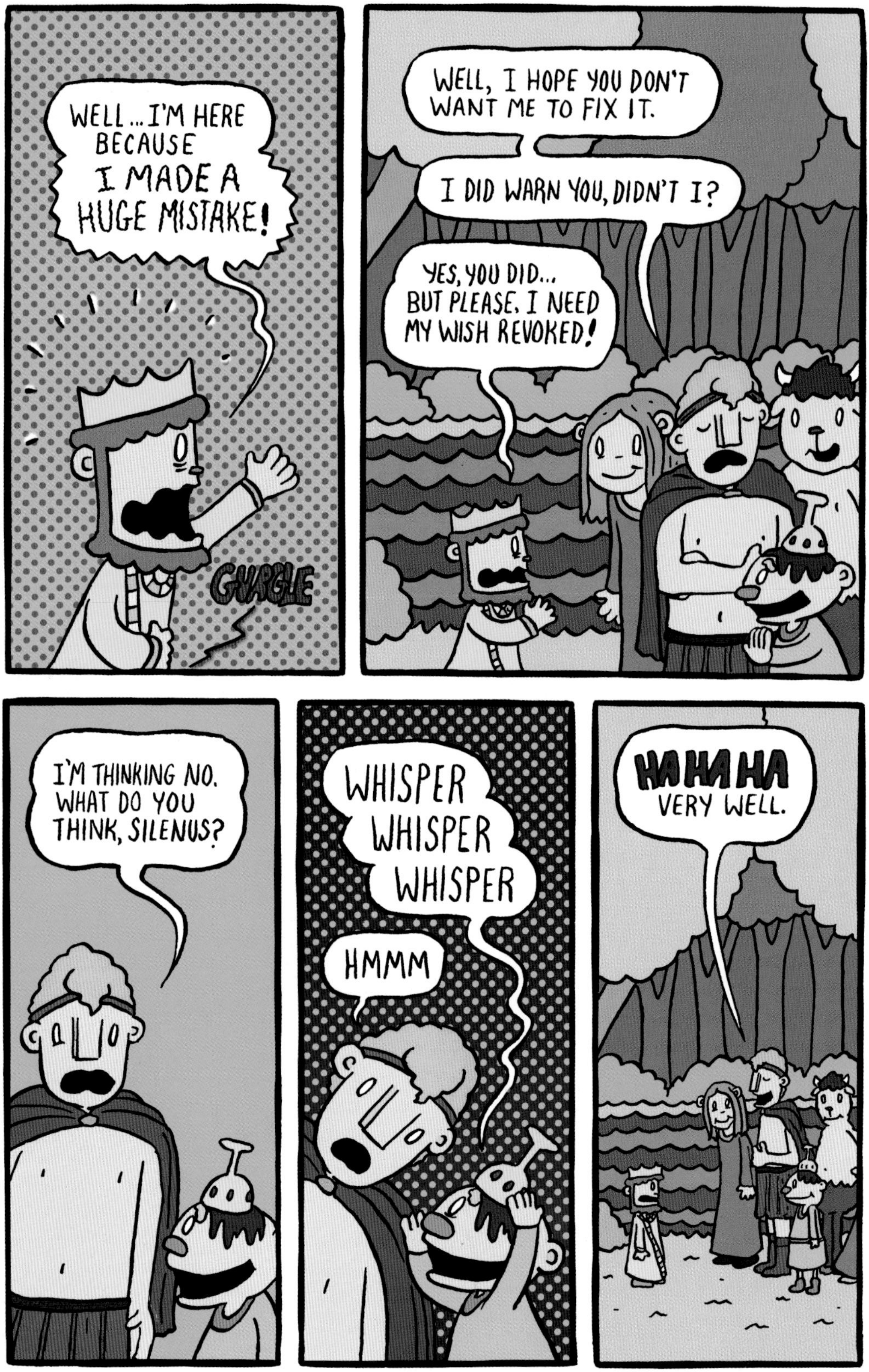
WELL... I'M HERE BECAUSE I MADE A HUGE MISTAKE!
GURGLE
WELL, I HOPE YOU DON'T WANT ME TO FIX IT.
I DID WARN YOU, DIDN'T I?
YES, YOU DID... BUT PLEASE, I NEED MY WISH REVOKED!
I'M THINKING NO. WHAT DO YOU THINK, SILENUS?
WHISPER WHISPER WHISPER
HMMM
HA HA HA HA
VERY WELL.

WELL, IT LOOKS LIKE YOU MADE A TRUE FRIEND OUT OF SILENUS BECAUSE...

HE'S SUGGESTED THAT I REVOKE YOUR WISH IN EXCHANGE FOR A VERY SPECIAL DANCE NUMBER PUT ON BY THE BOTH OF YOU.

CHUCKLE

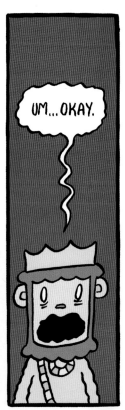

UM... OKAY.

AND SO, AFTER A BIT OF REHERSAL, MIDAS AND SILENUS WERE READY TO PERFORM A VERY SPECTACULAR DUCKY DANCE!

HE HE HE THAT IS SOOO HOW DUCKS WOULD DANCE.

QUACK QUACK QUACK

QUACK QUACK QUACK

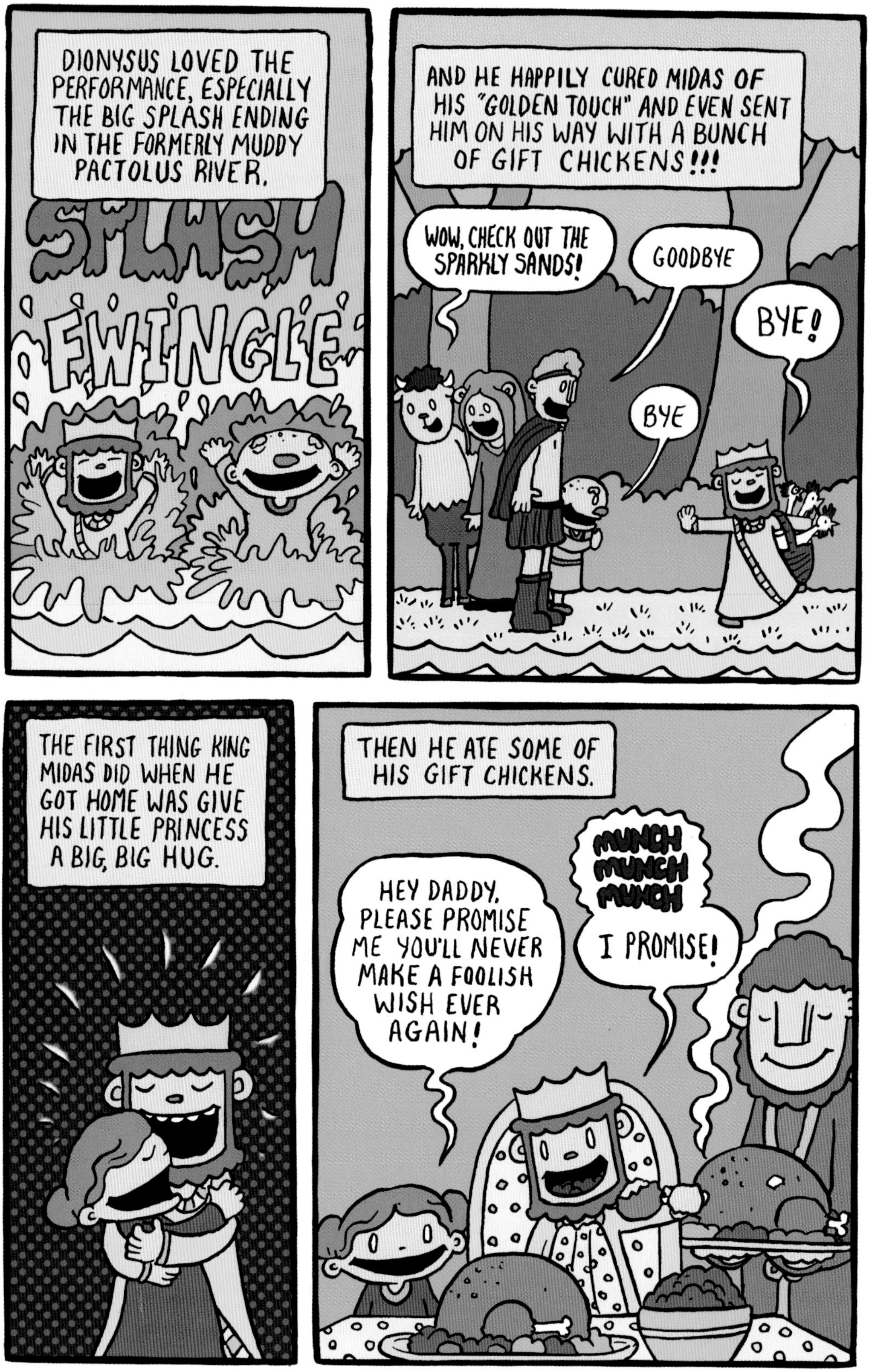
DIONYSUS LOVED THE PERFORMANCE, ESPECIALLY THE BIG SPLASH ENDING IN THE FORMERLY MUDDY PACTOLUS RIVER.
SPLASH
FWINGLE
AND HE HAPPILY CURED MIDAS OF HIS "GOLDEN TOUCH" AND EVEN SENT HIM ON HIS WAY WITH A BUNCH OF GIFT CHICKENS!!!
WOW, CHECK OUT THE SPARKLY SANDS!
GOODBYE
BYE!
BYE
THE FIRST THING KING MIDAS DID WHEN HE GOT HOME WAS GIVE HIS LITTLE PRINCESS A BIG, BIG HUG.
THEN HE ATE SOME OF HIS GIFT CHICKENS.
HEY DADDY, PLEASE PROMISE ME YOU'LL NEVER MAKE A FOOLISH WISH EVER AGAIN!
MUNCH MUNCH MUNCH
I PROMISE!

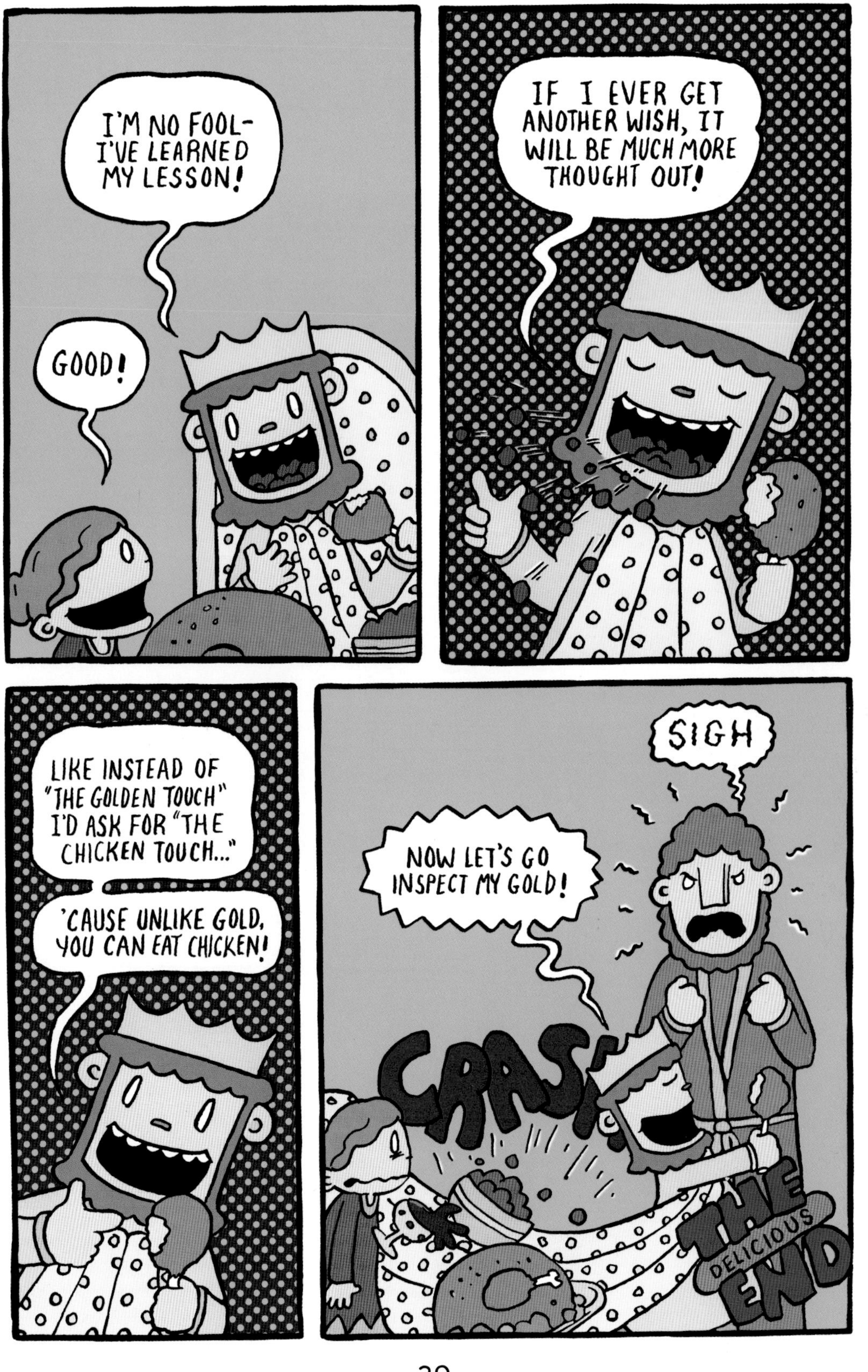
I'M NO FOOL-
I'VE LEARNED
MY LESSON!
GOOD!
IF I EVER GET
ANOTHER WISH, IT
WILL BE MUCH MORE
THOUGHT OUT!
LIKE INSTEAD OF
"THE GOLDEN TOUCH"
I'D ASK FOR "THE
CHICKEN TOUCH..."
'CAUSE UNLIKE GOLD,
YOU CAN EAT CHICKEN!
SIGH
NOW LET'S GO
INSPECT MY GOLD!
CRASH
THE DELICIOUS END

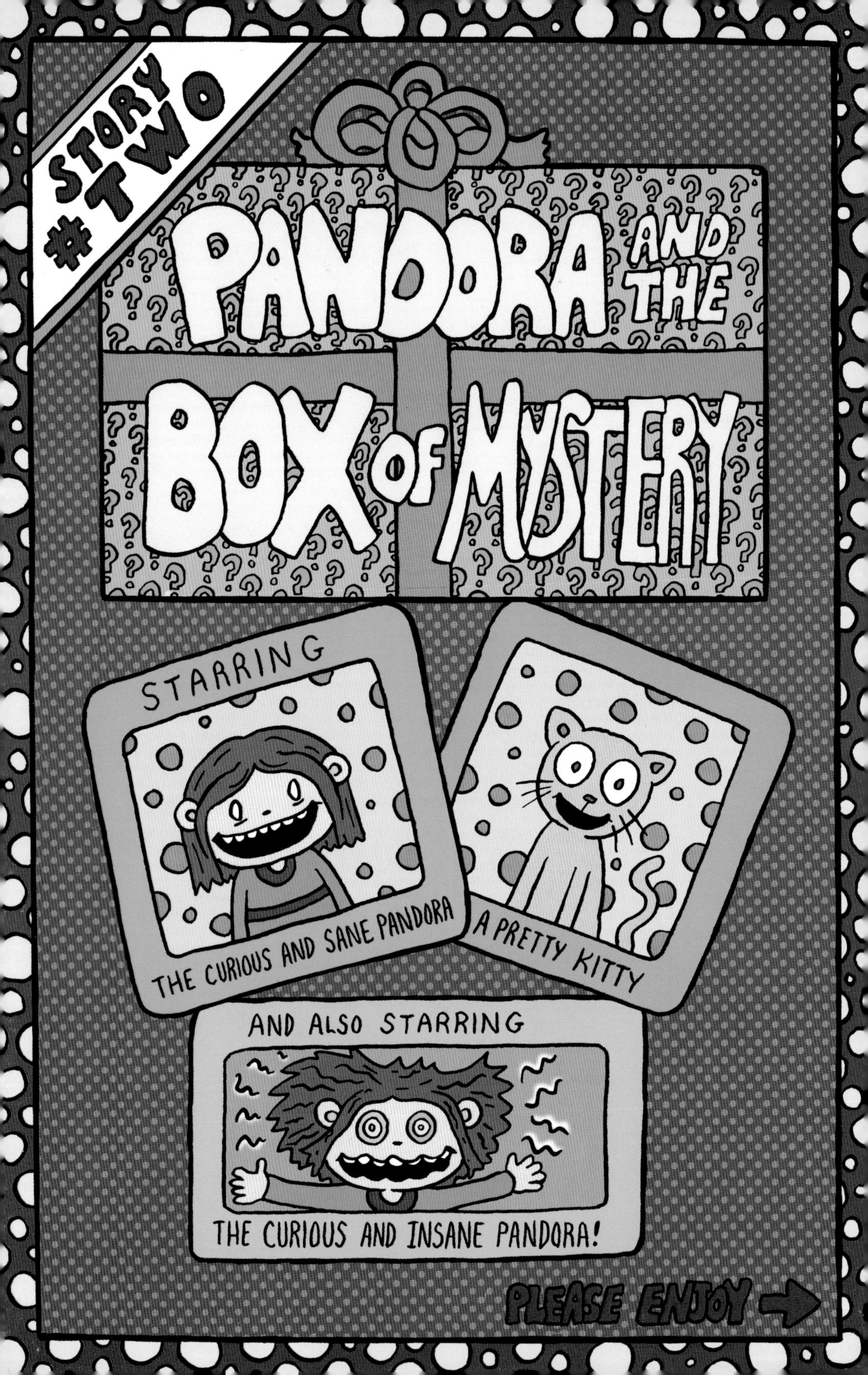
STORY #TWO
PANDORA AND THE BOX OF MYSTERY
STARRING
THE CURIOUS AND SANE PANDORA
A PRETTY KITTY
AND ALSO STARRING
THE CURIOUS AND INSANE PANDORA!
PLEASE ENJOY

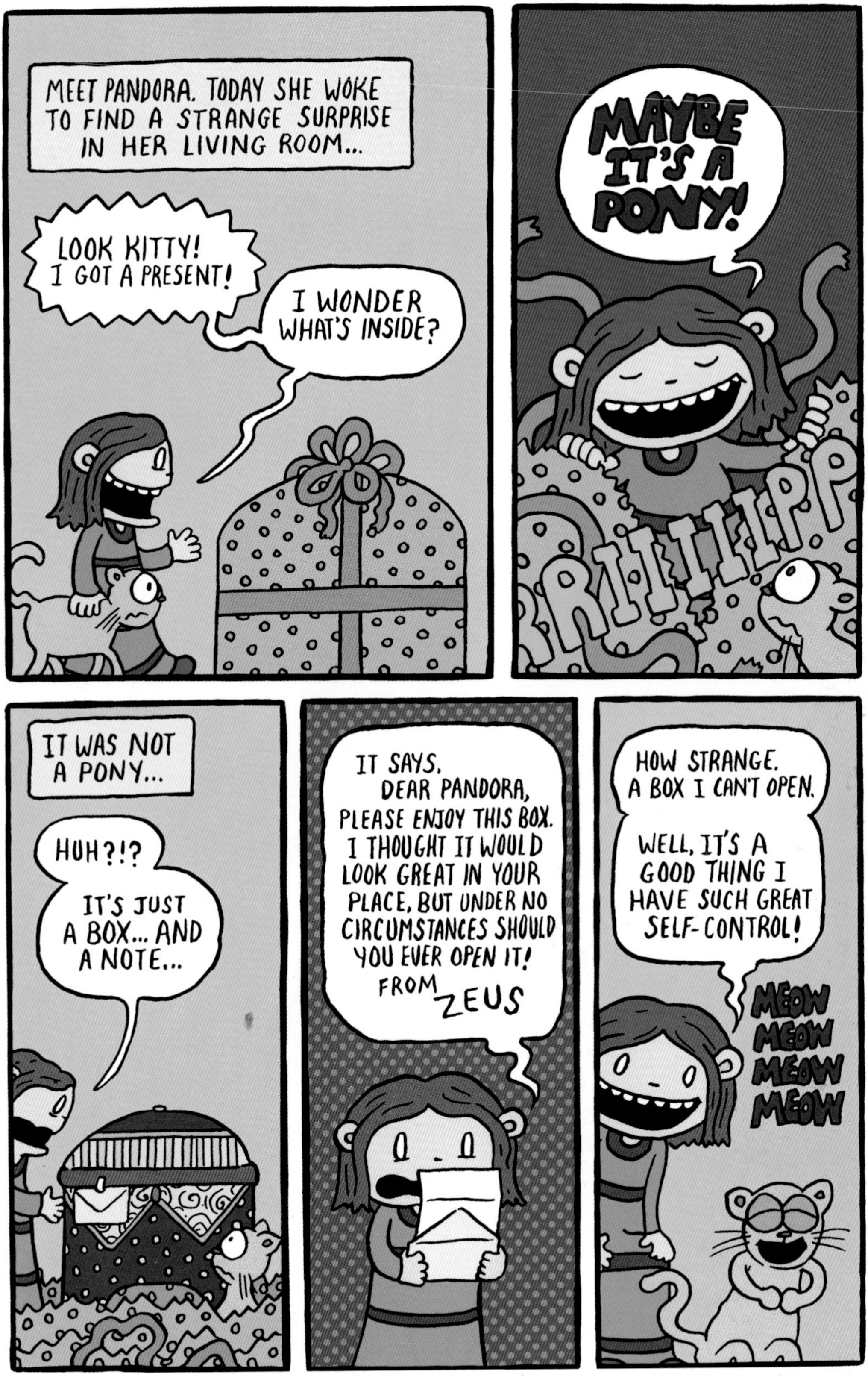

MEET PANDORA. TODAY SHE WOKE TO FIND A STRANGE SURPRISE IN HER LIVING ROOM...
LOOK KITTY! I GOT A PRESENT!
I WONDER WHAT'S INSIDE?
MAYBE IT'S A PONY!
RRIIIIIIPP
IT WAS NOT A PONY...
HUH?!?
IT'S JUST A BOX... AND A NOTE...
IT SAYS, DEAR PANDORA, PLEASE ENJOY THIS BOX. I THOUGHT IT WOULD LOOK GREAT IN YOUR PLACE, BUT UNDER NO CIRCUMSTANCES SHOULD YOU EVER OPEN IT! FROM ZEUS
HOW STRANGE. A BOX I CAN'T OPEN.
WELL, IT'S A GOOD THING I HAVE SUCH GREAT SELF-CONTROL!
MEOW MEOW MEOW MEOW

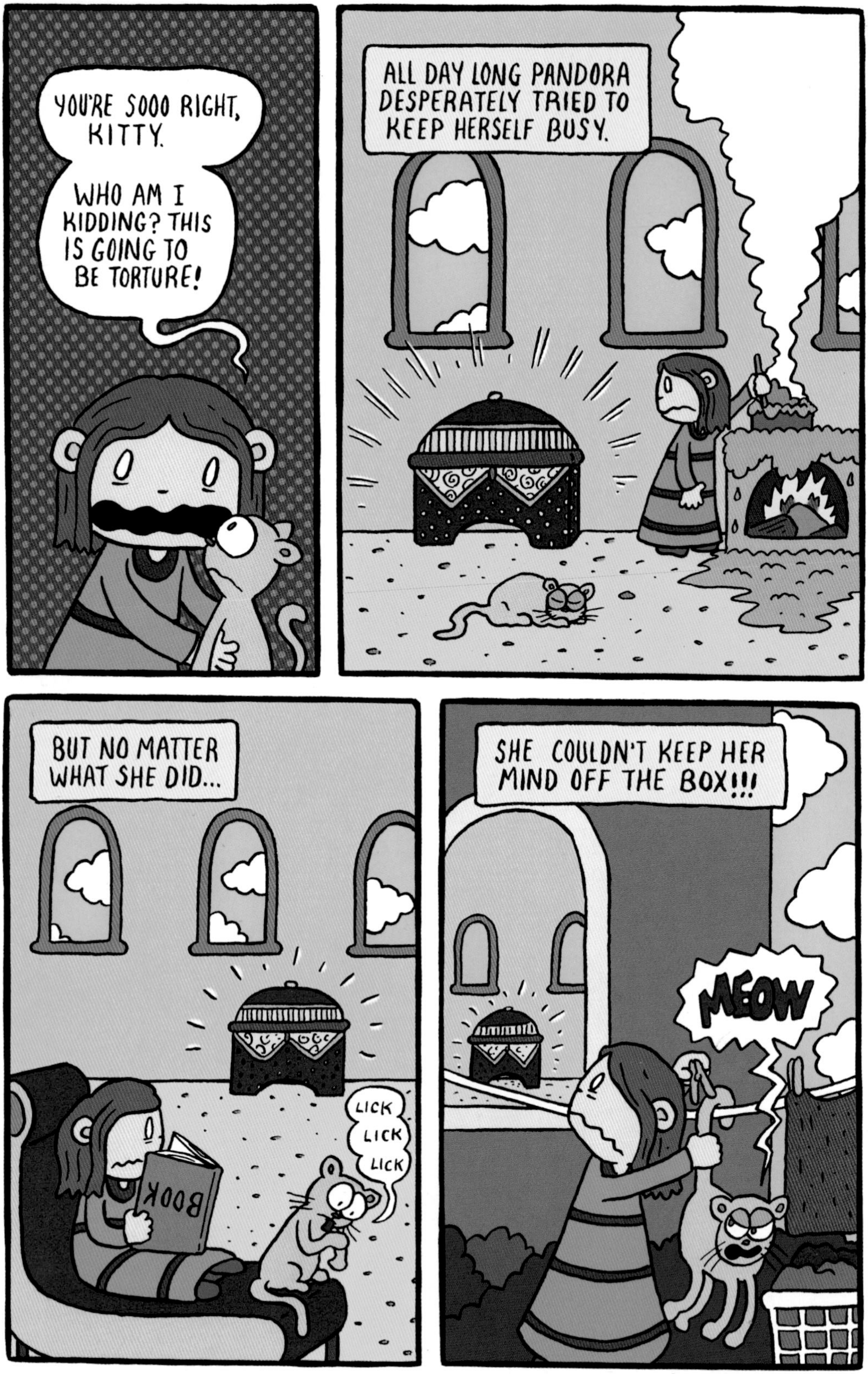
YOU'RE SOOO RIGHT, KITTY.
WHO AM I KIDDING? THIS IS GOING TO BE TORTURE!
ALL DAY LONG PANDORA DESPERATELY TRIED TO KEEP HERSELF BUSY.
BUT NO MATTER WHAT SHE DID...
BOOK
LICK LICK LICK
SHE COULDN'T KEEP HER MIND OFF THE BOX!!!
MEOW

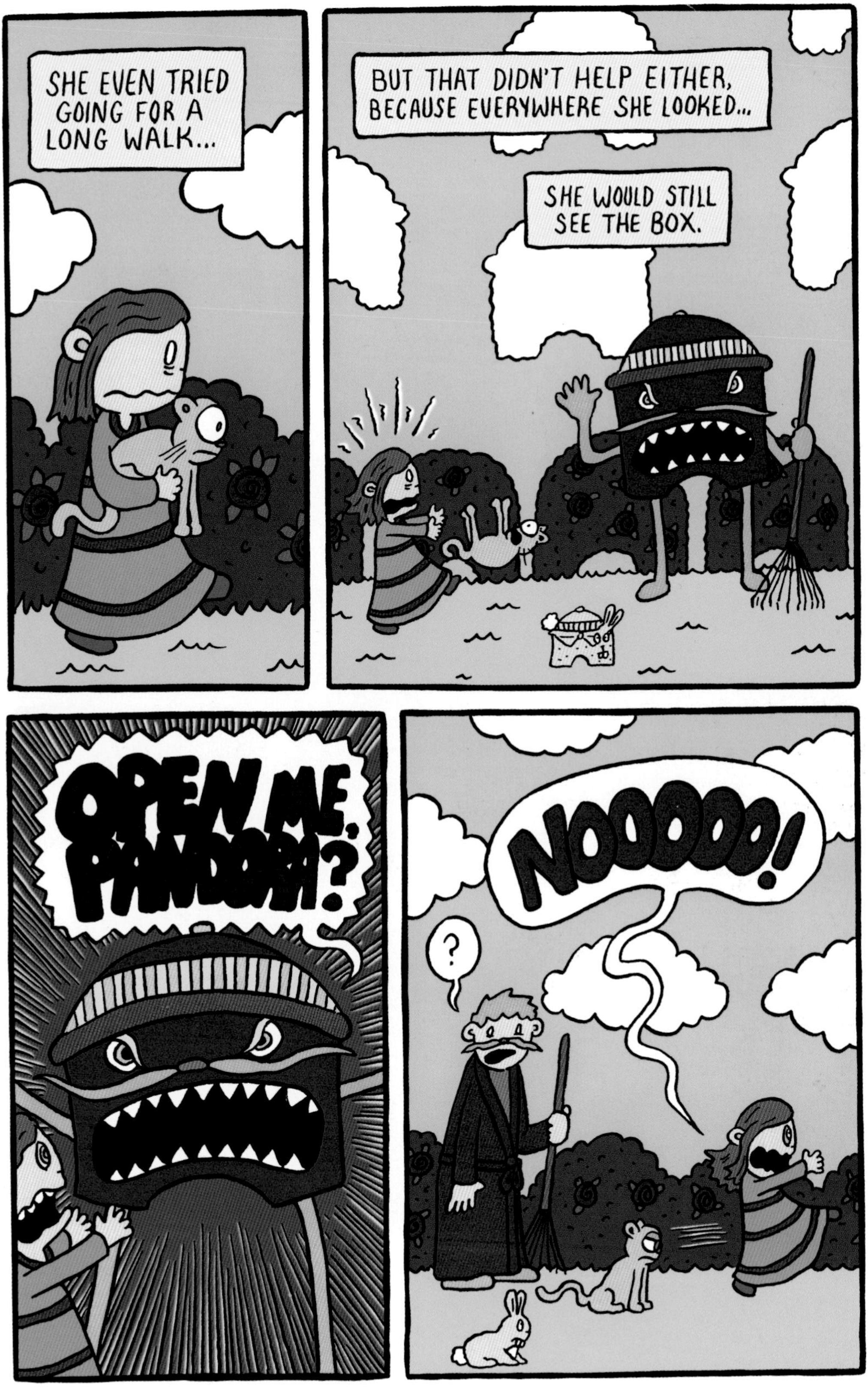
SHE EVEN TRIED GOING FOR A LONG WALK...
BUT THAT DIDN'T HELP EITHER, BECAUSE EVERYWHERE SHE LOOKED...
SHE WOULD STILL SEE THE BOX.
OPEN ME, PANDORA?
NOOOOOO!
?

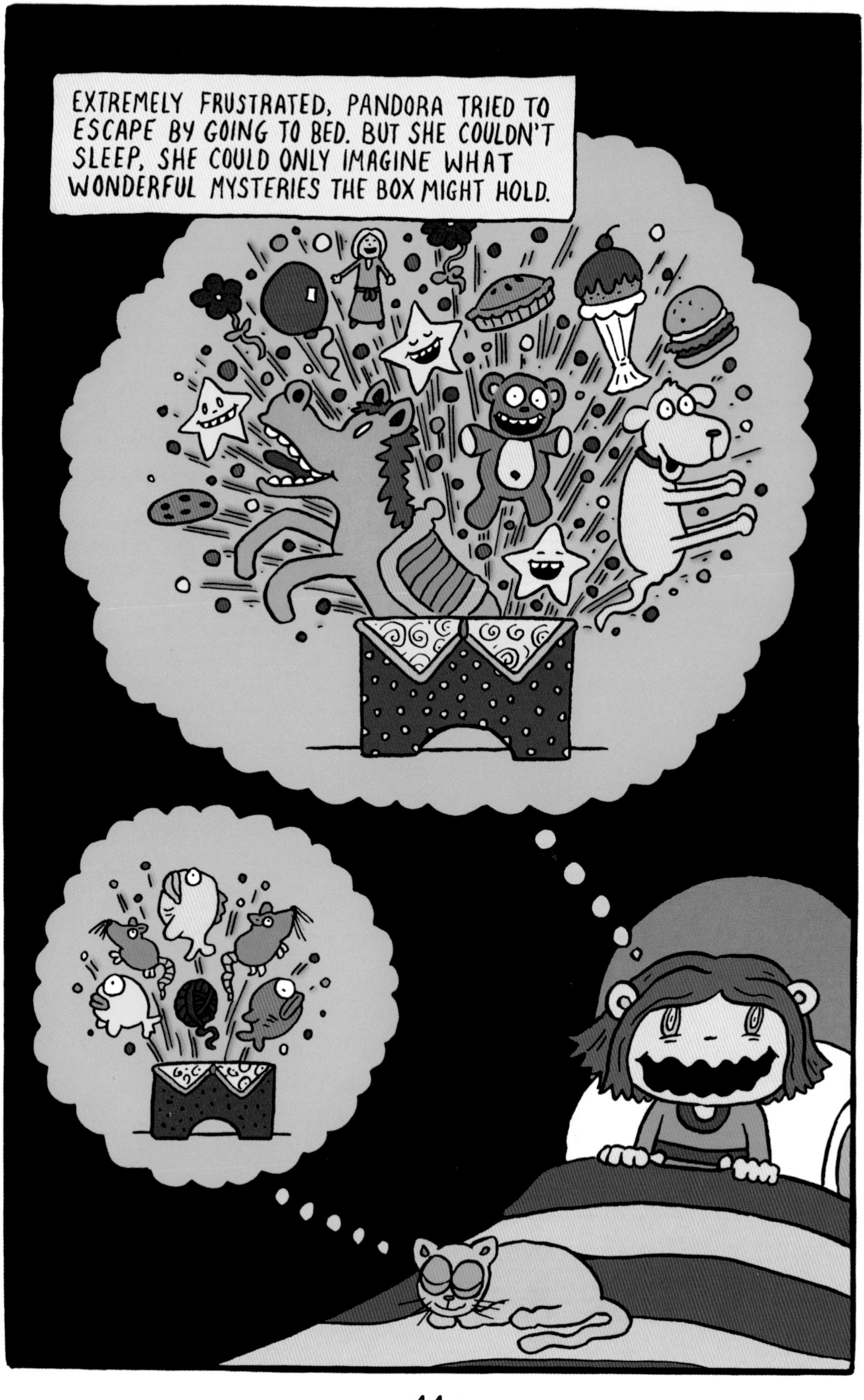
EXTREMELY FRUSTRATED, PANDORA TRIED TO ESCAPE BY GOING TO BED. BUT SHE COULDN'T SLEEP, SHE COULD ONLY IMAGINE WHAT WONDERFUL MYSTERIES THE BOX MIGHT HOLD.

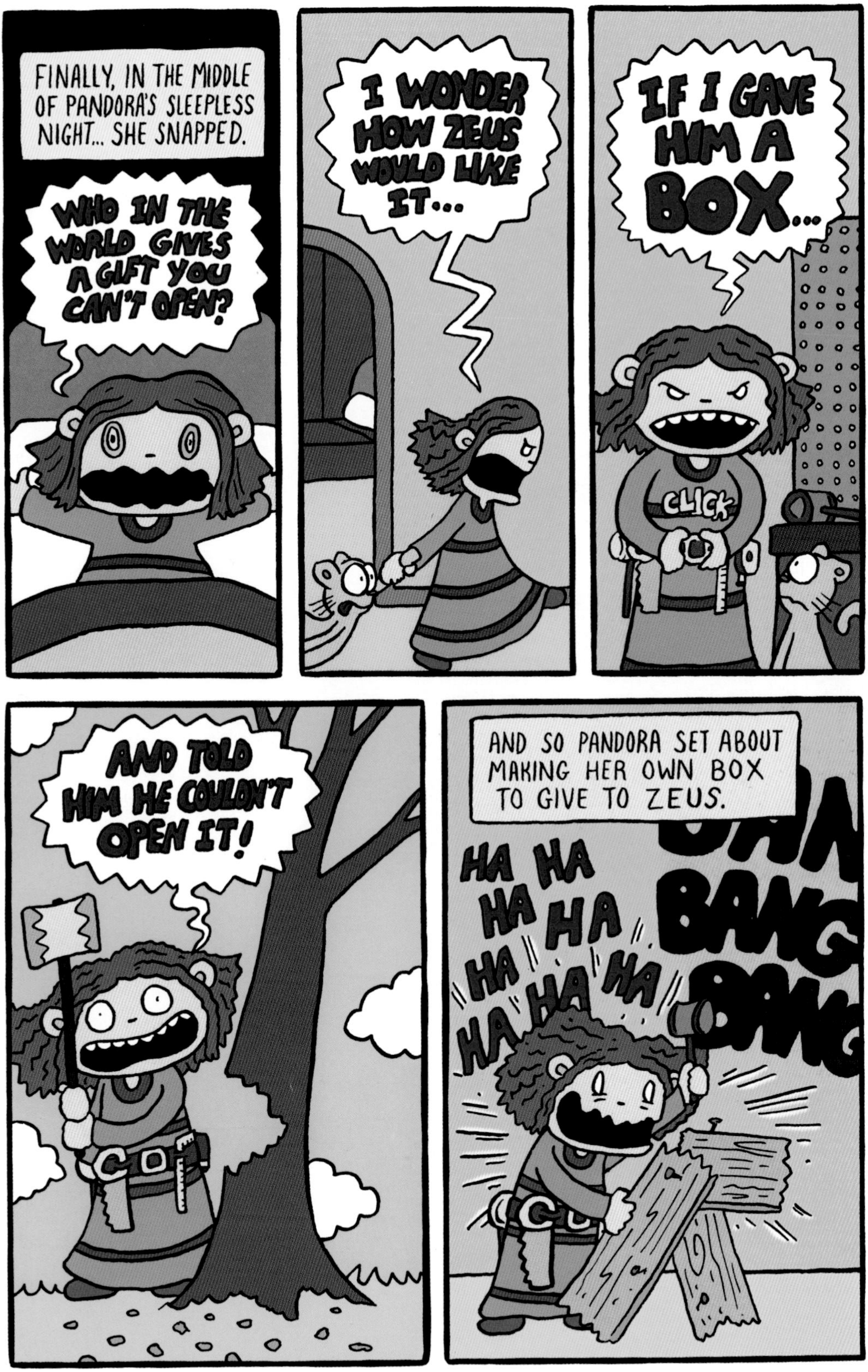

FINALLY, IN THE MIDDLE OF PANDORA'S SLEEPLESS NIGHT... SHE SNAPPED.
WHO IN THE WORLD GIVES A GIFT YOU CAN'T OPEN?
I WONDER HOW ZEUS WOULD LIKE IT...
IF I GAVE HIM A BOX...
CLICK
AND TOLD HIM HE COULDN'T OPEN IT!
AND SO PANDORA SET ABOUT MAKING HER OWN BOX TO GIVE TO ZEUS.
HA HA HA HA HA HA HA HA
BANG

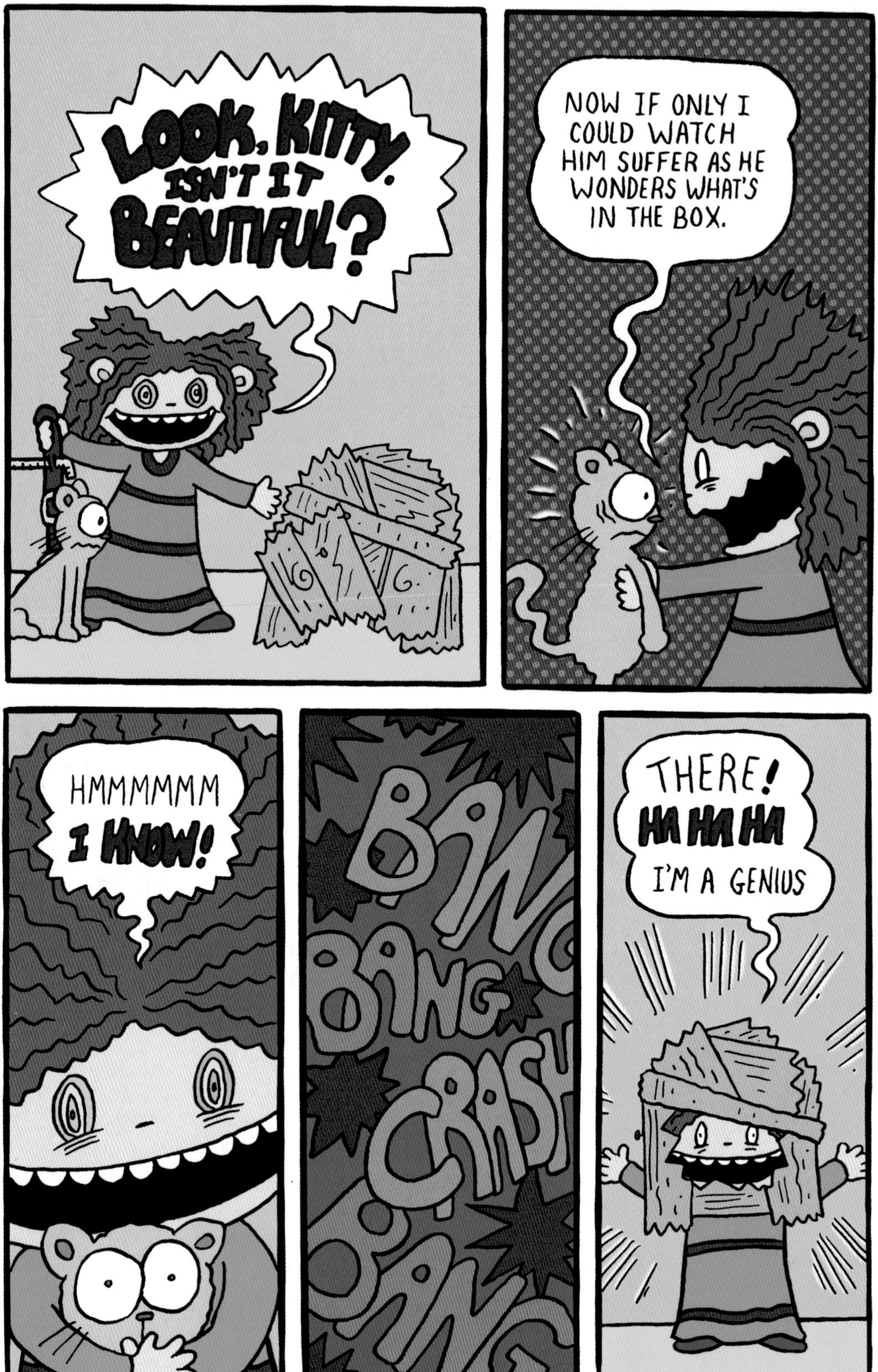
LOOK, KITTY. ISN'T IT BEAUTIFUL?
NOW IF ONLY I COULD WATCH HIM SUFFER AS HE WONDERS WHAT'S IN THE BOX.
HMMMMMM
I KNOW!
BANG
BANG
CRASH
THERE!
HA HA HA
I'M A GENIUS

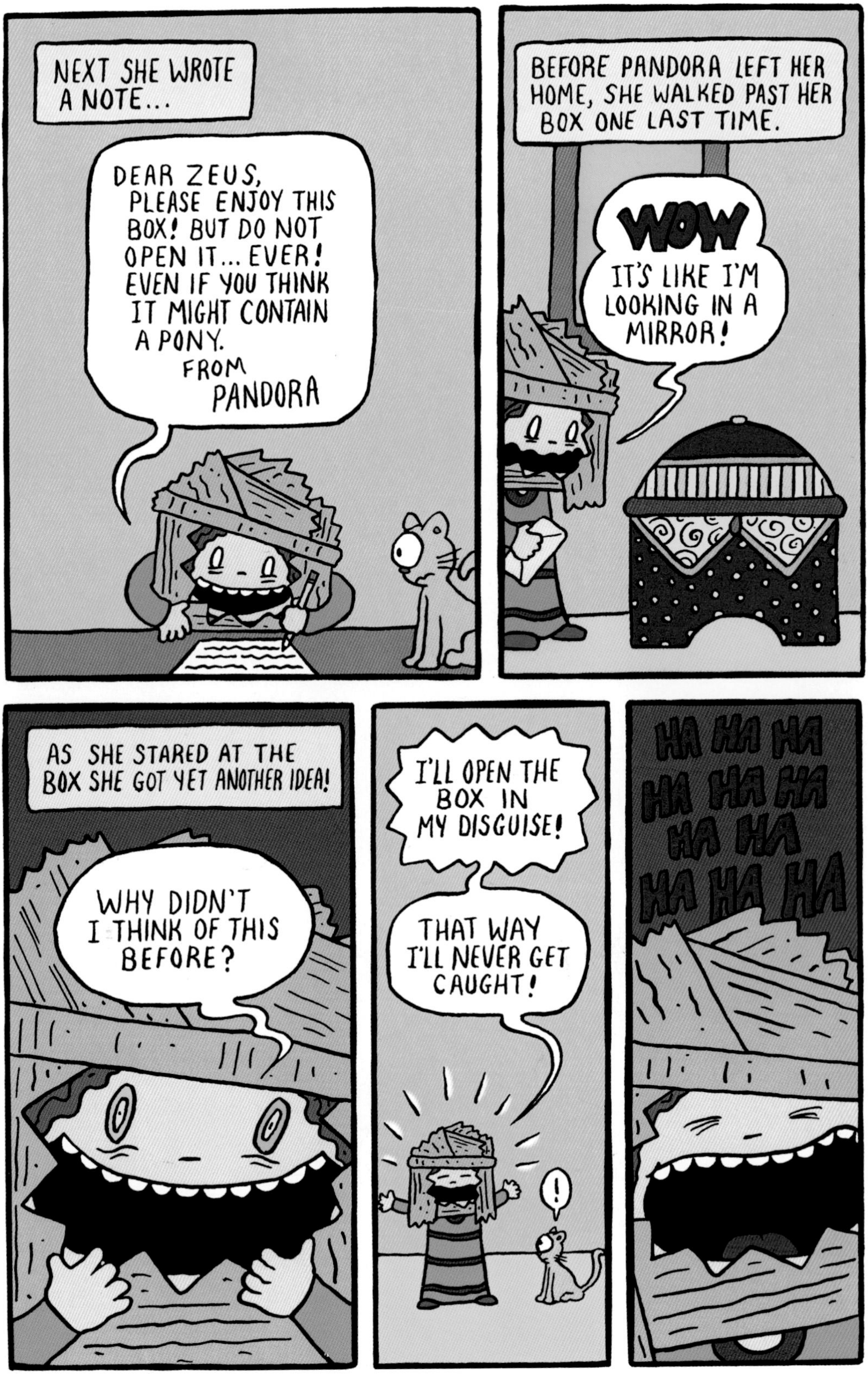
NEXT SHE WROTE A NOTE...
DEAR ZEUS, PLEASE ENJOY THIS BOX! BUT DO NOT OPEN IT... EVER! EVEN IF YOU THINK IT MIGHT CONTAIN A PONY. FROM PANDORA
BEFORE PANDORA LEFT HER HOME, SHE WALKED PAST HER BOX ONE LAST TIME.
WOW
IT'S LIKE I'M LOOKING IN A MIRROR!
AS SHE STARED AT THE BOX SHE GOT YET ANOTHER IDEA!
WHY DIDN'T I THINK OF THIS BEFORE?
I'LL OPEN THE BOX IN MY DISGUISE!
THAT WAY I'LL NEVER GET CAUGHT!
!
HA HA HA HA HA HA HA HA HA HA HA

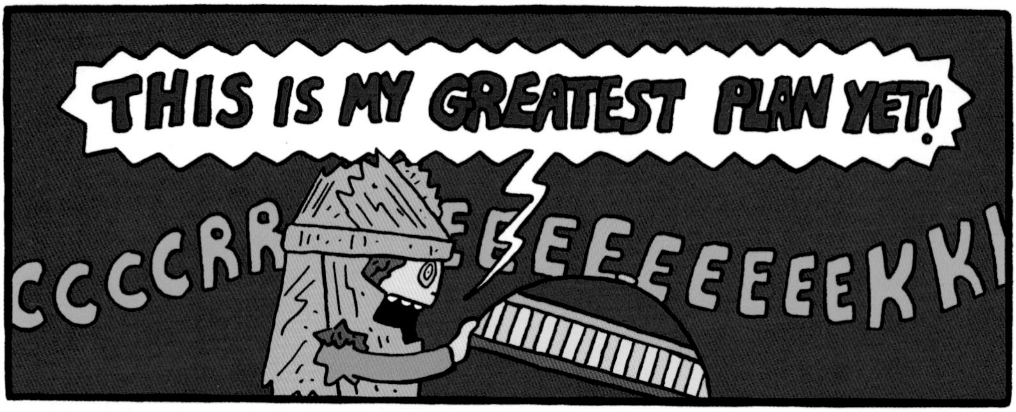
THIS IS MY GREATEST PLAN YET!
CCCCRREEEEEEEEEEKK!

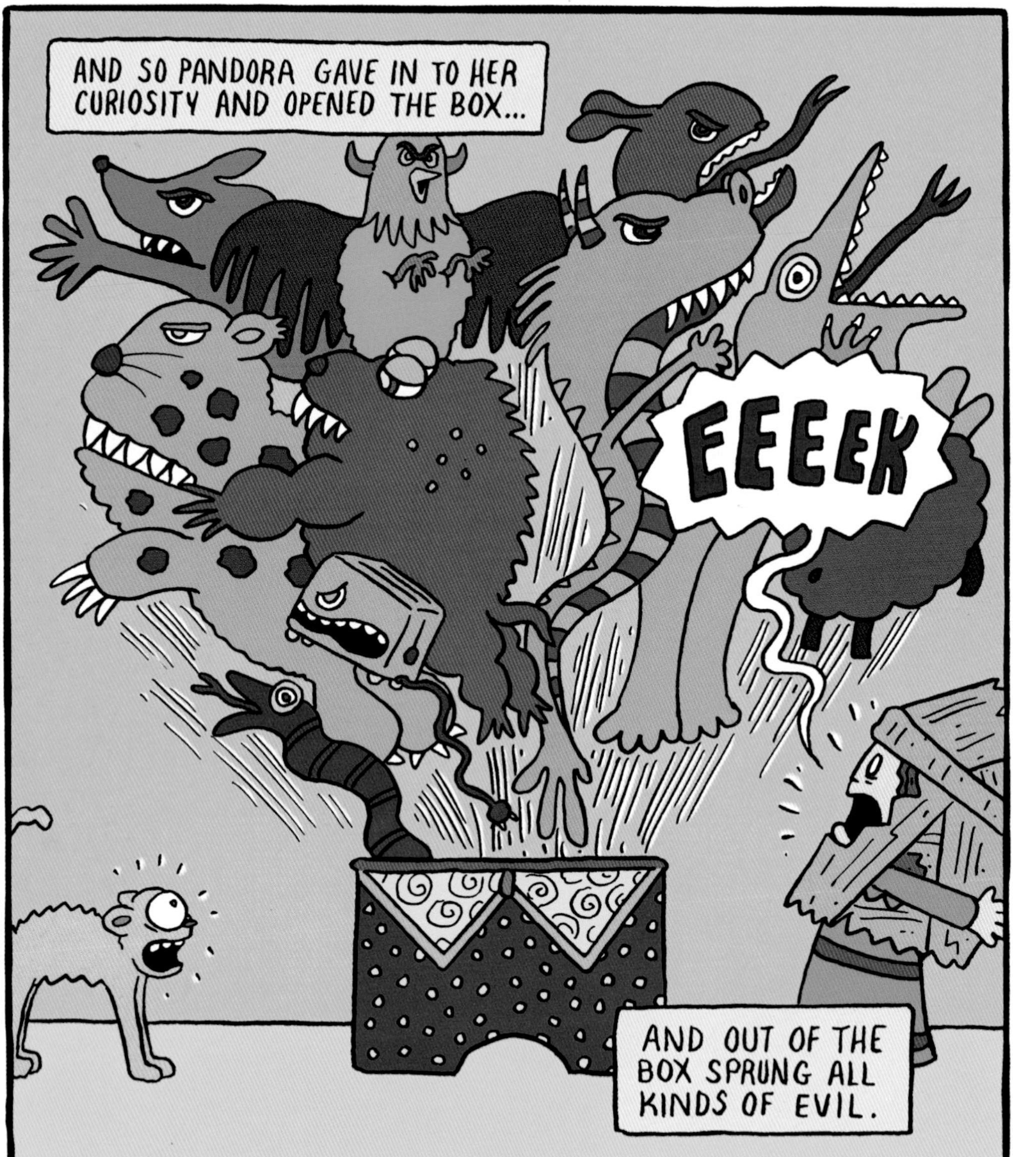
AND SO PANDORA GAVE IN TO HER CURIOSITY AND OPENED THE BOX...
EEEEK
AND OUT OF THE BOX SPRUNG ALL KINDS OF EVIL.

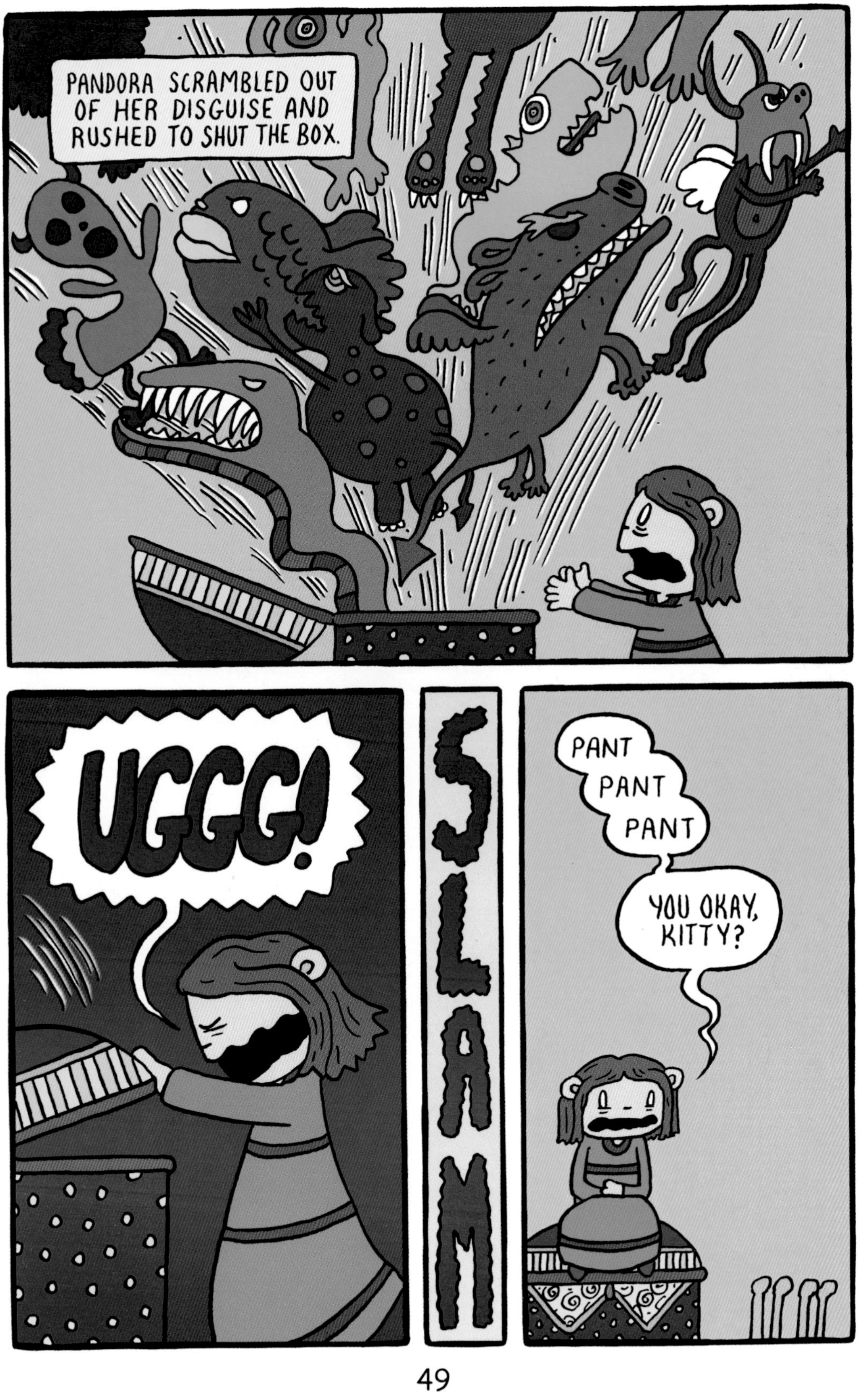
PANDORA SCRAMBLED OUT OF HER DISGUISE AND RUSHED TO SHUT THE BOX.
UGGG!
SLAM
PANT
PANT
PANT
YOU OKAY, KITTY?

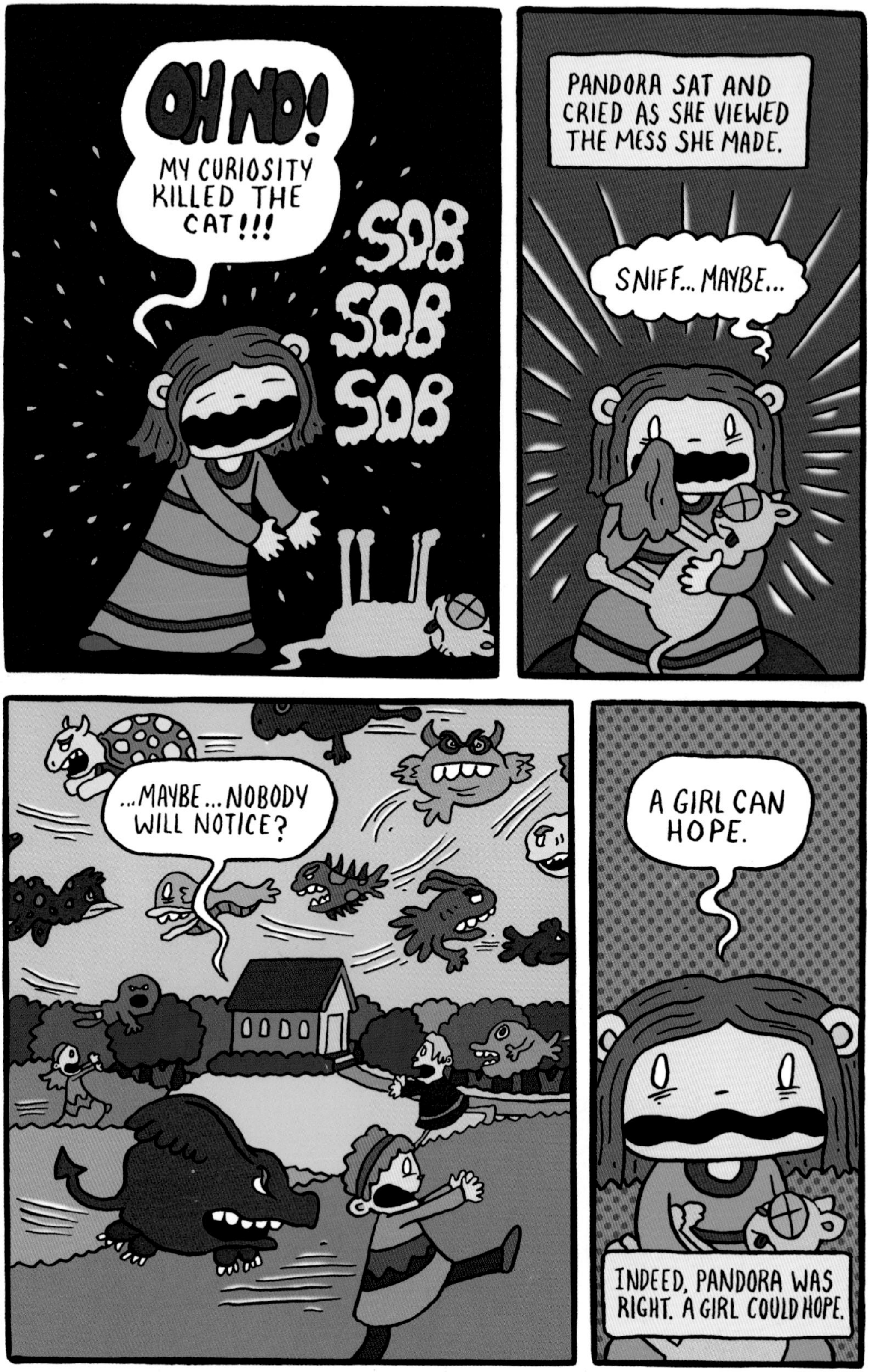
OH NO!
MY CURIOSITY KILLED THE CAT!!!
SOB SOB SOB
PANDORA SAT AND CRIED AS SHE VIEWED THE MESS SHE MADE.
SNIFF... MAYBE...
...MAYBE... NOBODY WILL NOTICE?
A GIRL CAN HOPE.
INDEED, PANDORA WAS RIGHT. A GIRL COULD HOPE.

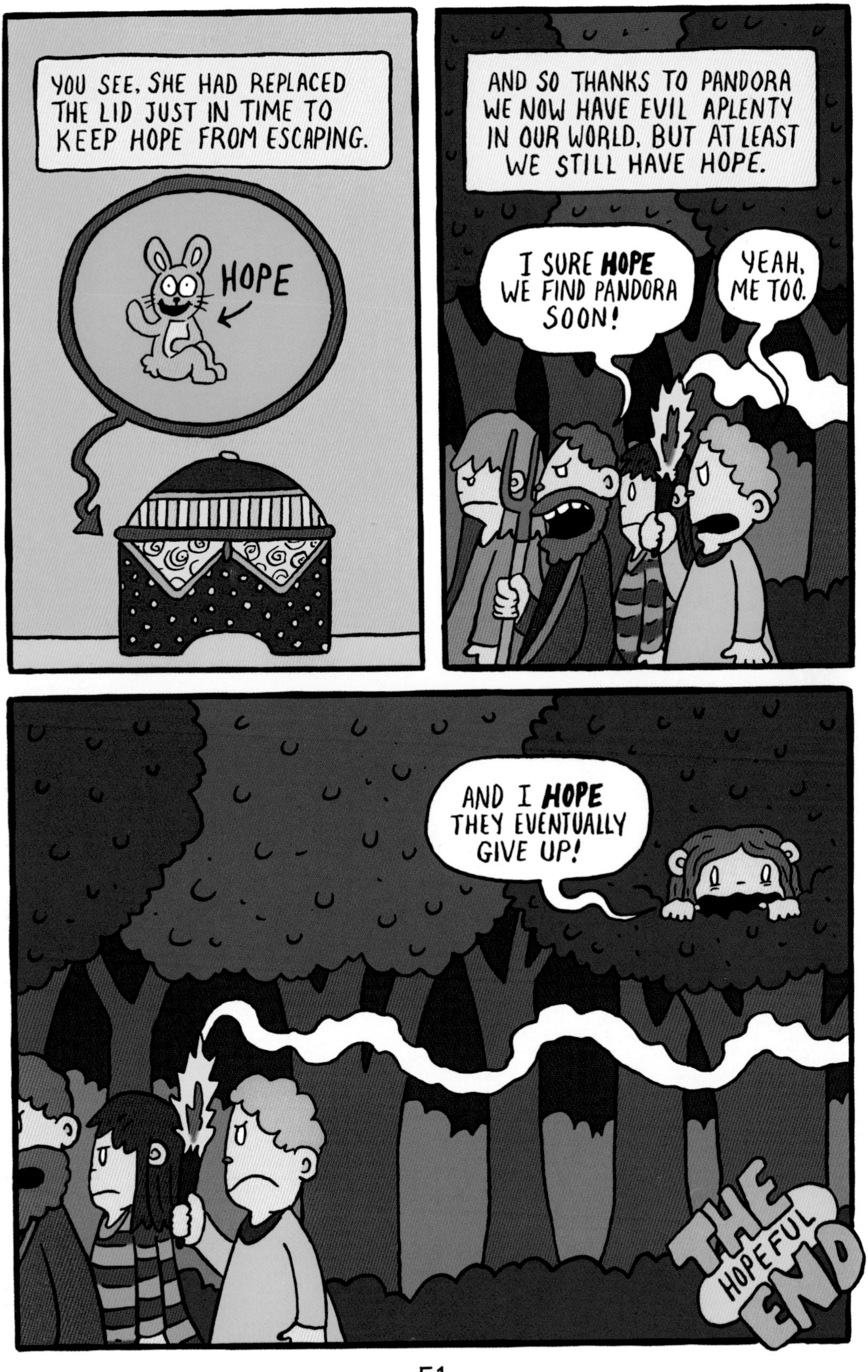
YOU SEE, SHE HAD REPLACED THE LID JUST IN TIME TO KEEP HOPE FROM ESCAPING.
HOPE
AND SO THANKS TO PANDORA WE NOW HAVE EVIL APLENTY IN OUR WORLD, BUT AT LEAST WE STILL HAVE HOPE.
I SURE HOPE WE FIND PANDORA SOON!
YEAH, ME TOO.
AND I HOPE THEY EVENTUALLY GIVE UP!
THE HOPEFUL END

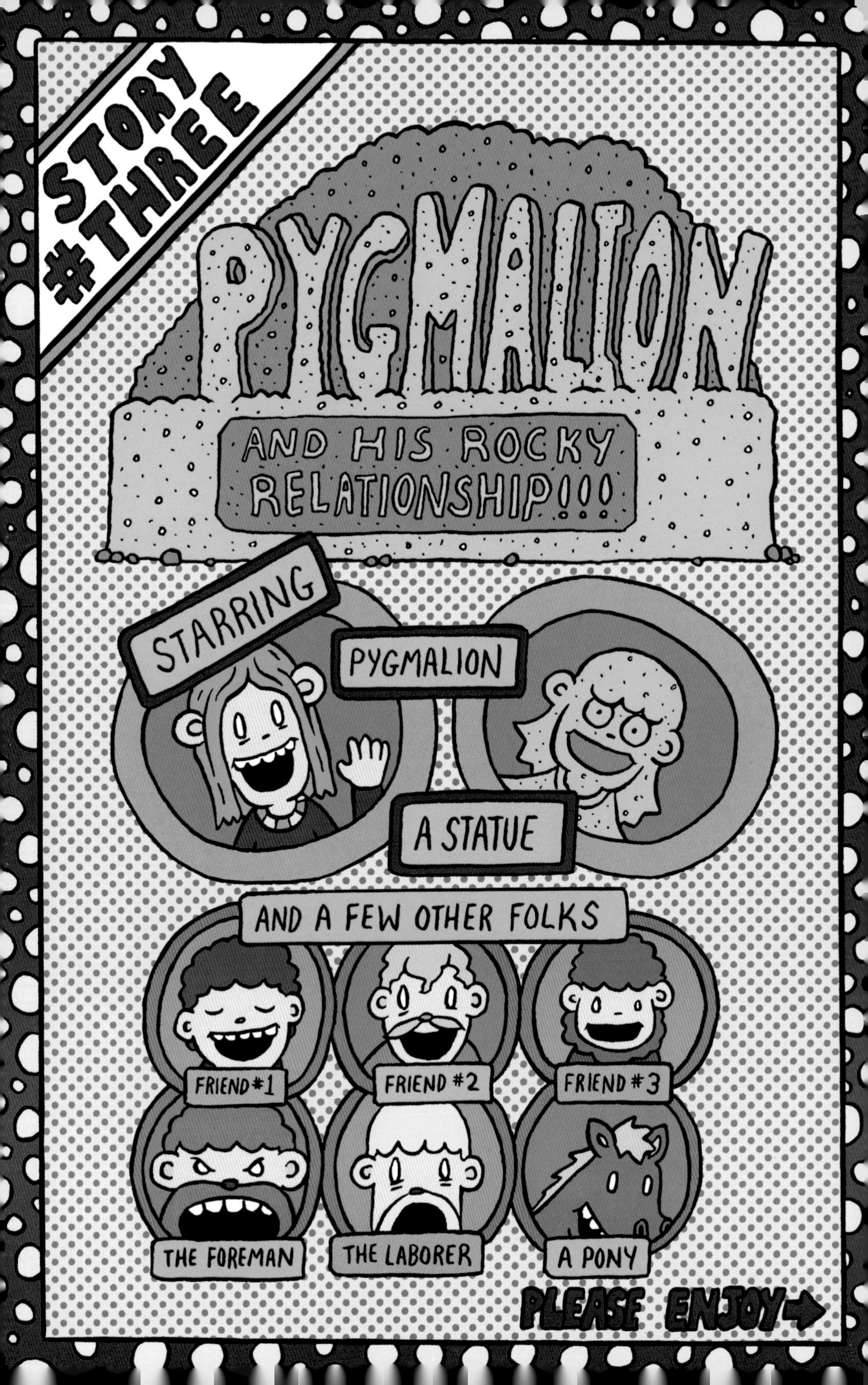
STORY #THREE
PYGMALION
AND HIS ROCKY RELATIONSHIP!!!
STARRING
PYGMALION
A STATUE
AND A FEW OTHER FOLKS
FRIEND #1
FRIEND #2
FRIEND #3
THE FOREMAN
THE LABORER
A PONY
PLEASE ENJOY

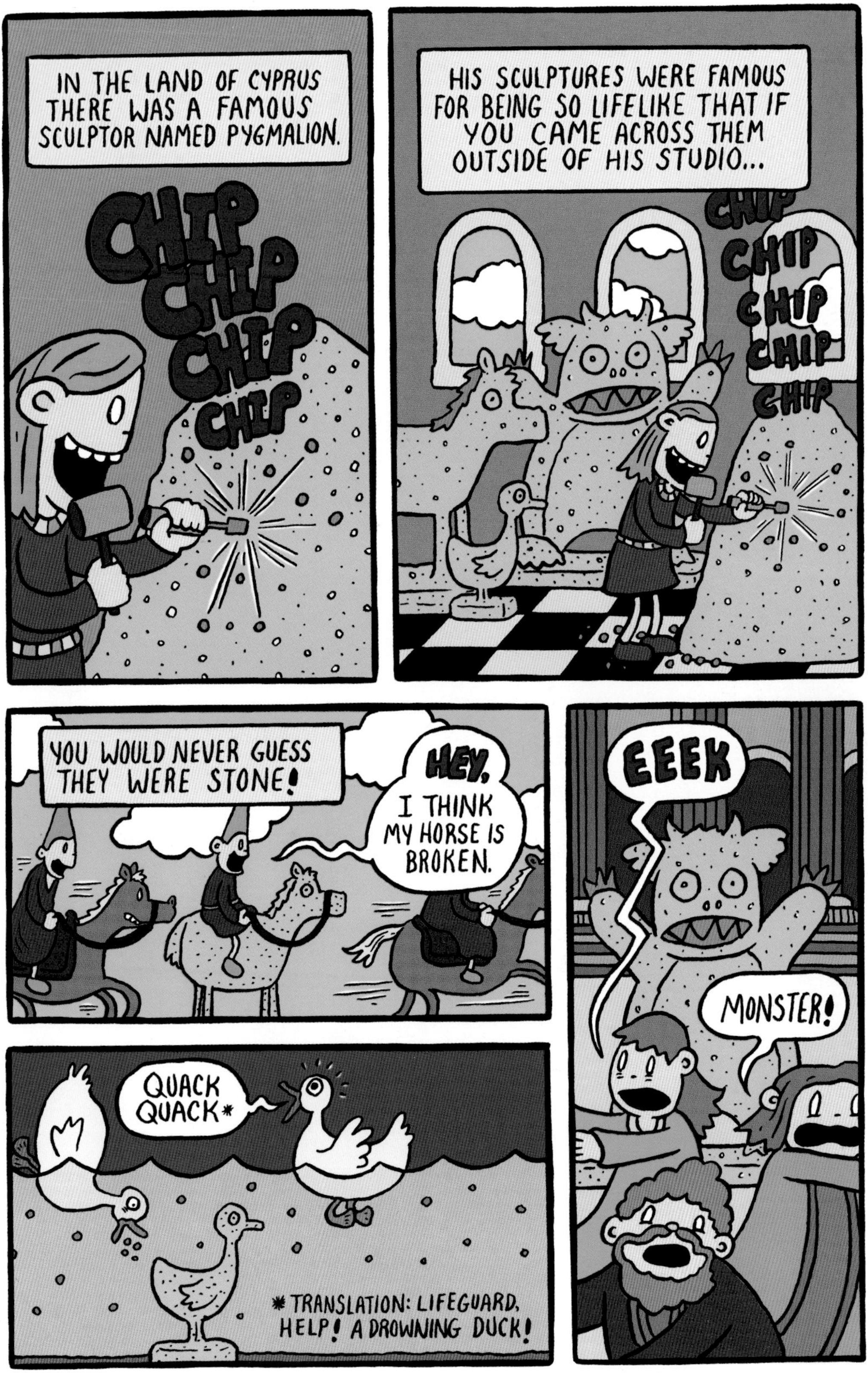
IN THE LAND OF CYPRUS THERE WAS A FAMOUS SCULPTOR NAMED PYGMALION.
CHIP CHIP CHIP CHIP
HIS SCULPTURES WERE FAMOUS FOR BEING SO LIFELIKE THAT IF YOU CAME ACROSS THEM OUTSIDE OF HIS STUDIO...
CHIP CHIP CHIP CHIP CHIP
YOU WOULD NEVER GUESS THEY WERE STONE!
HEY, I THINK MY HORSE IS BROKEN.
EEEK
MONSTER!
QUACK QUACK*
* TRANSLATION: LIFEGUARD, HELP! A DROWNING DUCK!

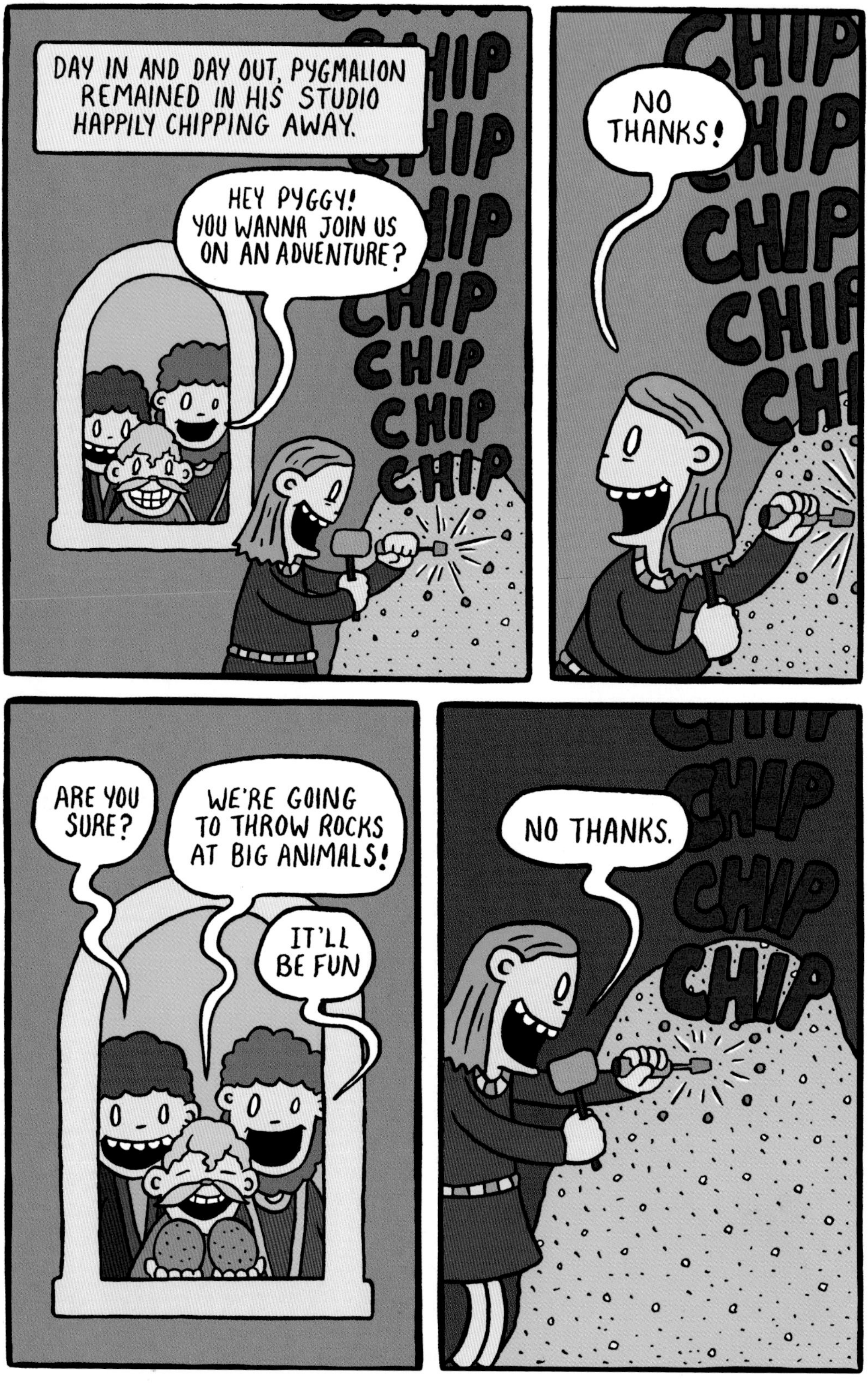
DAY IN AND DAY OUT, PYGMALION REMAINED IN HIS STUDIO HAPPILY CHIPPING AWAY.
HEY PYGGY! YOU WANNA JOIN US ON AN ADVENTURE?
CHIP CHIP CHIP CHIP CHIP CHIP CHIP
NO THANKS!
CHIP CHIP CHIP CHIP
ARE YOU SURE?
WE'RE GOING TO THROW ROCKS AT BIG ANIMALS!
IT'LL BE FUN
NO THANKS.
CHIP CHIP CHIP

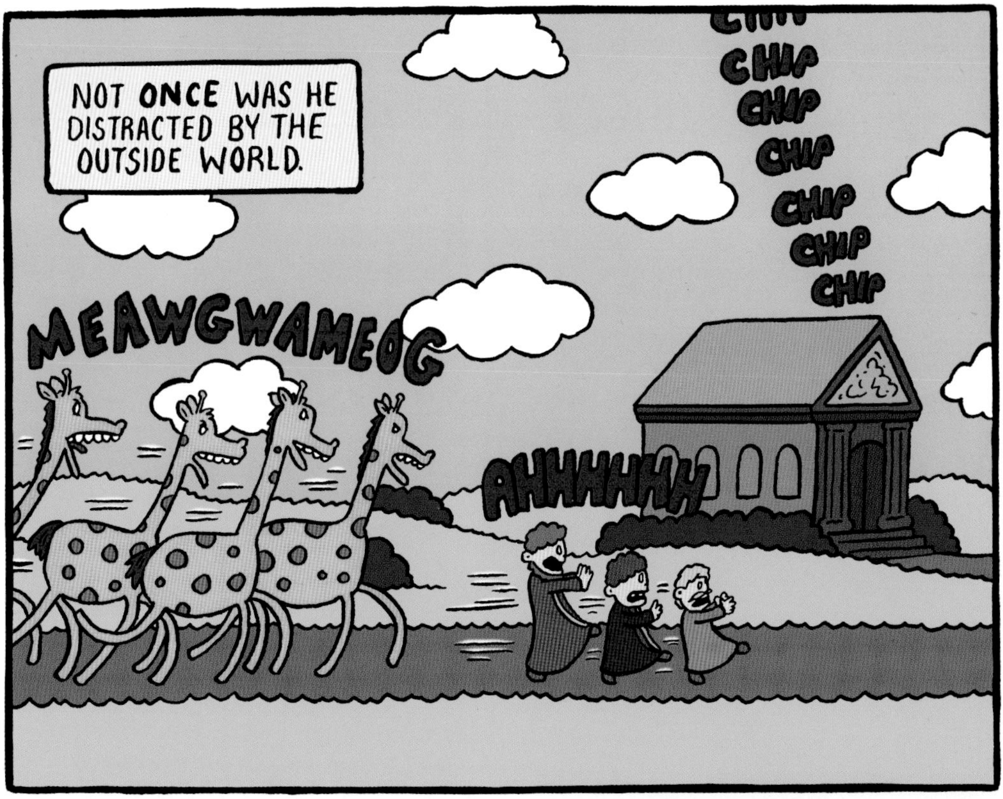
NOT ONCE WAS HE DISTRACTED BY THE OUTSIDE WORLD.
CHIP
CHIP
CHIP
CHIP
CHIP
CHIP
MEAWGWAMEOG
AHHHHHH
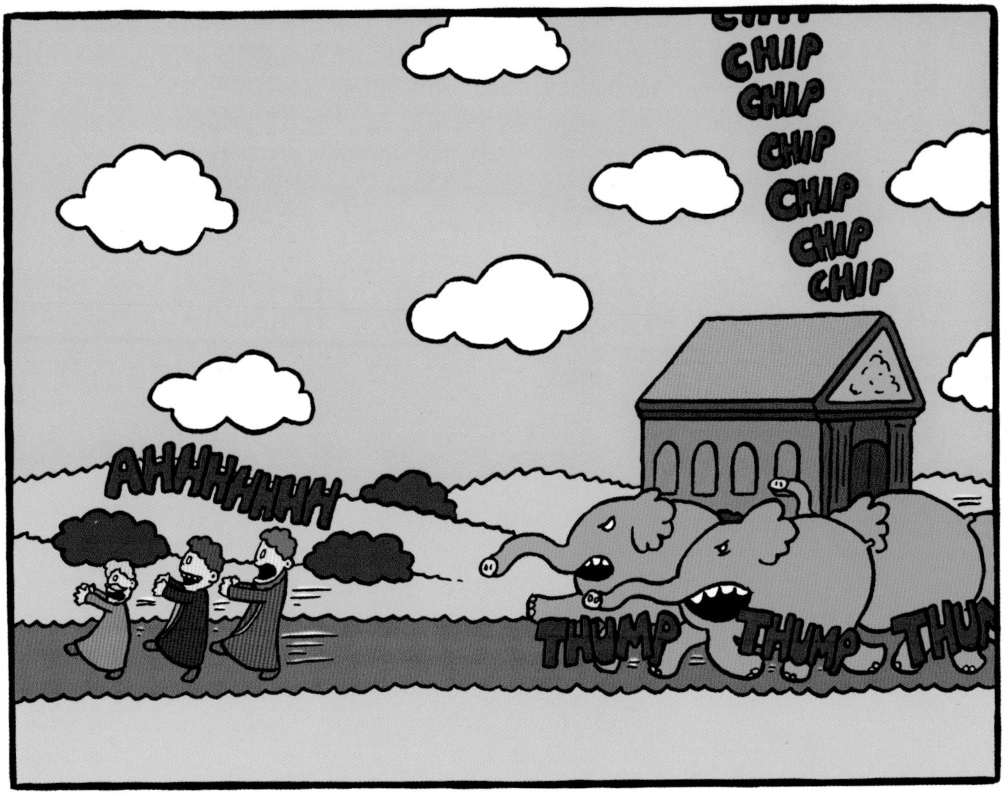
CHIP
CHIP
CHIP
CHIP
CHIP
CHIP
AHHHHHHH
THUMP
THUMP

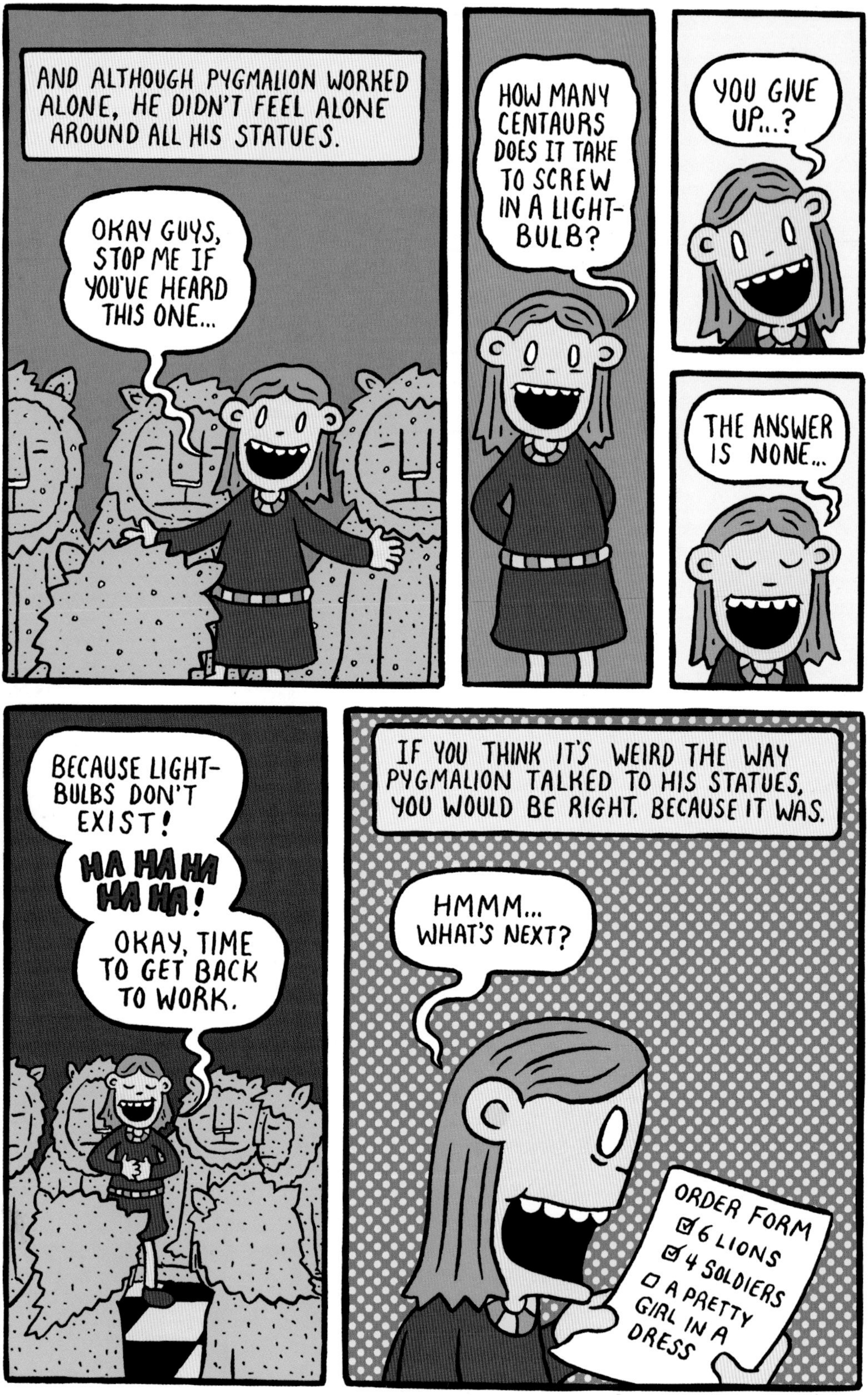
AND ALTHOUGH PYGMALION WORKED ALONE, HE DIDN'T FEEL ALONE AROUND ALL HIS STATUES.
OKAY GUYS, STOP ME IF YOU'VE HEARD THIS ONE...
HOW MANY CENTAURS DOES IT TAKE TO SCREW IN A LIGHT-BULB?
YOU GIVE UP...?
THE ANSWER IS NONE...
BECAUSE LIGHT-BULBS DON'T EXIST!
HA HA HA HA HA!
OKAY, TIME TO GET BACK TO WORK.
IF YOU THINK IT'S WEIRD THE WAY PYGMALION TALKED TO HIS STATUES, YOU WOULD BE RIGHT. BECAUSE IT WAS.
HMMM... WHAT'S NEXT?
ORDER FORM
☑ 6 LIONS
☑ 4 SOLDIERS
☐ A PRETTY GIRL IN A DRESS

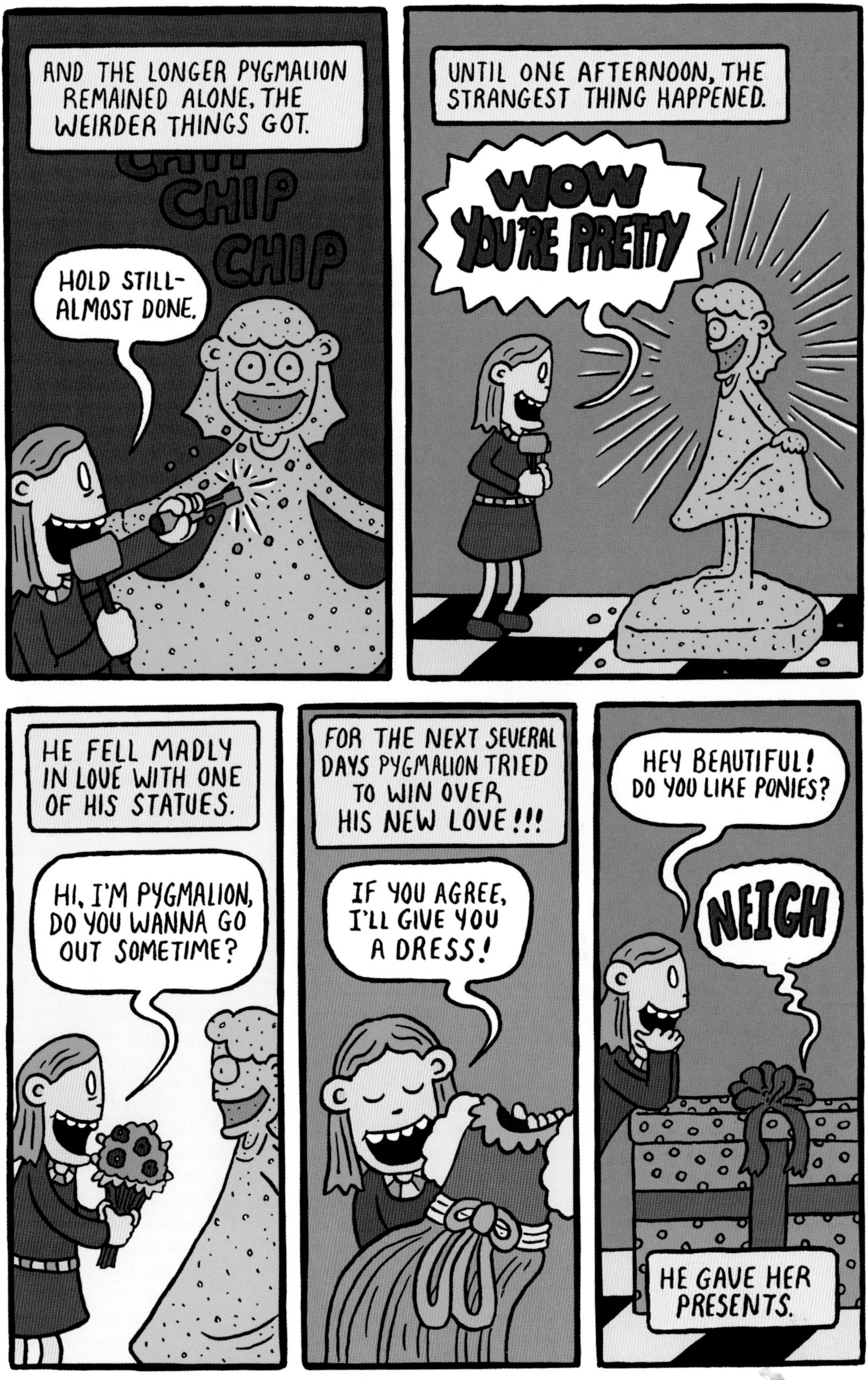

AND THE LONGER PYGMALION REMAINED ALONE, THE WEIRDER THINGS GOT.
CHIP
CHIP
HOLD STILL- ALMOST DONE.
UNTIL ONE AFTERNOON, THE STRANGEST THING HAPPENED.
WOW YOU'RE PRETTY
HE FELL MADLY IN LOVE WITH ONE OF HIS STATUES.
HI, I'M PYGMALION, DO YOU WANNA GO OUT SOMETIME?
FOR THE NEXT SEVERAL DAYS PYGMALION TRIED TO WIN OVER HIS NEW LOVE!!!
IF YOU AGREE, I'LL GIVE YOU A DRESS!
HEY BEAUTIFUL! DO YOU LIKE PONIES?
NEIGH
HE GAVE HER PRESENTS.

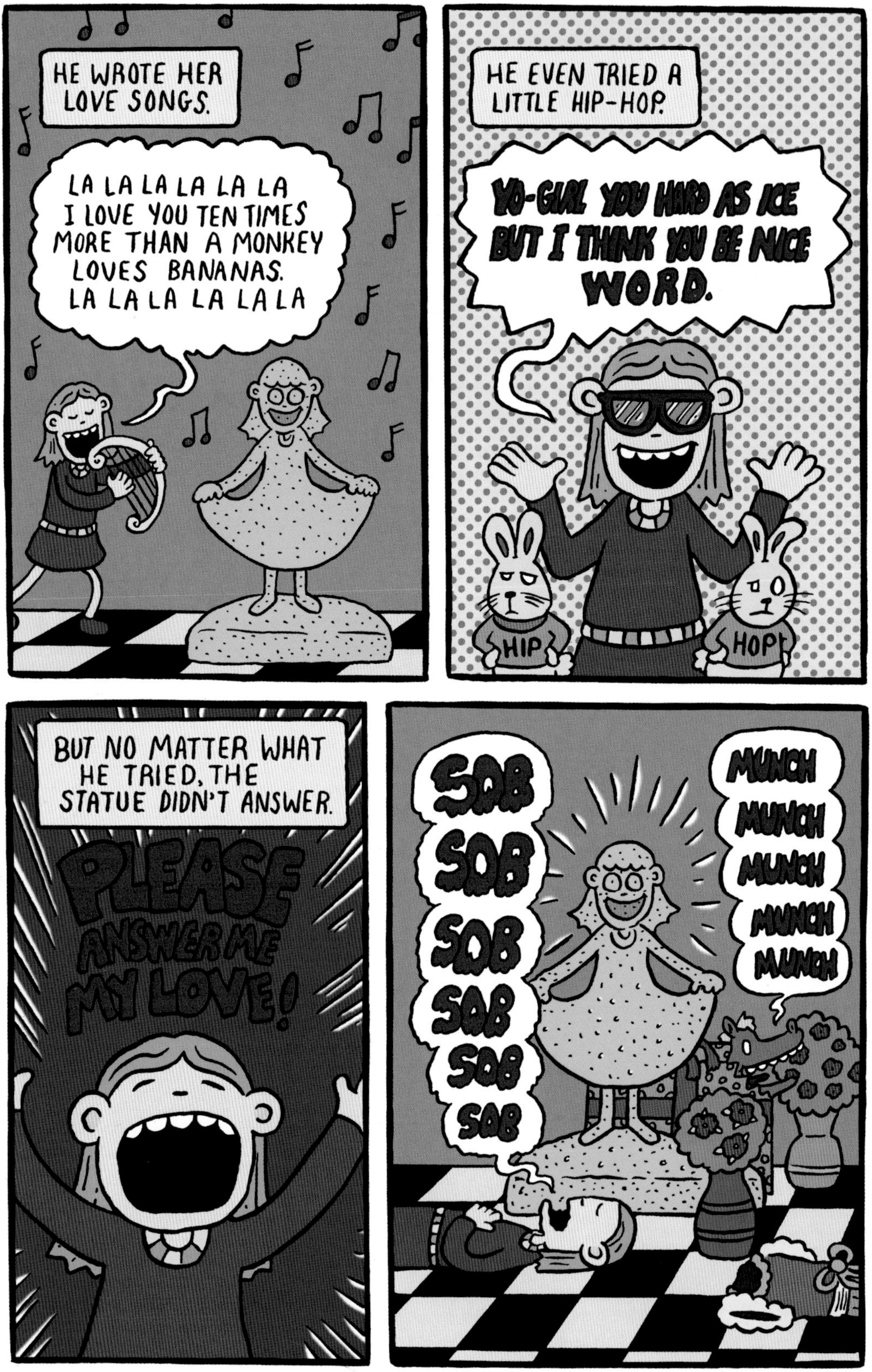
HE WROTE HER LOVE SONGS.
LA LA LA LA LA LA I LOVE YOU TEN TIMES MORE THAN A MONKEY LOVES BANANAS. LA LA LA LA LA LA
HE EVEN TRIED A LITTLE HIP-HOP.
YO-GIRL YOU HARD AS ICE BUT I THINK YOU BE NICE WORD.
HIP
HOP
BUT NO MATTER WHAT HE TRIED, THE STATUE DIDN'T ANSWER.
PLEASE ANSWER ME MY LOVE!
SOB SOB SOB SOB SOB SOB
MUNCH MUNCH MUNCH MUNCH MUNCH

OVERCOME WITH SADNESS, PYGMALION STOPPED WORKING.

SNIFF SNIFF

THE NORMAL NOISES OF HIS WORK STOPPED...

CHIP CHIP CHIP CHIP CHIP CHIP CHIP

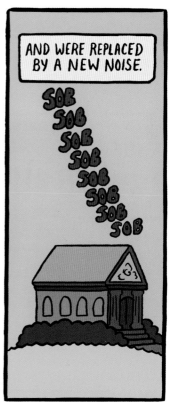

AND WERE REPLACED BY A NEW NOISE.

SOB SOB SOB SOB SOB SOB SOB SOB

MEANWHILE...

HEY! WHERE IS MY PRETTY GIRL STATUE?

UMM... IT HASN'T ARRIVED YET.

WELL, I HAVE DEADLINES TO MEET, SO UNLESS YOU WANT TO PUT ON A DRESS AND FILL THE VOID...

GET ME MY STATUE!

YES, SIR.

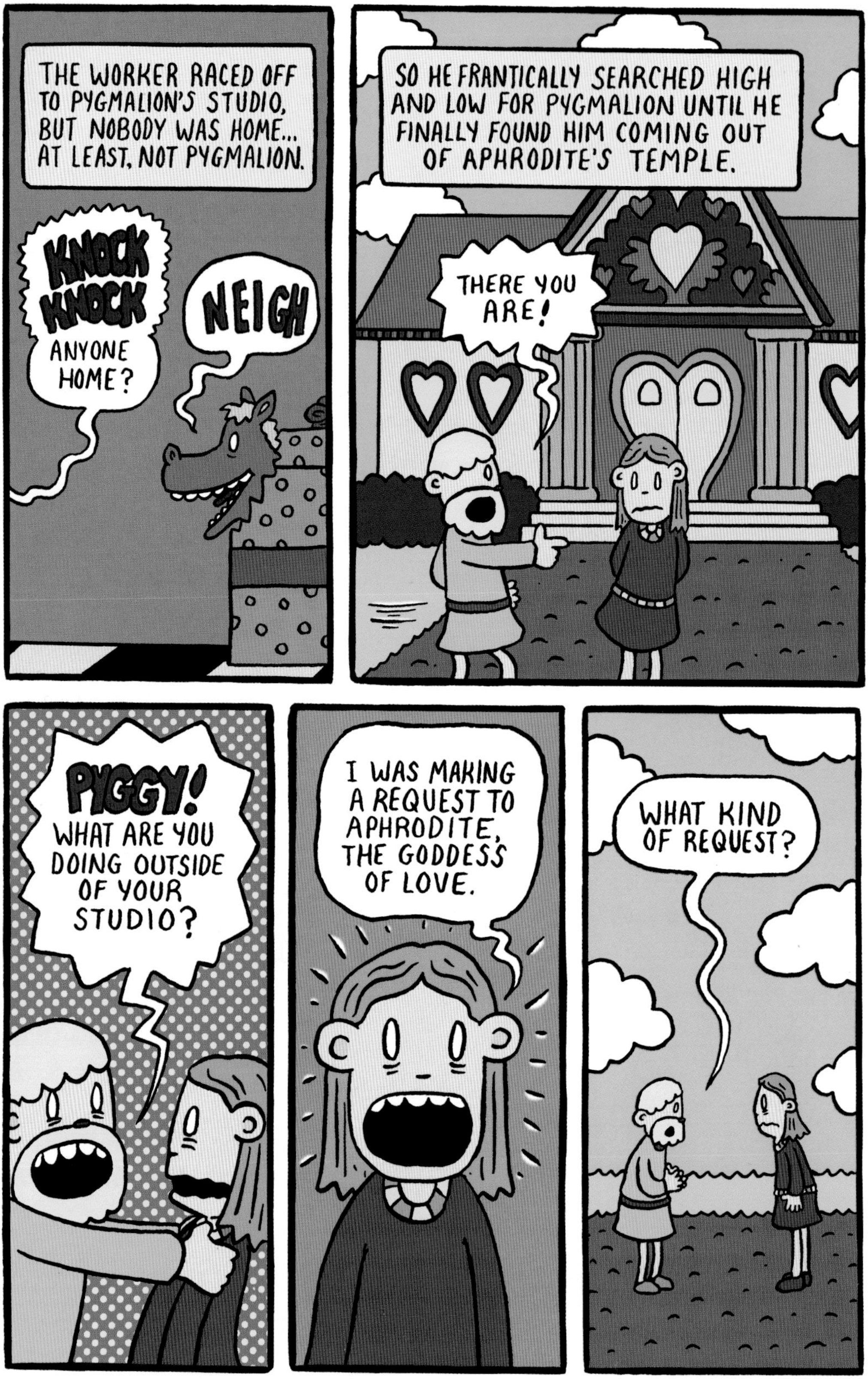
THE WORKER RACED OFF TO PYGMALION'S STUDIO, BUT NOBODY WAS HOME... AT LEAST, NOT PYGMALION.
KNOCK KNOCK
ANYONE HOME?
NEIGH
SO HE FRANTICALLY SEARCHED HIGH AND LOW FOR PYGMALION UNTIL HE FINALLY FOUND HIM COMING OUT OF APHRODITE'S TEMPLE.
THERE YOU ARE!
PYGGY! WHAT ARE YOU DOING OUTSIDE OF YOUR STUDIO?
I WAS MAKING A REQUEST TO APHRODITE, THE GODDESS OF LOVE.
WHAT KIND OF REQUEST?

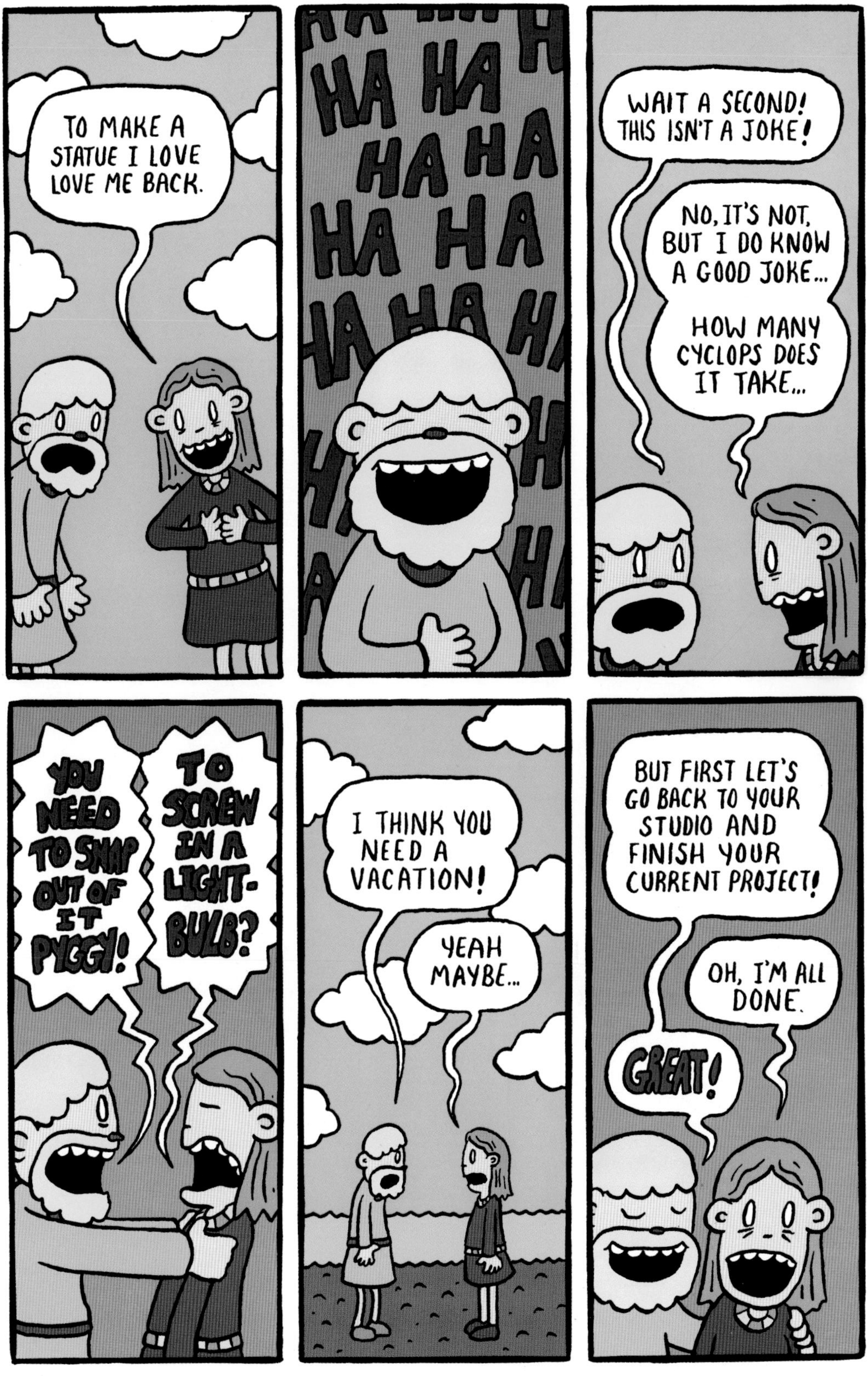
TO MAKE A STATUE I LOVE LOVE ME BACK.
HA HA HA HA HA HA HA HA HA HA
WAIT A SECOND! THIS ISN'T A JOKE!
NO, IT'S NOT, BUT I DO KNOW A GOOD JOKE...
HOW MANY CYCLOPS DOES IT TAKE...
YOU NEED TO SNAP OUT OF IT PYGGY!
TO SCREW IN A LIGHT-BULB?
I THINK YOU NEED A VACATION!
YEAH MAYBE...
BUT FIRST LET'S GO BACK TO YOUR STUDIO AND FINISH YOUR CURRENT PROJECT!
OH, I'M ALL DONE.
GREAT!

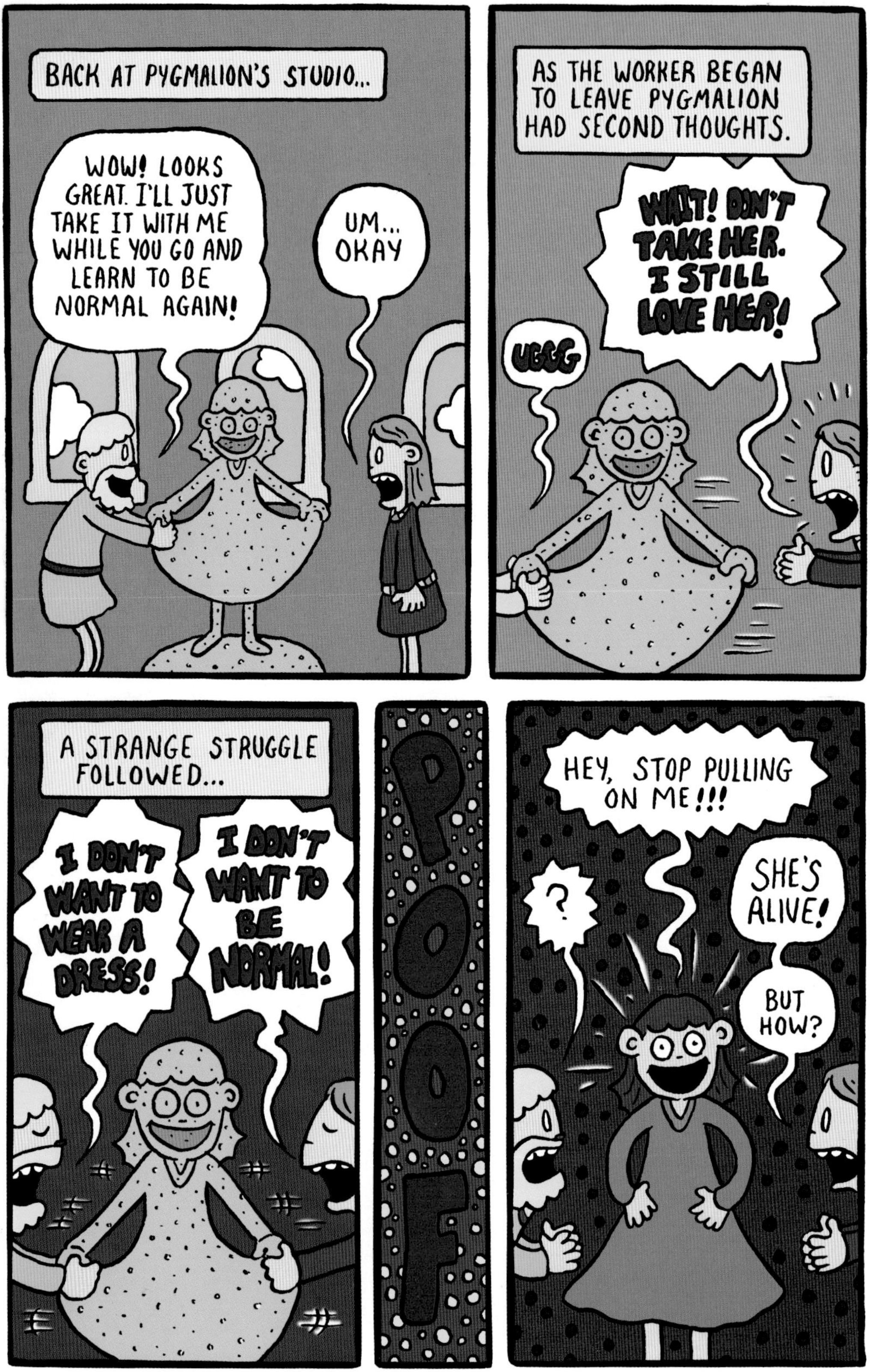

BACK AT PYGMALION'S STUDIO...
WOW! LOOKS GREAT. I'LL JUST TAKE IT WITH ME WHILE YOU GO AND LEARN TO BE NORMAL AGAIN!
UM... OKAY
AS THE WORKER BEGAN TO LEAVE PYGMALION HAD SECOND THOUGHTS.
WAIT! DON'T TAKE HER. I STILL LOVE HER!
UGGG
A STRANGE STRUGGLE FOLLOWED...
I DON'T WANT TO WEAR A DRESS!
I DON'T WANT TO BE NORMAL!
POOF
HEY, STOP PULLING ON ME!!!
?
SHE'S ALIVE!
BUT HOW?

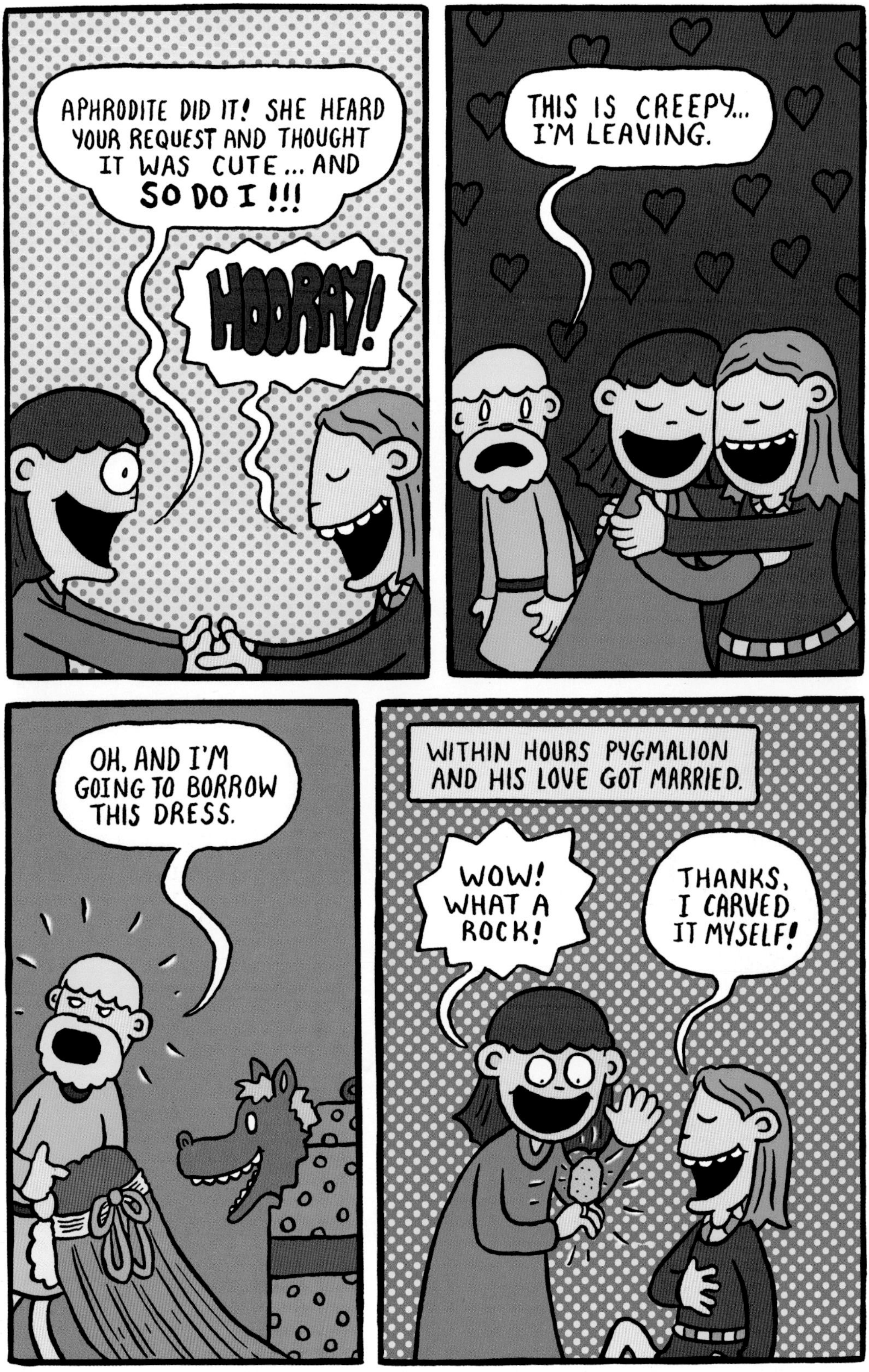
APHRODITE DID IT! SHE HEARD YOUR REQUEST AND THOUGHT IT WAS CUTE... AND SO DO I!!!
HOORAY!
THIS IS CREEPY... I'M LEAVING.
OH, AND I'M GOING TO BORROW THIS DRESS.
WITHIN HOURS PYGMALION AND HIS LOVE GOT MARRIED.
WOW! WHAT A ROCK!
THANKS, I CARVED IT MYSELF!

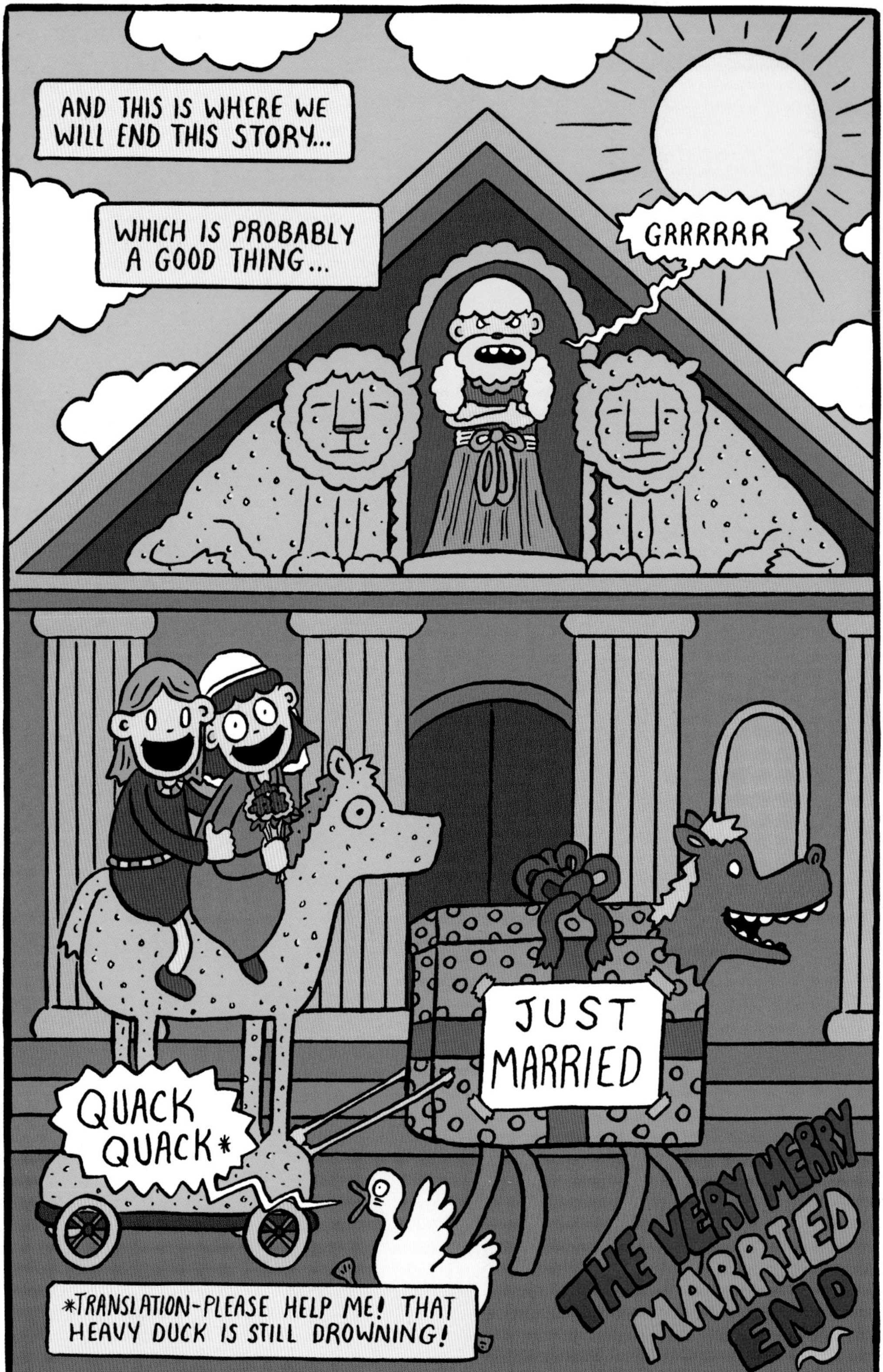
AND THIS IS WHERE WE WILL END THIS STORY...
WHICH IS PROBABLY A GOOD THING...
GRRRRRR
JUST MARRIED
QUACK QUACK*
*TRANSLATION-PLEASE HELP ME! THAT HEAVY DUCK IS STILL DROWNING!
THE VERY MERRY MARRIED END

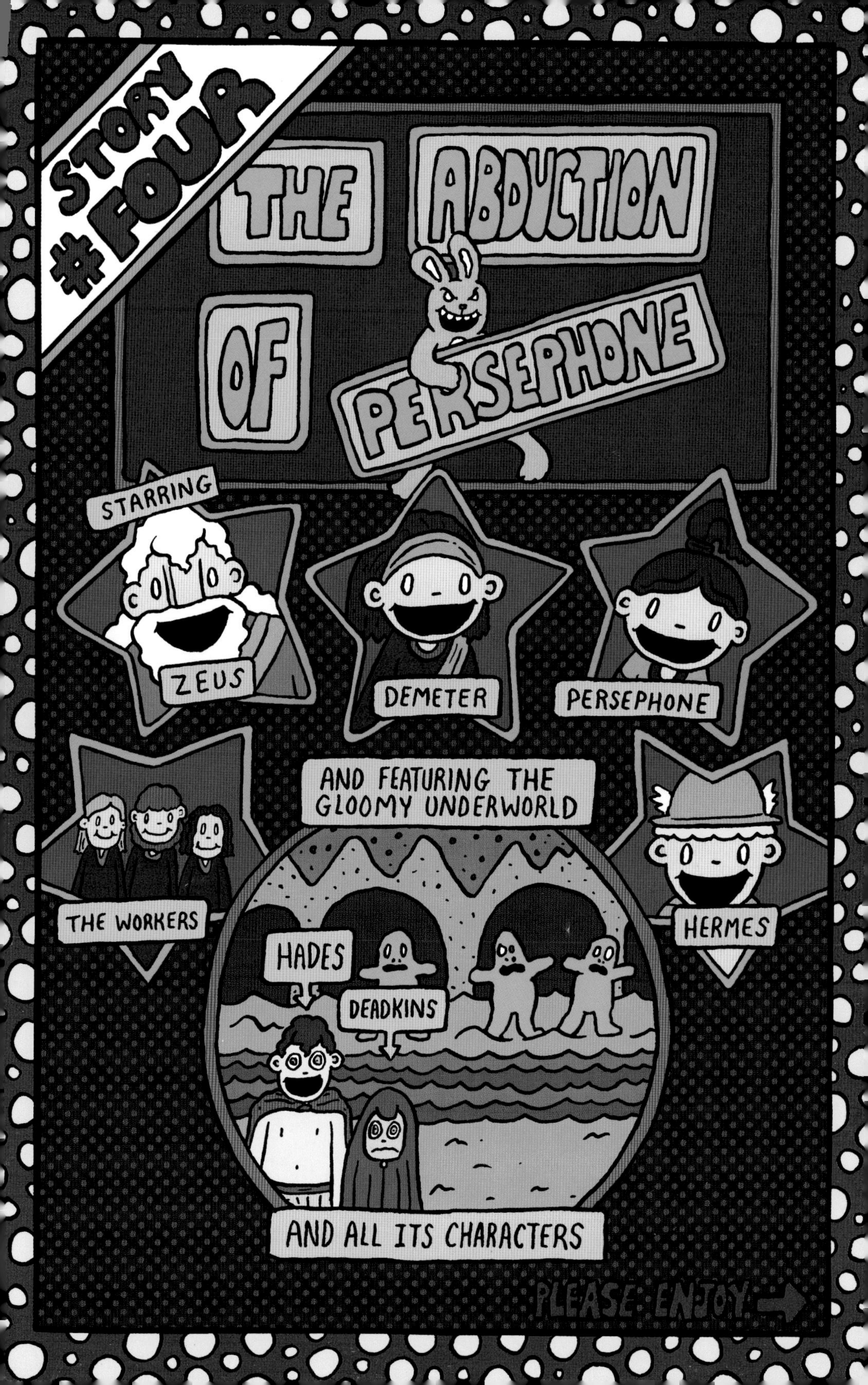
STORY #FOUR
THE ABDUCTION OF PERSEPHONE
STARRING
ZEUS
DEMETER
PERSEPHONE
AND FEATURING THE GLOOMY UNDERWORLD
THE WORKERS
HERMES
HADES
DEADKINS
AND ALL ITS CHARACTERS
PLEASE ENJOY

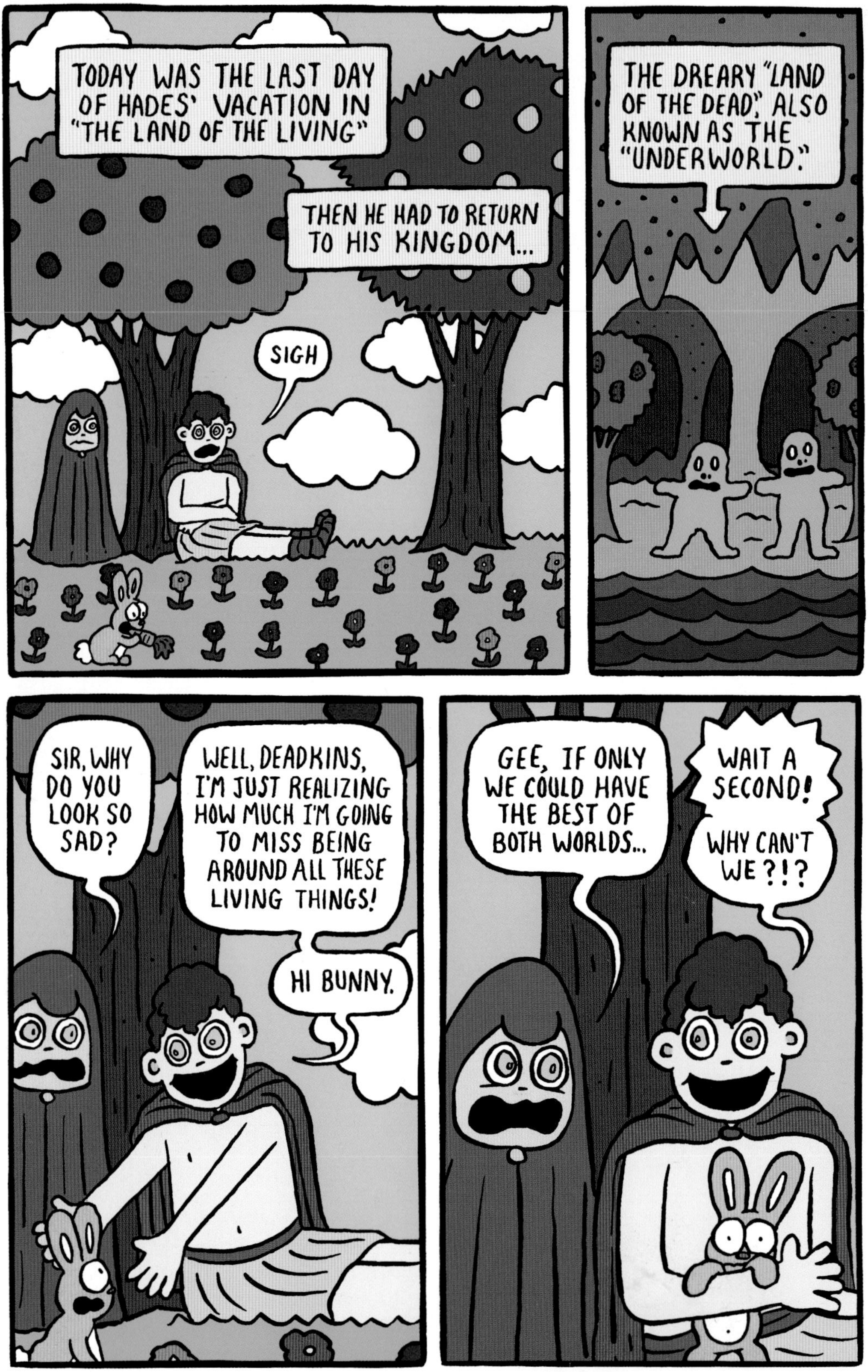

TODAY WAS THE LAST DAY OF HADES' VACATION IN "THE LAND OF THE LIVING"
THEN HE HAD TO RETURN TO HIS KINGDOM...
SIGH
THE DREARY "LAND OF THE DEAD," ALSO KNOWN AS THE "UNDERWORLD."
SIR, WHY DO YOU LOOK SO SAD?
WELL, DEADKINS, I'M JUST REALIZING HOW MUCH I'M GOING TO MISS BEING AROUND ALL THESE LIVING THINGS!
HI BUNNY.
GEE, IF ONLY WE COULD HAVE THE BEST OF BOTH WORLDS...
WAIT A SECOND!
WHY CAN'T WE?!?

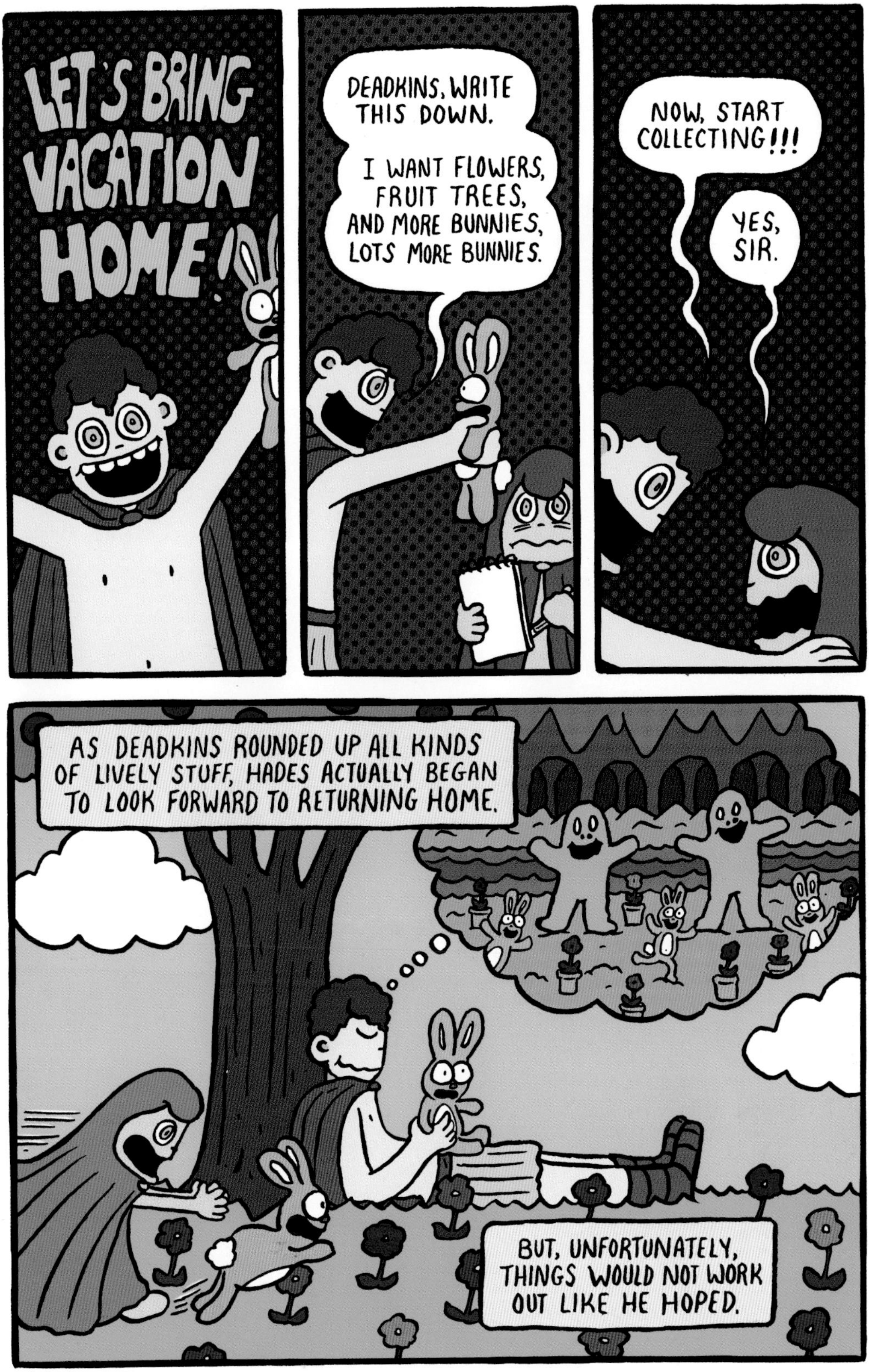
LET'S BRING VACATION HOME!
DEADKINS, WRITE THIS DOWN.
I WANT FLOWERS, FRUIT TREES, AND MORE BUNNIES, LOTS MORE BUNNIES.
NOW, START COLLECTING!!!
YES, SIR.
AS DEADKINS ROUNDED UP ALL KINDS OF LIVELY STUFF, HADES ACTUALLY BEGAN TO LOOK FORWARD TO RETURNING HOME.
BUT, UNFORTUNATELY, THINGS WOULD NOT WORK OUT LIKE HE HOPED.

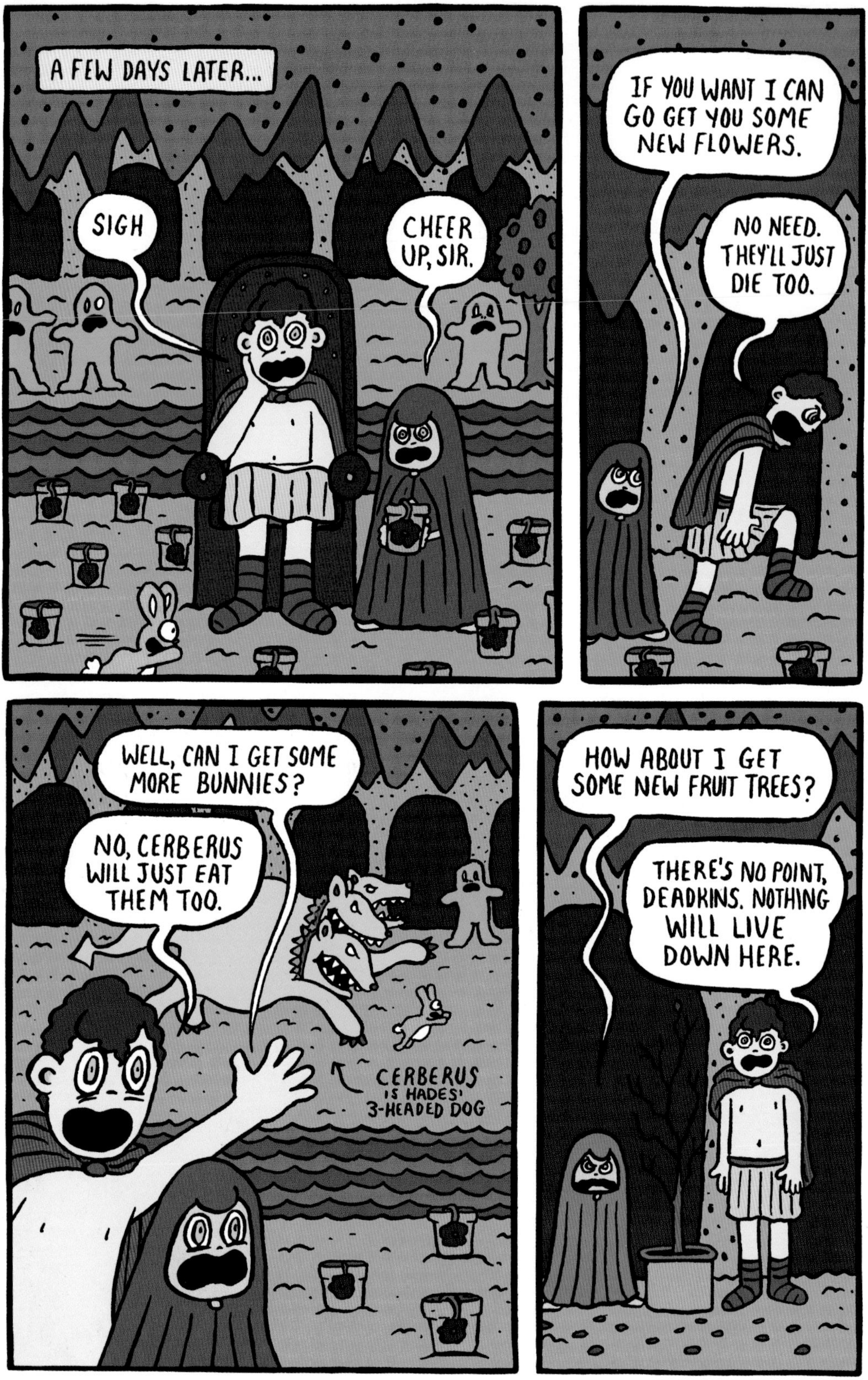
A FEW DAYS LATER...
SIGH
CHEER UP, SIR.
IF YOU WANT I CAN GO GET YOU SOME NEW FLOWERS.
NO NEED. THEY'LL JUST DIE TOO.
WELL, CAN I GET SOME MORE BUNNIES?
NO, CERBERUS WILL JUST EAT THEM TOO.
CERBERUS IS HADES' 3-HEADED DOG
HOW ABOUT I GET SOME NEW FRUIT TREES?
THERE'S NO POINT, DEADKINS. NOTHING WILL LIVE DOWN HERE.

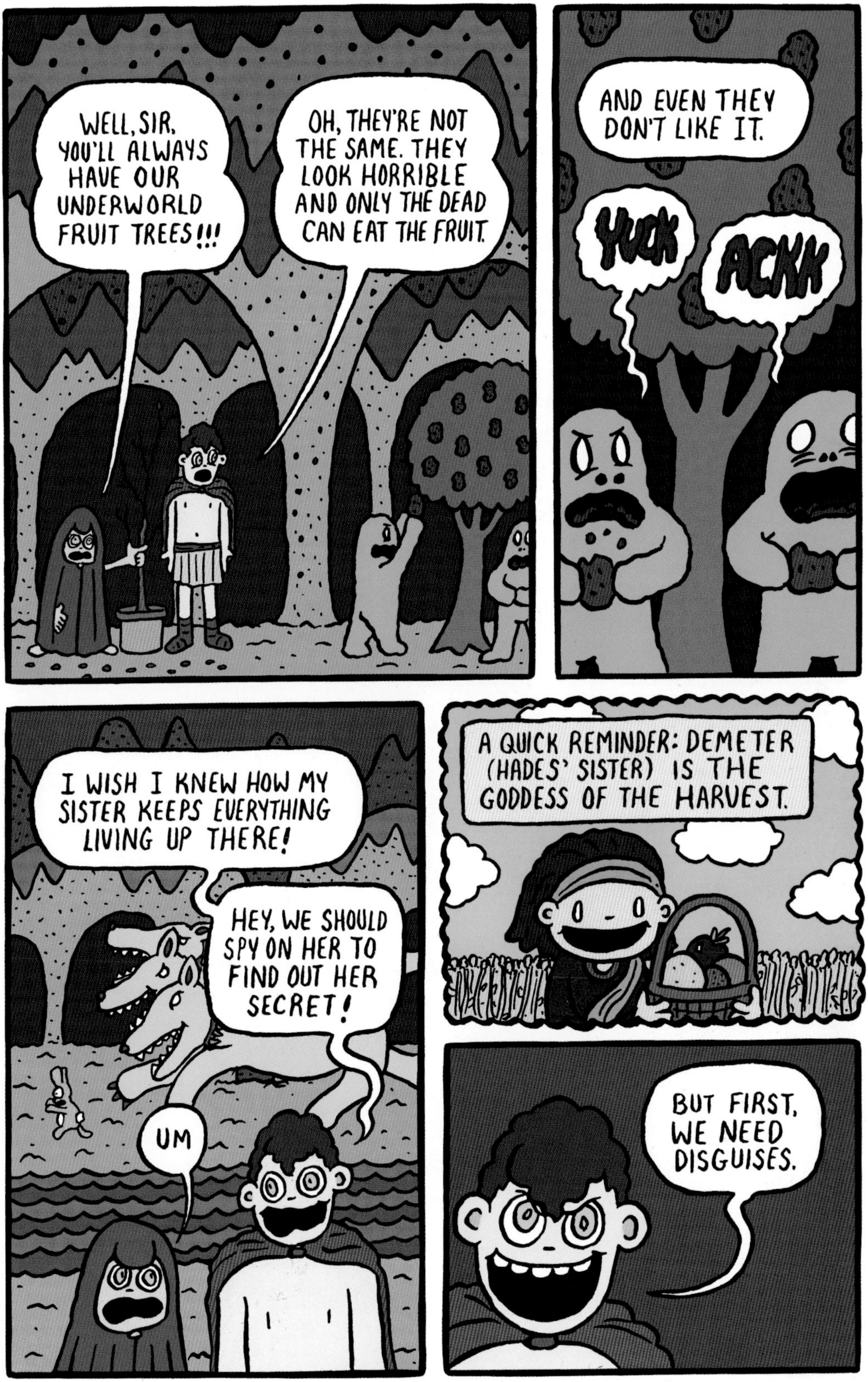
WELL, SIR, YOU'LL ALWAYS HAVE OUR UNDERWORLD FRUIT TREES!!!
OH, THEY'RE NOT THE SAME. THEY LOOK HORRIBLE AND ONLY THE DEAD CAN EAT THE FRUIT.
AND EVEN THEY DON'T LIKE IT.
YUCK
ACKK
I WISH I KNEW HOW MY SISTER KEEPS EVERYTHING LIVING UP THERE!
HEY, WE SHOULD SPY ON HER TO FIND OUT HER SECRET!
UM
A QUICK REMINDER: DEMETER (HADES' SISTER) IS THE GODDESS OF THE HARVEST.
BUT FIRST, WE NEED DISGUISES.

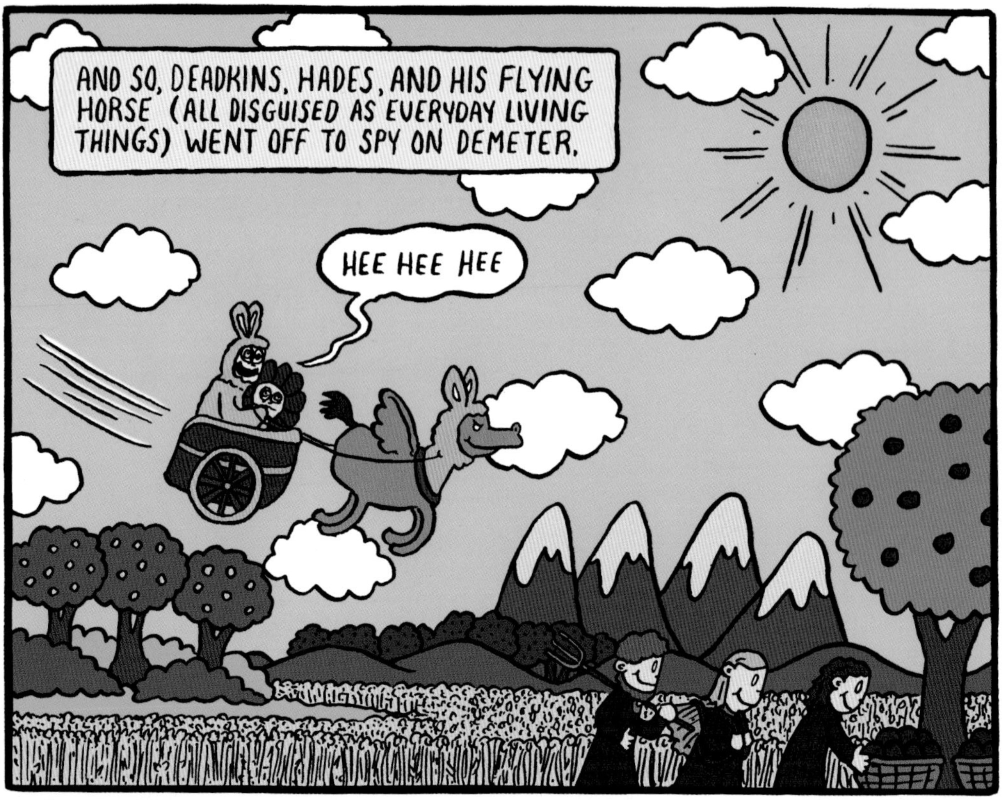
AND SO, DEADKINS, HADES, AND HIS FLYING HORSE (ALL DISGUISED AS EVERYDAY LIVING THINGS) WENT OFF TO SPY ON DEMETER.
HEE HEE HEE

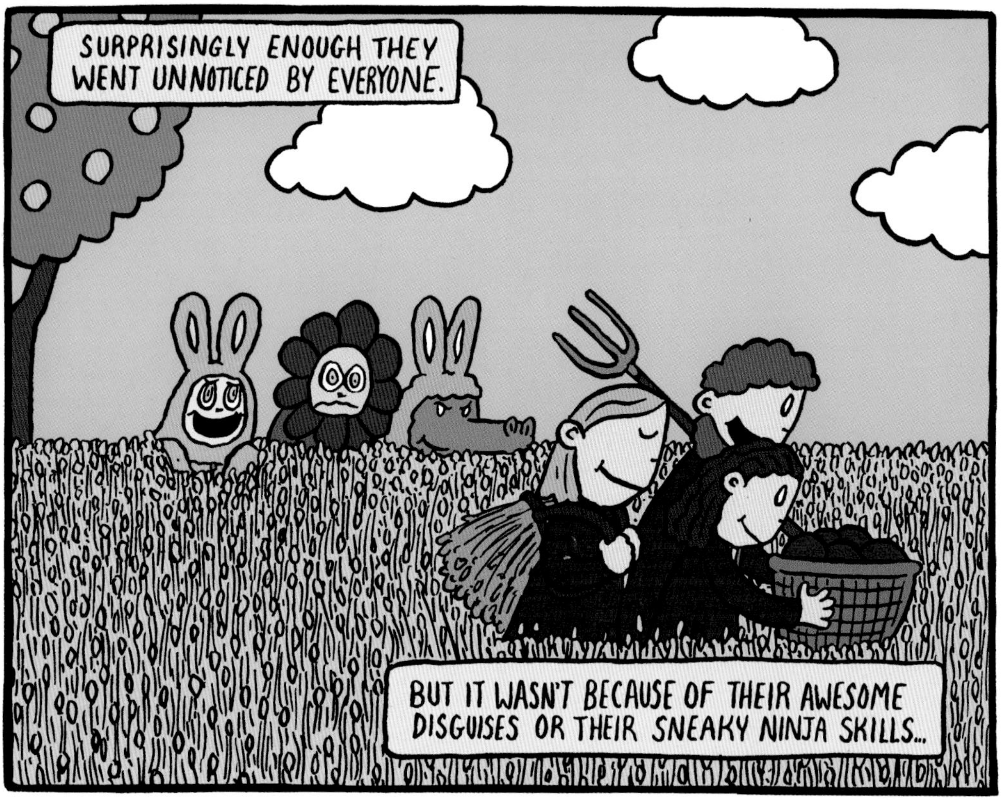
SURPRISINGLY ENOUGH THEY WENT UNNOTICED BY EVERYONE.
BUT IT WASN'T BECAUSE OF THEIR AWESOME DISGUISES OR THEIR SNEAKY NINJA SKILLS...

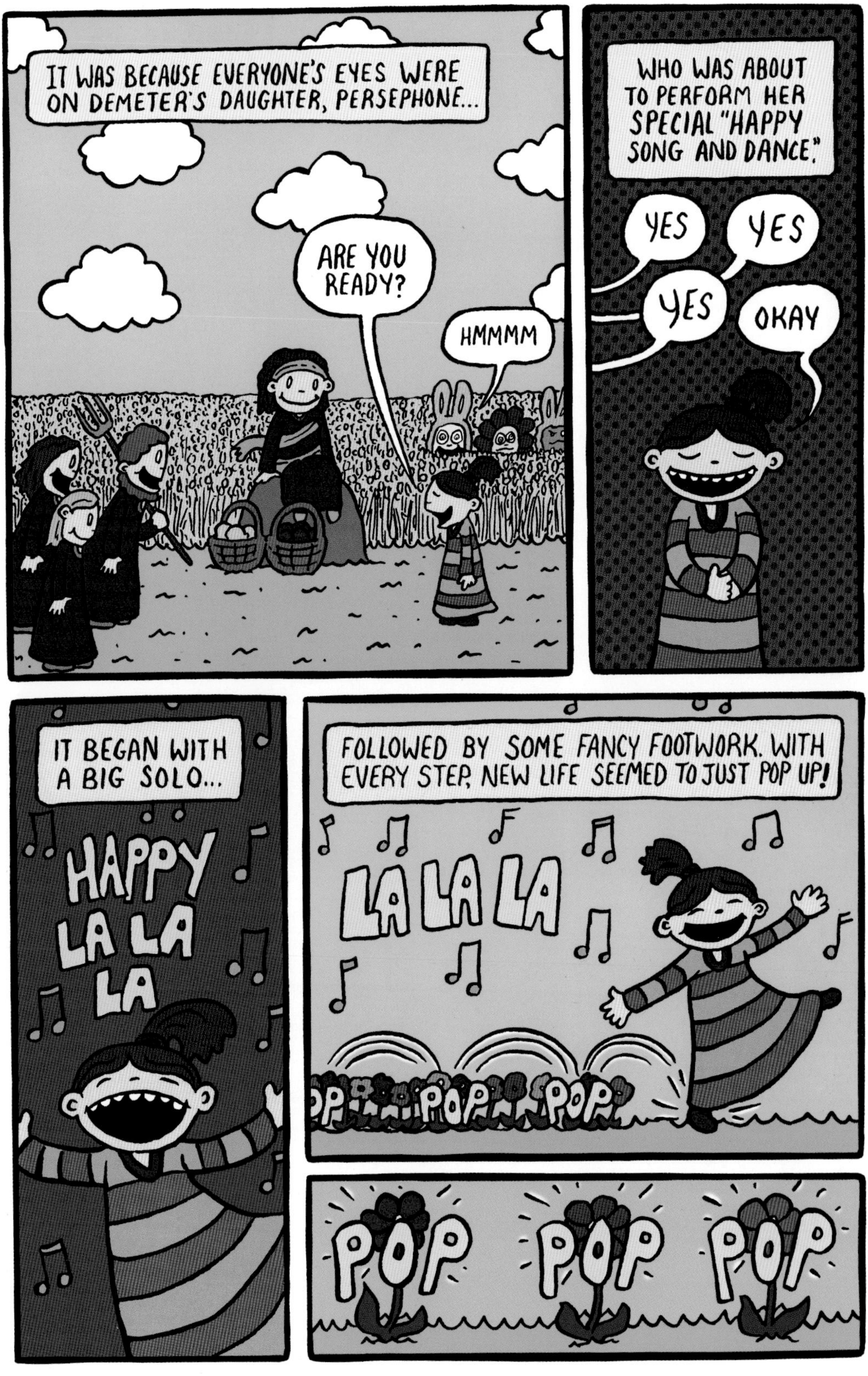

IT WAS BECAUSE EVERYONE'S EYES WERE ON DEMETER'S DAUGHTER, PERSEPHONE...
ARE YOU READY?
HMMMM
WHO WAS ABOUT TO PERFORM HER SPECIAL "HAPPY SONG AND DANCE."
YES
YES
YES
OKAY
IT BEGAN WITH A BIG SOLO...
HAPPY LA LA LA
FOLLOWED BY SOME FANCY FOOTWORK. WITH EVERY STEP, NEW LIFE SEEMED TO JUST POP UP!
LA LA LA
POP POP POP
POP POP POP

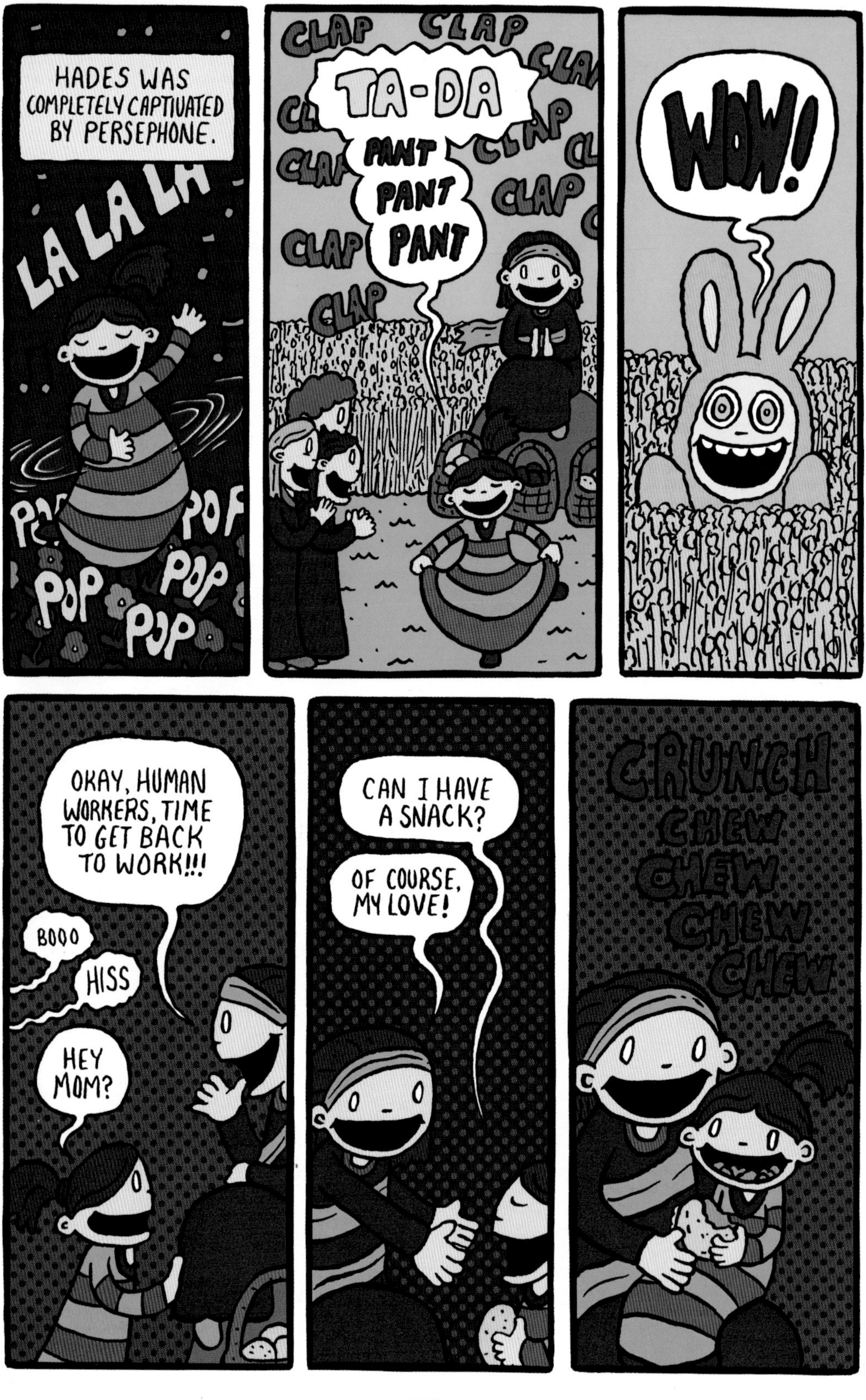
HADES WAS COMPLETELY CAPTIVATED BY PERSEPHONE.
LA LA LA
POP POP POP POP POP
CLAP CLAP CLAP
TA-DA
PANT PANT PANT
CLAP CLAP CLAP CLAP CLAP
WOW!
OKAY, HUMAN WORKERS, TIME TO GET BACK TO WORK!!!
BOOO
HISS
HEY MOM?
CAN I HAVE A SNACK?
OF COURSE, MY LOVE!
CRUNCH
CHEW
CHEW
CHEW
CHEW

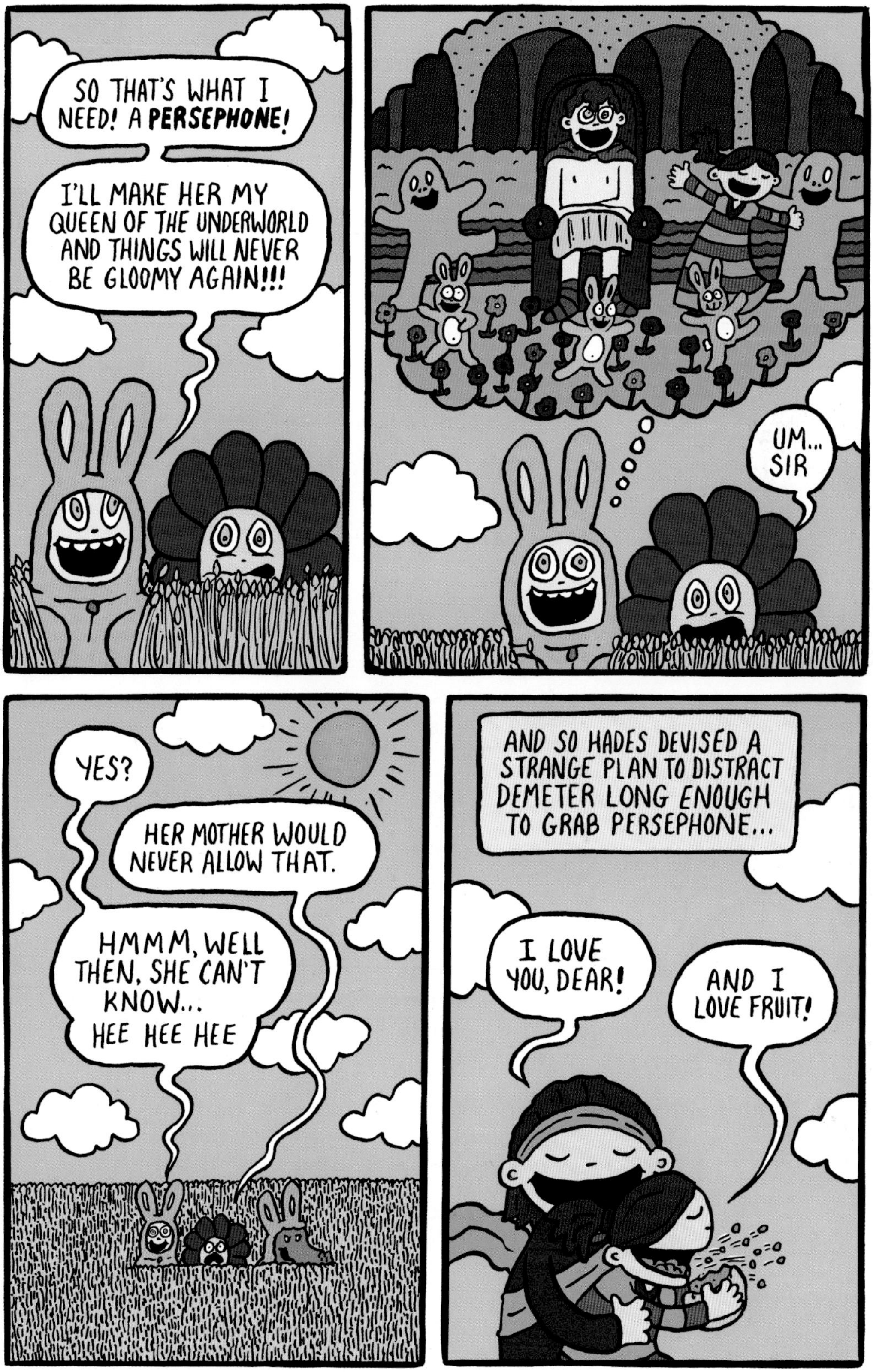
SO THAT'S WHAT I NEED! A PERSEPHONE!
I'LL MAKE HER MY QUEEN OF THE UNDERWORLD AND THINGS WILL NEVER BE GLOOMY AGAIN!!!
UM... SIR
YES?
HER MOTHER WOULD NEVER ALLOW THAT.
HMMM, WELL THEN, SHE CAN'T KNOW... HEE HEE HEE
AND SO HADES DEVISED A STRANGE PLAN TO DISTRACT DEMETER LONG ENOUGH TO GRAB PERSEPHONE...
I LOVE YOU, DEAR!
AND I LOVE FRUIT!

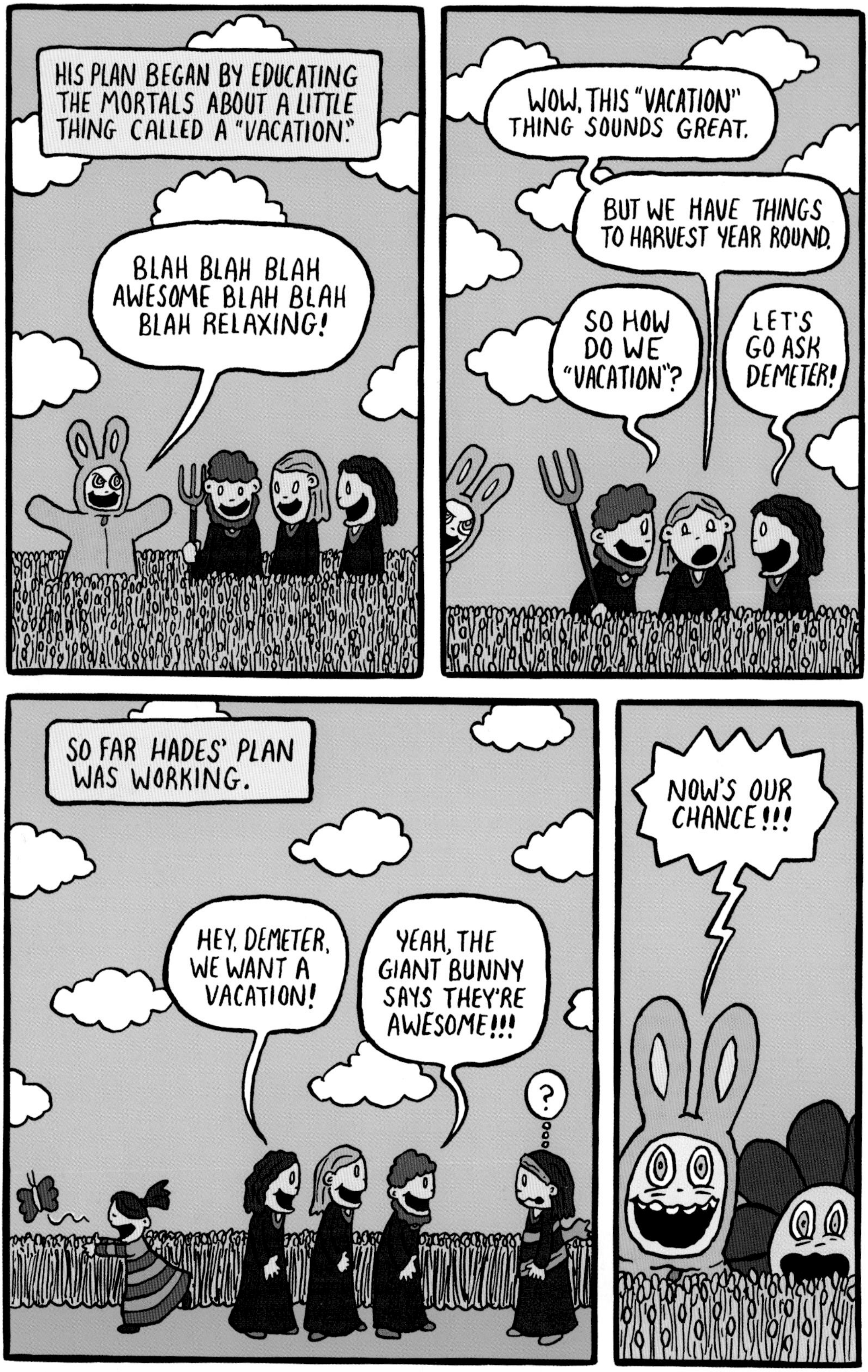
HIS PLAN BEGAN BY EDUCATING THE MORTALS ABOUT A LITTLE THING CALLED A "VACATION."
BLAH BLAH BLAH AWESOME BLAH BLAH BLAH RELAXING!
WOW, THIS "VACATION" THING SOUNDS GREAT.
BUT WE HAVE THINGS TO HARVEST YEAR ROUND.
SO HOW DO WE "VACATION"?
LET'S GO ASK DEMETER!
SO FAR HADES' PLAN WAS WORKING.
HEY, DEMETER, WE WANT A VACATION!
YEAH, THE GIANT BUNNY SAYS THEY'RE AWESOME!!!
?
NOW'S OUR CHANCE!!!

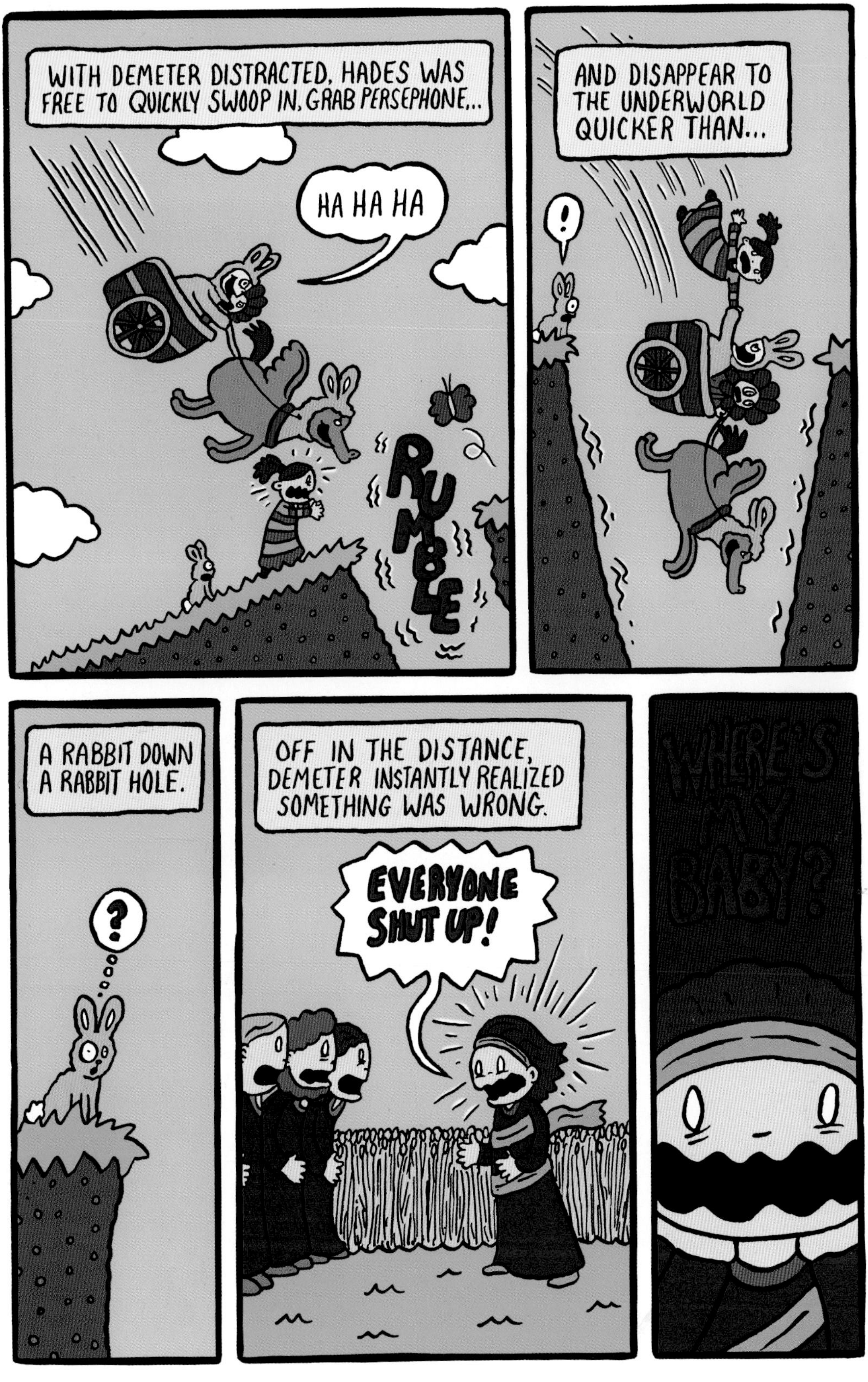
WITH DEMETER DISTRACTED, HADES WAS FREE TO QUICKLY SWOOP IN, GRAB PERSEPHONE...
HA HA HA
RUMBLE
AND DISAPPEAR TO THE UNDERWORLD QUICKER THAN...
!
A RABBIT DOWN A RABBIT HOLE.
?
OFF IN THE DISTANCE, DEMETER INSTANTLY REALIZED SOMETHING WAS WRONG.
EVERYONE SHUT UP!
WHERE'S MY BABY?

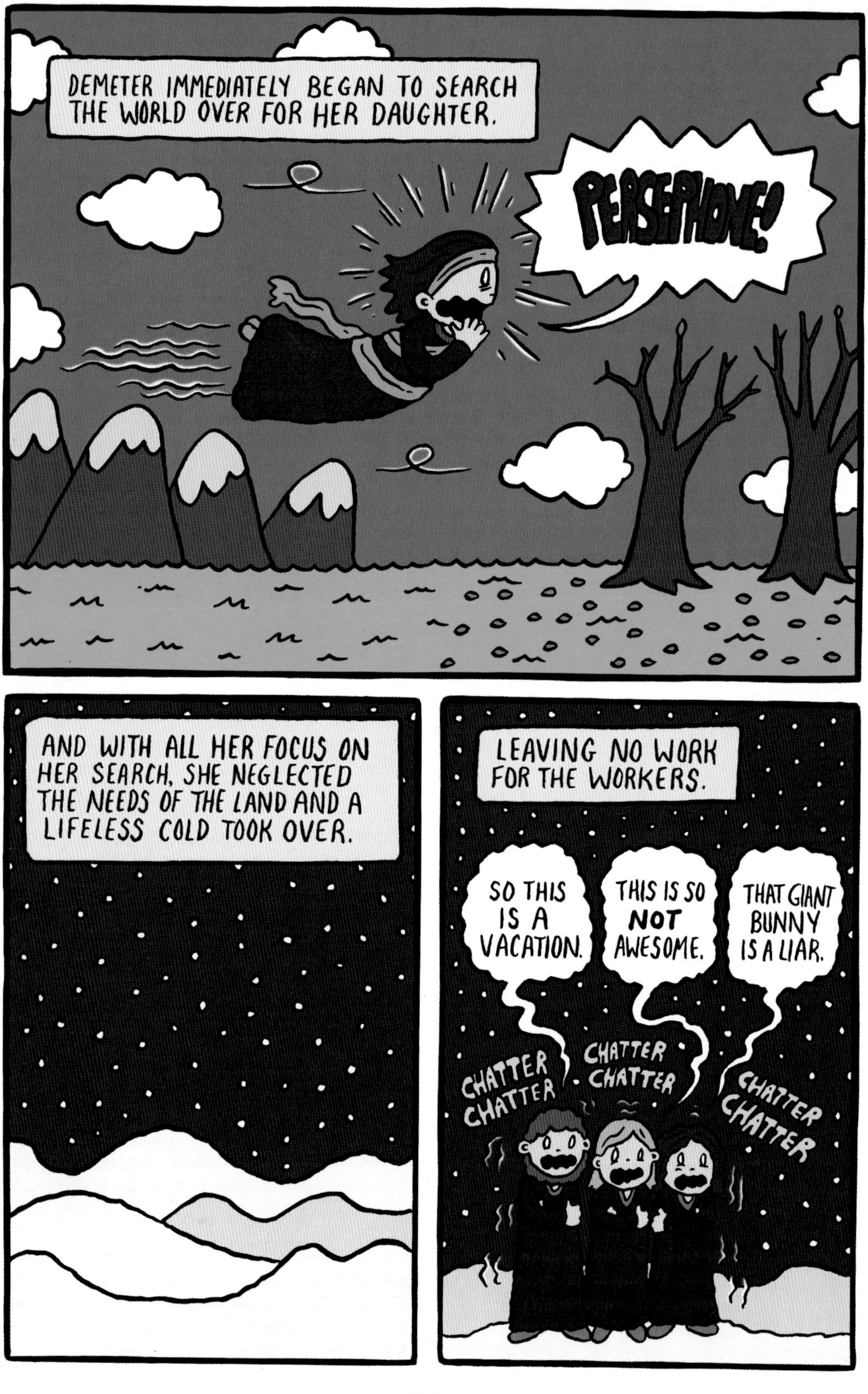
DEMETER IMMEDIATELY BEGAN TO SEARCH THE WORLD OVER FOR HER DAUGHTER.
PERSEPHONE!
AND WITH ALL HER FOCUS ON HER SEARCH, SHE NEGLECTED THE NEEDS OF THE LAND AND A LIFELESS COLD TOOK OVER.
LEAVING NO WORK FOR THE WORKERS.
SO THIS IS A VACATION.
THIS IS SO NOT AWESOME.
THAT GIANT BUNNY IS A LIAR.
CHATTER CHATTER
CHATTER CHATTER
CHATTER CHATTER

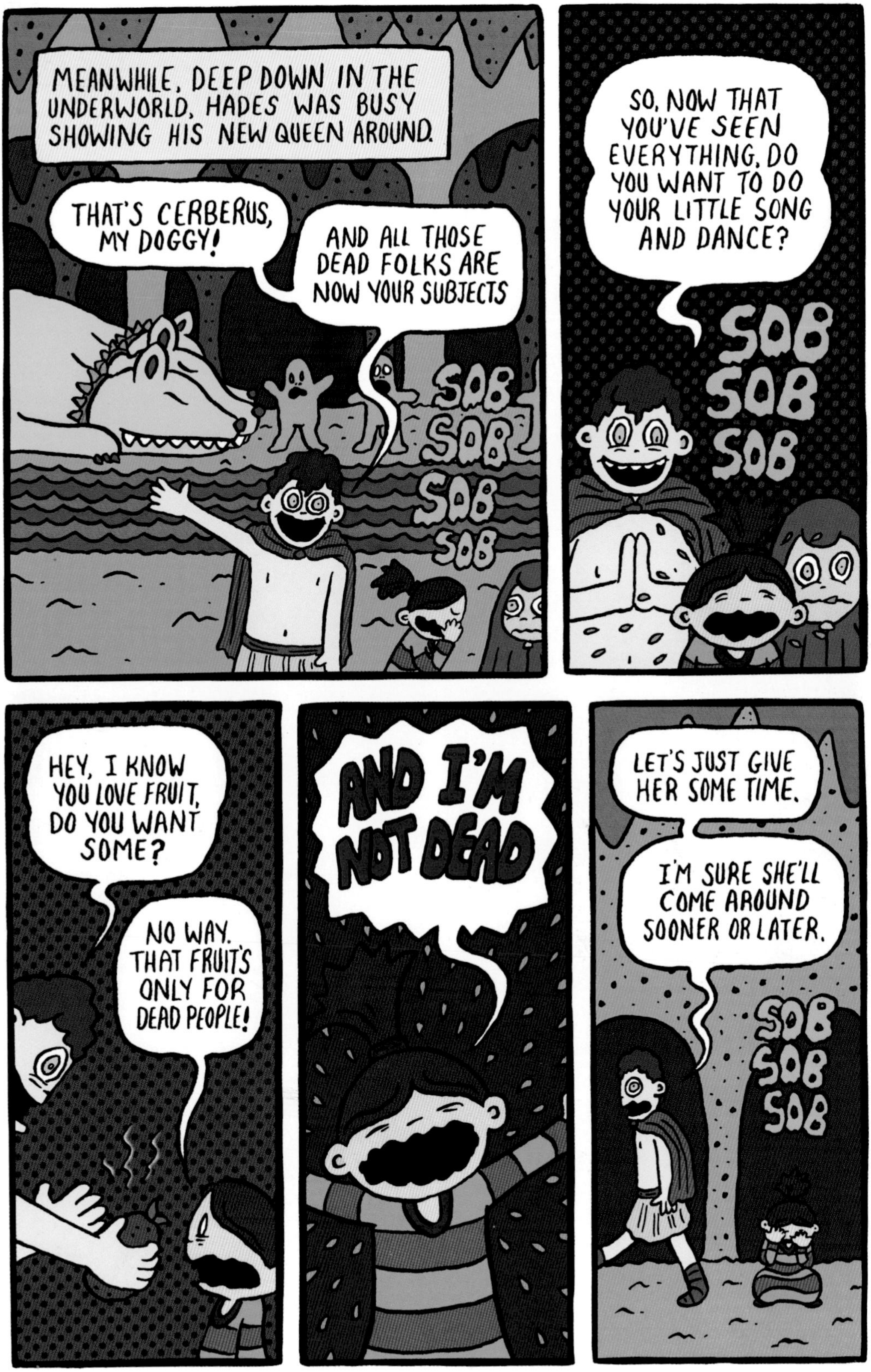
MEANWHILE, DEEP DOWN IN THE UNDERWORLD, HADES WAS BUSY SHOWING HIS NEW QUEEN AROUND.
THAT'S CERBERUS, MY DOGGY!
AND ALL THOSE DEAD FOLKS ARE NOW YOUR SUBJECTS
SOB SOB SOB SOB
SO, NOW THAT YOU'VE SEEN EVERYTHING, DO YOU WANT TO DO YOUR LITTLE SONG AND DANCE?
SOB SOB SOB
HEY, I KNOW YOU LOVE FRUIT, DO YOU WANT SOME?
NO WAY. THAT FRUIT'S ONLY FOR DEAD PEOPLE!
AND I'M NOT DEAD
LET'S JUST GIVE HER SOME TIME.
I'M SURE SHE'LL COME AROUND SOONER OR LATER.
SOB SOB SOB

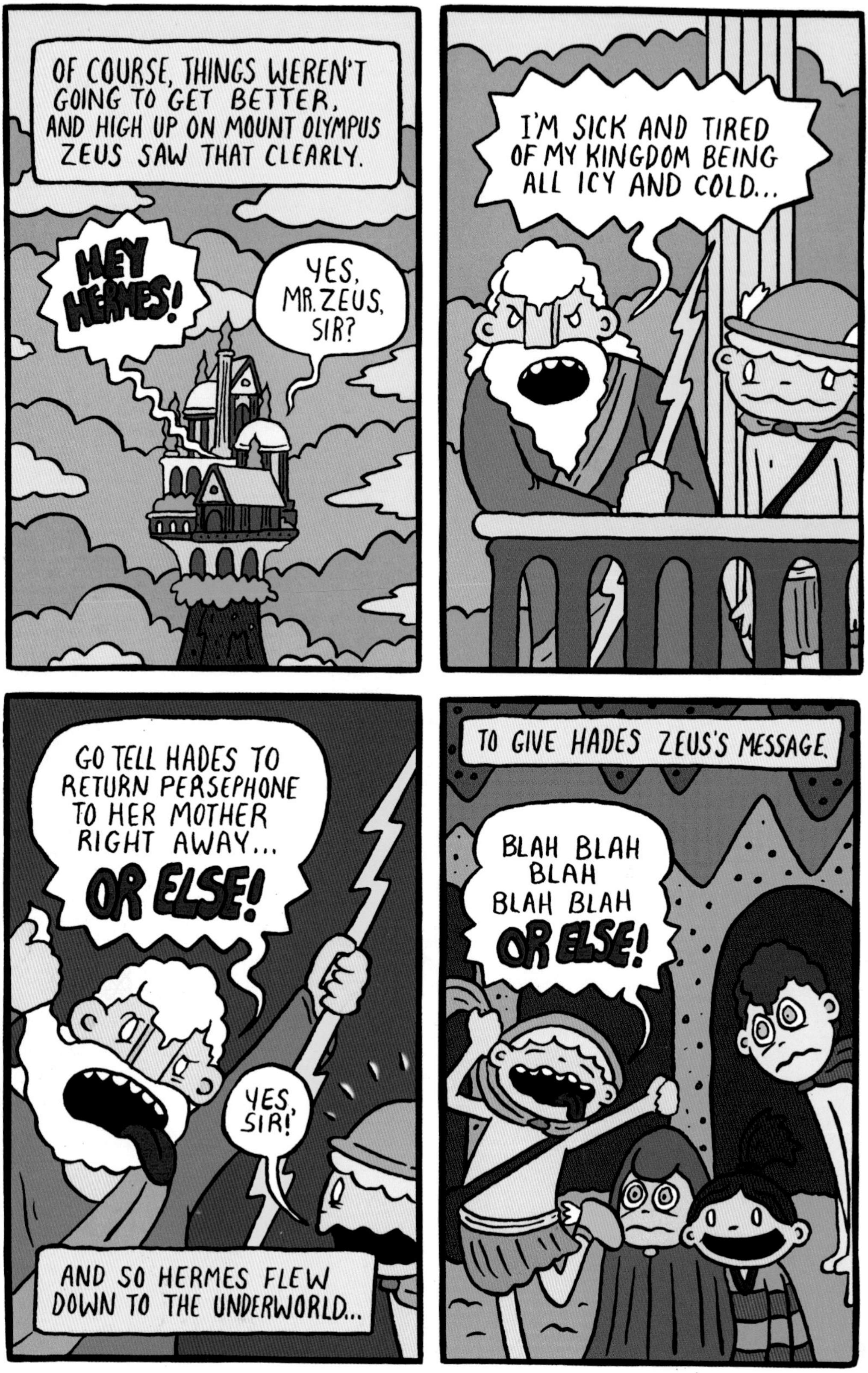
OF COURSE, THINGS WEREN'T GOING TO GET BETTER, AND HIGH UP ON MOUNT OLYMPUS ZEUS SAW THAT CLEARLY.
HEY HERMES!
YES, MR. ZEUS, SIR?
I'M SICK AND TIRED OF MY KINGDOM BEING ALL ICY AND COLD...
GO TELL HADES TO RETURN PERSEPHONE TO HER MOTHER RIGHT AWAY... OR ELSE!
YES, SIR!
AND SO HERMES FLEW DOWN TO THE UNDERWORLD...
TO GIVE HADES ZEUS'S MESSAGE.
BLAH BLAH BLAH BLAH BLAH OR ELSE!

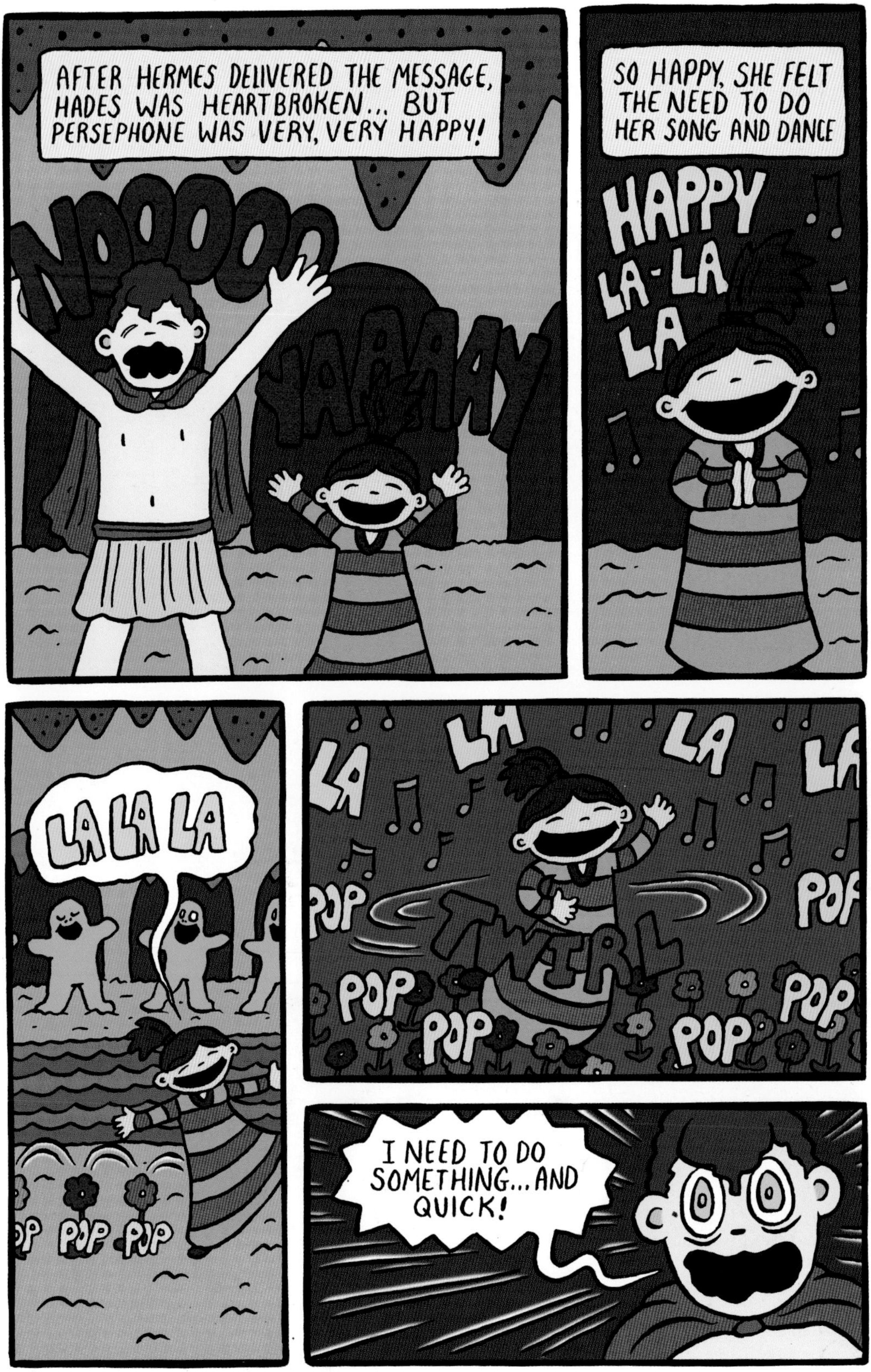
AFTER HERMES DELIVERED THE MESSAGE, HADES WAS HEARTBROKEN... BUT PERSEPHONE WAS VERY, VERY HAPPY!
NOOOOOO
YAAAAY
SO HAPPY, SHE FELT THE NEED TO DO HER SONG AND DANCE
HAPPY
LA-LA
LA
LA LA LA
POP POP POP
LA
LA
LA
LA
POP
POP
TWIRL
POP
POP
POP
POP
I NEED TO DO SOMETHING... AND QUICK!

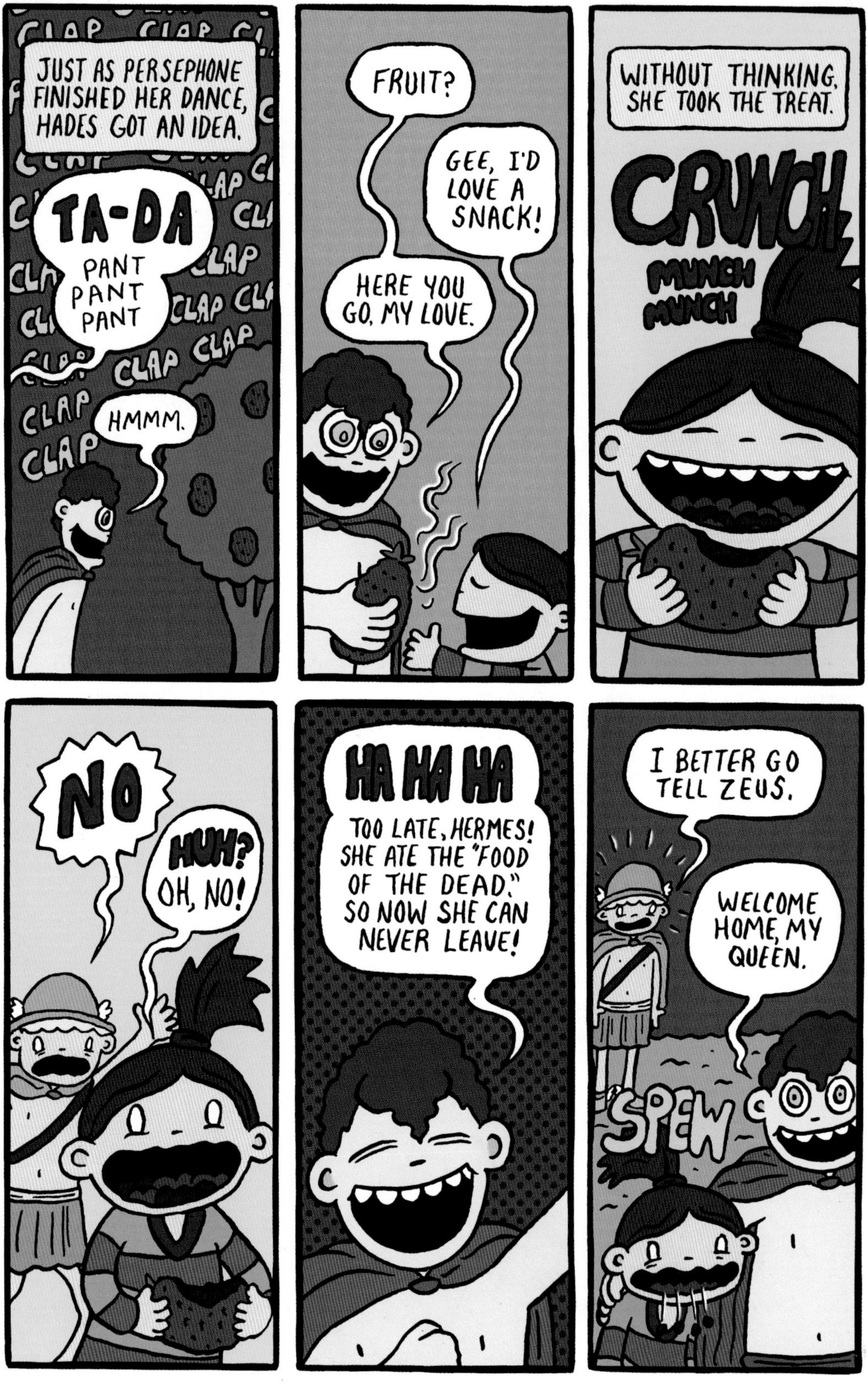
JUST AS PERSEPHONE FINISHED HER DANCE, HADES GOT AN IDEA.
TA-DA
PANT PANT PANT
CLAP CLAP CLAP
HMMM.
FRUIT?
GEE, I'D LOVE A SNACK!
HERE YOU GO, MY LOVE.
WITHOUT THINKING, SHE TOOK THE TREAT.
CRUNCH
MUNCH MUNCH
NO
HUH? OH, NO!
HA HA HA
TOO LATE, HERMES! SHE ATE THE "FOOD OF THE DEAD," SO NOW SHE CAN NEVER LEAVE!
I BETTER GO TELL ZEUS.
WELCOME HOME, MY QUEEN.
SPEW

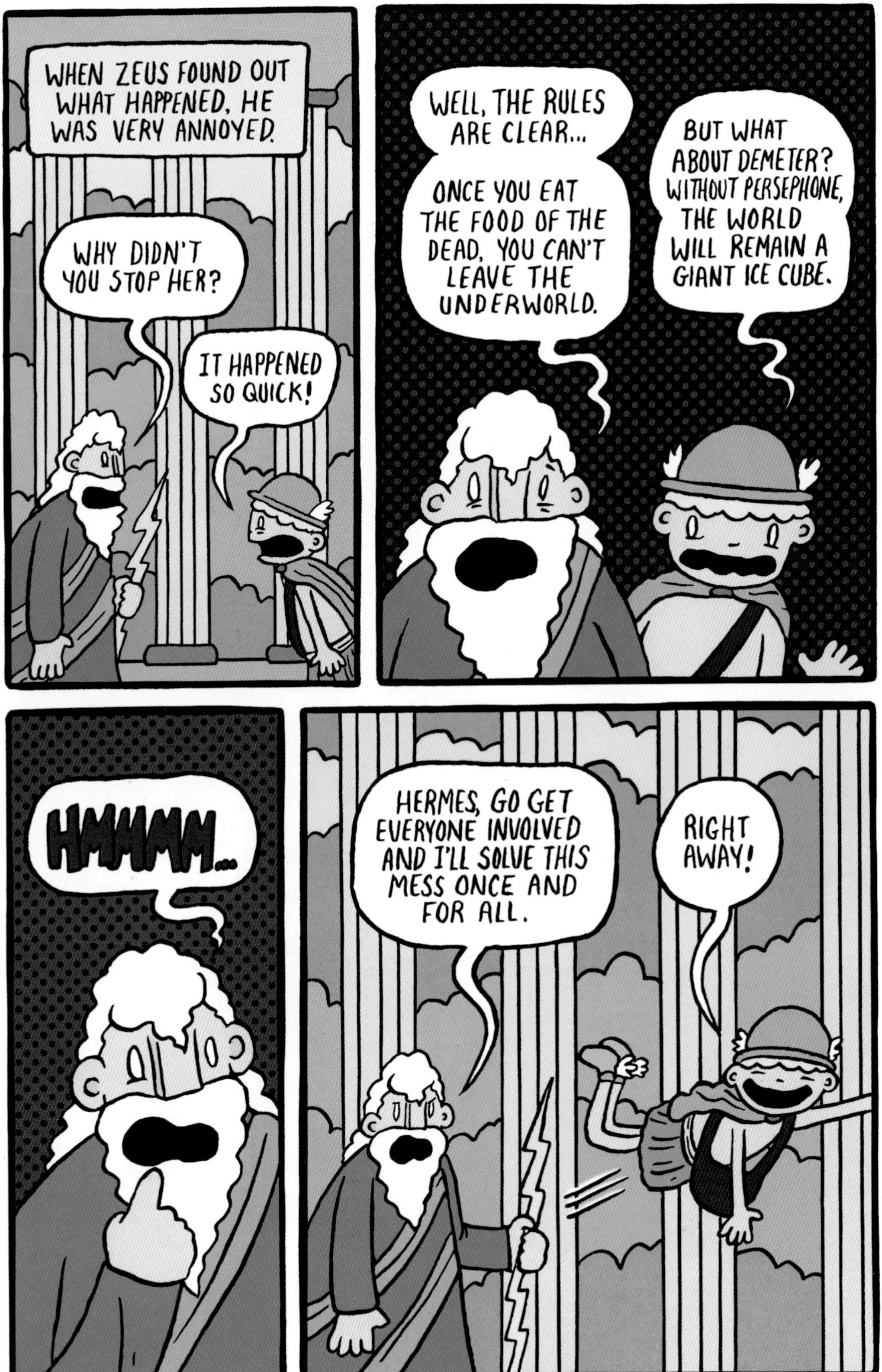
WHEN ZEUS FOUND OUT WHAT HAPPENED, HE WAS VERY ANNOYED.
WHY DIDN'T YOU STOP HER?
IT HAPPENED SO QUICK!
WELL, THE RULES ARE CLEAR...
ONCE YOU EAT THE FOOD OF THE DEAD, YOU CAN'T LEAVE THE UNDERWORLD.
BUT WHAT ABOUT DEMETER? WITHOUT PERSEPHONE, THE WORLD WILL REMAIN A GIANT ICE CUBE.
HMMMM...
HERMES, GO GET EVERYONE INVOLVED AND I'LL SOLVE THIS MESS ONCE AND FOR ALL.
RIGHT AWAY!

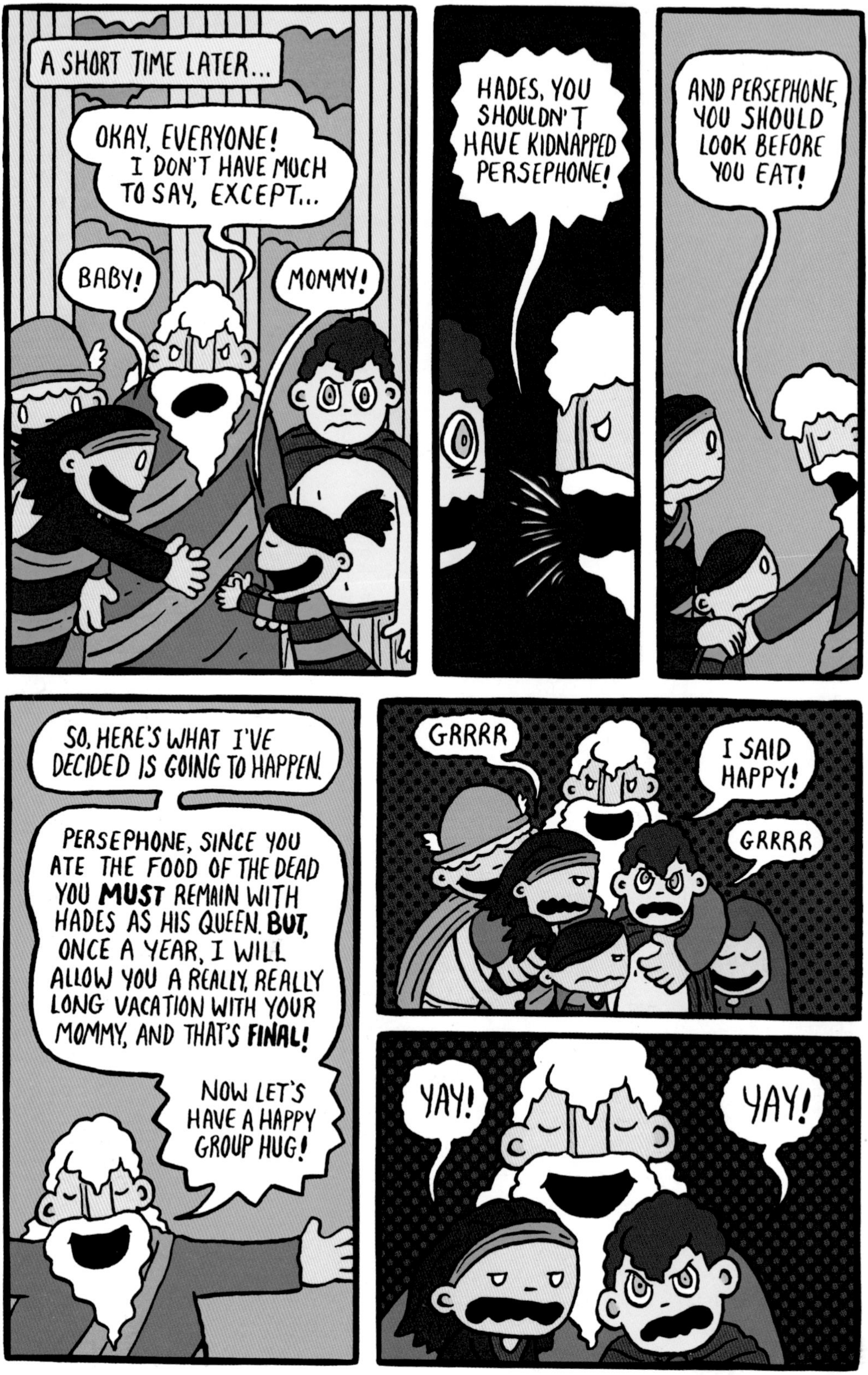
A SHORT TIME LATER...
OKAY, EVERYONE! I DON'T HAVE MUCH TO SAY, EXCEPT...
BABY!
MOMMY!
HADES, YOU SHOULDN'T HAVE KIDNAPPED PERSEPHONE!
AND PERSEPHONE, YOU SHOULD LOOK BEFORE YOU EAT!
SO, HERE'S WHAT I'VE DECIDED IS GOING TO HAPPEN.
PERSEPHONE, SINCE YOU ATE THE FOOD OF THE DEAD YOU MUST REMAIN WITH HADES AS HIS QUEEN. BUT, ONCE A YEAR, I WILL ALLOW YOU A REALLY, REALLY LONG VACATION WITH YOUR MOMMY, AND THAT'S FINAL!
NOW LET'S HAVE A HAPPY GROUP HUG!
GRRRR
I SAID HAPPY!
GRRRR
YAY!
YAY!

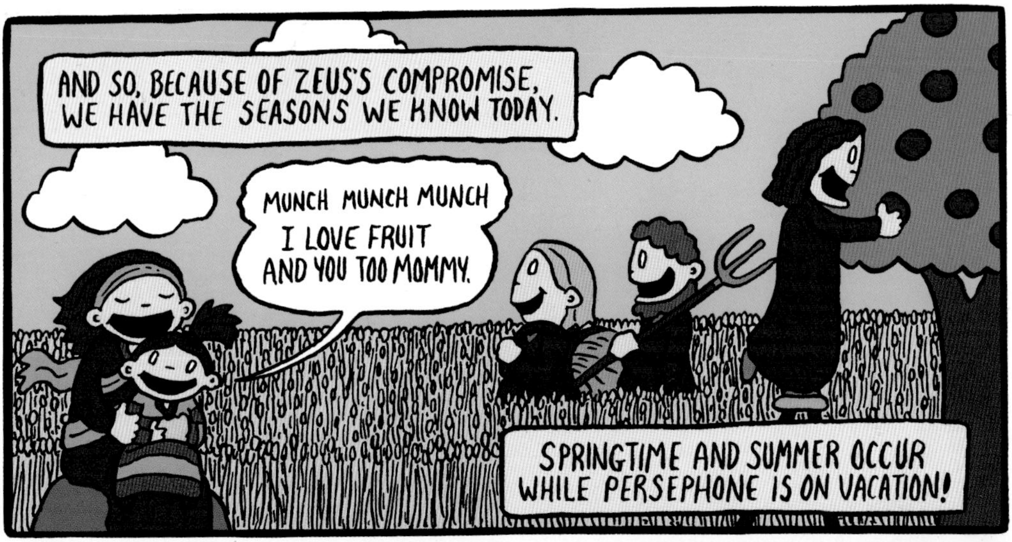
AND SO, BECAUSE OF ZEUS'S COMPROMISE, WE HAVE THE SEASONS WE KNOW TODAY.
MUNCH MUNCH MUNCH I LOVE FRUIT AND YOU TOO MOMMY.
SPRINGTIME AND SUMMER OCCUR WHILE PERSEPHONE IS ON VACATION!

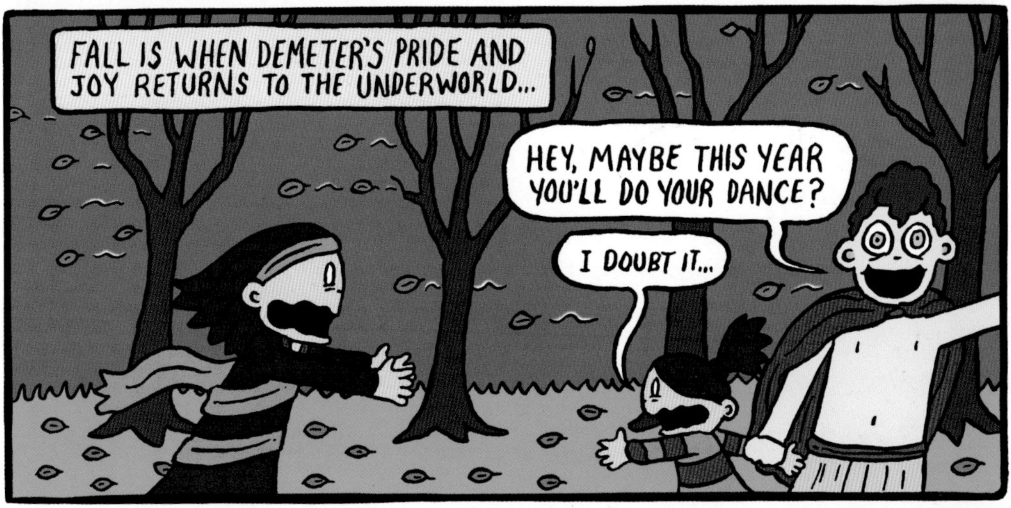
FALL IS WHEN DEMETER'S PRIDE AND JOY RETURNS TO THE UNDERWORLD...
HEY, MAYBE THIS YEAR YOU'LL DO YOUR DANCE?
I DOUBT IT...

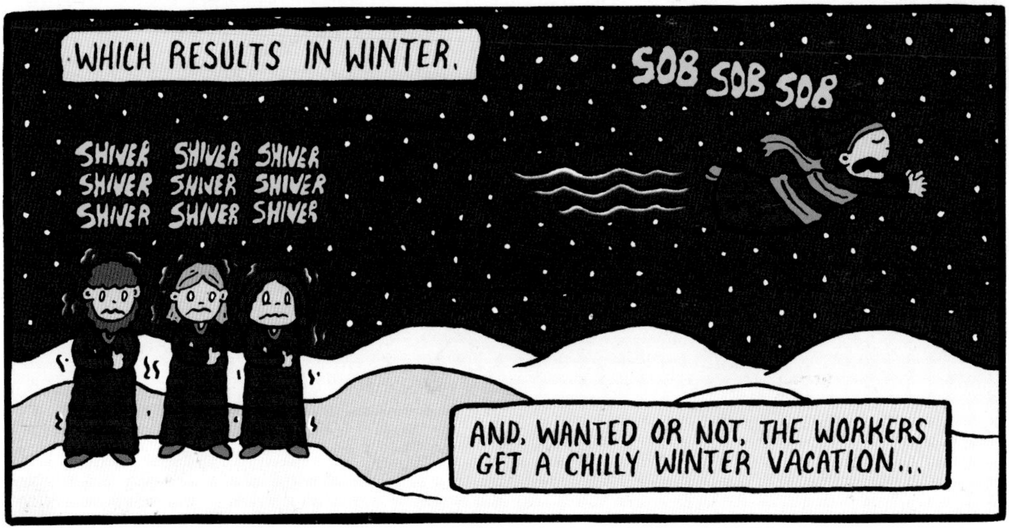
WHICH RESULTS IN WINTER.
SOB SOB SOB
SHIVER SHIVER SHIVER SHIVER SHIVER SHIVER SHIVER SHIVER SHIVER
AND, WANTED OR NOT, THE WORKERS GET A CHILLY WINTER VACATION...

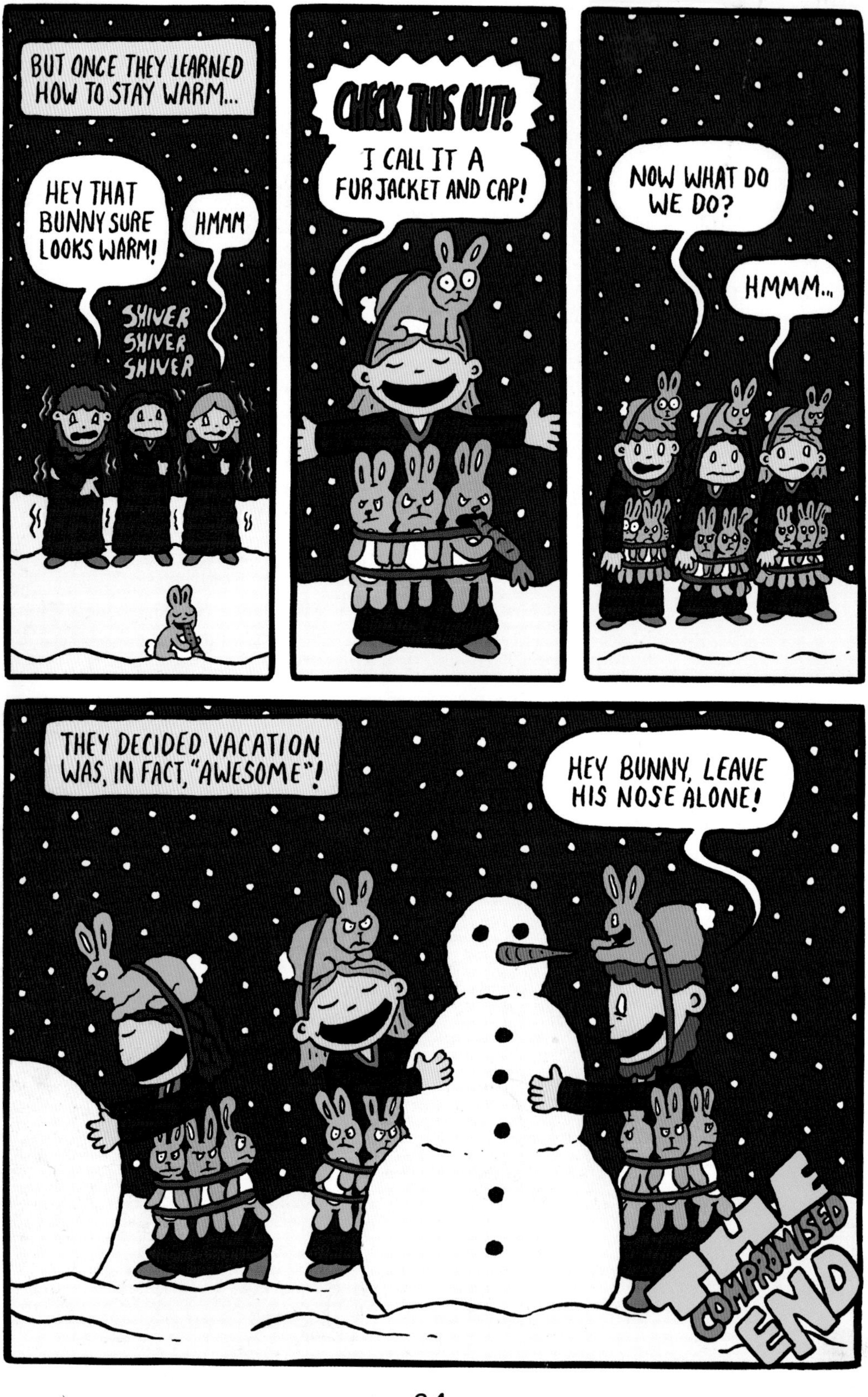
BUT ONCE THEY LEARNED HOW TO STAY WARM...
HEY THAT BUNNY SURE LOOKS WARM!
HMMM
SHIVER SHIVER SHIVER
CHECK THIS OUT!
I CALL IT A FUR JACKET AND CAP!
NOW WHAT DO WE DO?
HMMM...
THEY DECIDED VACATION WAS, IN FACT, "AWESOME"!
HEY BUNNY, LEAVE HIS NOSE ALONE!
THE COMPROMISED END

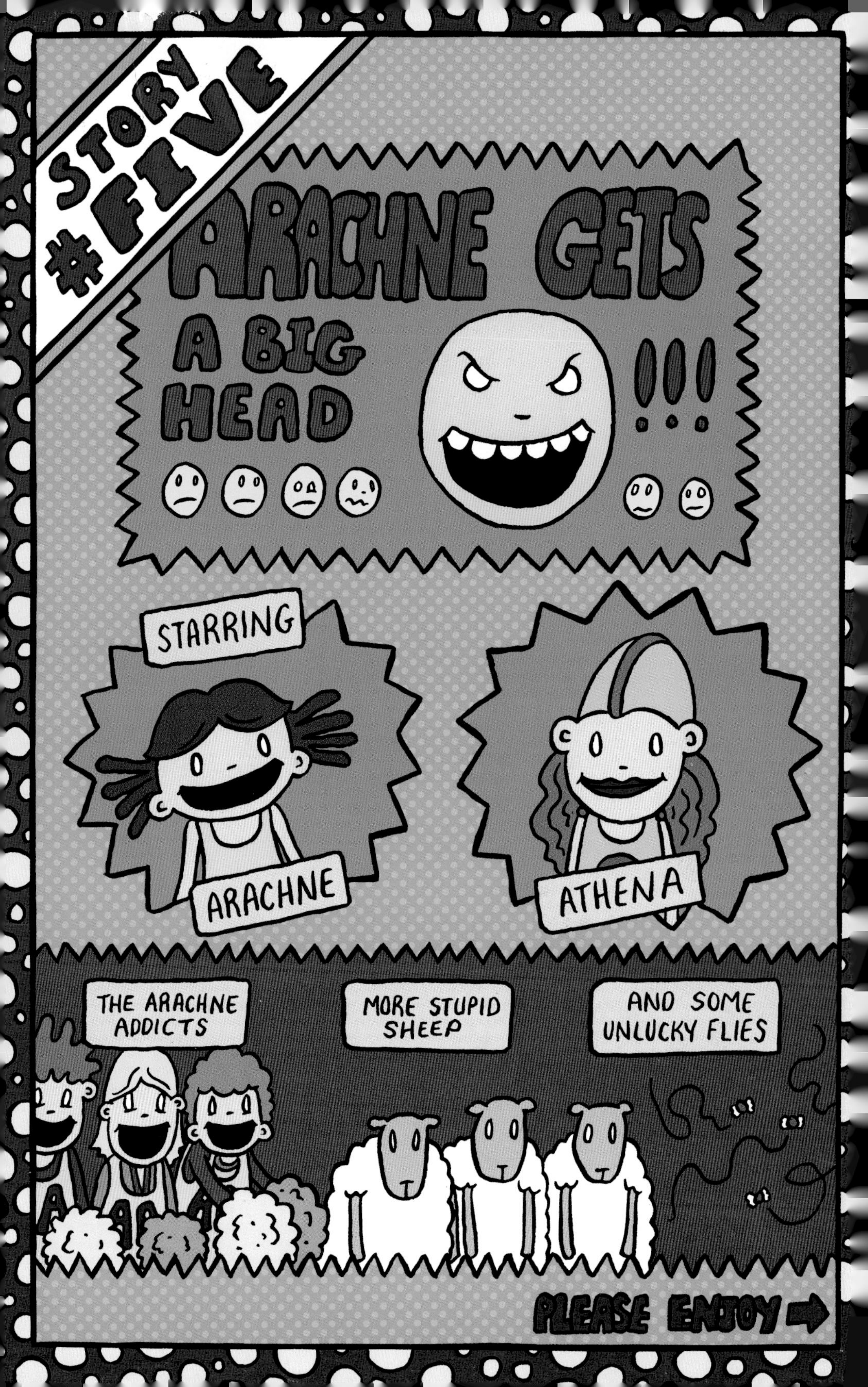
STORY #FIVE
ARACHNE GETS A BIG HEAD!!!
STARRING
ARACHNE
ATHENA
THE ARACHNE ADDICTS
MORE STUPID SHEEP
AND SOME UNLUCKY FLIES
PLEASE ENJOY

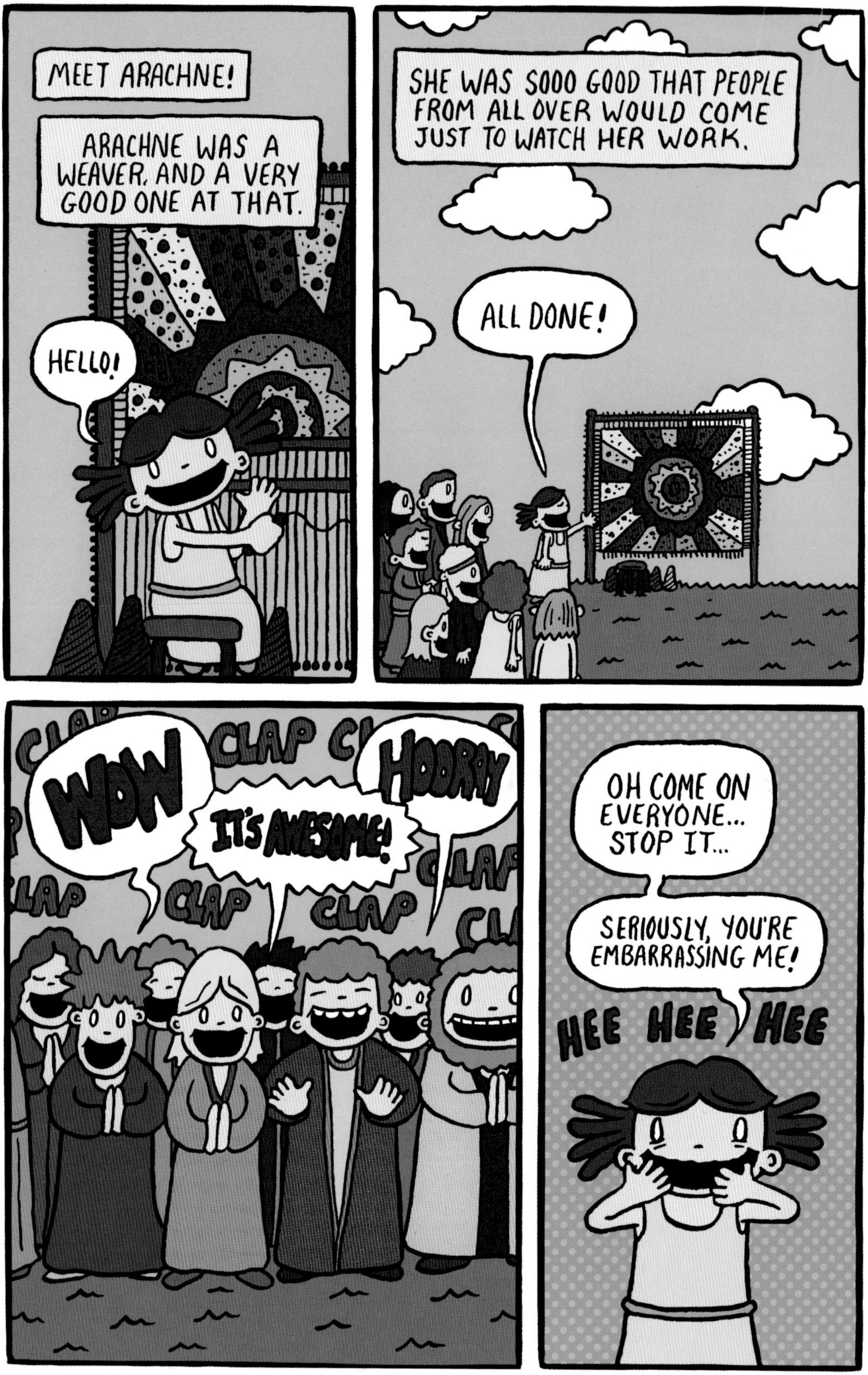
MEET ARACHNE!
ARACHNE WAS A WEAVER, AND A VERY GOOD ONE AT THAT.
HELLO!
SHE WAS SOOO GOOD THAT PEOPLE FROM ALL OVER WOULD COME JUST TO WATCH HER WORK.
ALL DONE!
WOW
CLAP
IT'S AWESOME!
HOORAY
CLAP
CLAP
OH COME ON EVERYONE... STOP IT...
SERIOUSLY, YOU'RE EMBARRASSING ME!
HEE HEE HEE

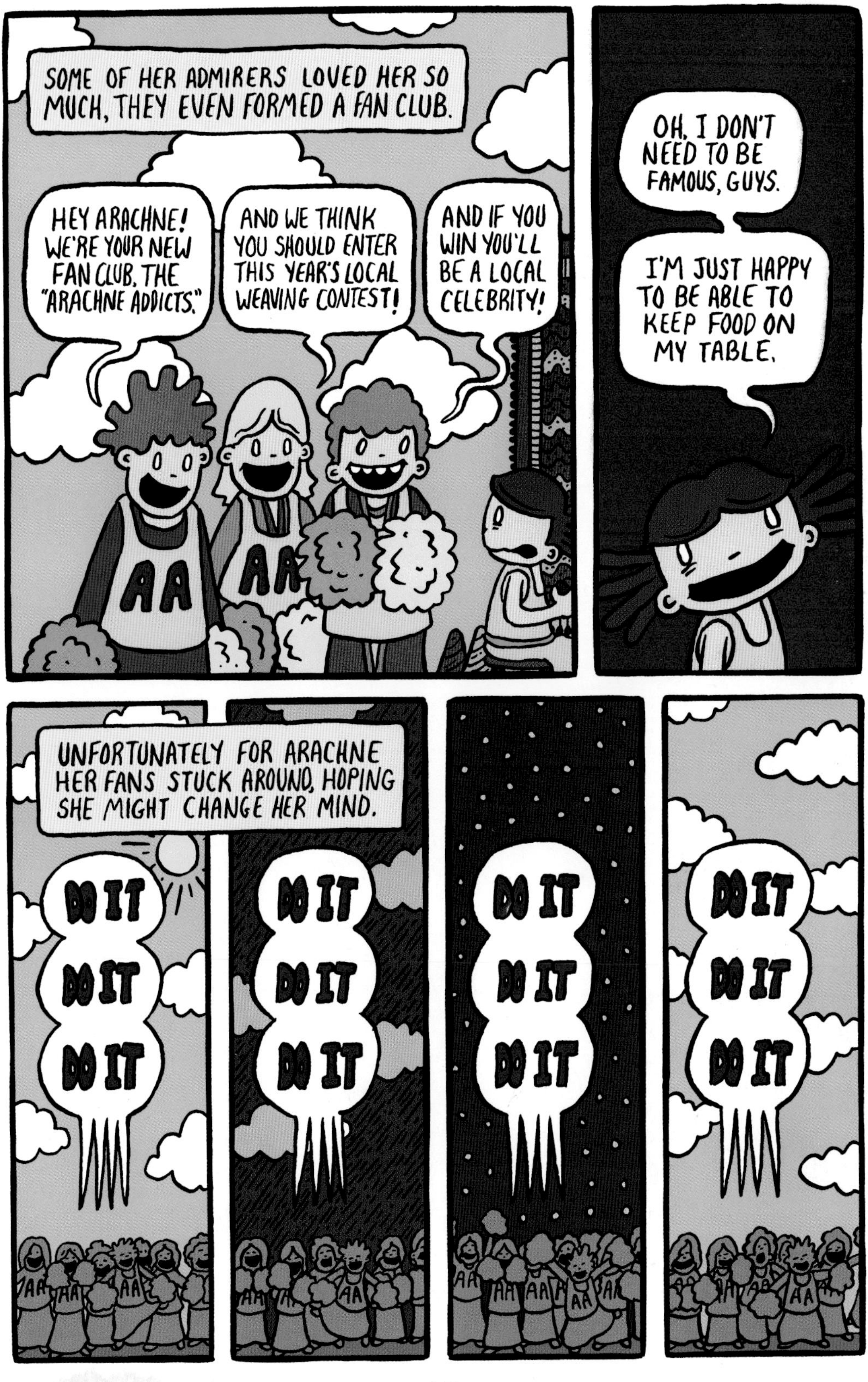
SOME OF HER ADMIRERS LOVED HER SO MUCH, THEY EVEN FORMED A FAN CLUB.
HEY ARACHNE! WE'RE YOUR NEW FAN CLUB, THE "ARACHNE ADDICTS."
AND WE THINK YOU SHOULD ENTER THIS YEAR'S LOCAL WEAVING CONTEST!
AND IF YOU WIN YOU'LL BE A LOCAL CELEBRITY!
AA
OH, I DON'T NEED TO BE FAMOUS, GUYS.
I'M JUST HAPPY TO BE ABLE TO KEEP FOOD ON MY TABLE.
UNFORTUNATELY FOR ARACHNE HER FANS STUCK AROUND, HOPING SHE MIGHT CHANGE HER MIND.
DO IT DO IT DO IT
DO IT DO IT DO IT
DO IT DO IT DO IT
DO IT DO IT DO IT

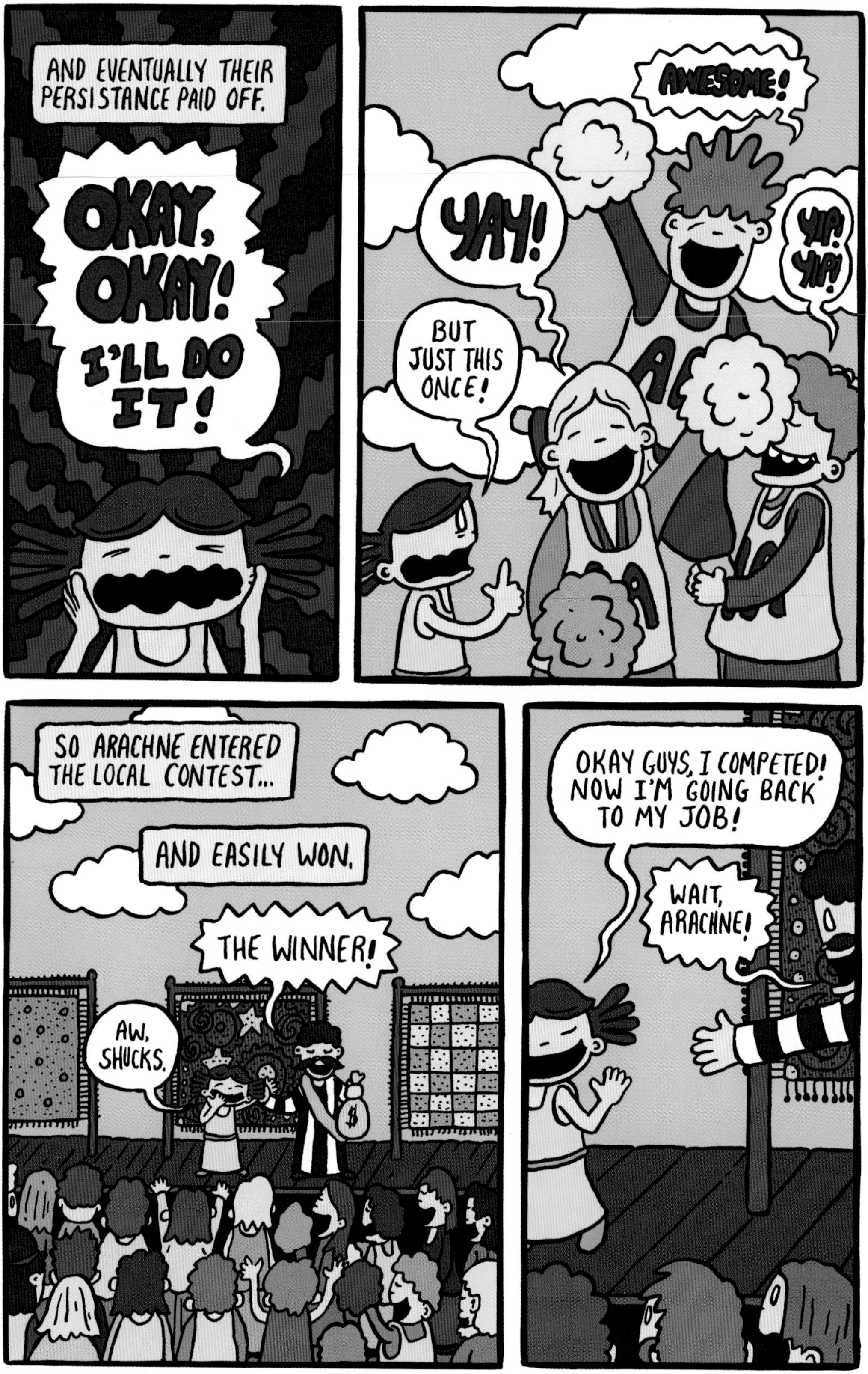
AND EVENTUALLY THEIR PERSISTANCE PAID OFF.
OKAY, OKAY! I'LL DO IT!
AWESOME!
YAY!
YIP! YIP!
BUT JUST THIS ONCE!
SO ARACHNE ENTERED THE LOCAL CONTEST...
AND EASILY WON.
THE WINNER!
AW, SHUCKS.
OKAY GUYS, I COMPETED! NOW I'M GOING BACK TO MY JOB!
WAIT, ARACHNE!

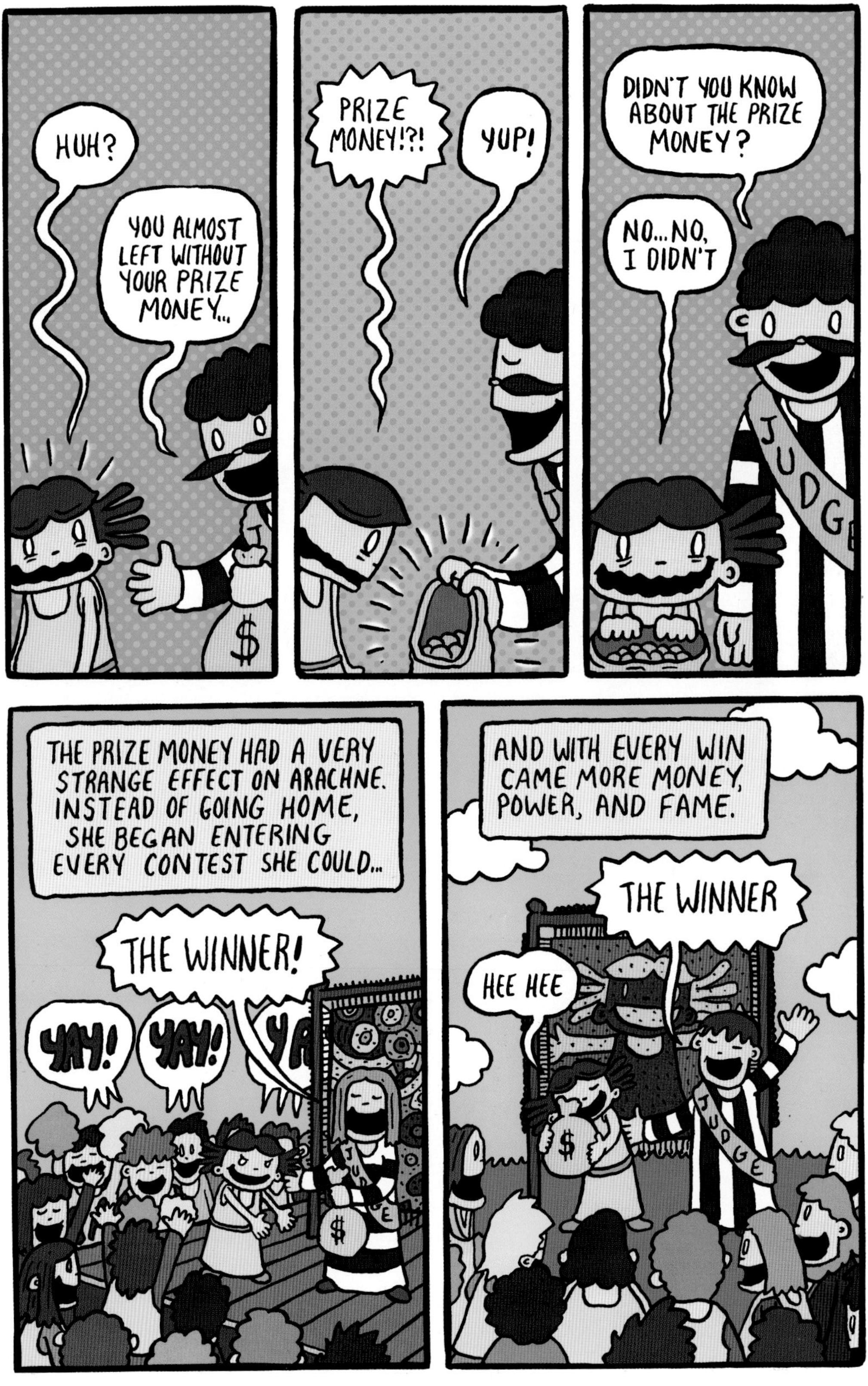
HUH?
YOU ALMOST LEFT WITHOUT YOUR PRIZE MONEY...
PRIZE MONEY!?!
YUP!
DIDN'T YOU KNOW ABOUT THE PRIZE MONEY?
NO...NO, I DIDN'T
JUDGE
$
THE PRIZE MONEY HAD A VERY STRANGE EFFECT ON ARACHNE. INSTEAD OF GOING HOME, SHE BEGAN ENTERING EVERY CONTEST SHE COULD...
THE WINNER!
YAY!
YAY!
AND WITH EVERY WIN CAME MORE MONEY, POWER, AND FAME.
THE WINNER
HEE HEE
JUDGE

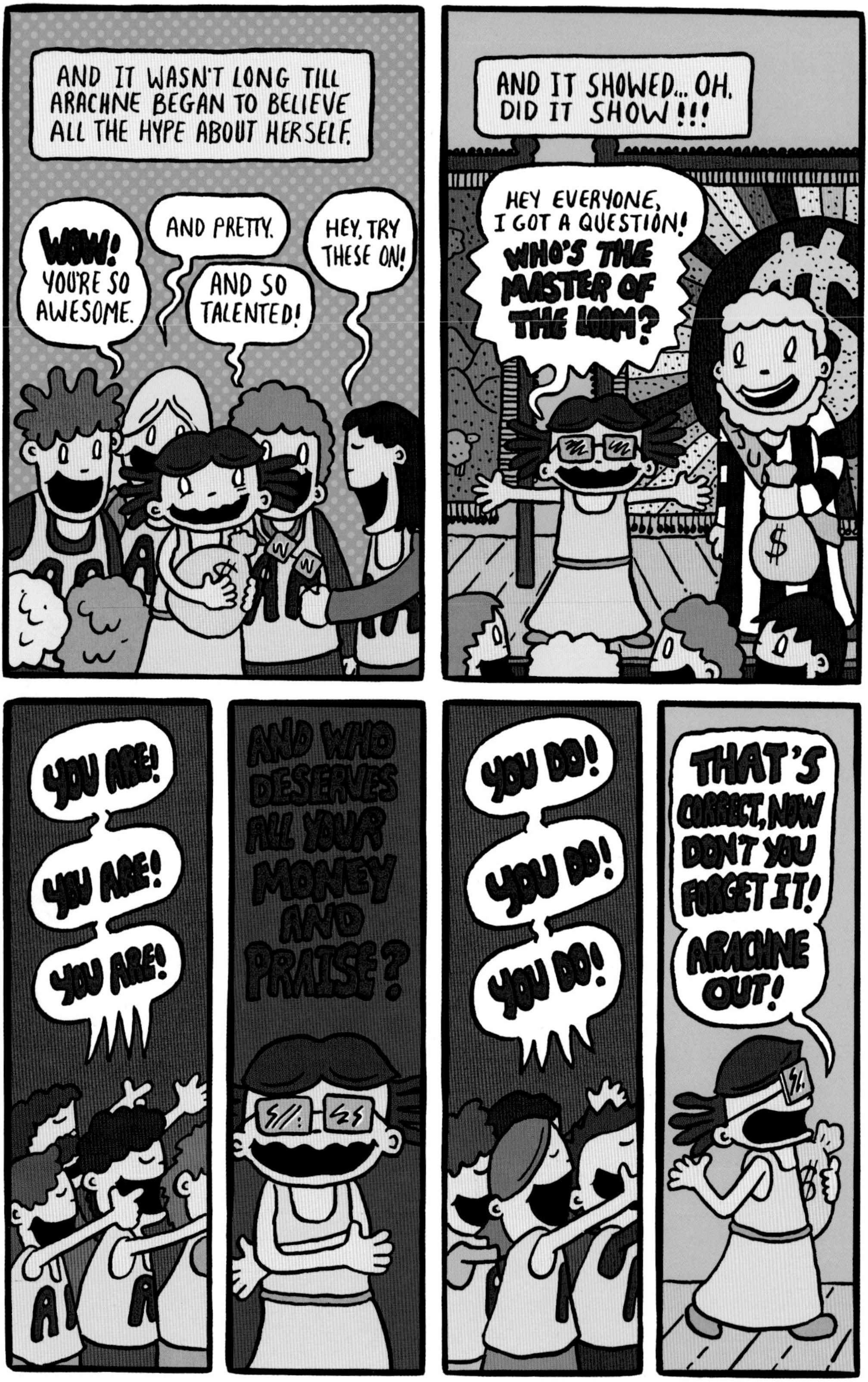
AND IT WASN'T LONG TILL ARACHNE BEGAN TO BELIEVE ALL THE HYPE ABOUT HERSELF.
WOW! YOU'RE SO AWESOME.
AND PRETTY.
AND SO TALENTED!
HEY, TRY THESE ON!
AND IT SHOWED... OH, DID IT SHOW!!!
HEY EVERYONE, I GOT A QUESTION! WHO'S THE MASTER OF THE LOOM?
YOU ARE!
YOU ARE!
YOU ARE!
AND WHO DESERVES ALL YOUR MONEY AND PRAISE?
YOU DO!
YOU DO!
YOU DO!
THAT'S CORRECT, NOW DON'T YOU FORGET IT! ARACHNE OUT!

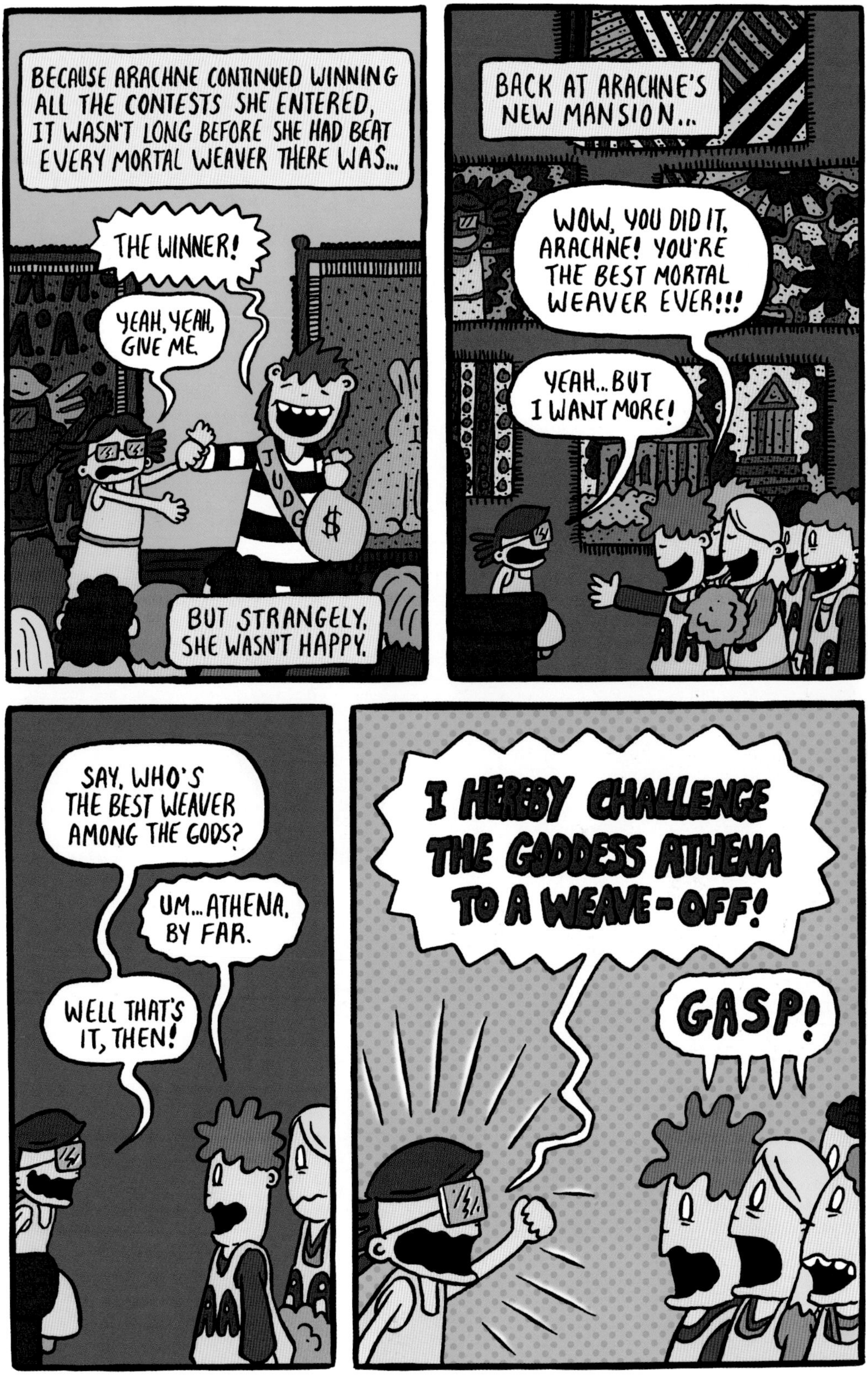
BECAUSE ARACHNE CONTINUED WINNING ALL THE CONTESTS SHE ENTERED, IT WASN'T LONG BEFORE SHE HAD BEAT EVERY MORTAL WEAVER THERE WAS...
THE WINNER!
YEAH, YEAH, GIVE ME.
JUDGE
$
BUT STRANGELY, SHE WASN'T HAPPY.
BACK AT ARACHNE'S NEW MANSION...
WOW, YOU DID IT, ARACHNE! YOU'RE THE BEST MORTAL WEAVER EVER!!!
YEAH... BUT I WANT MORE!
SAY, WHO'S THE BEST WEAVER AMONG THE GODS?
UM... ATHENA, BY FAR.
WELL THAT'S IT, THEN!
I HEREBY CHALLENGE THE GODDESS ATHENA TO A WEAVE-OFF!
GASP!

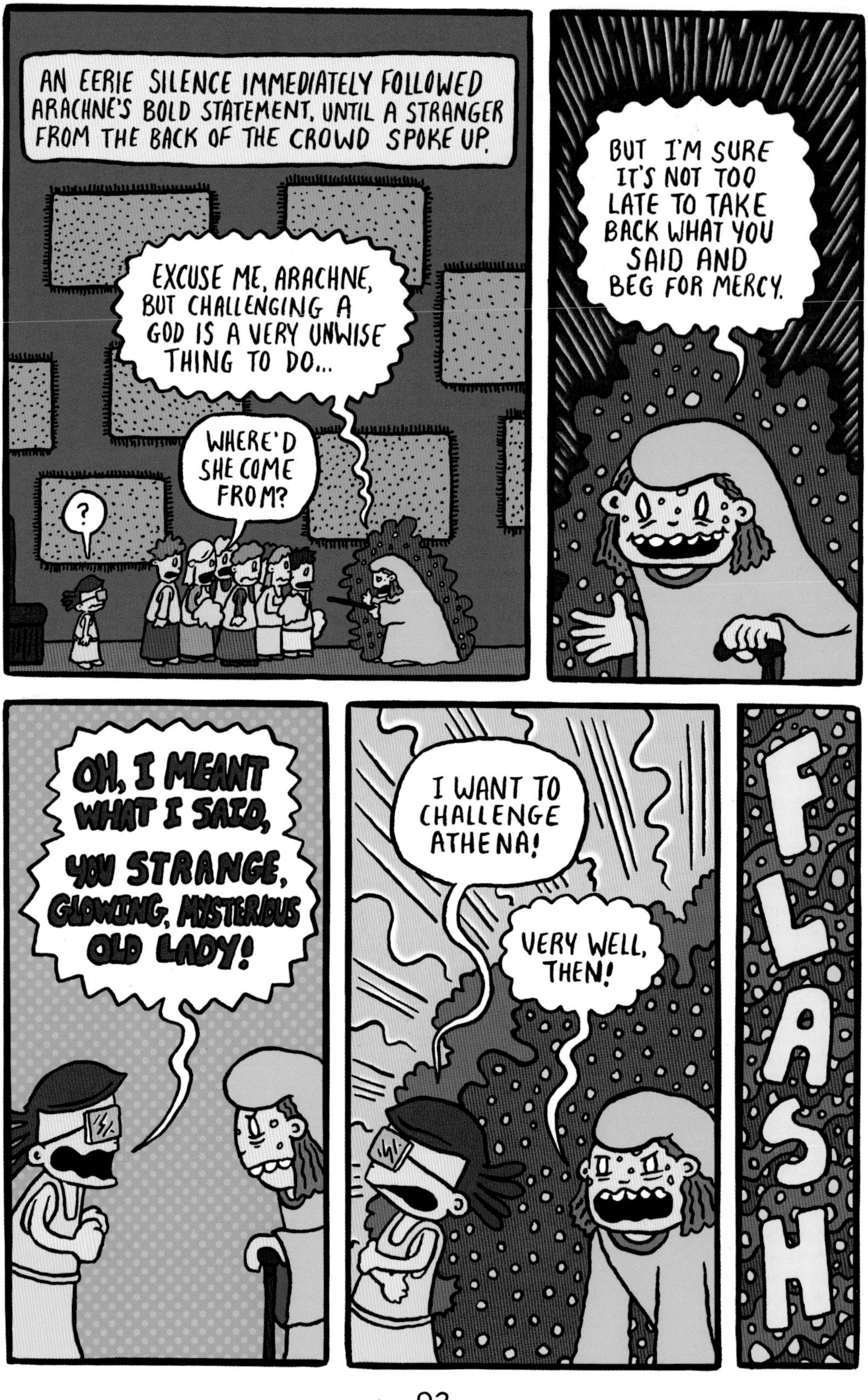
AN EERIE SILENCE IMMEDIATELY FOLLOWED ARACHNE'S BOLD STATEMENT, UNTIL A STRANGER FROM THE BACK OF THE CROWD SPOKE UP.
EXCUSE ME, ARACHNE, BUT CHALLENGING A GOD IS A VERY UNWISE THING TO DO...
?
WHERE'D SHE COME FROM?
BUT I'M SURE IT'S NOT TOO LATE TO TAKE BACK WHAT YOU SAID AND BEG FOR MERCY.
OH, I MEANT WHAT I SAID, YOU STRANGE, GLOWING, MYSTERIOUS OLD LADY!
I WANT TO CHALLENGE ATHENA!
VERY WELL, THEN!
FLASH

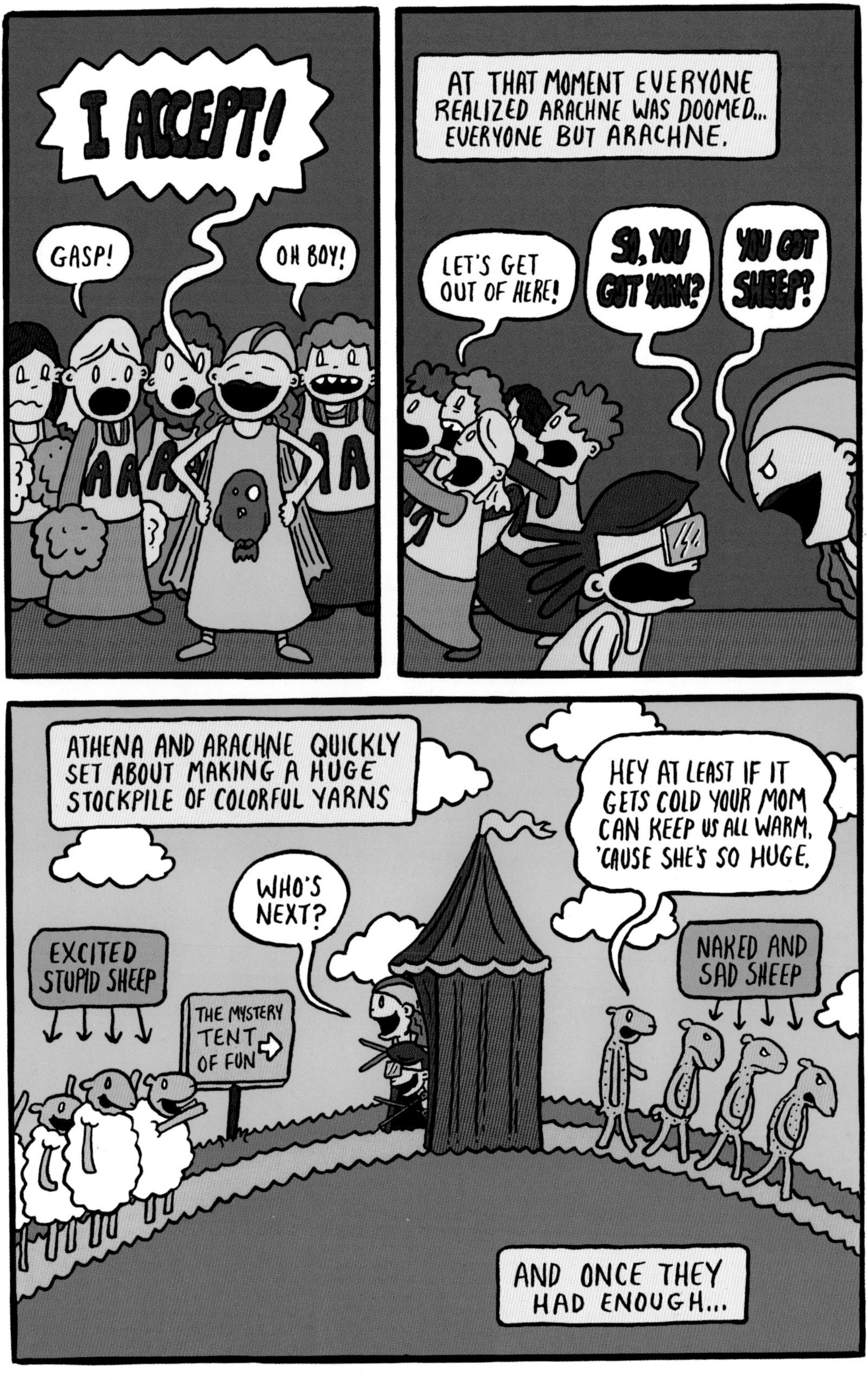
I ACCEPT!
GASP!
OH BOY!
AT THAT MOMENT EVERYONE REALIZED ARACHNE WAS DOOMED... EVERYONE BUT ARACHNE.
LET'S GET OUT OF HERE!
SO, YOU GOT YARN?
YOU GOT SHEEP?
ATHENA AND ARACHNE QUICKLY SET ABOUT MAKING A HUGE STOCKPILE OF COLORFUL YARNS
HEY AT LEAST IF IT GETS COLD YOUR MOM CAN KEEP US ALL WARM, 'CAUSE SHE'S SO HUGE.
WHO'S NEXT?
EXCITED STUPID SHEEP
THE MYSTERY TENT OF FUN
NAKED AND SAD SHEEP
AND ONCE THEY HAD ENOUGH...

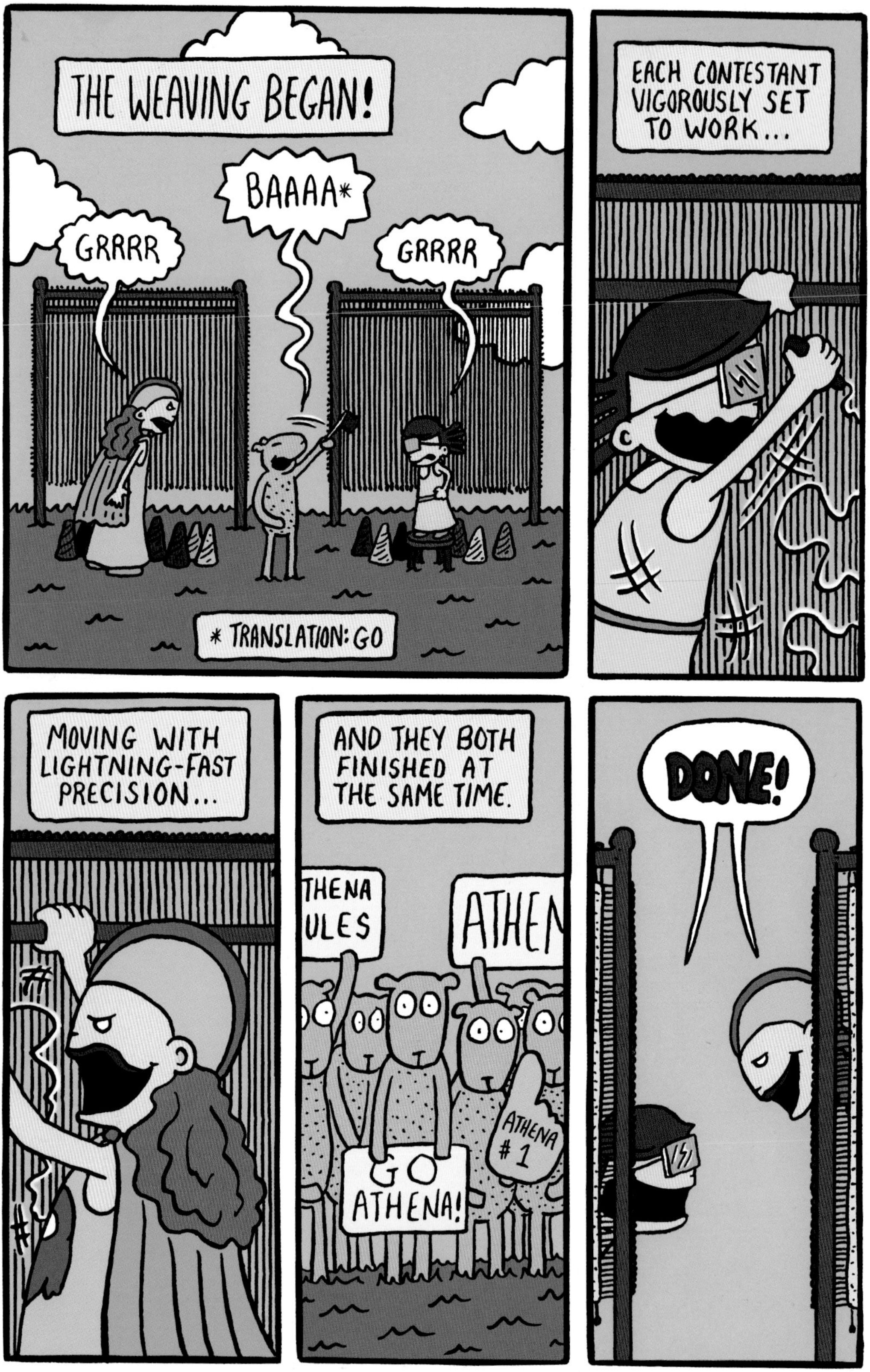
THE WEAVING BEGAN!
BAAAA*
GRRRR
GRRRR
* TRANSLATION: GO
EACH CONTESTANT VIGOROUSLY SET TO WORK...
MOVING WITH LIGHTNING-FAST PRECISION...
AND THEY BOTH FINISHED AT THE SAME TIME.
THENA
ULES
ATHEN
GO ATHENA!
ATHENA #1
DONE!

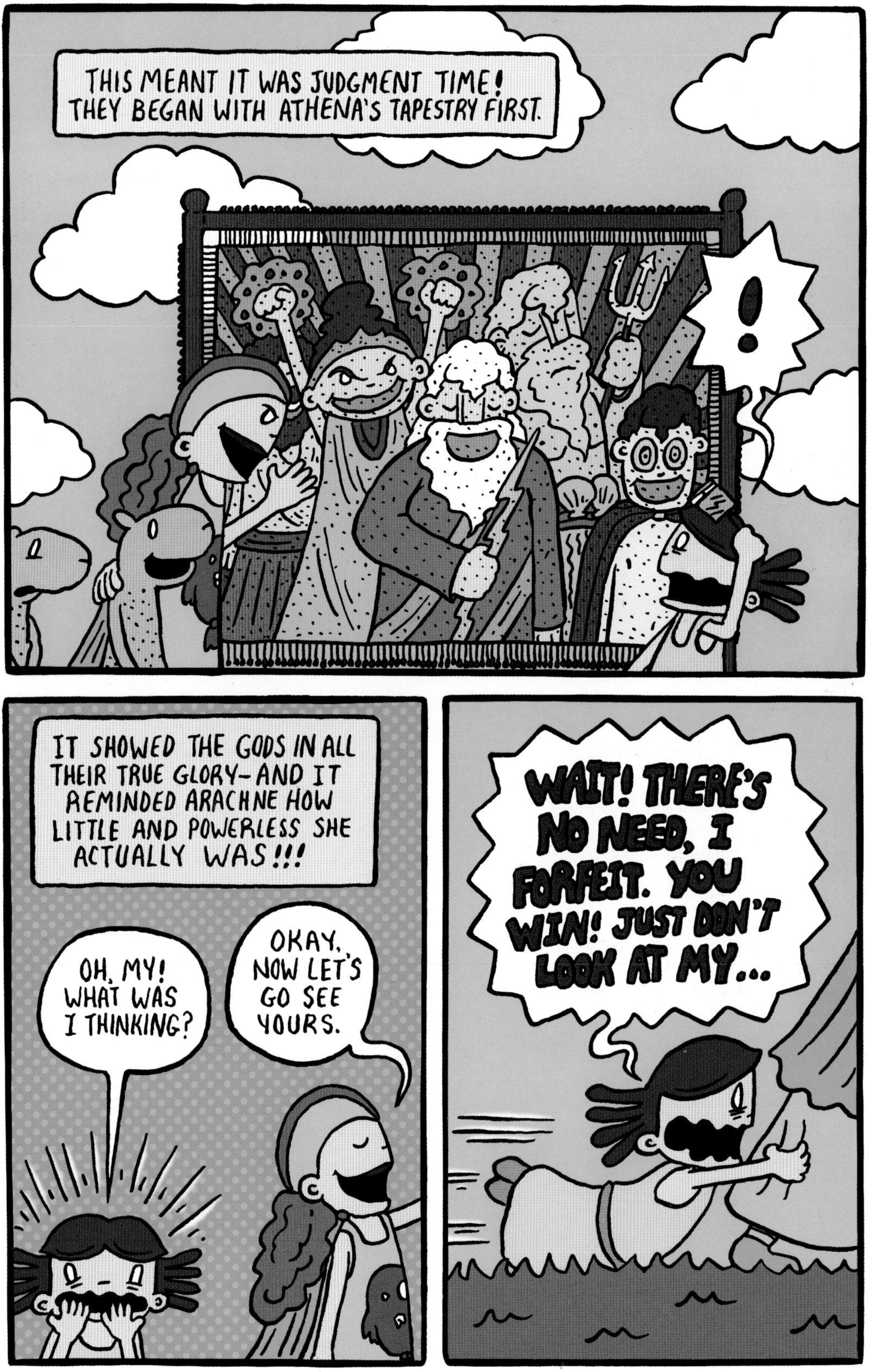
THIS MEANT IT WAS JUDGMENT TIME! THEY BEGAN WITH ATHENA'S TAPESTRY FIRST.
!
IT SHOWED THE GODS IN ALL THEIR TRUE GLORY– AND IT REMINDED ARACHNE HOW LITTLE AND POWERLESS SHE ACTUALLY WAS!!!
OH, MY! WHAT WAS I THINKING?
OKAY, NOW LET'S GO SEE YOURS.
WAIT! THERE'S NO NEED, I FORFEIT. YOU WIN! JUST DON'T LOOK AT MY...

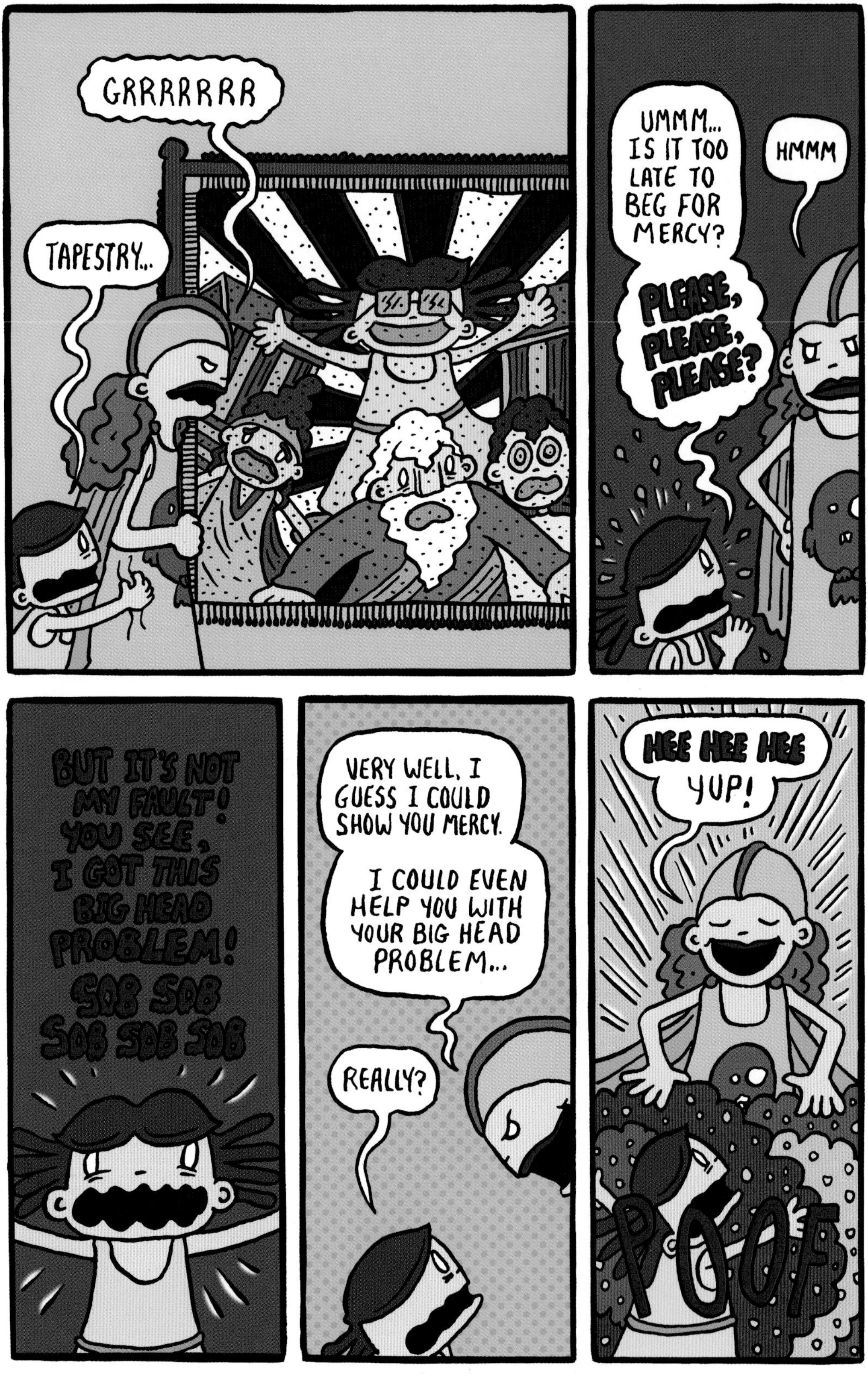

GRRRRRRR
TAPESTRY...
UMMM... IS IT TOO LATE TO BEG FOR MERCY?
PLEASE, PLEASE, PLEASE?
HMMM
BUT IT'S NOT MY FAULT! YOU SEE, I GOT THIS BIG HEAD PROBLEM!
SOB SOB SOB SOB SOB
VERY WELL, I GUESS I COULD SHOW YOU MERCY.
I COULD EVEN HELP YOU WITH YOUR BIG HEAD PROBLEM...
REALLY?
HEE HEE HEE
YUP!
POOF

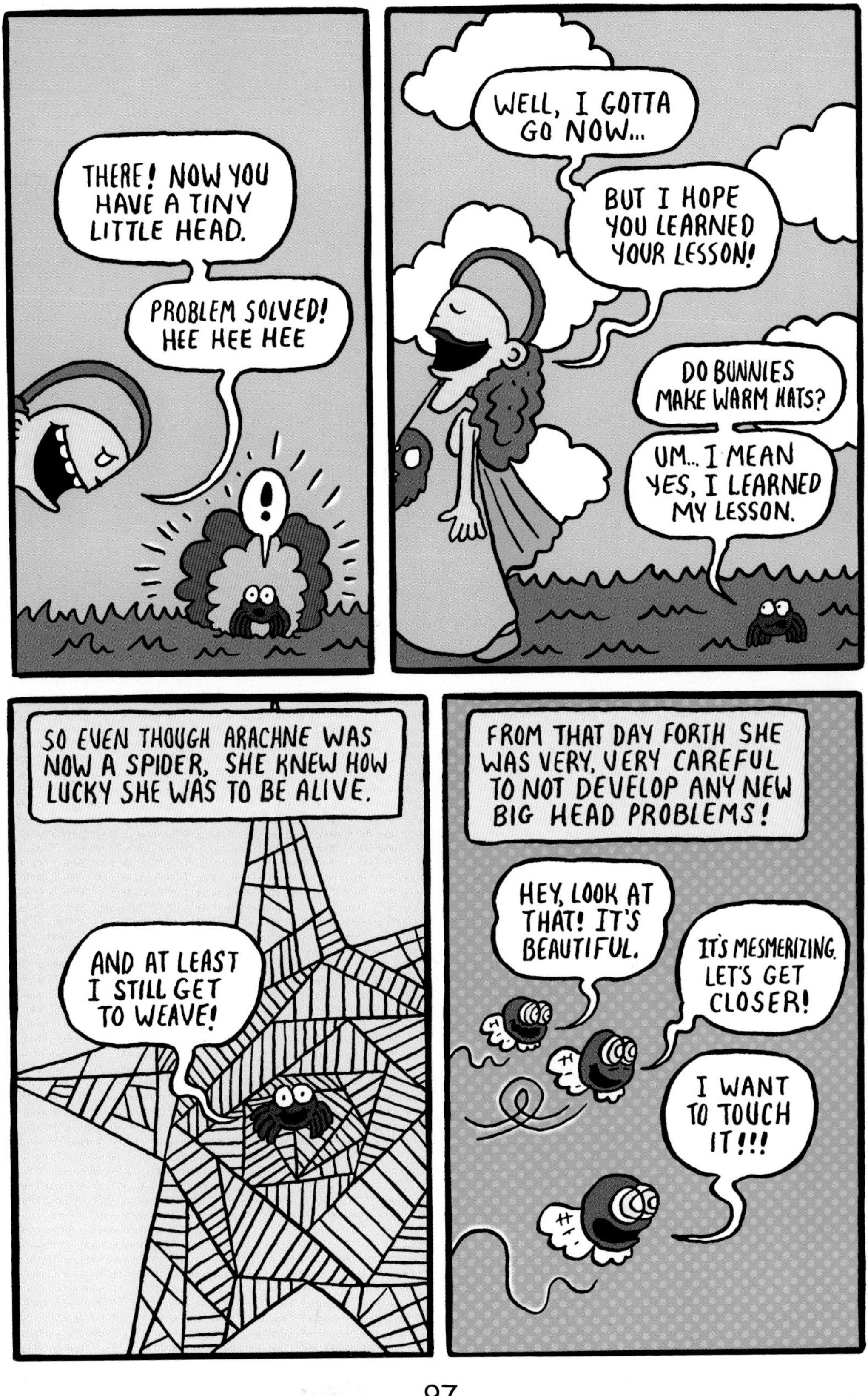
THERE! NOW YOU HAVE A TINY LITTLE HEAD.
PROBLEM SOLVED! HEE HEE HEE
!
WELL, I GOTTA GO NOW...
BUT I HOPE YOU LEARNED YOUR LESSON!
DO BUNNIES MAKE WARM HATS?
UM... I MEAN YES, I LEARNED MY LESSON.
SO EVEN THOUGH ARACHNE WAS NOW A SPIDER, SHE KNEW HOW LUCKY SHE WAS TO BE ALIVE.
AND AT LEAST I STILL GET TO WEAVE!
FROM THAT DAY FORTH SHE WAS VERY, VERY CAREFUL TO NOT DEVELOP ANY NEW BIG HEAD PROBLEMS!
HEY, LOOK AT THAT! IT'S BEAUTIFUL.
IT'S MESMERIZING. LET'S GET CLOSER!
I WANT TO TOUCH IT!!!

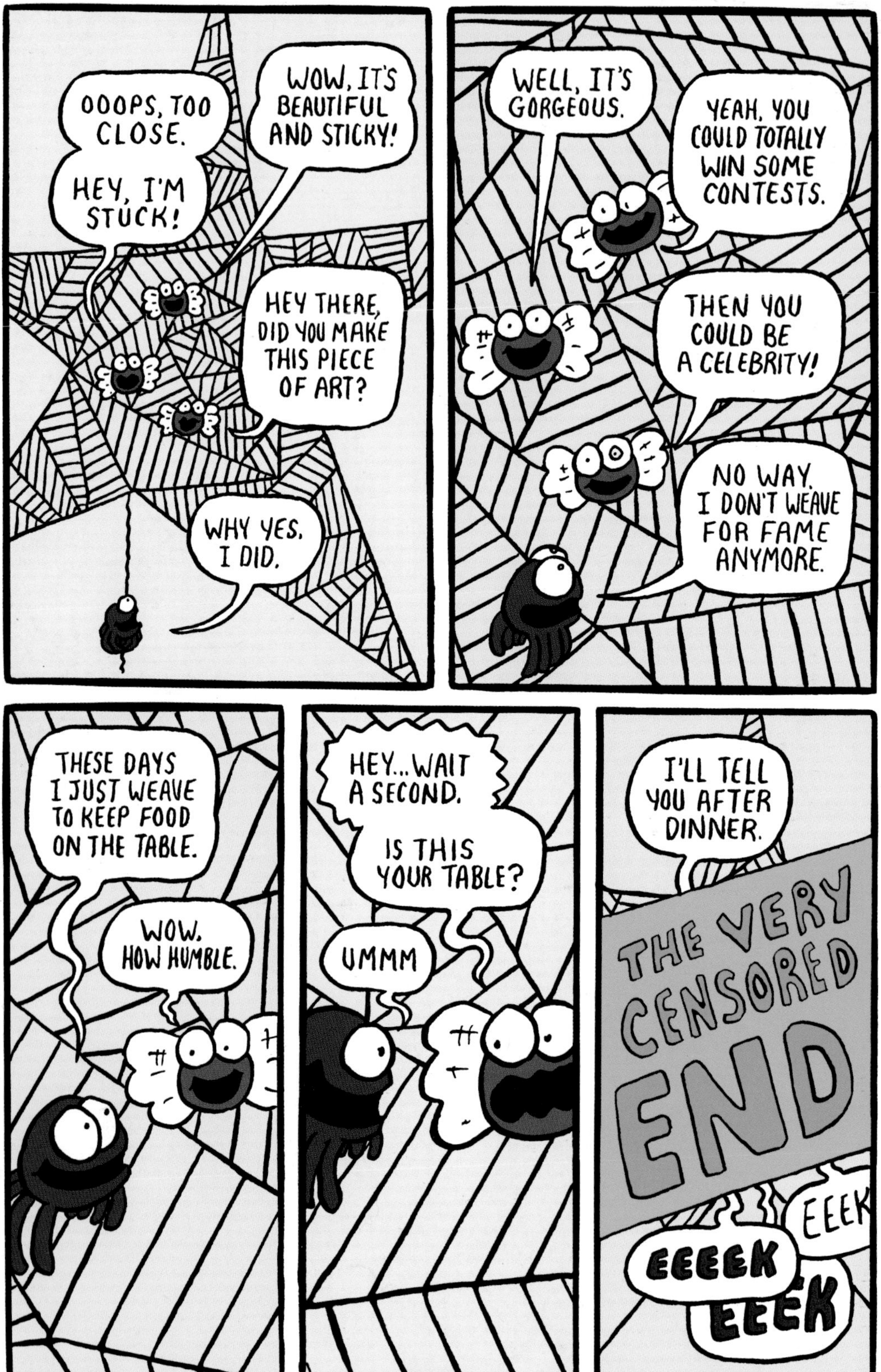
OOOPS, TOO CLOSE.
HEY, I'M STUCK!
WOW, IT'S BEAUTIFUL AND STICKY!
HEY THERE, DID YOU MAKE THIS PIECE OF ART?
WHY YES. I DID.
WELL, IT'S GORGEOUS.
YEAH, YOU COULD TOTALLY WIN SOME CONTESTS.
THEN YOU COULD BE A CELEBRITY!
NO WAY. I DON'T WEAVE FOR FAME ANYMORE.
THESE DAYS I JUST WEAVE TO KEEP FOOD ON THE TABLE.
WOW. HOW HUMBLE.
HEY... WAIT A SECOND.
IS THIS YOUR TABLE?
UMMM
I'LL TELL YOU AFTER DINNER.
THE VERY CENSORED END
EEEK
EEEEK
EEEK

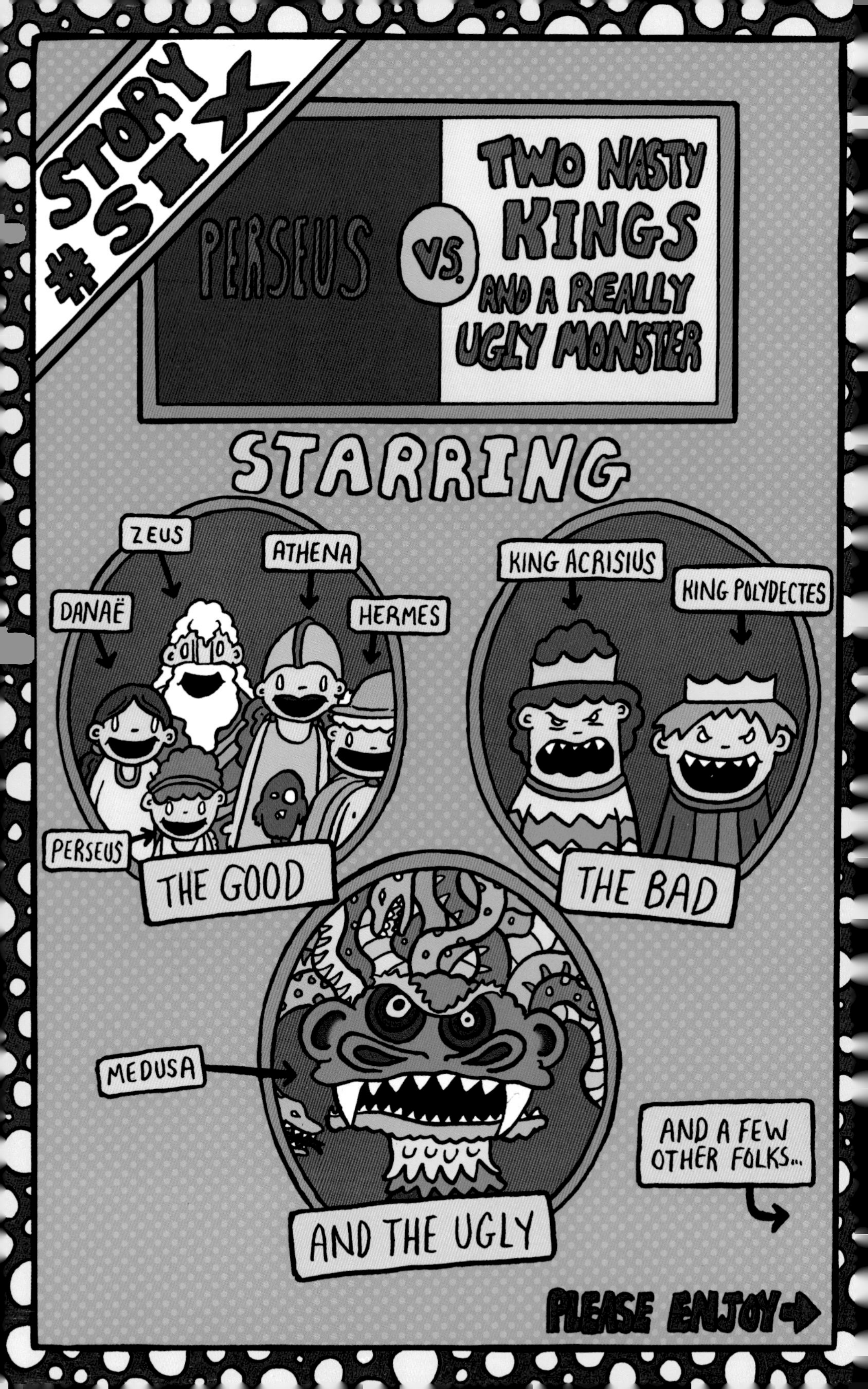
STORY #SIX
PERSEUS VS. TWO NASTY KINGS AND A REALLY UGLY MONSTER
STARRING
ZEUS
ATHENA
DANAË
HERMES
PERSEUS
THE GOOD
KING ACRISIUS
KING POLYDECTES
THE BAD
MEDUSA
AND THE UGLY
AND A FEW OTHER FOLKS...
PLEASE ENJOY

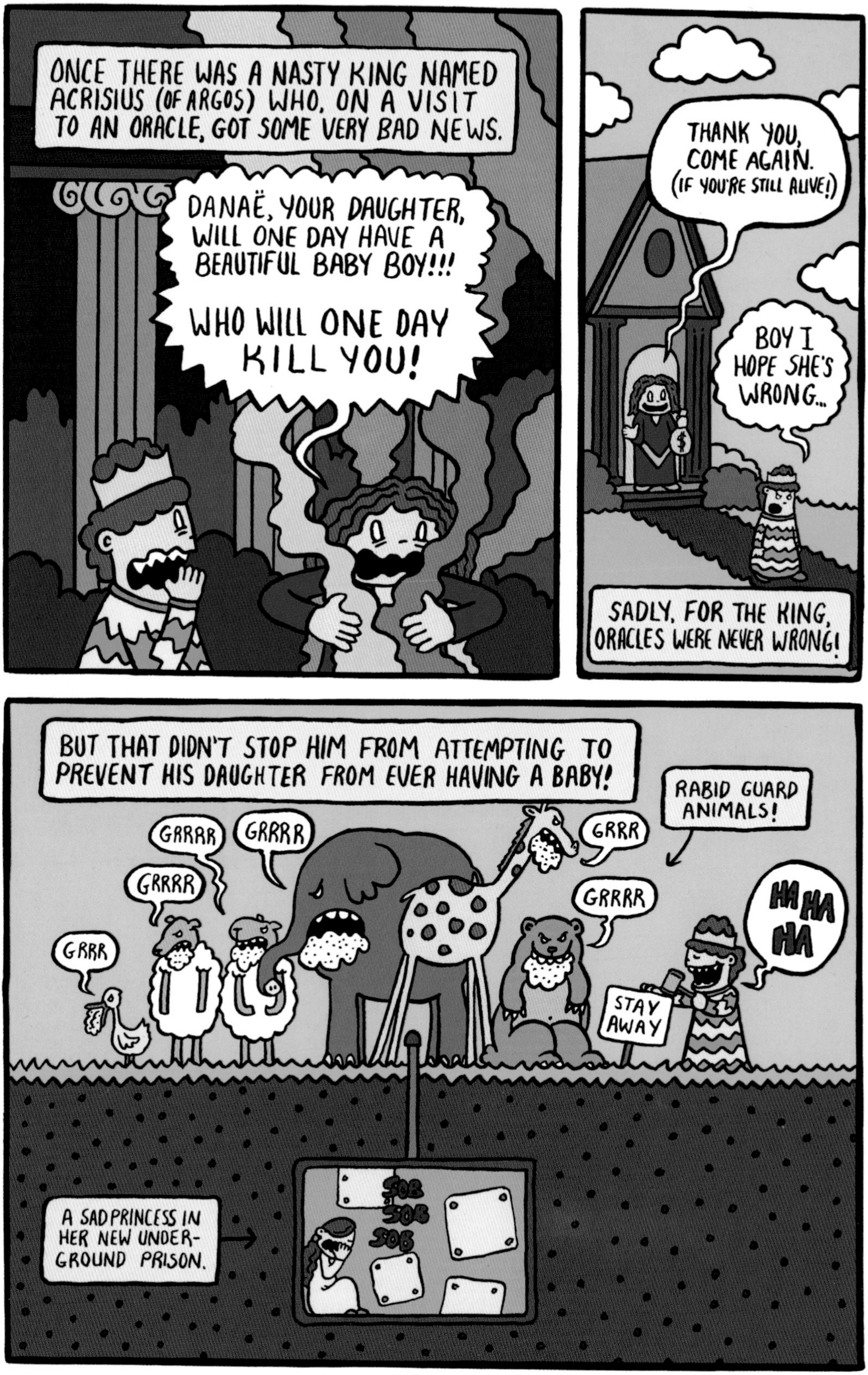

ONCE THERE WAS A NASTY KING NAMED ACRISIUS (OF ARGOS) WHO, ON A VISIT TO AN ORACLE, GOT SOME VERY BAD NEWS.
DANAË, YOUR DAUGHTER, WILL ONE DAY HAVE A BEAUTIFUL BABY BOY!!!
WHO WILL ONE DAY KILL YOU!
THANK YOU, COME AGAIN. (IF YOU'RE STILL ALIVE!)
$
BOY I HOPE SHE'S WRONG...
SADLY, FOR THE KING, ORACLES WERE NEVER WRONG!
BUT THAT DIDN'T STOP HIM FROM ATTEMPTING TO PREVENT HIS DAUGHTER FROM EVER HAVING A BABY!
RABID GUARD ANIMALS!
GRRR
GRRRR
GRRRR
GRRRR
GRRR
GRRRR
HA HA HA
STAY AWAY
SOB SOB SOB
A SAD PRINCESS IN HER NEW UNDER-GROUND PRISON.

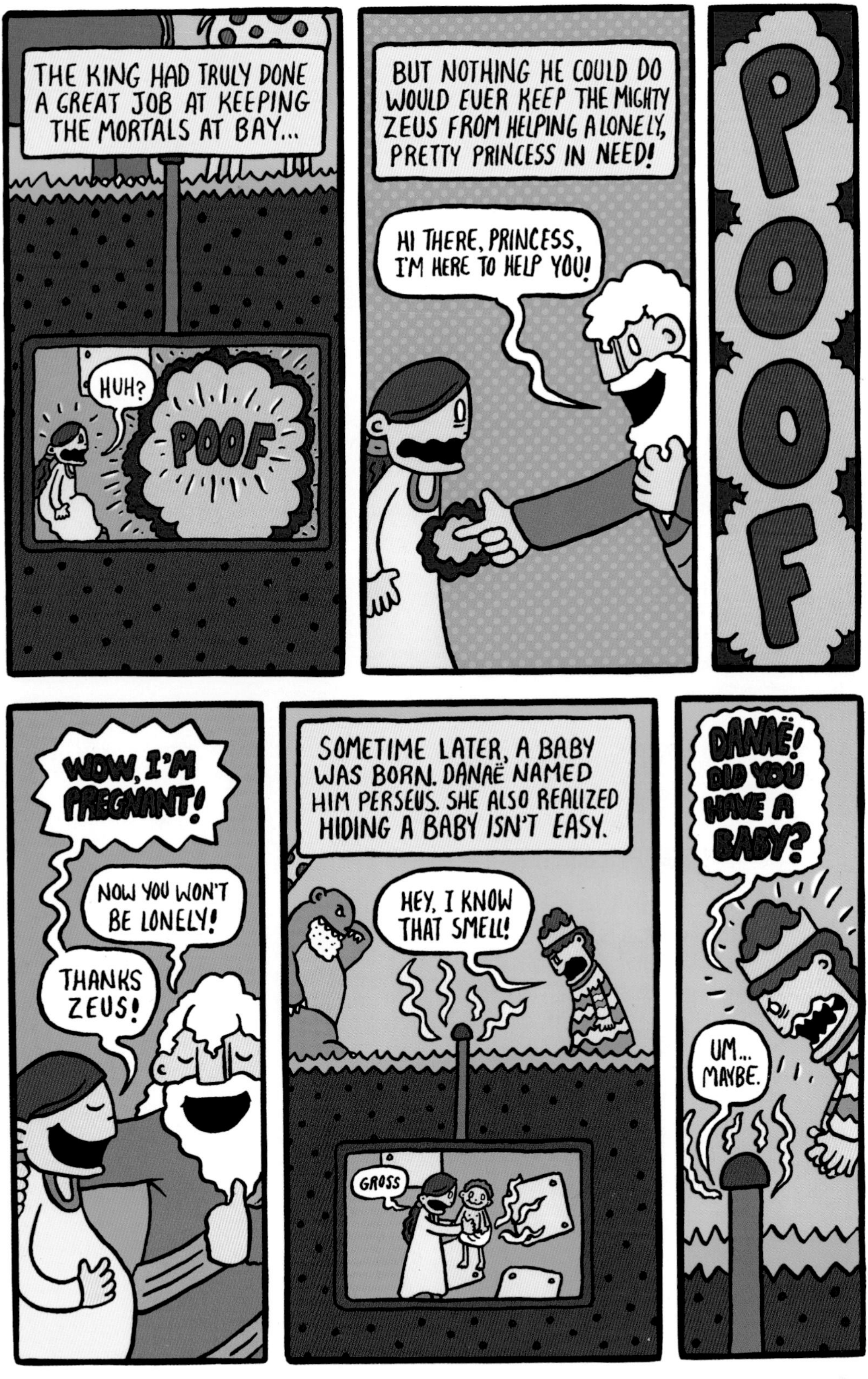
THE KING HAD TRULY DONE A GREAT JOB AT KEEPING THE MORTALS AT BAY...
HUH?
POOF
BUT NOTHING HE COULD DO WOULD EVER KEEP THE MIGHTY ZEUS FROM HELPING A LONELY, PRETTY PRINCESS IN NEED!
HI THERE, PRINCESS, I'M HERE TO HELP YOU!
POOF
WOW, I'M PREGNANT!
NOW YOU WON'T BE LONELY!
THANKS ZEUS!
SOMETIME LATER, A BABY WAS BORN. DANAË NAMED HIM PERSEUS. SHE ALSO REALIZED HIDING A BABY ISN'T EASY.
HEY, I KNOW THAT SMELL!
GROSS
DANAË! DID YOU HAVE A BABY?
UM... MAYBE.

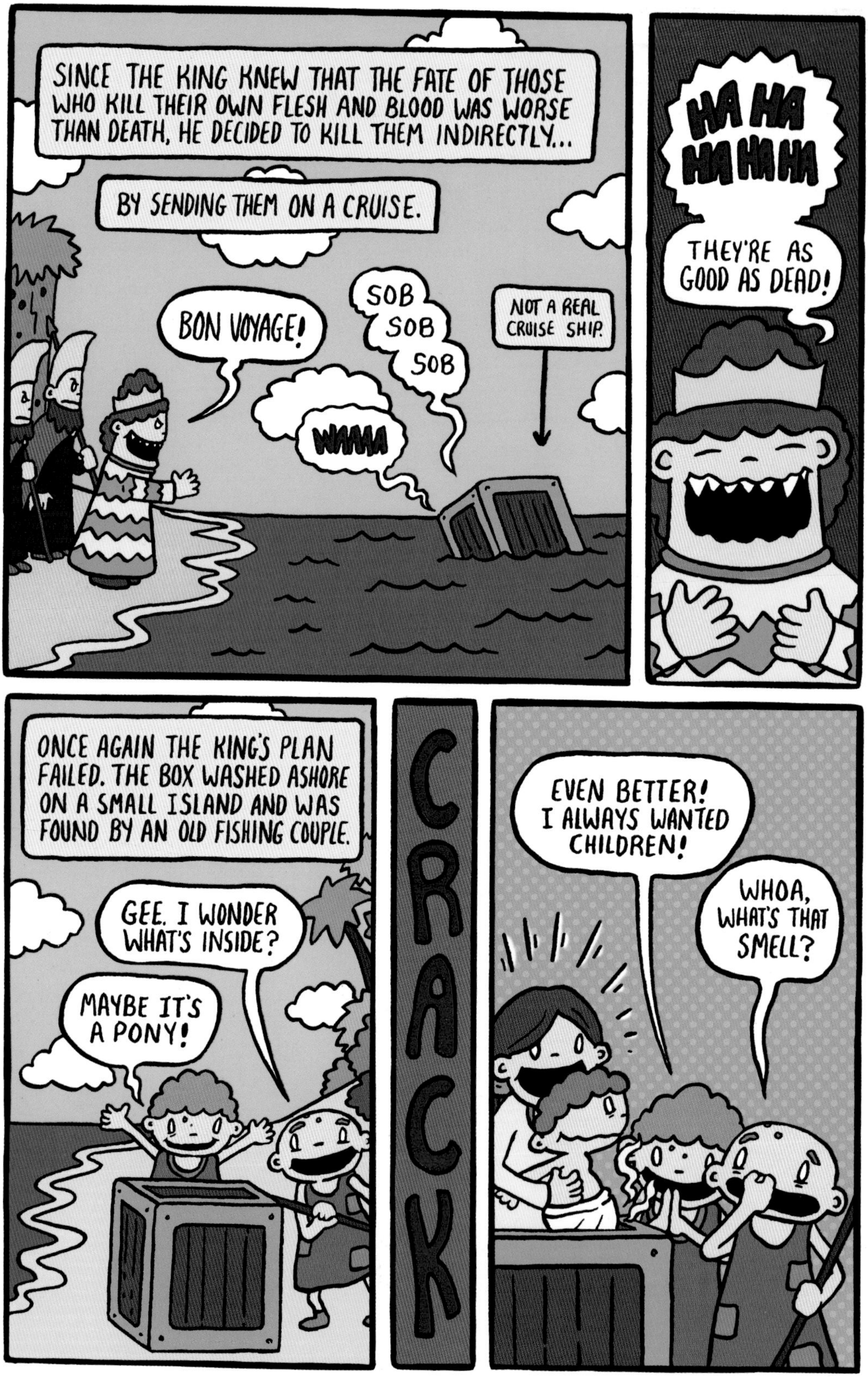
SINCE THE KING KNEW THAT THE FATE OF THOSE WHO KILL THEIR OWN FLESH AND BLOOD WAS WORSE THAN DEATH, HE DECIDED TO KILL THEM INDIRECTLY...
BY SENDING THEM ON A CRUISE.
BON VOYAGE!
SOB SOB SOB
WAAHA
NOT A REAL CRUISE SHIP.
HA HA HA HA HA
THEY'RE AS GOOD AS DEAD!
ONCE AGAIN THE KING'S PLAN FAILED. THE BOX WASHED ASHORE ON A SMALL ISLAND AND WAS FOUND BY AN OLD FISHING COUPLE.
GEE. I WONDER WHAT'S INSIDE?
MAYBE IT'S A PONY!
CRACK
EVEN BETTER! I ALWAYS WANTED CHILDREN!
WHOA, WHAT'S THAT SMELL?

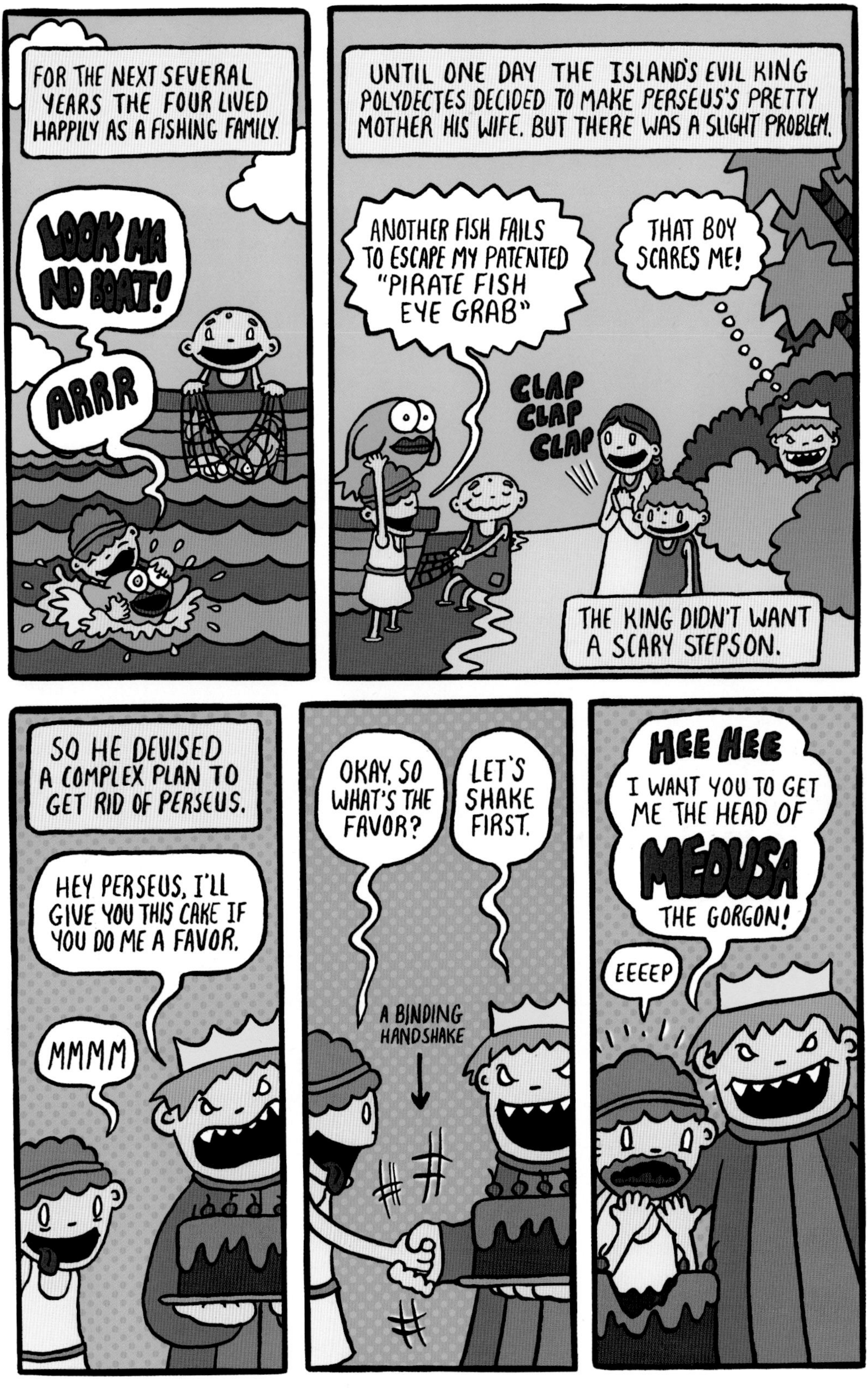
FOR THE NEXT SEVERAL YEARS THE FOUR LIVED HAPPILY AS A FISHING FAMILY.
LOOK MA NO BOAT!
ARRR
UNTIL ONE DAY THE ISLAND'S EVIL KING POLYDECTES DECIDED TO MAKE PERSEUS'S PRETTY MOTHER HIS WIFE. BUT THERE WAS A SLIGHT PROBLEM.
ANOTHER FISH FAILS TO ESCAPE MY PATENTED "PIRATE FISH EYE GRAB"
THAT BOY SCARES ME!
CLAP CLAP CLAP
THE KING DIDN'T WANT A SCARY STEPSON.
SO HE DEVISED A COMPLEX PLAN TO GET RID OF PERSEUS.
HEY PERSEUS, I'LL GIVE YOU THIS CAKE IF YOU DO ME A FAVOR.
MMMM
OKAY, SO WHAT'S THE FAVOR?
LET'S SHAKE FIRST.
A BINDING HANDSHAKE
HEE HEE
I WANT YOU TO GET ME THE HEAD OF MEDUSA THE GORGON!
EEEEP

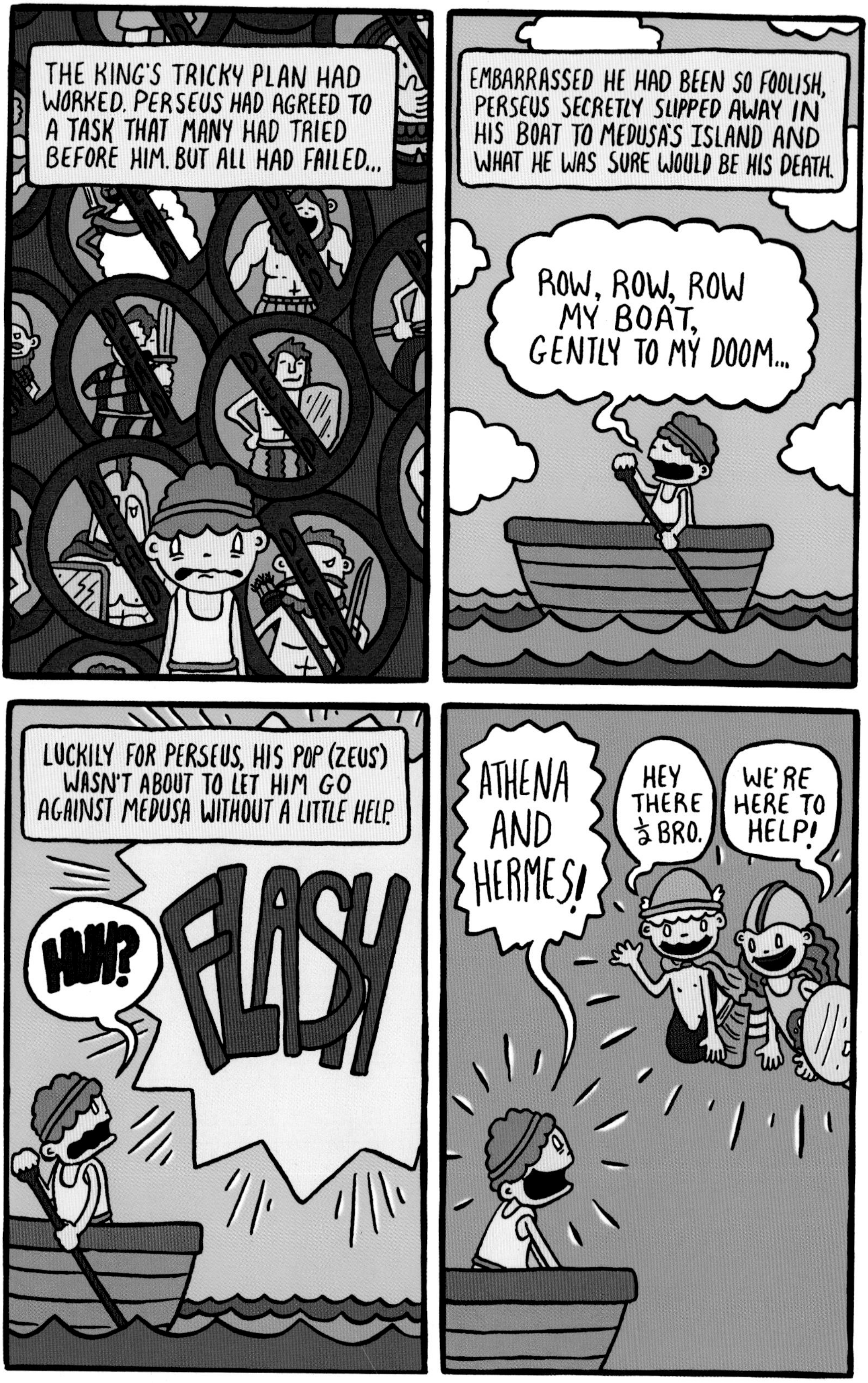
THE KING'S TRICKY PLAN HAD WORKED. PERSEUS HAD AGREED TO A TASK THAT MANY HAD TRIED BEFORE HIM. BUT ALL HAD FAILED...
EMBARRASSED HE HAD BEEN SO FOOLISH, PERSEUS SECRETLY SLIPPED AWAY IN HIS BOAT TO MEDUSA'S ISLAND AND WHAT HE WAS SURE WOULD BE HIS DEATH.
ROW, ROW, ROW MY BOAT, GENTLY TO MY DOOM...
LUCKILY FOR PERSEUS, HIS POP (ZEUS) WASN'T ABOUT TO LET HIM GO AGAINST MEDUSA WITHOUT A LITTLE HELP.
HUH?
FLASH
ATHENA AND HERMES!
HEY THERE ½ BRO.
WE'RE HERE TO HELP!

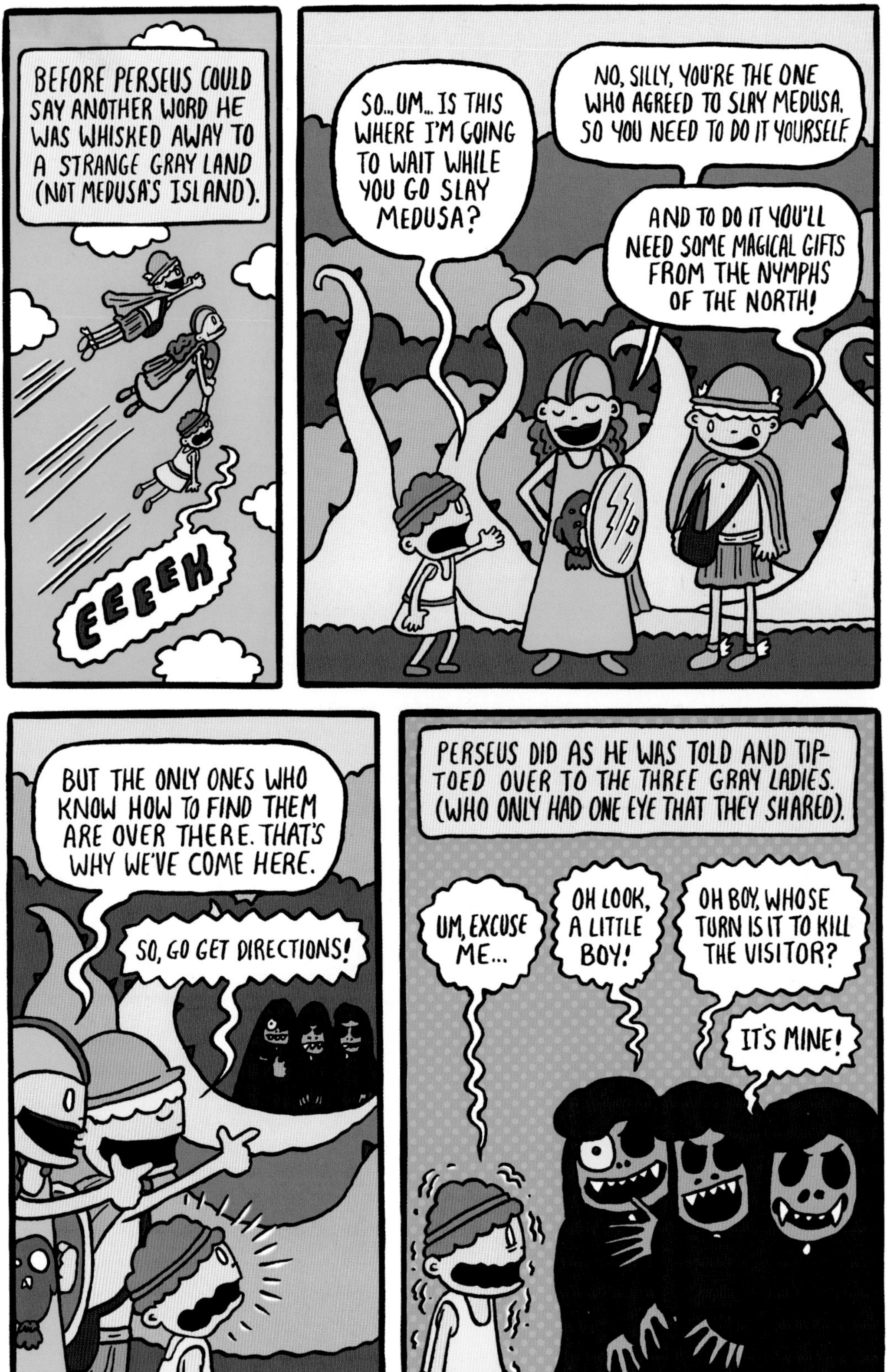
BEFORE PERSEUS COULD SAY ANOTHER WORD HE WAS WHISKED AWAY TO A STRANGE GRAY LAND (NOT MEDUSA'S ISLAND).
EEEEK
SO...UM... IS THIS WHERE I'M GOING TO WAIT WHILE YOU GO SLAY MEDUSA?
NO, SILLY, YOU'RE THE ONE WHO AGREED TO SLAY MEDUSA. SO YOU NEED TO DO IT YOURSELF.
AND TO DO IT YOU'LL NEED SOME MAGICAL GIFTS FROM THE NYMPHS OF THE NORTH!
BUT THE ONLY ONES WHO KNOW HOW TO FIND THEM ARE OVER THERE. THAT'S WHY WE'VE COME HERE.
SO, GO GET DIRECTIONS!
PERSEUS DID AS HE WAS TOLD AND TIP-TOED OVER TO THE THREE GRAY LADIES. (WHO ONLY HAD ONE EYE THAT THEY SHARED).
UM, EXCUSE ME...
OH LOOK, A LITTLE BOY!
OH BOY, WHOSE TURN IS IT TO KILL THE VISITOR?
IT'S MINE!

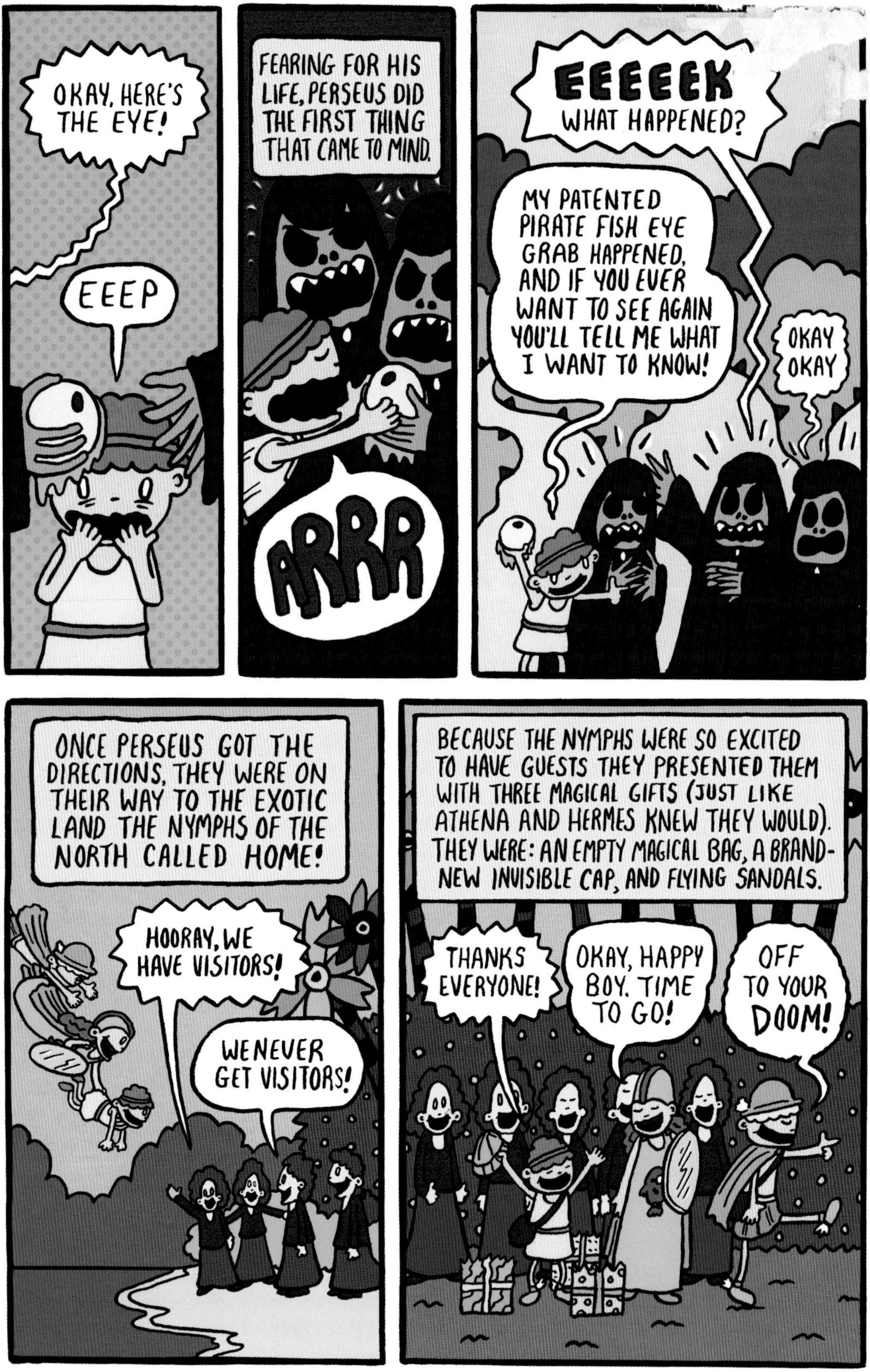

OKAY, HERE'S THE EYE!
EEEP
FEARING FOR HIS LIFE, PERSEUS DID THE FIRST THING THAT CAME TO MIND.
ARRR
EEEEEK WHAT HAPPENED?
MY PATENTED PIRATE FISH EYE GRAB HAPPENED, AND IF YOU EVER WANT TO SEE AGAIN YOU'LL TELL ME WHAT I WANT TO KNOW!
OKAY OKAY
ONCE PERSEUS GOT THE DIRECTIONS, THEY WERE ON THEIR WAY TO THE EXOTIC LAND THE NYMPHS OF THE NORTH CALLED HOME!
HOORAY, WE HAVE VISITORS!
WE NEVER GET VISITORS!
BECAUSE THE NYMPHS WERE SO EXCITED TO HAVE GUESTS THEY PRESENTED THEM WITH THREE MAGICAL GIFTS (JUST LIKE ATHENA AND HERMES KNEW THEY WOULD). THEY WERE: AN EMPTY MAGICAL BAG, A BRAND-NEW INVISIBLE CAP, AND FLYING SANDALS.
THANKS EVERYONE!
OKAY, HAPPY BOY. TIME TO GO!
OFF TO YOUR DOOM!

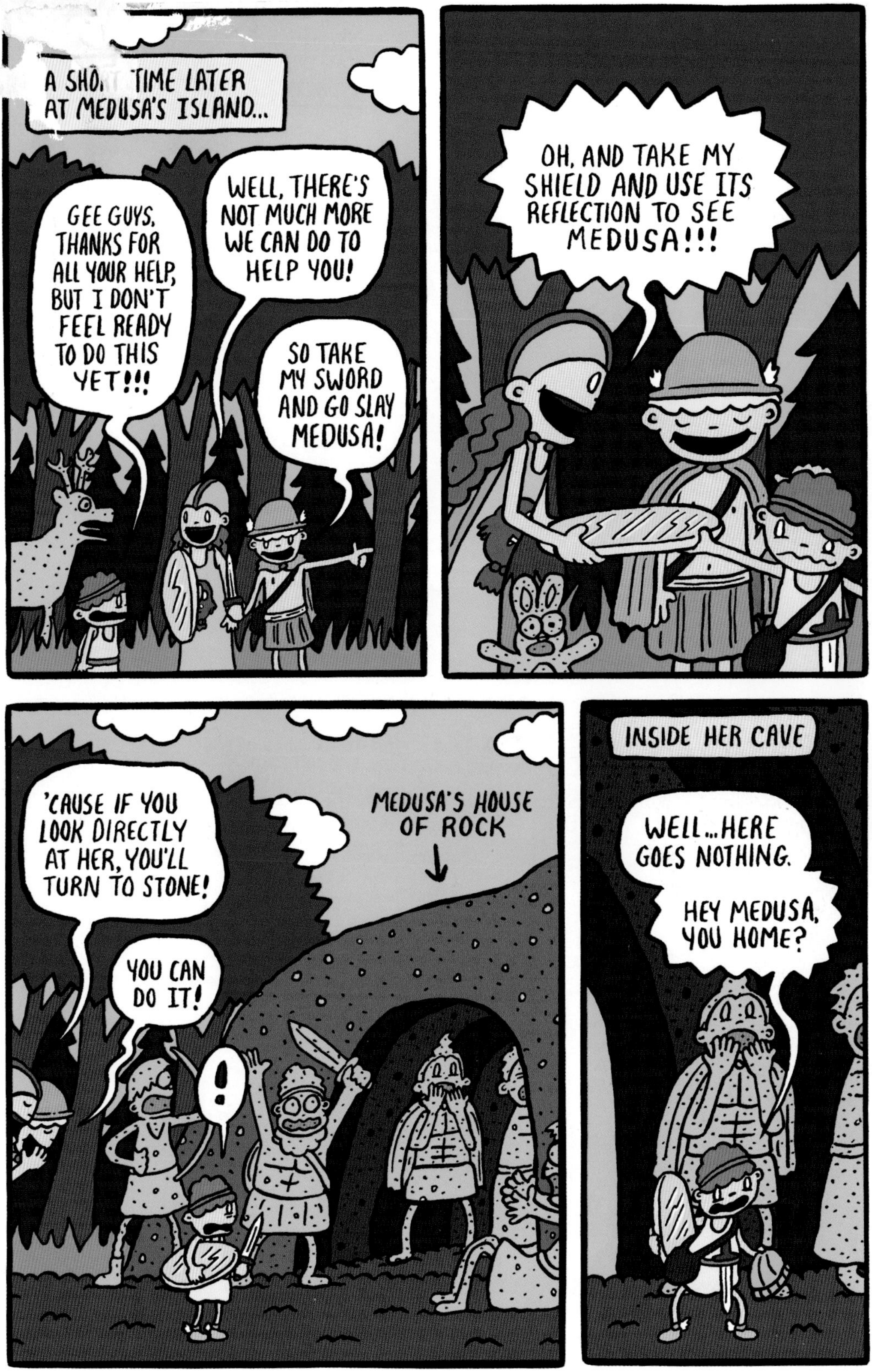
A SHO[R]T TIME LATER AT MEDUSA'S ISLAND...
GEE GUYS, THANKS FOR ALL YOUR HELP, BUT I DON'T FEEL READY TO DO THIS YET!!!
WELL, THERE'S NOT MUCH MORE WE CAN DO TO HELP YOU!
SO TAKE MY SWORD AND GO SLAY MEDUSA!
OH, AND TAKE MY SHIELD AND USE ITS REFLECTION TO SEE MEDUSA!!!
'CAUSE IF YOU LOOK DIRECTLY AT HER, YOU'LL TURN TO STONE!
MEDUSA'S HOUSE OF ROCK
YOU CAN DO IT!
!
INSIDE HER CAVE
WELL...HERE GOES NOTHING.
HEY MEDUSA, YOU HOME?

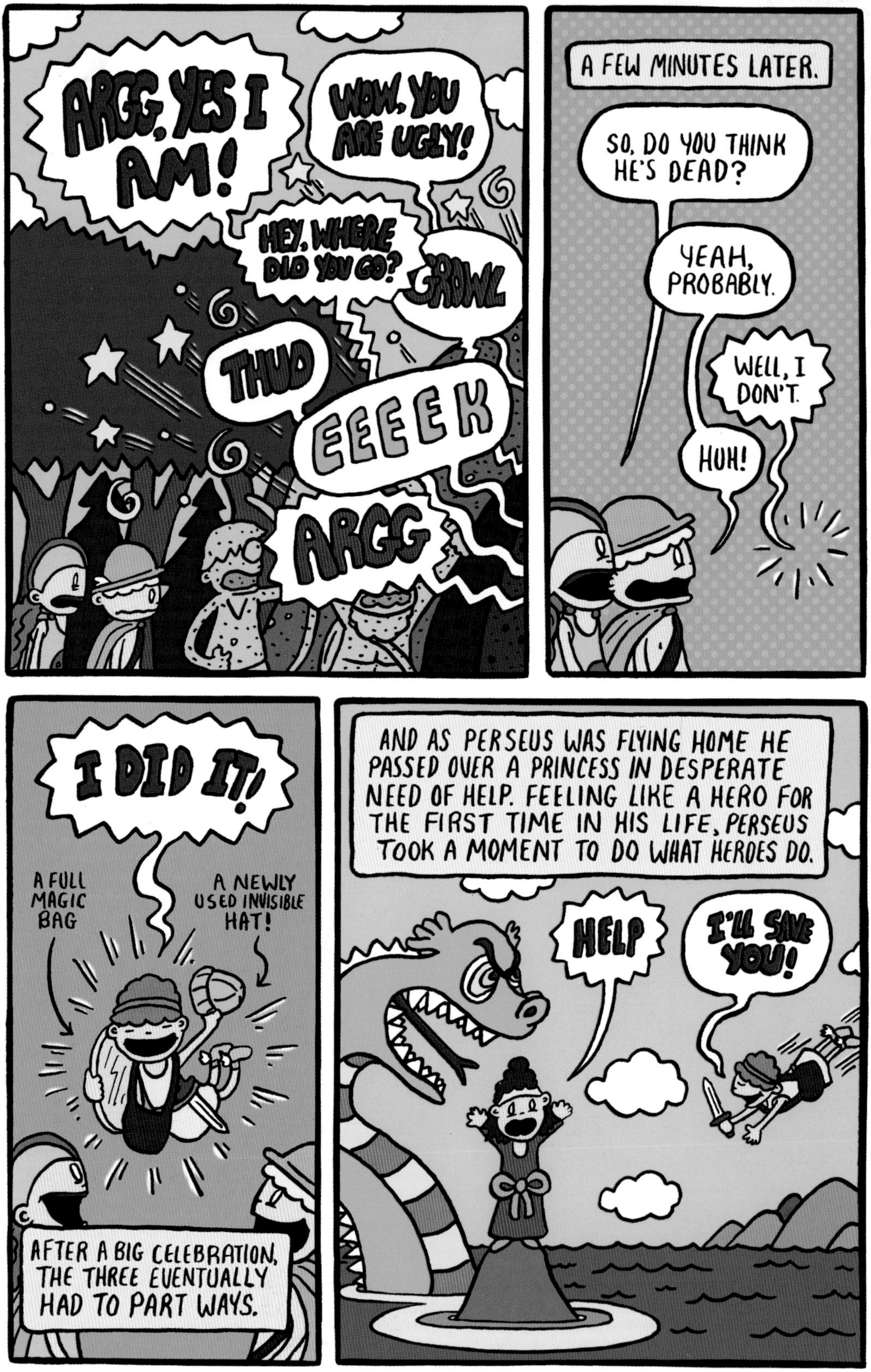
ARGG, YES I AM!
WOW, YOU ARE UGLY!
HEY, WHERE DID YOU GO?
GROWL
THUD
EEEEK
ARGG
A FEW MINUTES LATER.
SO, DO YOU THINK HE'S DEAD?
YEAH, PROBABLY.
WELL, I DON'T.
HUH!
I DID IT!
A FULL MAGIC BAG
A NEWLY USED INVISIBLE HAT!
AFTER A BIG CELEBRATION, THE THREE EVENTUALLY HAD TO PART WAYS.
AND AS PERSEUS WAS FLYING HOME HE PASSED OVER A PRINCESS IN DESPERATE NEED OF HELP. FEELING LIKE A HERO FOR THE FIRST TIME IN HIS LIFE, PERSEUS TOOK A MOMENT TO DO WHAT HEROES DO.
HELP
I'LL SAVE YOU!

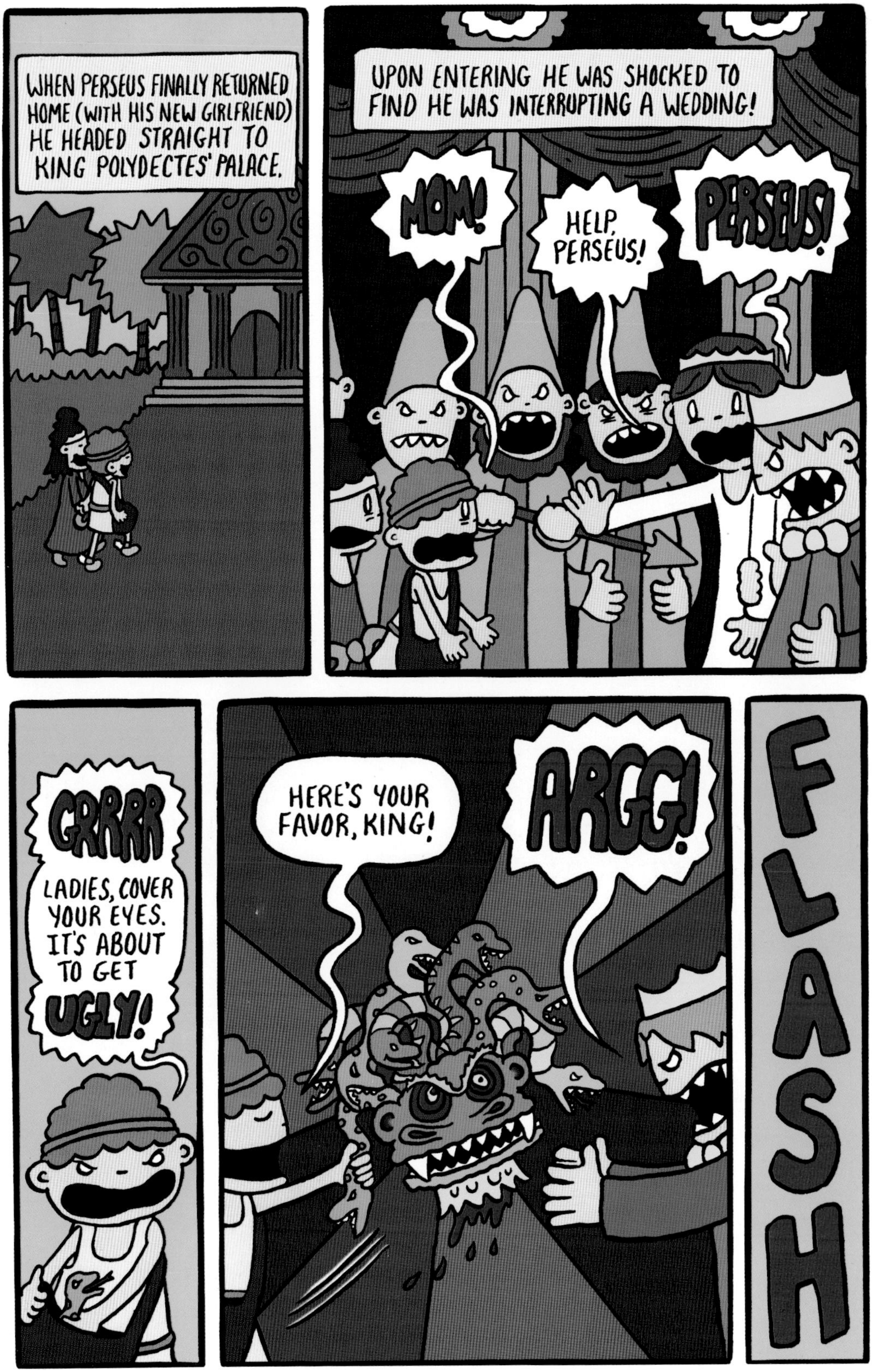
WHEN PERSEUS FINALLY RETURNED HOME (WITH HIS NEW GIRLFRIEND) HE HEADED STRAIGHT TO KING POLYDECTES' PALACE.
UPON ENTERING HE WAS SHOCKED TO FIND HE WAS INTERRUPTING A WEDDING!
MOM!
HELP, PERSEUS!
PERSEUS!
GRRRR
LADIES, COVER YOUR EYES. IT'S ABOUT TO GET UGLY!
HERE'S YOUR FAVOR, KING!
ARGG!
FLASH

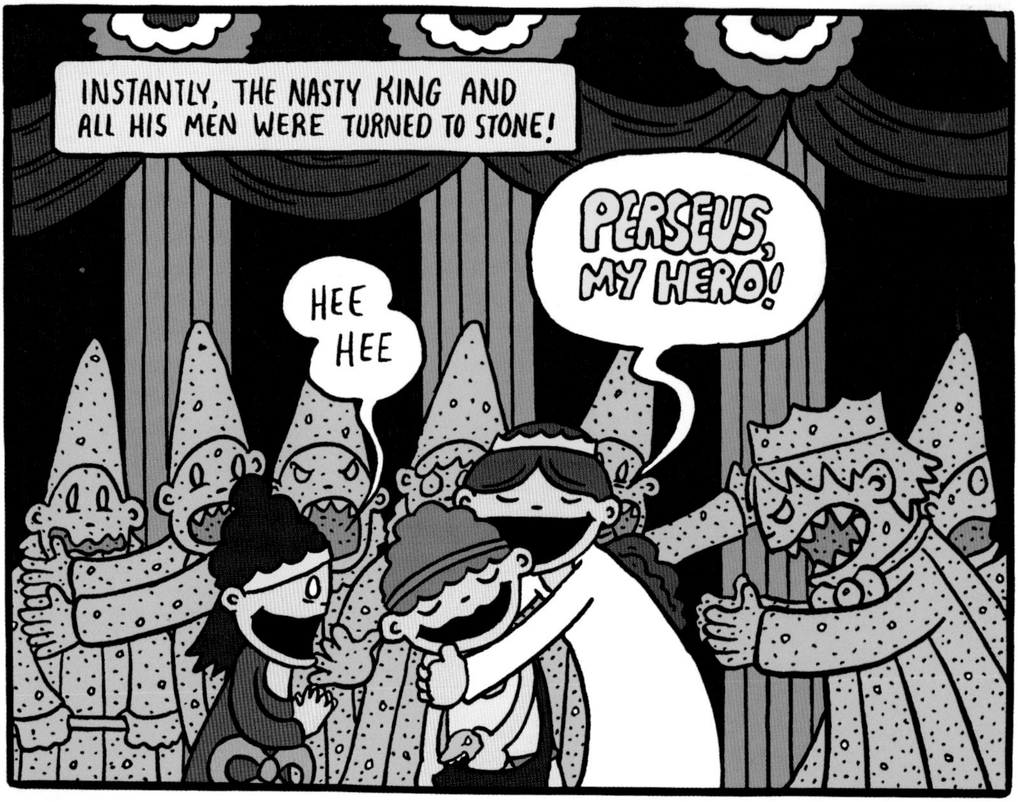
INSTANTLY, THE NASTY KING AND ALL HIS MEN WERE TURNED TO STONE!
HEE HEE
PERSEUS, MY HERO!

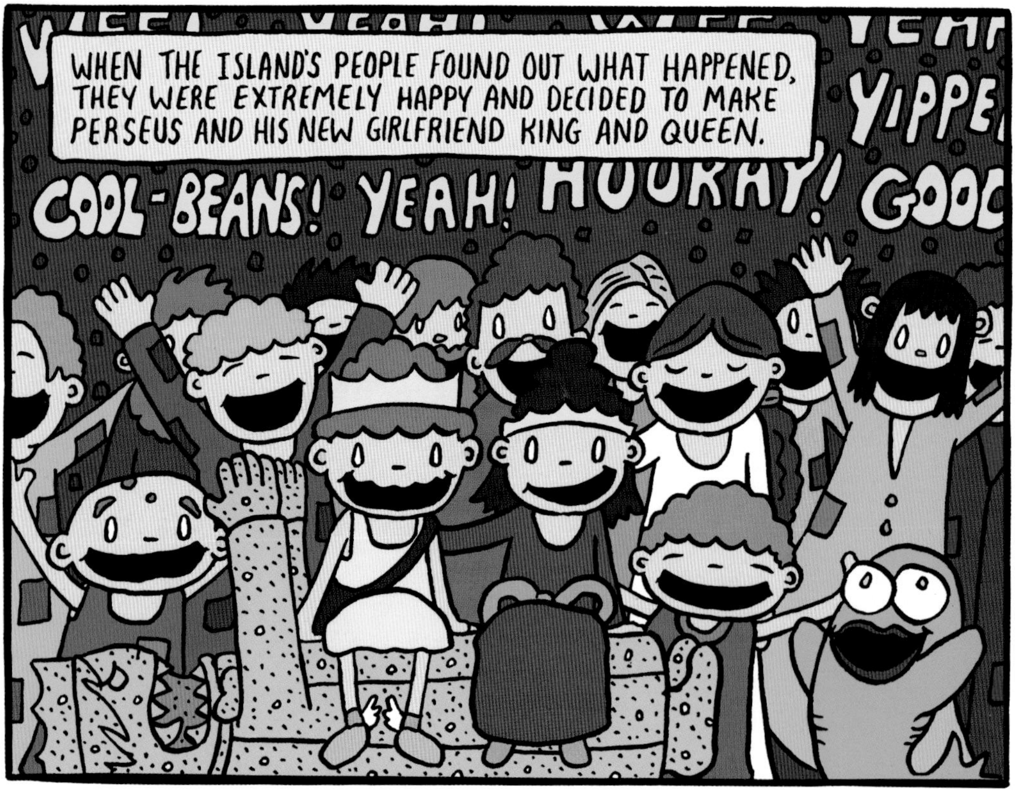
WHEN THE ISLAND'S PEOPLE FOUND OUT WHAT HAPPENED, THEY WERE EXTREMELY HAPPY AND DECIDED TO MAKE PERSEUS AND HIS NEW GIRLFRIEND KING AND QUEEN.
COOL-BEANS!
YEAH!
HOORAY!

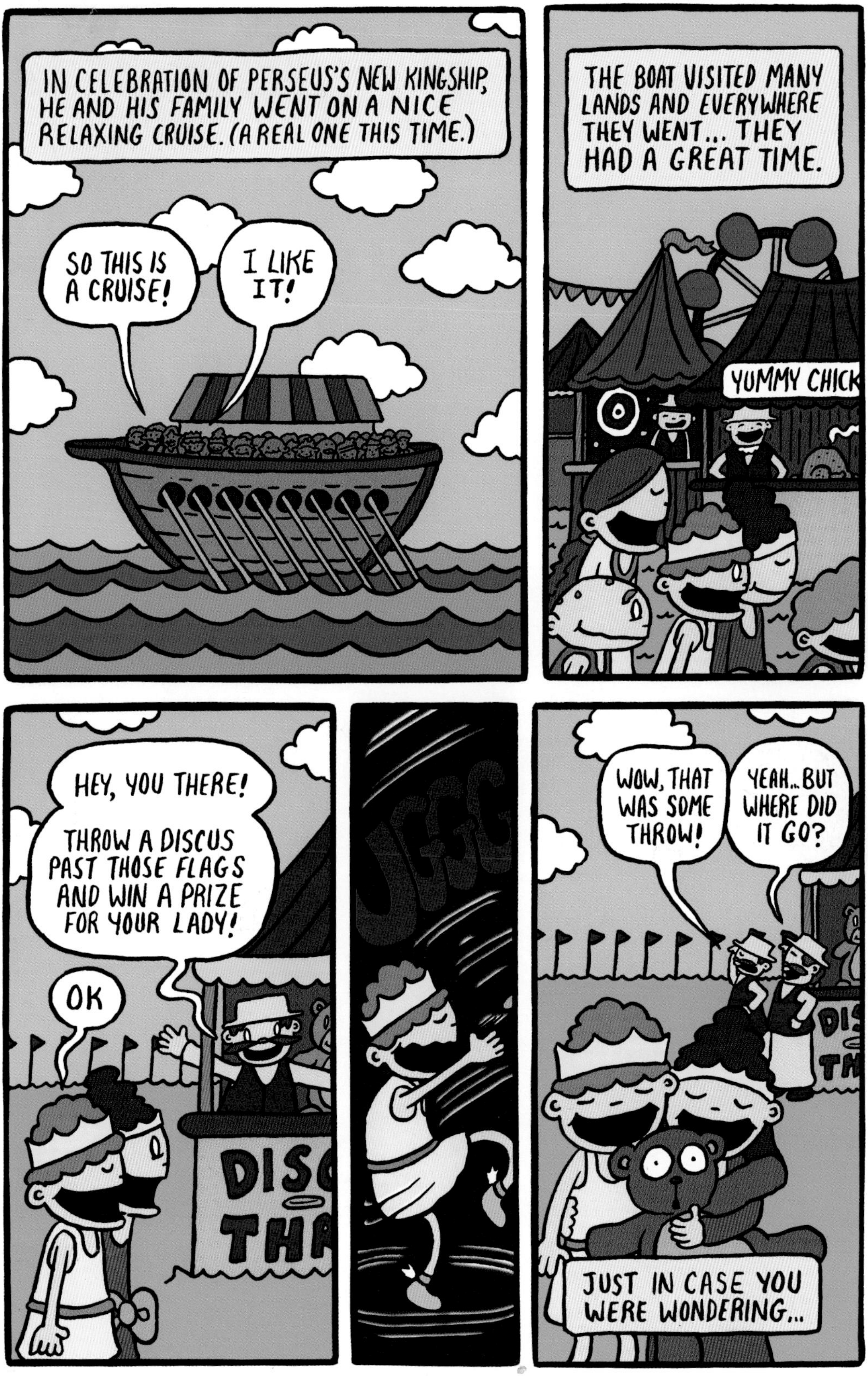
IN CELEBRATION OF PERSEUS'S NEW KINGSHIP, HE AND HIS FAMILY WENT ON A NICE RELAXING CRUISE. (A REAL ONE THIS TIME.)
SO THIS IS A CRUISE!
I LIKE IT!
THE BOAT VISITED MANY LANDS AND EVERYWHERE THEY WENT... THEY HAD A GREAT TIME.
YUMMY CHICK
HEY, YOU THERE!
THROW A DISCUS PAST THOSE FLAGS AND WIN A PRIZE FOR YOUR LADY!
OK
DISC
THR
WOW, THAT WAS SOME THROW!
YEAH... BUT WHERE DID IT GO?
DIS
TH
JUST IN CASE YOU WERE WONDERING...

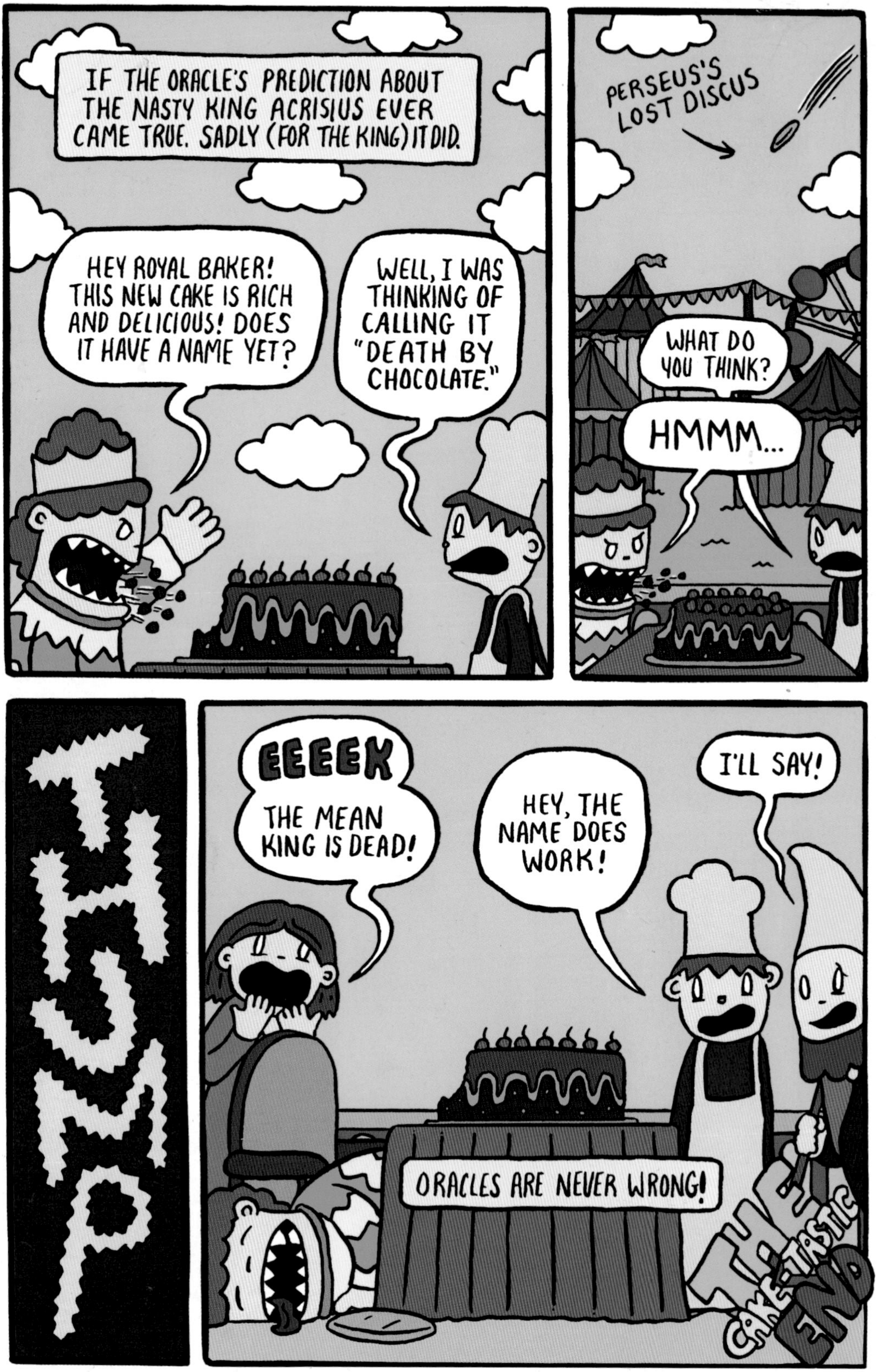
IF THE ORACLE'S PREDICTION ABOUT THE NASTY KING ACRISIUS EVER CAME TRUE. SADLY (FOR THE KING) IT DID.
HEY ROYAL BAKER! THIS NEW CAKE IS RICH AND DELICIOUS! DOES IT HAVE A NAME YET?
WELL, I WAS THINKING OF CALLING IT "DEATH BY CHOCOLATE."
PERSEUS'S LOST DISCUS
WHAT DO YOU THINK?
HMMM...
THUMP
EEEEK
THE MEAN KING IS DEAD!
HEY, THE NAME DOES WORK!
I'LL SAY!
ORACLES ARE NEVER WRONG!
THE CAKE-TASTIC END

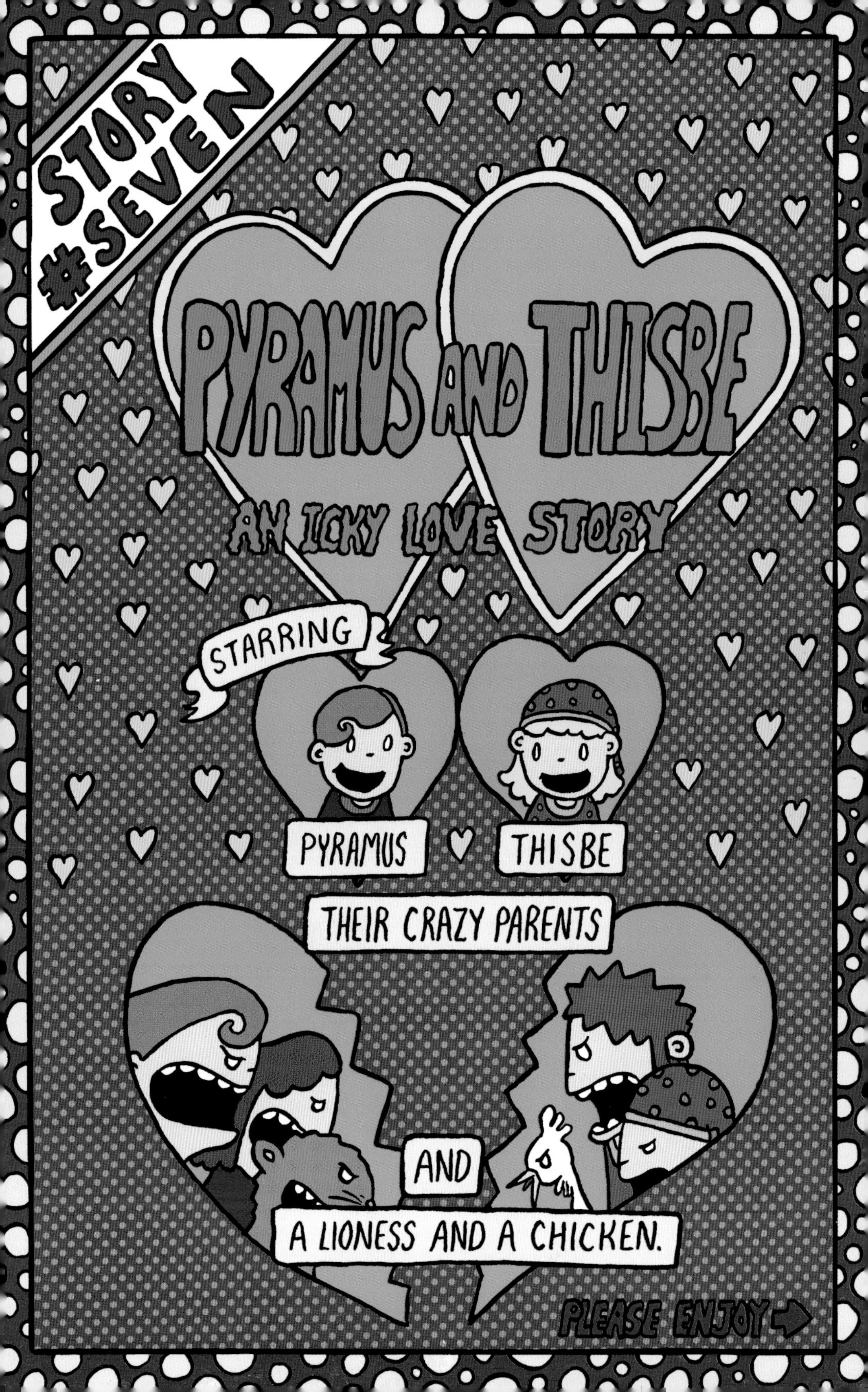
STORY #SEVEN
PYRAMUS AND THISBE
AN ICKY LOVE STORY
STARRING
PYRAMUS
THISBE
THEIR CRAZY PARENTS
AND
A LIONESS AND A CHICKEN.
PLEASE ENJOY

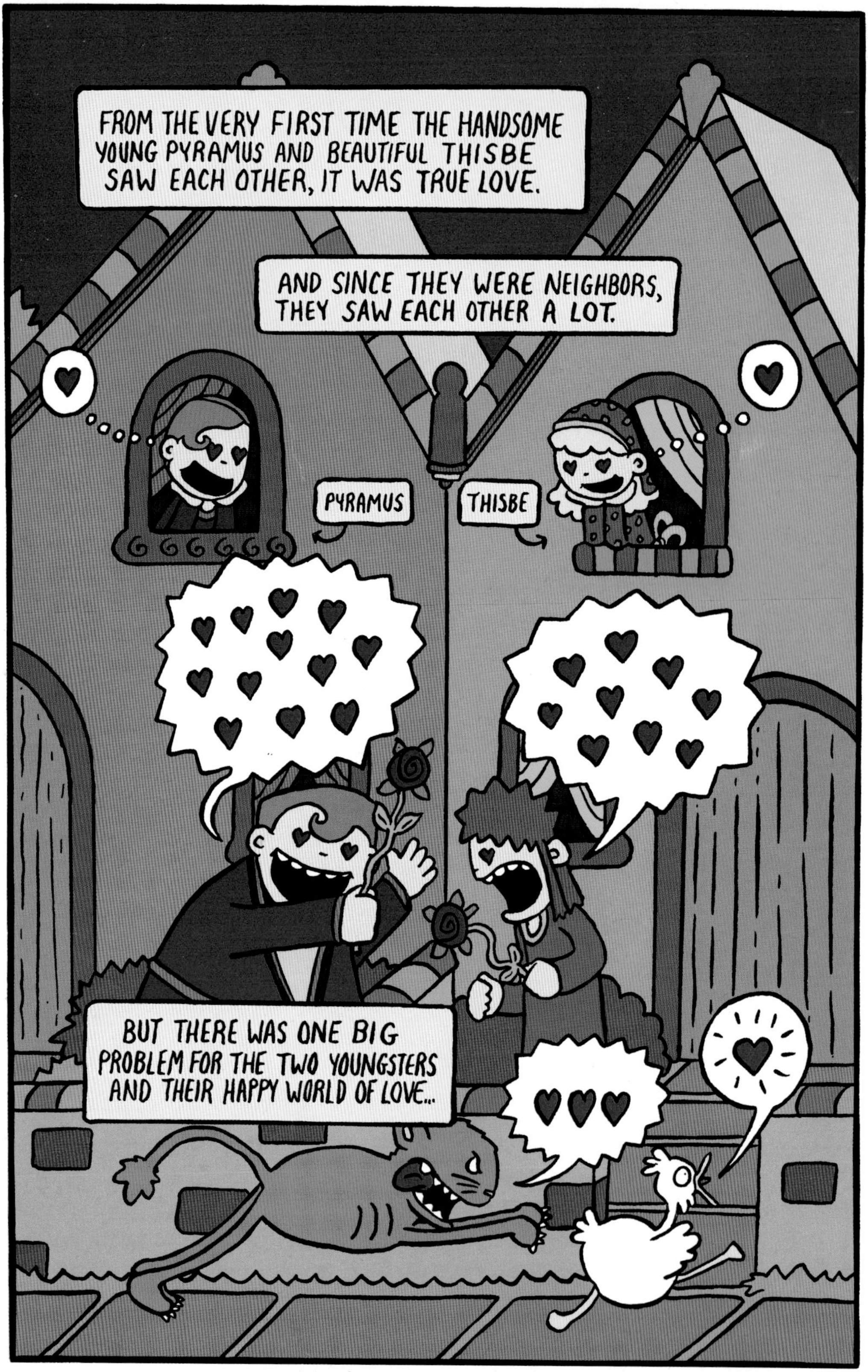
FROM THE VERY FIRST TIME THE HANDSOME YOUNG PYRAMUS AND BEAUTIFUL THISBE SAW EACH OTHER, IT WAS TRUE LOVE.
AND SINCE THEY WERE NEIGHBORS, THEY SAW EACH OTHER A LOT.
PYRAMUS
THISBE
BUT THERE WAS ONE BIG PROBLEM FOR THE TWO YOUNGSTERS AND THEIR HAPPY WORLD OF LOVE...

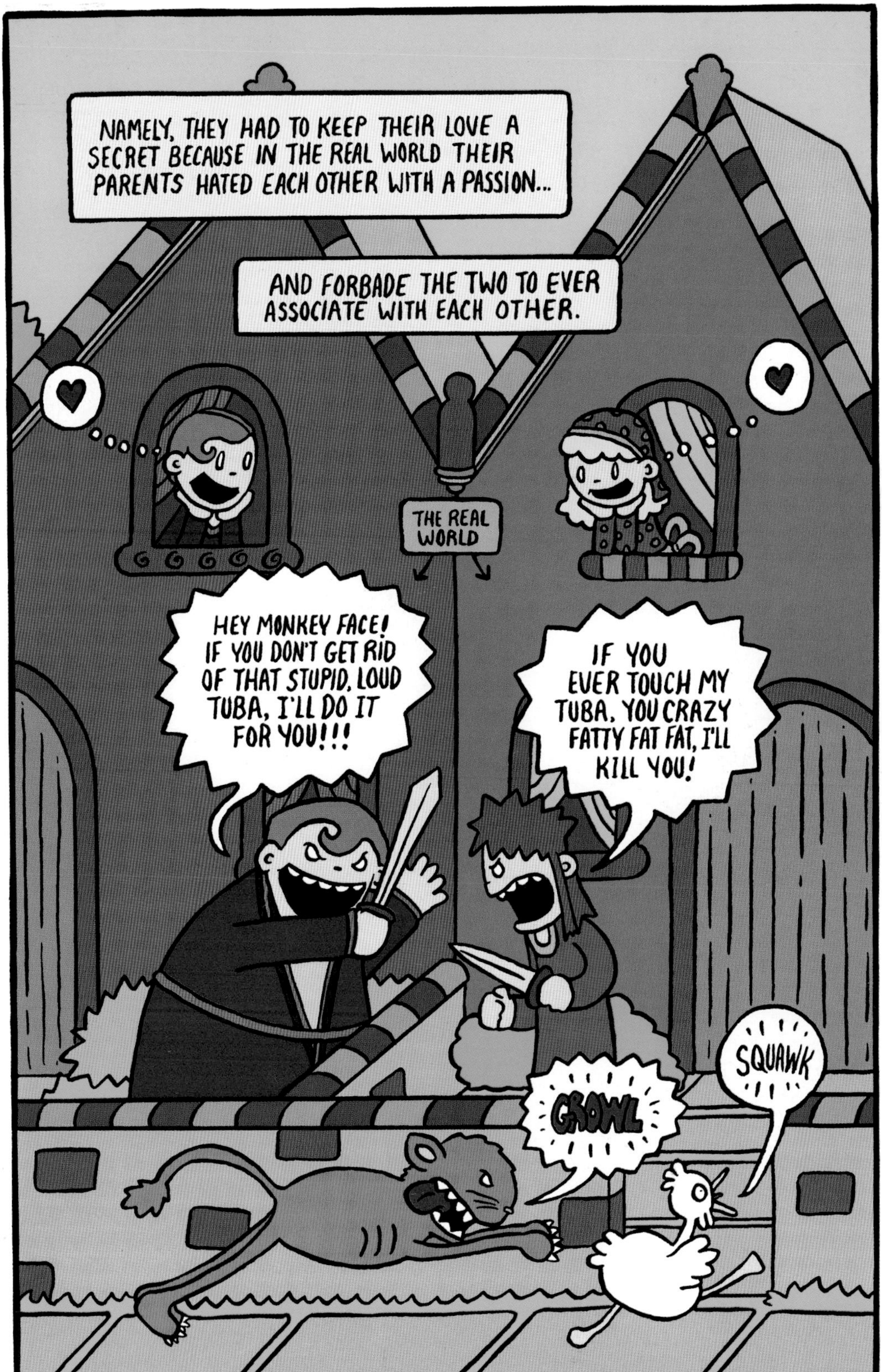
NAMELY, THEY HAD TO KEEP THEIR LOVE A SECRET BECAUSE IN THE REAL WORLD THEIR PARENTS HATED EACH OTHER WITH A PASSION...
AND FORBADE THE TWO TO EVER ASSOCIATE WITH EACH OTHER.
THE REAL WORLD
HEY MONKEY FACE! IF YOU DON'T GET RID OF THAT STUPID, LOUD TUBA, I'LL DO IT FOR YOU!!!
IF YOU EVER TOUCH MY TUBA, YOU CRAZY FATTY FAT FAT, I'LL KILL YOU!
GROWL
SQUAWK

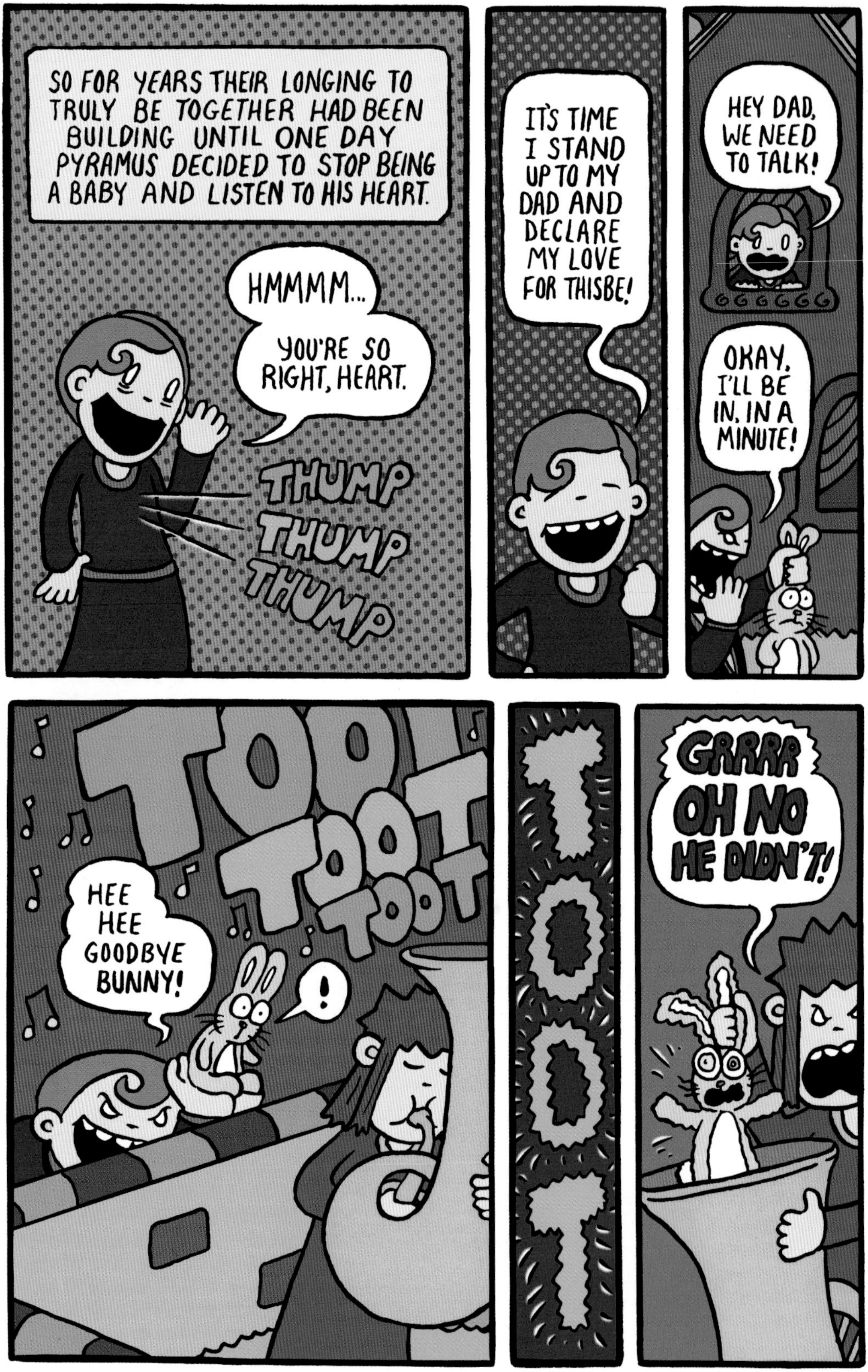
SO FOR YEARS THEIR LONGING TO TRULY BE TOGETHER HAD BEEN BUILDING UNTIL ONE DAY PYRAMUS DECIDED TO STOP BEING A BABY AND LISTEN TO HIS HEART.
HMMMM...
YOU'RE SO RIGHT, HEART.
THUMP
THUMP
THUMP
IT'S TIME I STAND UP TO MY DAD AND DECLARE MY LOVE FOR THISBE!
HEY DAD, WE NEED TO TALK!
OKAY, I'LL BE IN, IN A MINUTE!
TOOT
TOOT
TOOT
HEE HEE GOODBYE BUNNY!
!
TOOT
GRRRR
OH NO HE DIDN'T!

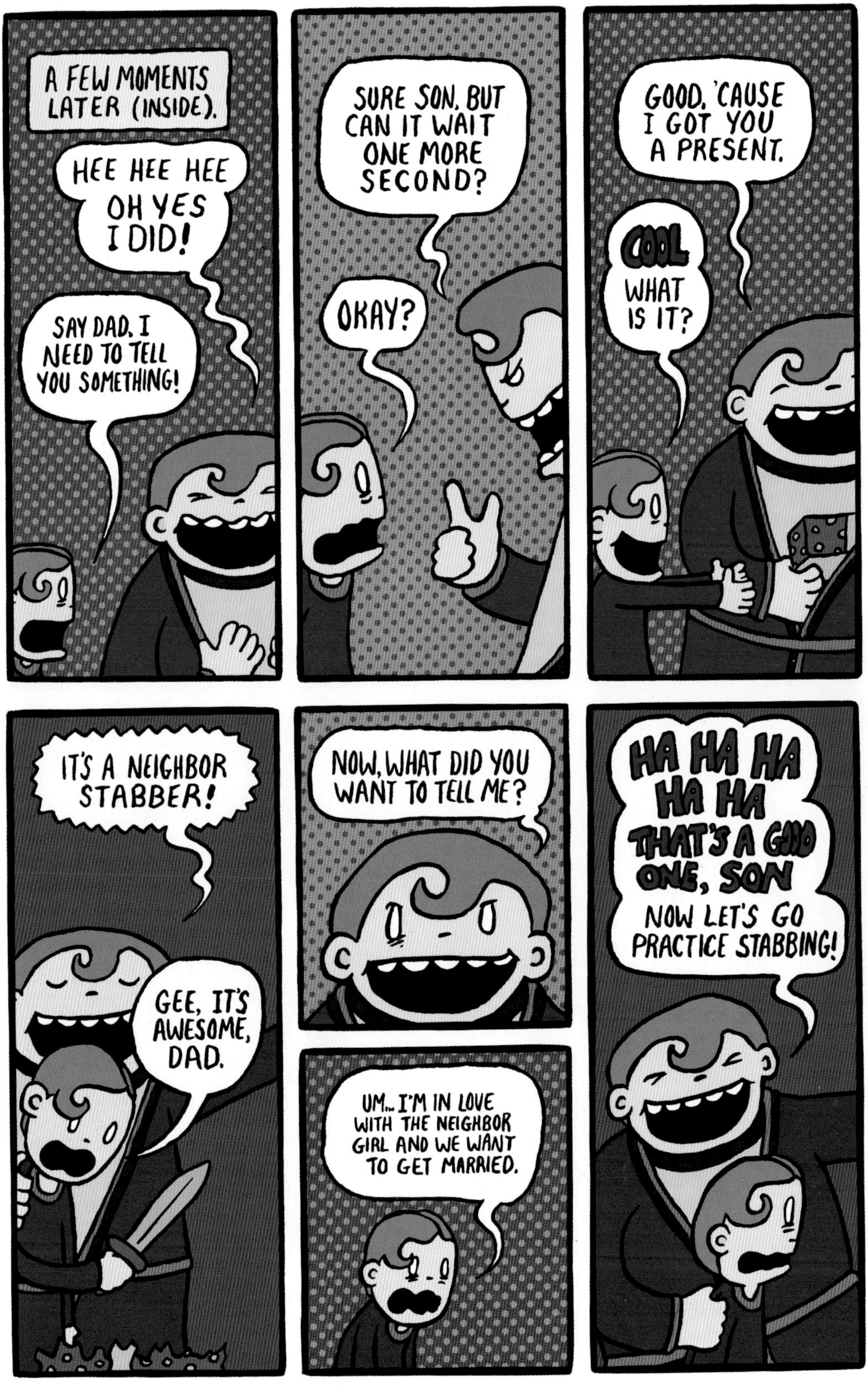
A FEW MOMENTS LATER (INSIDE).
HEE HEE HEE OH YES I DID!
SAY DAD, I NEED TO TELL YOU SOMETHING!
SURE SON, BUT CAN IT WAIT ONE MORE SECOND?
OKAY?
GOOD, 'CAUSE I GOT YOU A PRESENT.
COOL WHAT IS IT?
IT'S A NEIGHBOR STABBER!
GEE, IT'S AWESOME, DAD.
NOW, WHAT DID YOU WANT TO TELL ME?
UM... I'M IN LOVE WITH THE NEIGHBOR GIRL AND WE WANT TO GET MARRIED.
HA HA HA HA HA THAT'S A GOOD ONE, SON
NOW LET'S GO PRACTICE STABBING!

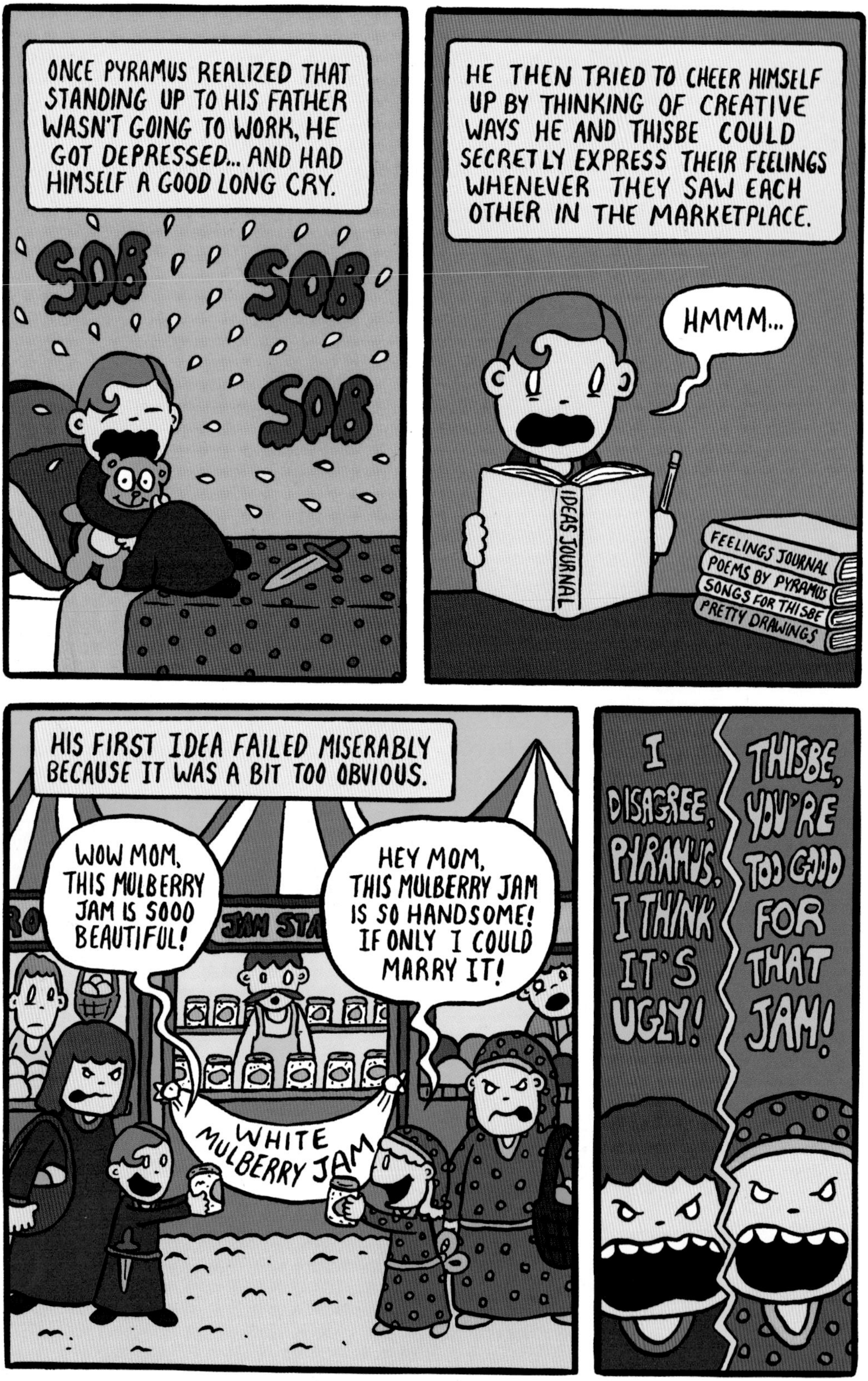
ONCE PYRAMUS REALIZED THAT STANDING UP TO HIS FATHER WASN'T GOING TO WORK, HE GOT DEPRESSED... AND HAD HIMSELF A GOOD LONG CRY.
SOB
SOB
SOB
HE THEN TRIED TO CHEER HIMSELF UP BY THINKING OF CREATIVE WAYS HE AND THISBE COULD SECRETLY EXPRESS THEIR FEELINGS WHENEVER THEY SAW EACH OTHER IN THE MARKETPLACE.
HMMM...
IDEAS JOURNAL
FEELINGS JOURNAL
POEMS BY PYRAMUS
SONGS FOR THISBE
PRETTY DRAWINGS
HIS FIRST IDEA FAILED MISERABLY BECAUSE IT WAS A BIT TOO OBVIOUS.
WOW MOM, THIS MULBERRY JAM IS SOOO BEAUTIFUL!
HEY MOM, THIS MULBERRY JAM IS SO HANDSOME! IF ONLY I COULD MARRY IT!
JAM STA
WHITE MULBERRY JAM
I DISAGREE, PYRAMUS. I THINK IT'S UGLY!
THISBE, YOU'RE TOO GOOD FOR THAT JAM!

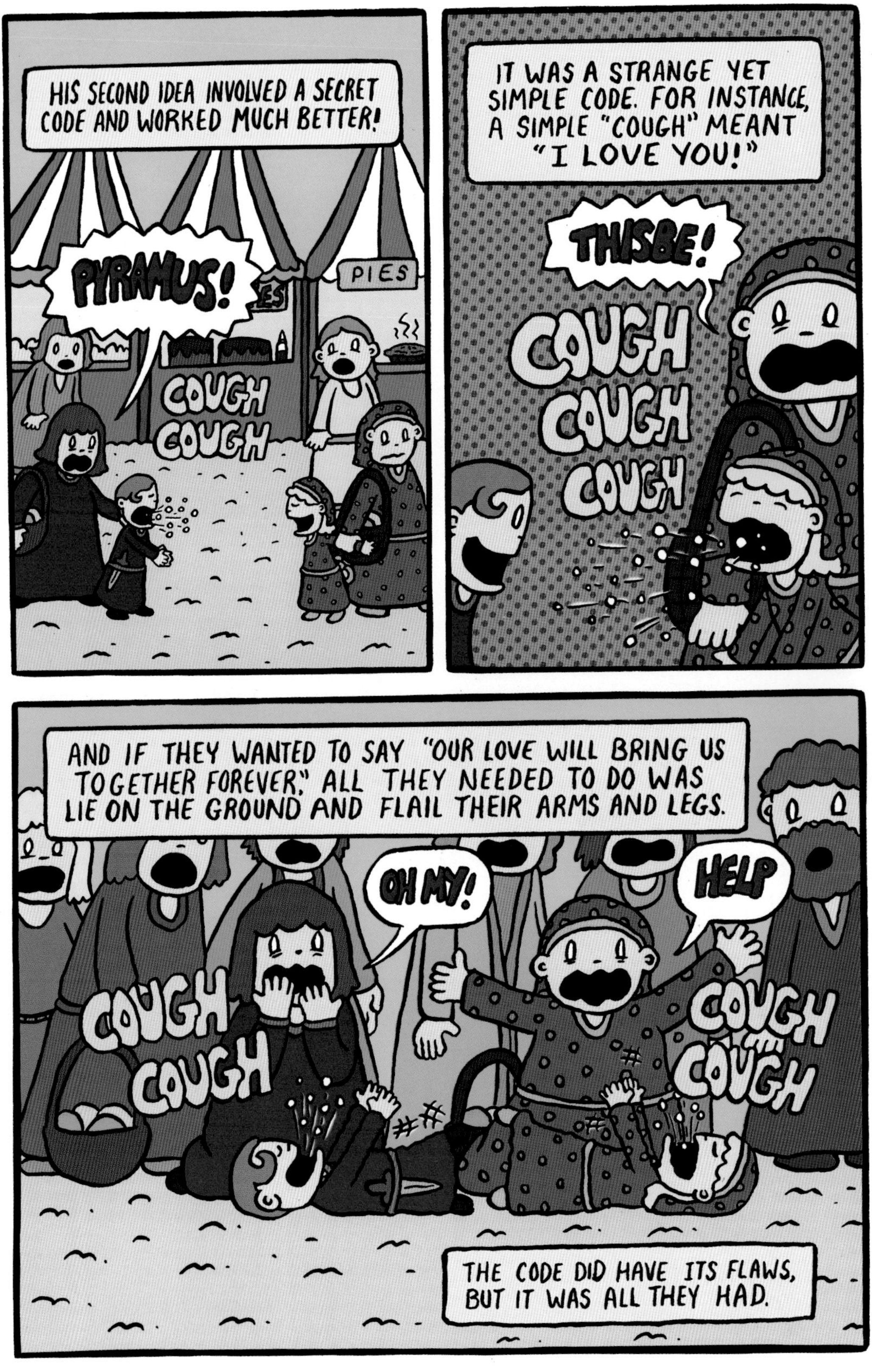
HIS SECOND IDEA INVOLVED A SECRET CODE AND WORKED MUCH BETTER!
PYRAMUS!
PIES
COUGH
COUGH
IT WAS A STRANGE YET SIMPLE CODE. FOR INSTANCE, A SIMPLE "COUGH" MEANT "I LOVE YOU!"
THISBE!
COUGH
COUGH
COUGH
AND IF THEY WANTED TO SAY "OUR LOVE WILL BRING US TOGETHER FOREVER," ALL THEY NEEDED TO DO WAS LIE ON THE GROUND AND FLAIL THEIR ARMS AND LEGS.
OH MY!
HELP
COUGH
COUGH
COUGH
COUGH
THE CODE DID HAVE ITS FLAWS, BUT IT WAS ALL THEY HAD.

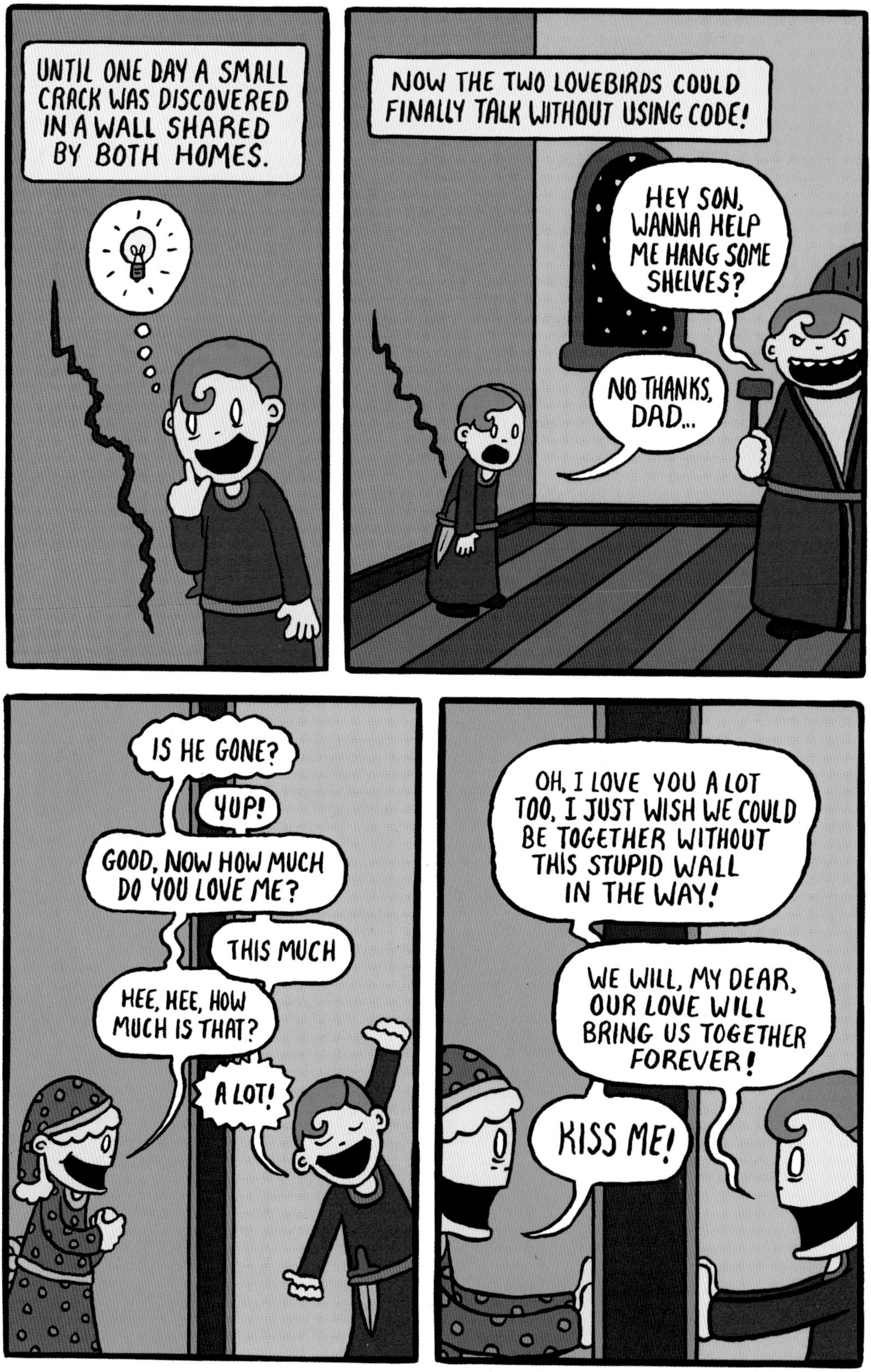
UNTIL ONE DAY A SMALL CRACK WAS DISCOVERED IN A WALL SHARED BY BOTH HOMES.
NOW THE TWO LOVEBIRDS COULD FINALLY TALK WITHOUT USING CODE!
HEY SON, WANNA HELP ME HANG SOME SHELVES?
NO THANKS, DAD...
IS HE GONE?
YUP!
GOOD, NOW HOW MUCH DO YOU LOVE ME?
THIS MUCH
HEE, HEE, HOW MUCH IS THAT?
A LOT!
OH, I LOVE YOU A LOT TOO, I JUST WISH WE COULD BE TOGETHER WITHOUT THIS STUPID WALL IN THE WAY!
WE WILL, MY DEAR, OUR LOVE WILL BRING US TOGETHER FOREVER!
KISS ME!

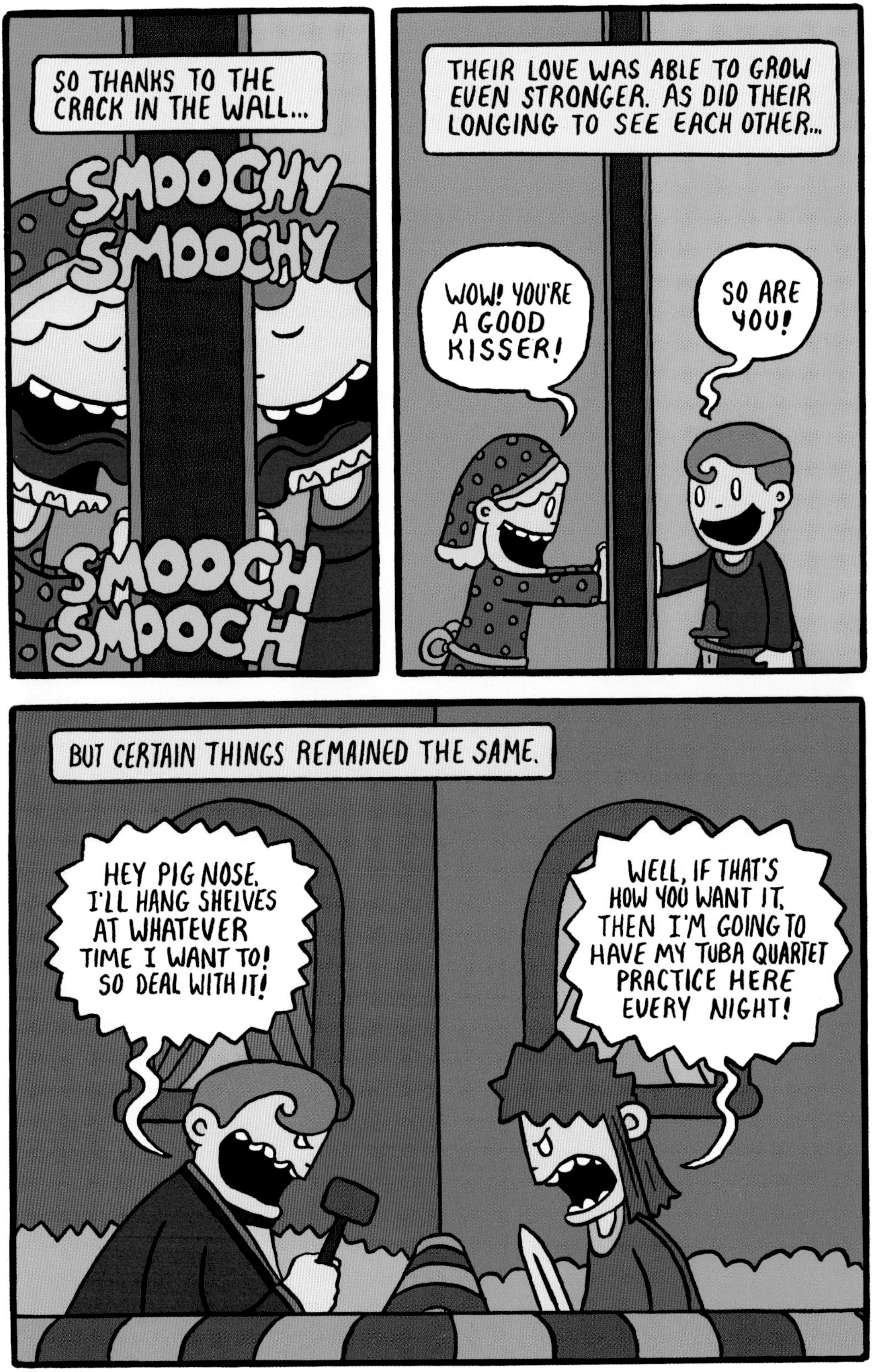
SO THANKS TO THE CRACK IN THE WALL...
SMOOCHY SMOOCHY
SMOOCH SMOOCH
THEIR LOVE WAS ABLE TO GROW EVEN STRONGER. AS DID THEIR LONGING TO SEE EACH OTHER...
WOW! YOU'RE A GOOD KISSER!
SO ARE YOU!
BUT CERTAIN THINGS REMAINED THE SAME.
HEY PIG NOSE, I'LL HANG SHELVES AT WHATEVER TIME I WANT TO! SO DEAL WITH IT!
WELL, IF THAT'S HOW YOU WANT IT, THEN I'M GOING TO HAVE MY TUBA QUARTET PRACTICE HERE EVERY NIGHT!

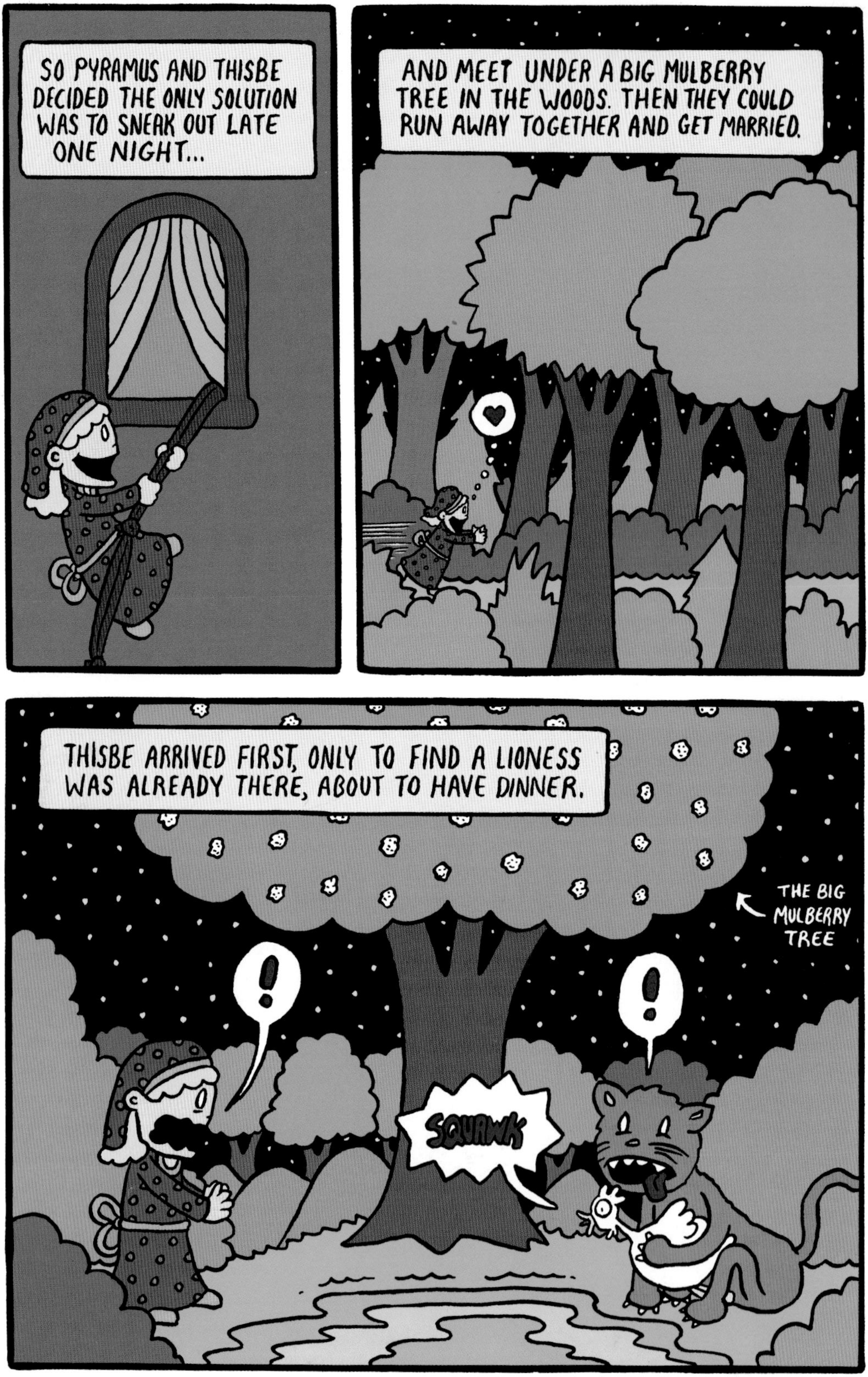
SO PYRAMUS AND THISBE DECIDED THE ONLY SOLUTION WAS TO SNEAK OUT LATE ONE NIGHT...
AND MEET UNDER A BIG MULBERRY TREE IN THE WOODS. THEN THEY COULD RUN AWAY TOGETHER AND GET MARRIED.
THISBE ARRIVED FIRST, ONLY TO FIND A LIONESS WAS ALREADY THERE, ABOUT TO HAVE DINNER.
THE BIG MULBERRY TREE
!
SQUAWK
!

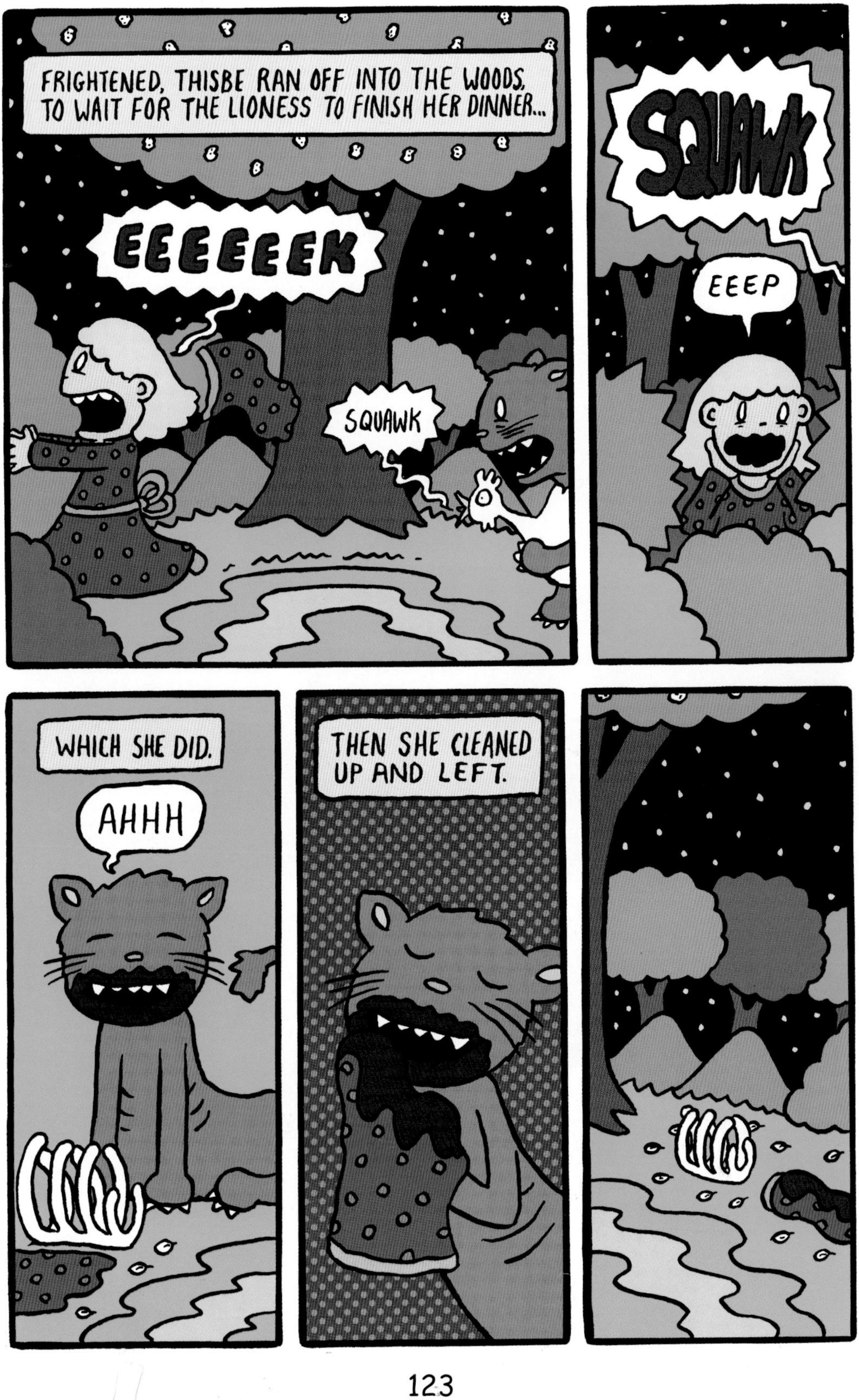
FRIGHTENED, THISBE RAN OFF INTO THE WOODS, TO WAIT FOR THE LIONESS TO FINISH HER DINNER...
EEEEEEK
SQUAWK
SQUAWK
EEEP
WHICH SHE DID.
AHHH
THEN SHE CLEANED UP AND LEFT.

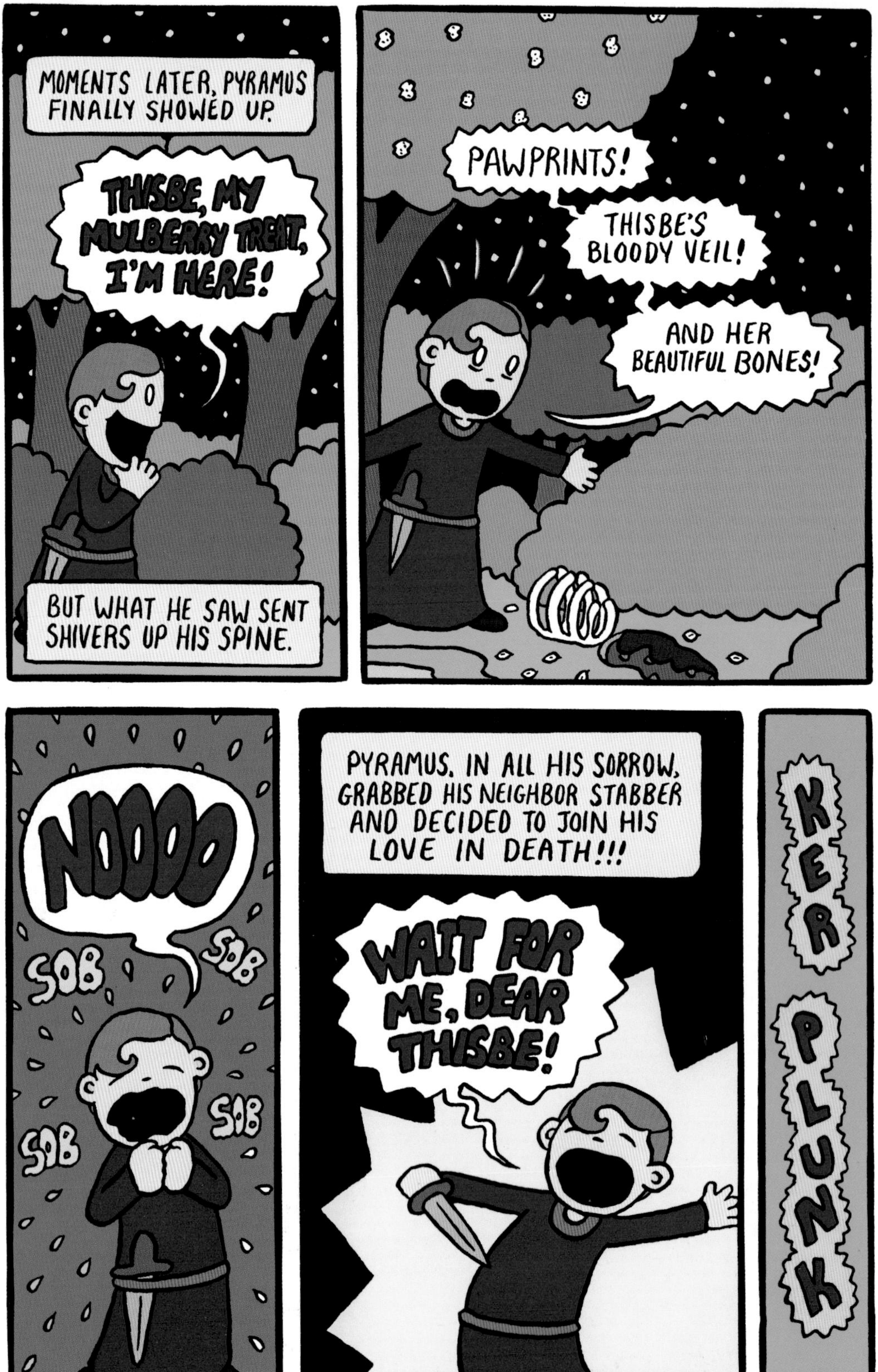
MOMENTS LATER, PYRAMUS FINALLY SHOWED UP.
THISBE, MY MULBERRY TREAT, I'M HERE!
BUT WHAT HE SAW SENT SHIVERS UP HIS SPINE.
PAWPRINTS!
THISBE'S BLOODY VEIL!
AND HER BEAUTIFUL BONES!
NOOOO
SOB
SOB
SOB
SOB
PYRAMUS, IN ALL HIS SORROW, GRABBED HIS NEIGHBOR STABBER AND DECIDED TO JOIN HIS LOVE IN DEATH!!!
WAIT FOR ME, DEAR THISBE!
KER
PLUNK

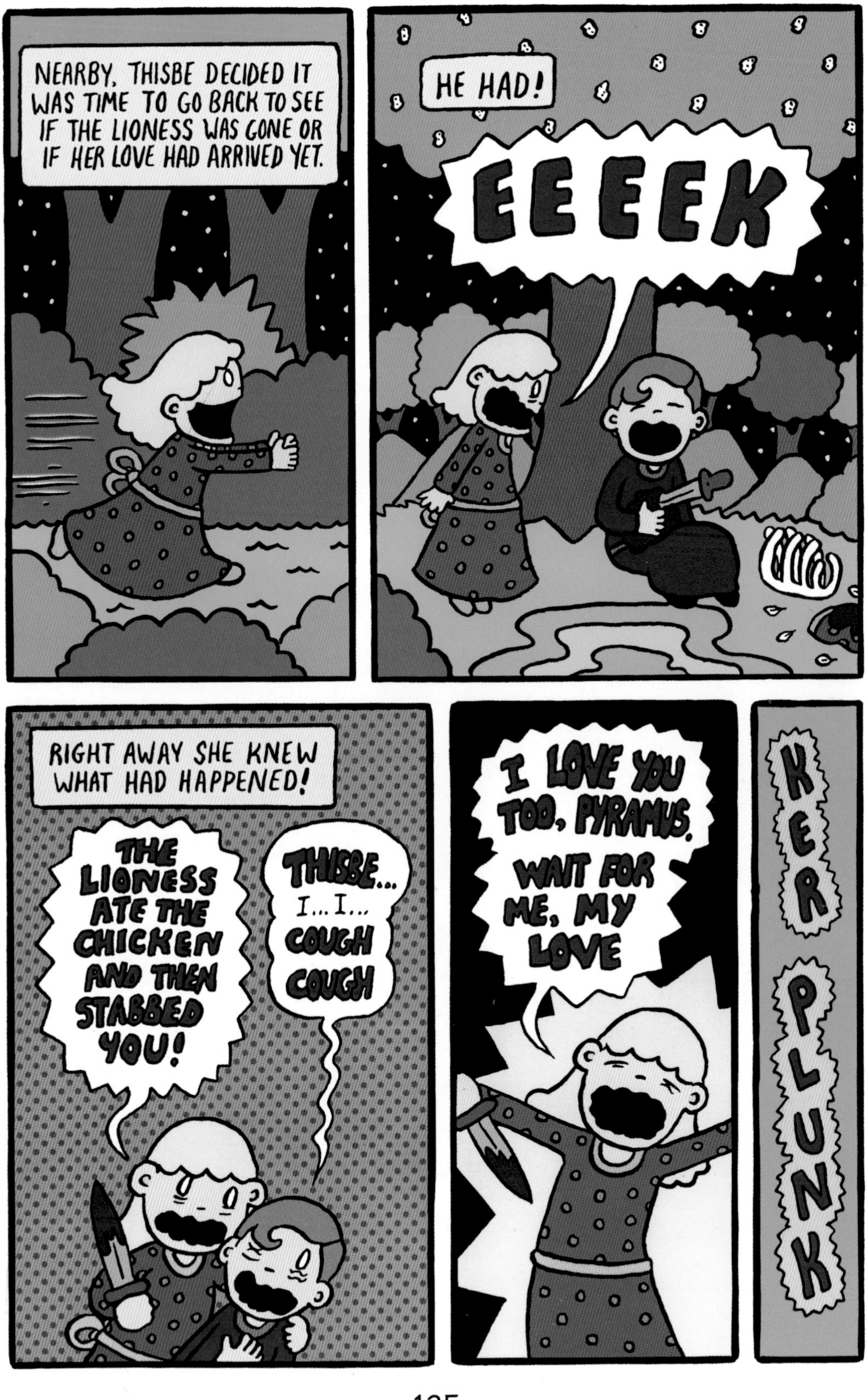
NEARBY, THISBE DECIDED IT WAS TIME TO GO BACK TO SEE IF THE LIONESS WAS GONE OR IF HER LOVE HAD ARRIVED YET.
HE HAD!
EEEEK
RIGHT AWAY SHE KNEW WHAT HAD HAPPENED!
THE LIONESS ATE THE CHICKEN AND THEN STABBED YOU!
THISBE... I... I... COUGH COUGH
I LOVE YOU TOO, PYRAMUS.
WAIT FOR ME, MY LOVE
KER PLUNK

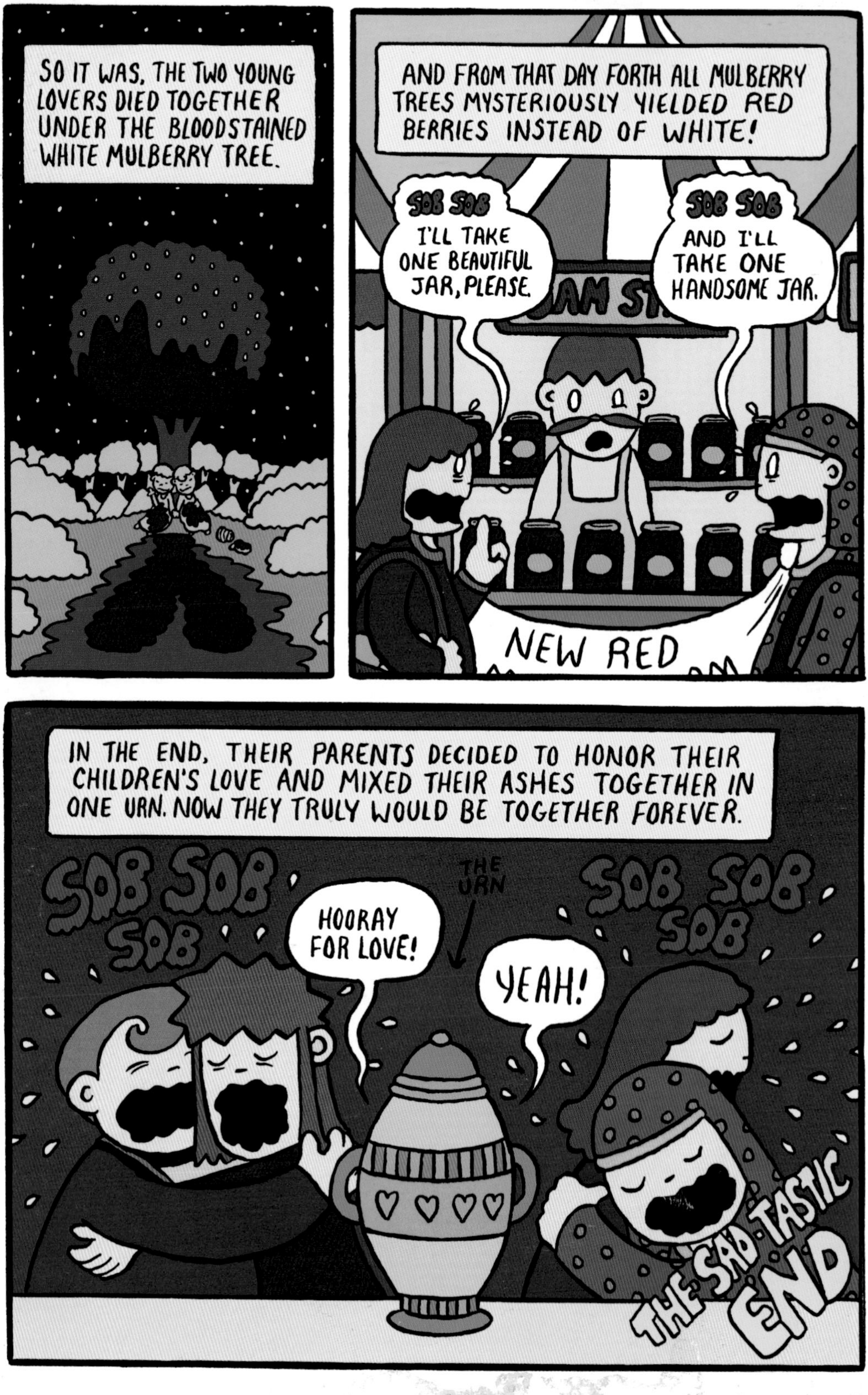
SO IT WAS, THE TWO YOUNG LOVERS DIED TOGETHER UNDER THE BLOODSTAINED WHITE MULBERRY TREE.
AND FROM THAT DAY FORTH ALL MULBERRY TREES MYSTERIOUSLY YIELDED RED BERRIES INSTEAD OF WHITE!
SOB SOB
I'LL TAKE ONE BEAUTIFUL JAR, PLEASE.
SOB SOB
AND I'LL TAKE ONE HANDSOME JAR.
NEW RED
IN THE END, THEIR PARENTS DECIDED TO HONOR THEIR CHILDREN'S LOVE AND MIXED THEIR ASHES TOGETHER IN ONE URN. NOW THEY TRULY WOULD BE TOGETHER FOREVER.
SOB SOB SOB
HOORAY FOR LOVE!
THE URN
YEAH!
SOB SOB SOB
THE SAD-TASTIC END

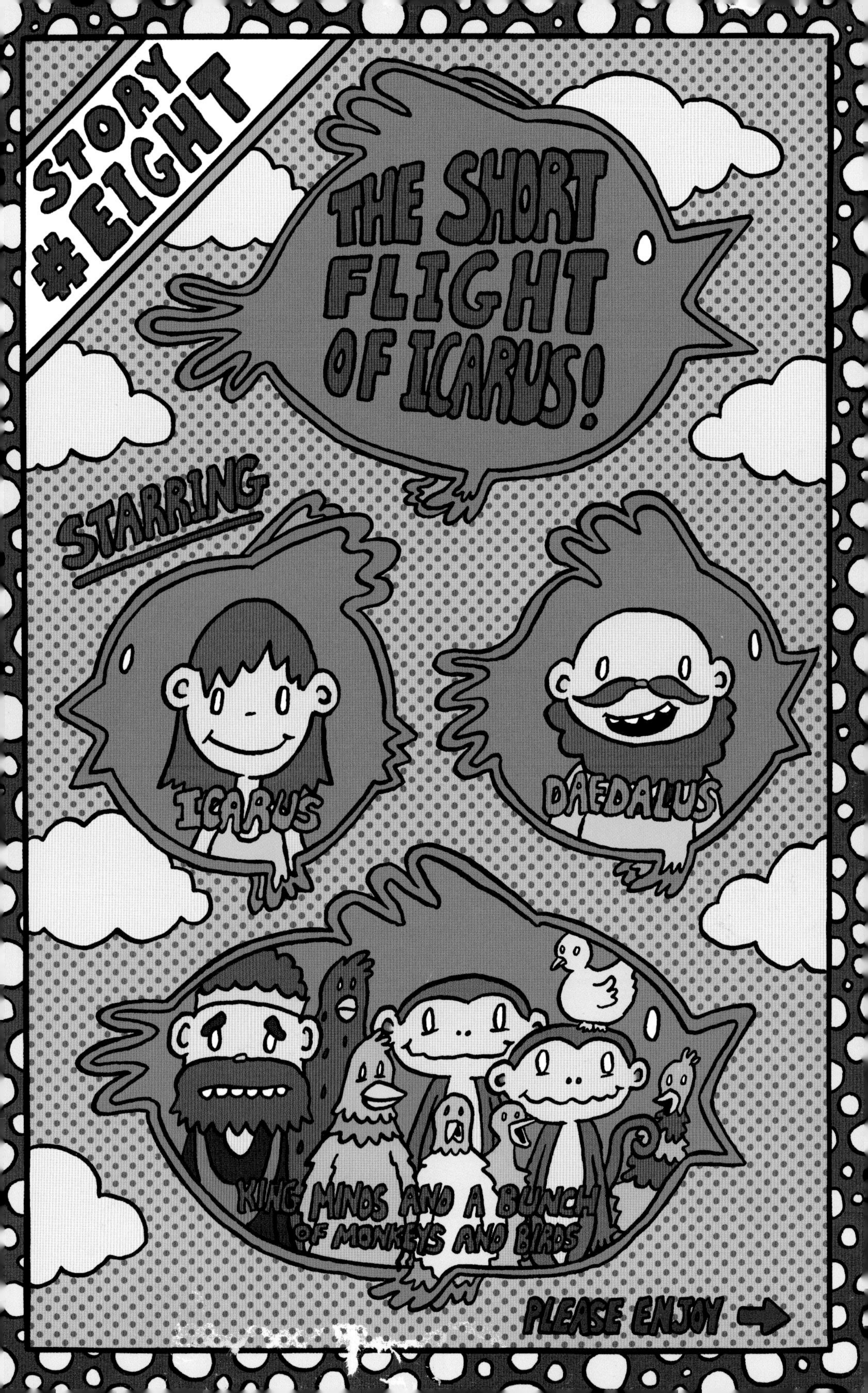
STORY #EIGHT
THE SHORT FLIGHT OF ICARUS!
STARRING
ICARUS
DAEDALUS
KING MINOS AND A BUNCH OF MONKEYS AND BIRDS
PLEASE ENJOY

ONCE UPON AN ISLAND, CALLED CRETE, THERE LIVED A KING NAMED MINOS...

WHO LIVED IN A BEAUTIFUL PALACE...

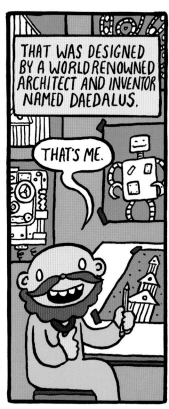

THAT WAS DESIGNED BY A WORLD RENOWNED ARCHITECT AND INVENTOR NAMED DAEDALUS.

THAT'S ME.

THE KING ALSO HAD DAEDALUS DESIGN AND BUILD AN INESCAPABLE MAZE UNDER THE PALACE CALLED THE...

LABYRINTH.

ITS PURPOSE WAS TO HOUSE THE KING'S HALF-MAN, HALF-BULL STEP-SON, THE MINOTAUR.

THAT'S ME!

MINOS WAS VERY PLEASED WITH DAEDALUS'S WORK... UNTIL A YOUNG HERO NAMED THESEUS KILLED THE MINOTAUR...

ESCAPED THE MAZE...

AND RAN OFF WITH THE KING'S DAUGHTER.

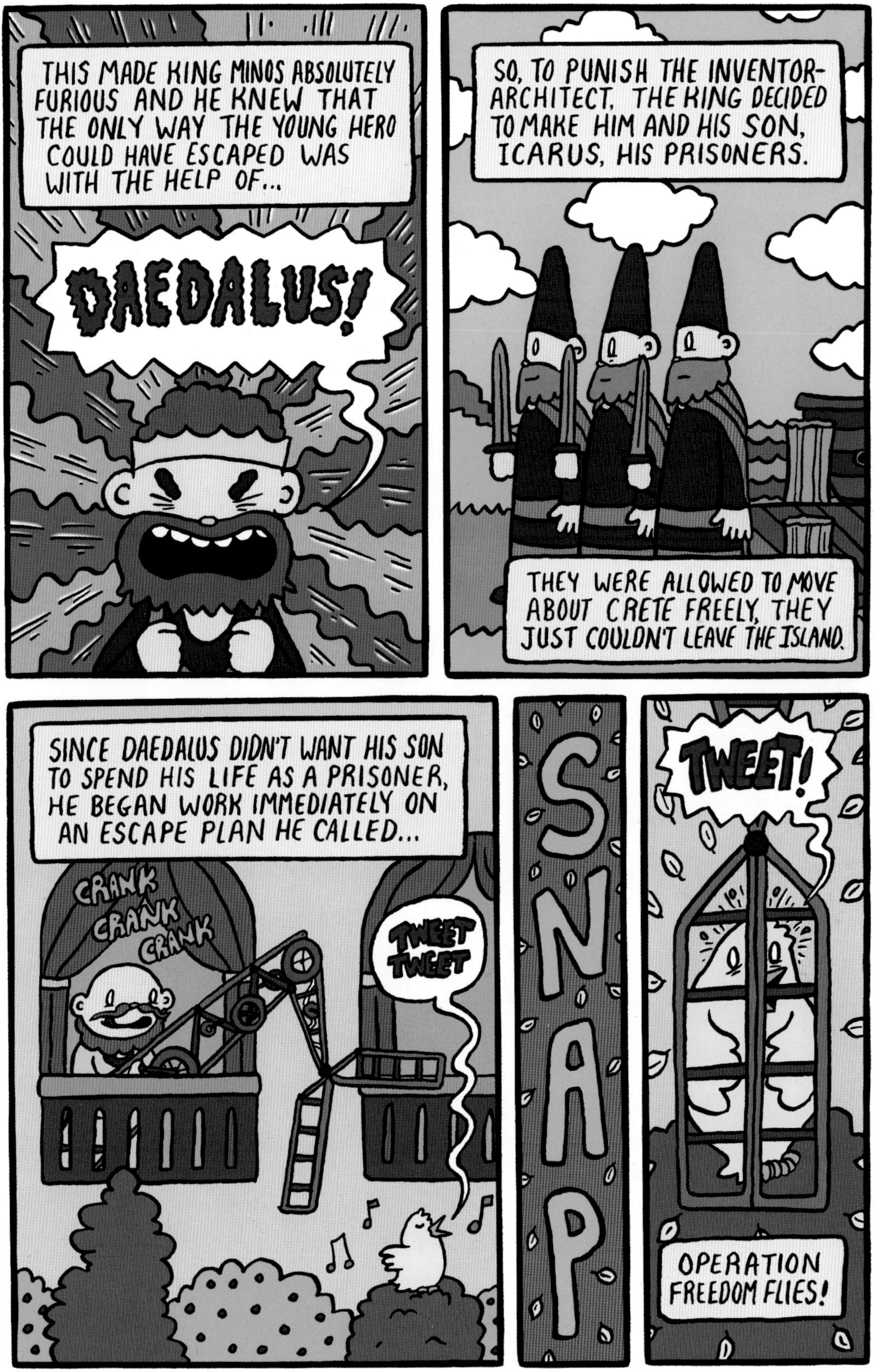
THIS MADE KING MINOS ABSOLUTELY FURIOUS AND HE KNEW THAT THE ONLY WAY THE YOUNG HERO COULD HAVE ESCAPED WAS WITH THE HELP OF...
DAEDALUS!
SO, TO PUNISH THE INVENTOR-ARCHITECT, THE KING DECIDED TO MAKE HIM AND HIS SON, ICARUS, HIS PRISONERS.
THEY WERE ALLOWED TO MOVE ABOUT CRETE FREELY, THEY JUST COULDN'T LEAVE THE ISLAND.
SINCE DAEDALUS DIDN'T WANT HIS SON TO SPEND HIS LIFE AS A PRISONER, HE BEGAN WORK IMMEDIATELY ON AN ESCAPE PLAN HE CALLED...
CRANK CRANK CRANK
TWEET TWEET
SNAP
TWEET!
OPERATION FREEDOM FLIES!

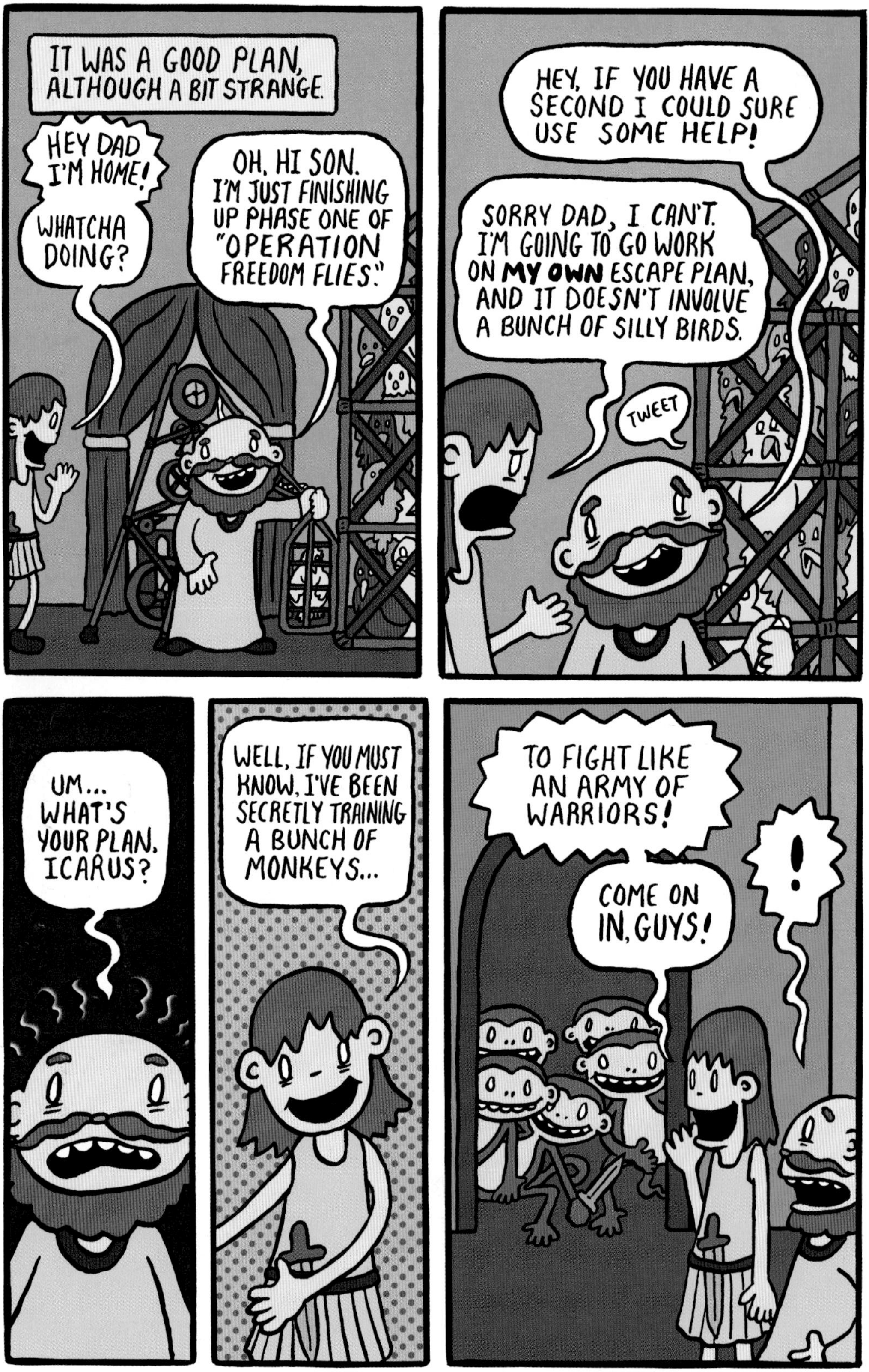
IT WAS A GOOD PLAN, ALTHOUGH A BIT STRANGE.
HEY DAD I'M HOME!
WHATCHA DOING?
OH, HI SON. I'M JUST FINISHING UP PHASE ONE OF "OPERATION FREEDOM FLIES."
HEY, IF YOU HAVE A SECOND I COULD SURE USE SOME HELP!
SORRY DAD, I CAN'T. I'M GOING TO GO WORK ON **MY OWN** ESCAPE PLAN, AND IT DOESN'T INVOLVE A BUNCH OF SILLY BIRDS.
TWEET
UM... WHAT'S YOUR PLAN, ICARUS?
WELL, IF YOU MUST KNOW, I'VE BEEN SECRETLY TRAINING A BUNCH OF MONKEYS...
TO FIGHT LIKE AN ARMY OF WARRIORS!
COME ON IN, GUYS!
!

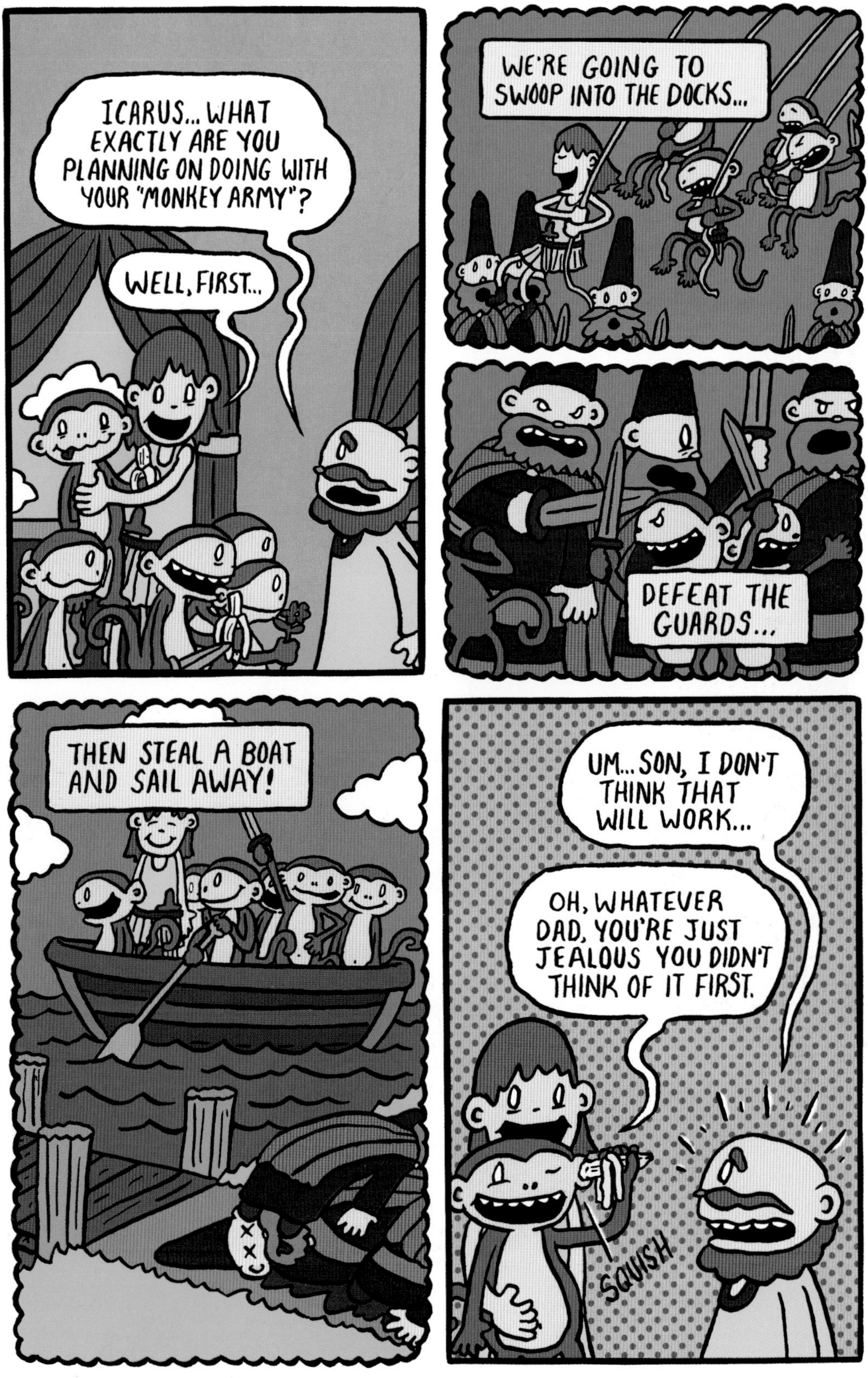
ICARUS... WHAT EXACTLY ARE YOU PLANNING ON DOING WITH YOUR "MONKEY ARMY"?
WELL, FIRST...
WE'RE GOING TO SWOOP INTO THE DOCKS...
DEFEAT THE GUARDS...
THEN STEAL A BOAT AND SAIL AWAY!
UM... SON, I DON'T THINK THAT WILL WORK...
OH, WHATEVER DAD, YOU'RE JUST JEALOUS YOU DIDN'T THINK OF IT FIRST.
SQUISH

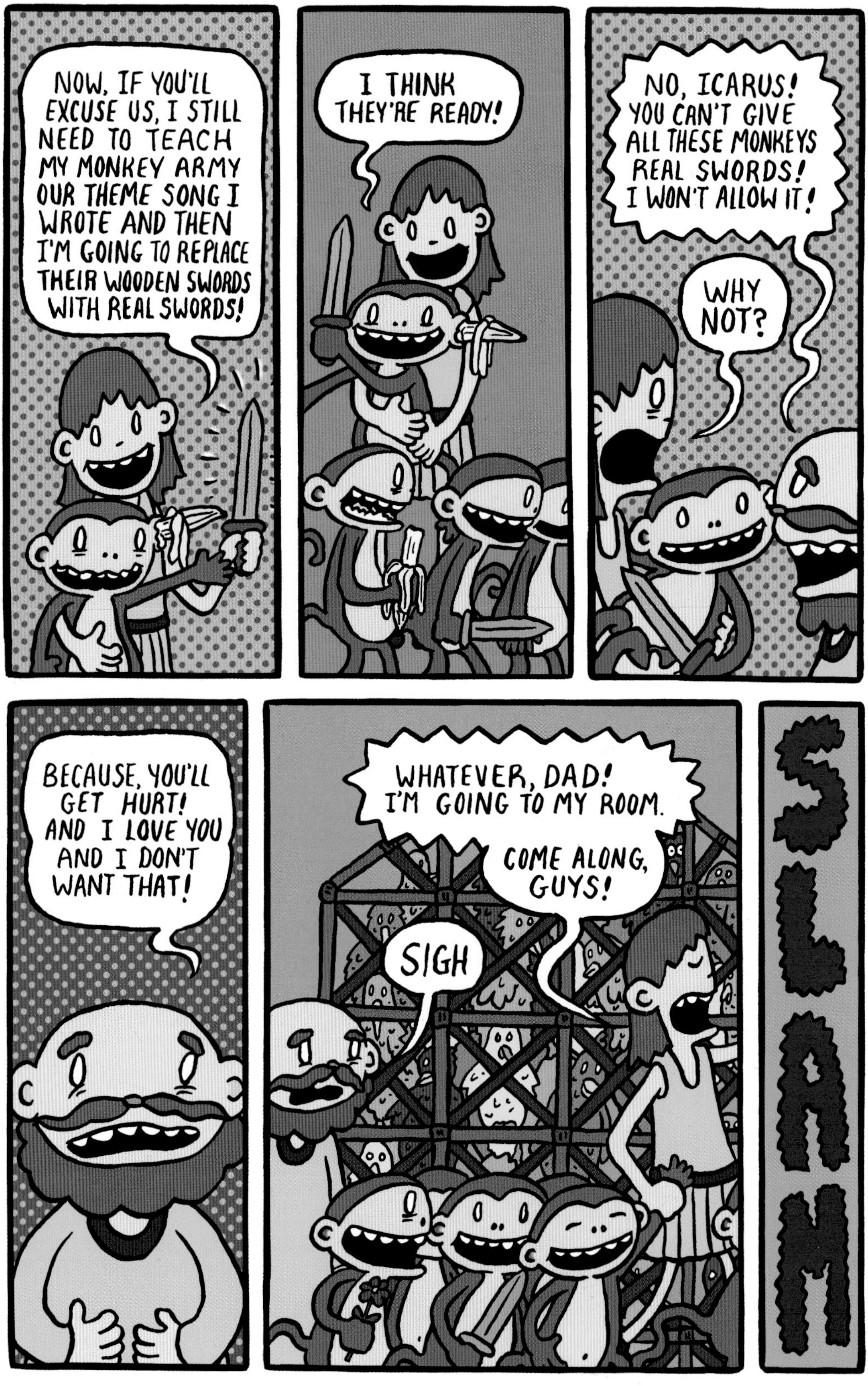
NOW, IF YOU'LL EXCUSE US, I STILL NEED TO TEACH MY MONKEY ARMY OUR THEME SONG I WROTE AND THEN I'M GOING TO REPLACE THEIR WOODEN SWORDS WITH REAL SWORDS!
I THINK THEY'RE READY!
NO, ICARUS! YOU CAN'T GIVE ALL THESE MONKEYS REAL SWORDS! I WON'T ALLOW IT!
WHY NOT?
BECAUSE, YOU'LL GET HURT! AND I LOVE YOU AND I DON'T WANT THAT!
WHATEVER, DAD! I'M GOING TO MY ROOM.
COME ALONG, GUYS!
SIGH
SLAM

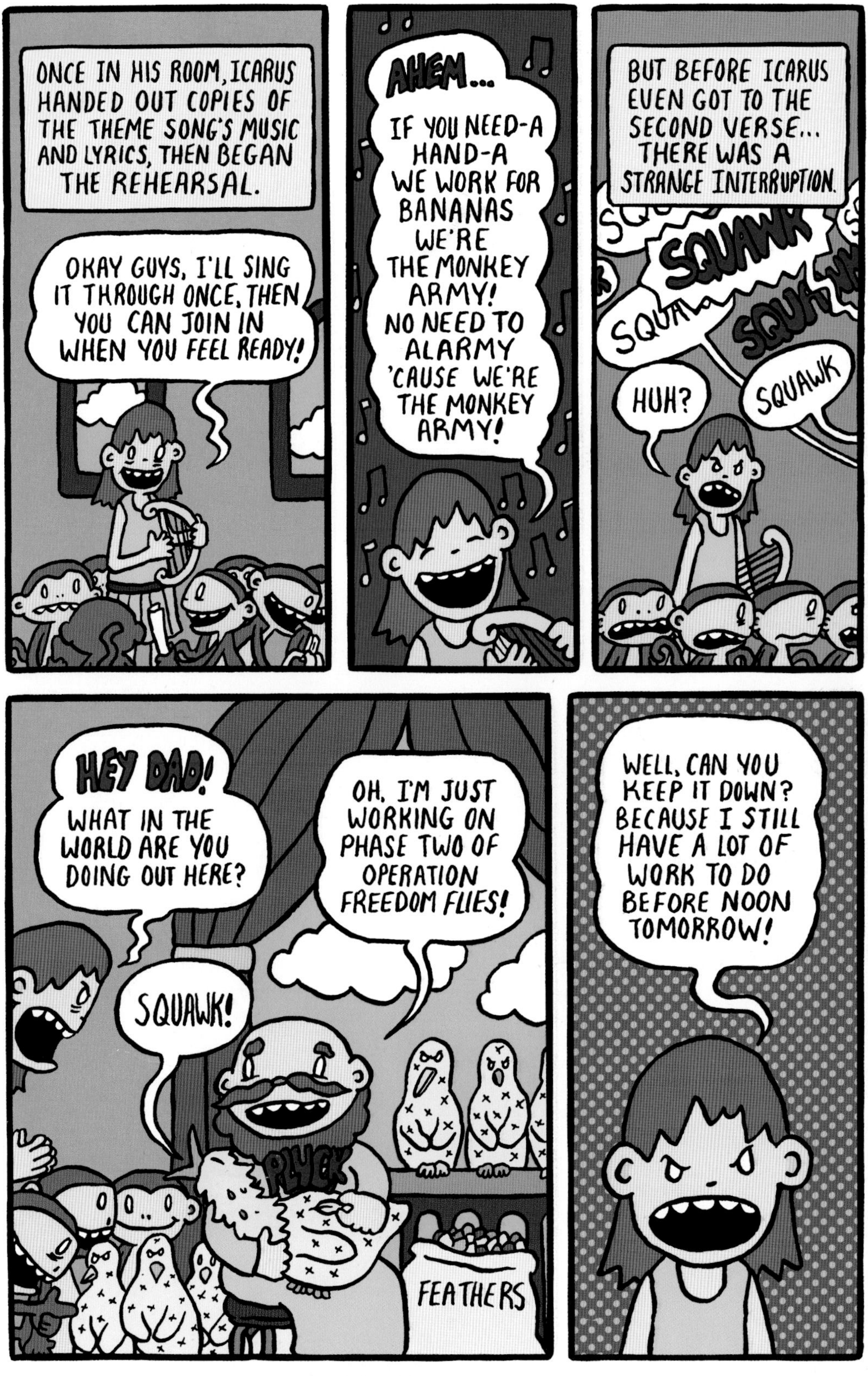
ONCE IN HIS ROOM, ICARUS HANDED OUT COPIES OF THE THEME SONG'S MUSIC AND LYRICS, THEN BEGAN THE REHEARSAL.
OKAY GUYS, I'LL SING IT THROUGH ONCE, THEN YOU CAN JOIN IN WHEN YOU FEEL READY!
AHEM...
IF YOU NEED-A HAND-A WE WORK FOR BANANAS WE'RE THE MONKEY ARMY! NO NEED TO ALARMY 'CAUSE WE'RE THE MONKEY ARMY!
BUT BEFORE ICARUS EVEN GOT TO THE SECOND VERSE... THERE WAS A STRANGE INTERRUPTION.
SQUAWK
HUH?
SQUAWK
HEY DAD! WHAT IN THE WORLD ARE YOU DOING OUT HERE?
OH, I'M JUST WORKING ON PHASE TWO OF OPERATION FREEDOM FLIES!
SQUAWK!
PLUCK
FEATHERS
WELL, CAN YOU KEEP IT DOWN? BECAUSE I STILL HAVE A LOT OF WORK TO DO BEFORE NOON TOMORROW!

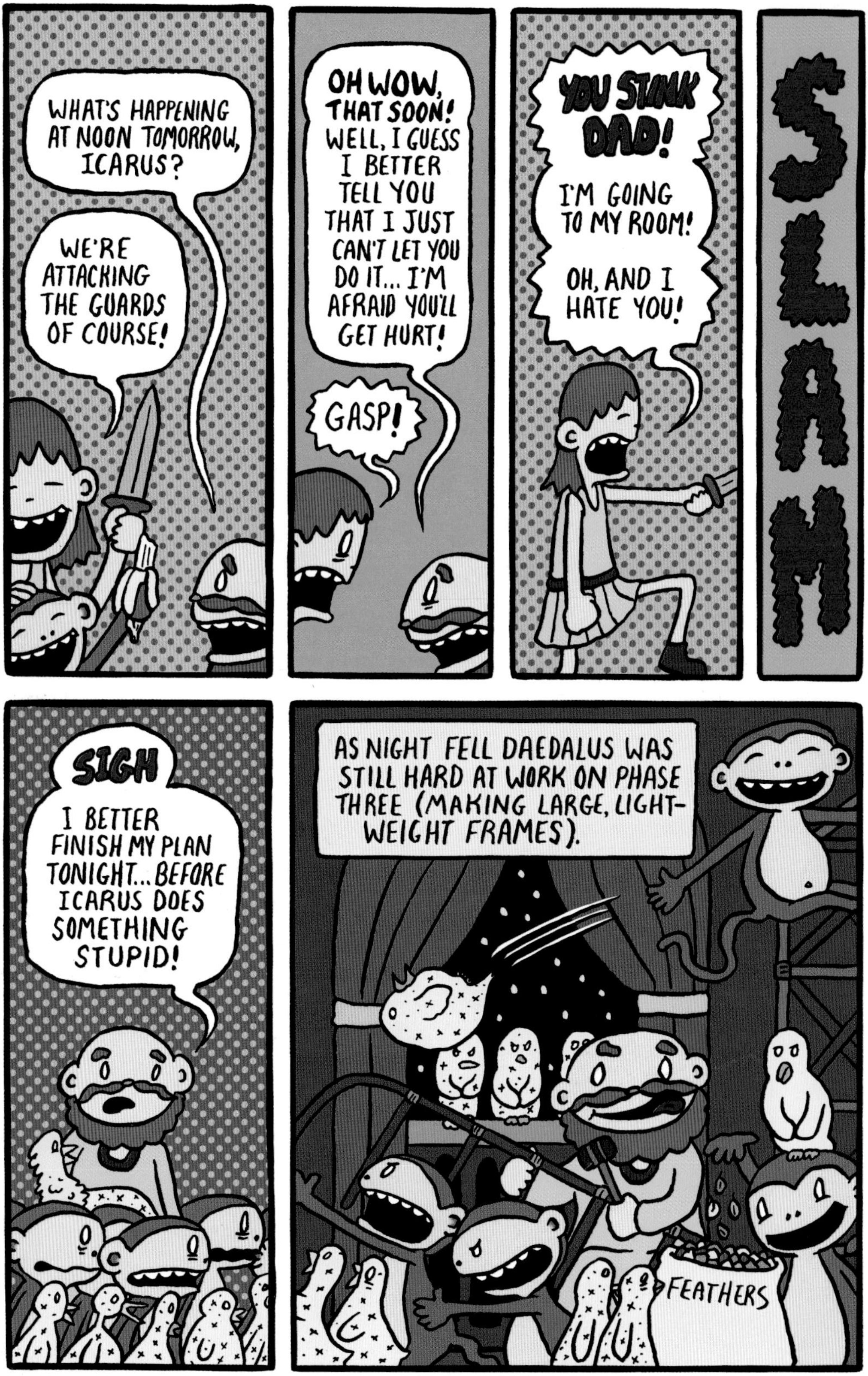
WHAT'S HAPPENING AT NOON TOMORROW, ICARUS?
WE'RE ATTACKING THE GUARDS OF COURSE!
OH WOW, THAT SOON! WELL, I GUESS I BETTER TELL YOU THAT I JUST CAN'T LET YOU DO IT... I'M AFRAID YOU'LL GET HURT!
GASP!
YOU STINK DAD!
I'M GOING TO MY ROOM!
OH, AND I HATE YOU!
SLAM
SIGH
I BETTER FINISH MY PLAN TONIGHT... BEFORE ICARUS DOES SOMETHING STUPID!
AS NIGHT FELL DAEDALUS WAS STILL HARD AT WORK ON PHASE THREE (MAKING LARGE, LIGHT-WEIGHT FRAMES).
FEATHERS

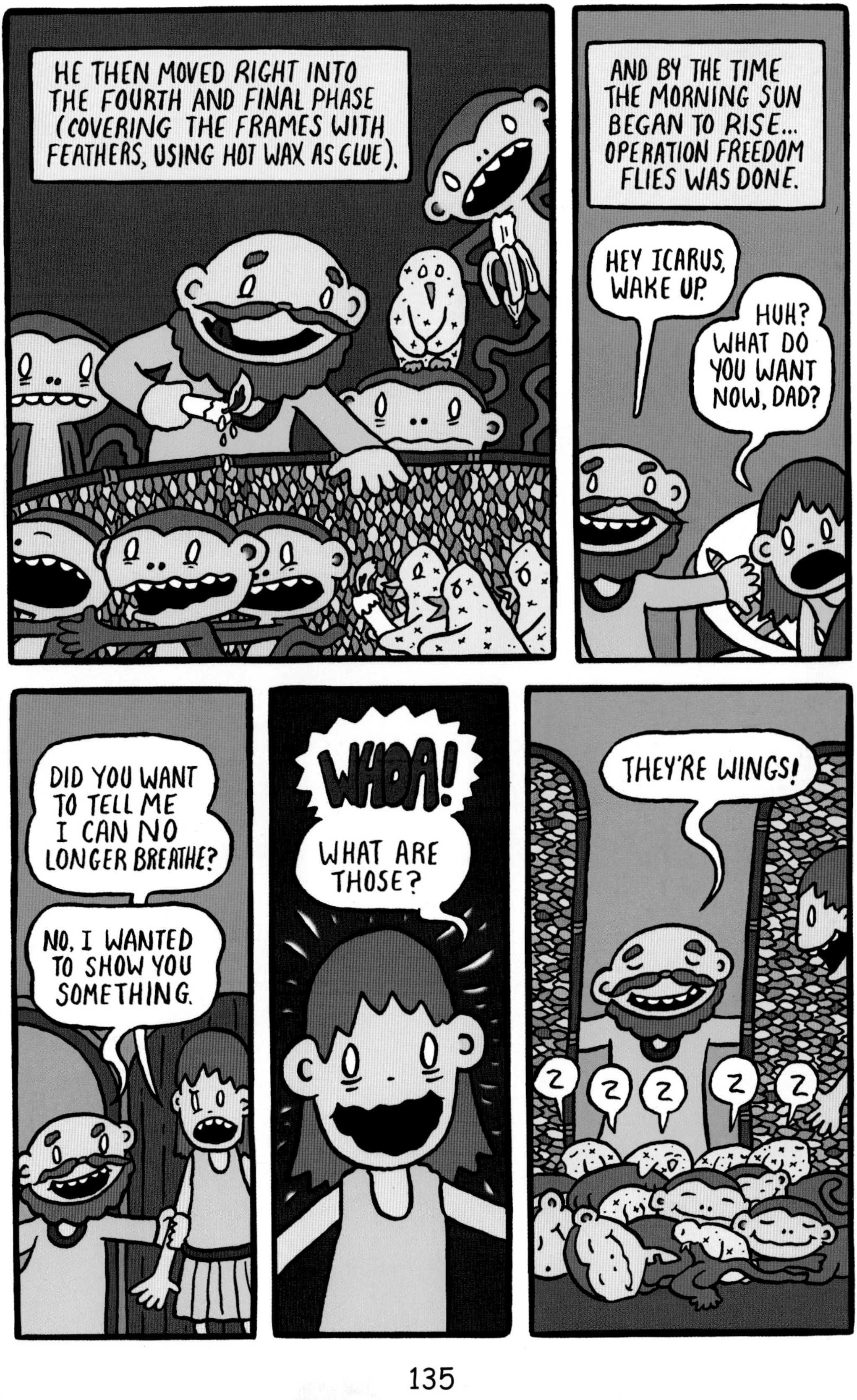

HE THEN MOVED RIGHT INTO THE FOURTH AND FINAL PHASE (COVERING THE FRAMES WITH FEATHERS, USING HOT WAX AS GLUE).
AND BY THE TIME THE MORNING SUN BEGAN TO RISE... OPERATION FREEDOM FLIES WAS DONE.
HEY ICARUS, WAKE UP.
HUH? WHAT DO YOU WANT NOW, DAD?
DID YOU WANT TO TELL ME I CAN NO LONGER BREATHE?
NO, I WANTED TO SHOW YOU SOMETHING.
WHOA!
WHAT ARE THOSE?
THEY'RE WINGS!
Z
Z
Z
Z
Z

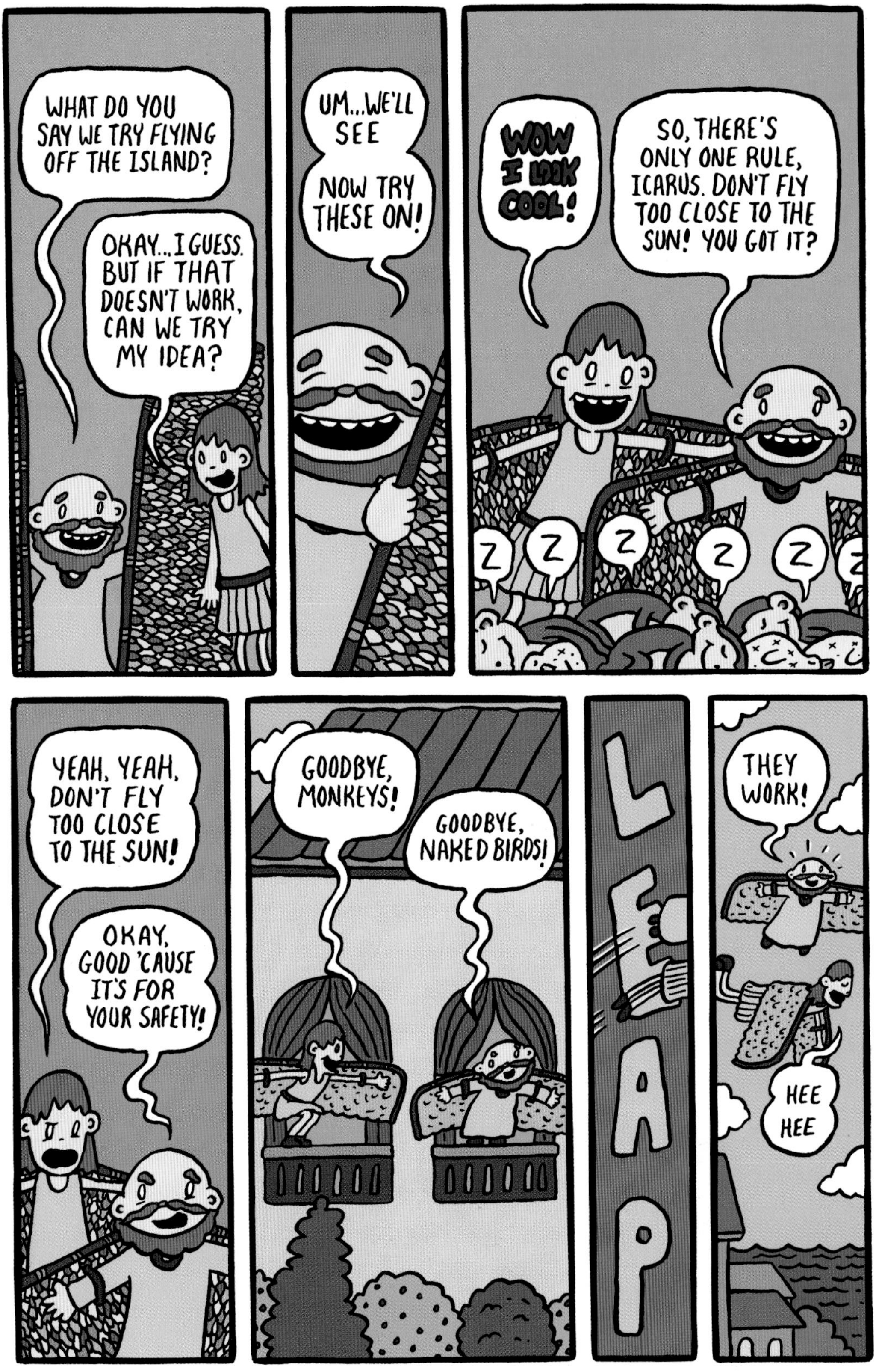
WHAT DO YOU SAY WE TRY FLYING OFF THE ISLAND?
OKAY... I GUESS. BUT IF THAT DOESN'T WORK, CAN WE TRY MY IDEA?
UM... WE'LL SEE
NOW TRY THESE ON!
WOW I LOOK COOL!
SO, THERE'S ONLY ONE RULE, ICARUS. DON'T FLY TOO CLOSE TO THE SUN! YOU GOT IT?
Z Z Z Z Z Z
YEAH, YEAH. DON'T FLY TOO CLOSE TO THE SUN!
OKAY, GOOD 'CAUSE IT'S FOR YOUR SAFETY!
GOODBYE, MONKEYS!
GOODBYE, NAKED BIRDS!
LEAP
THEY WORK!
HEE HEE

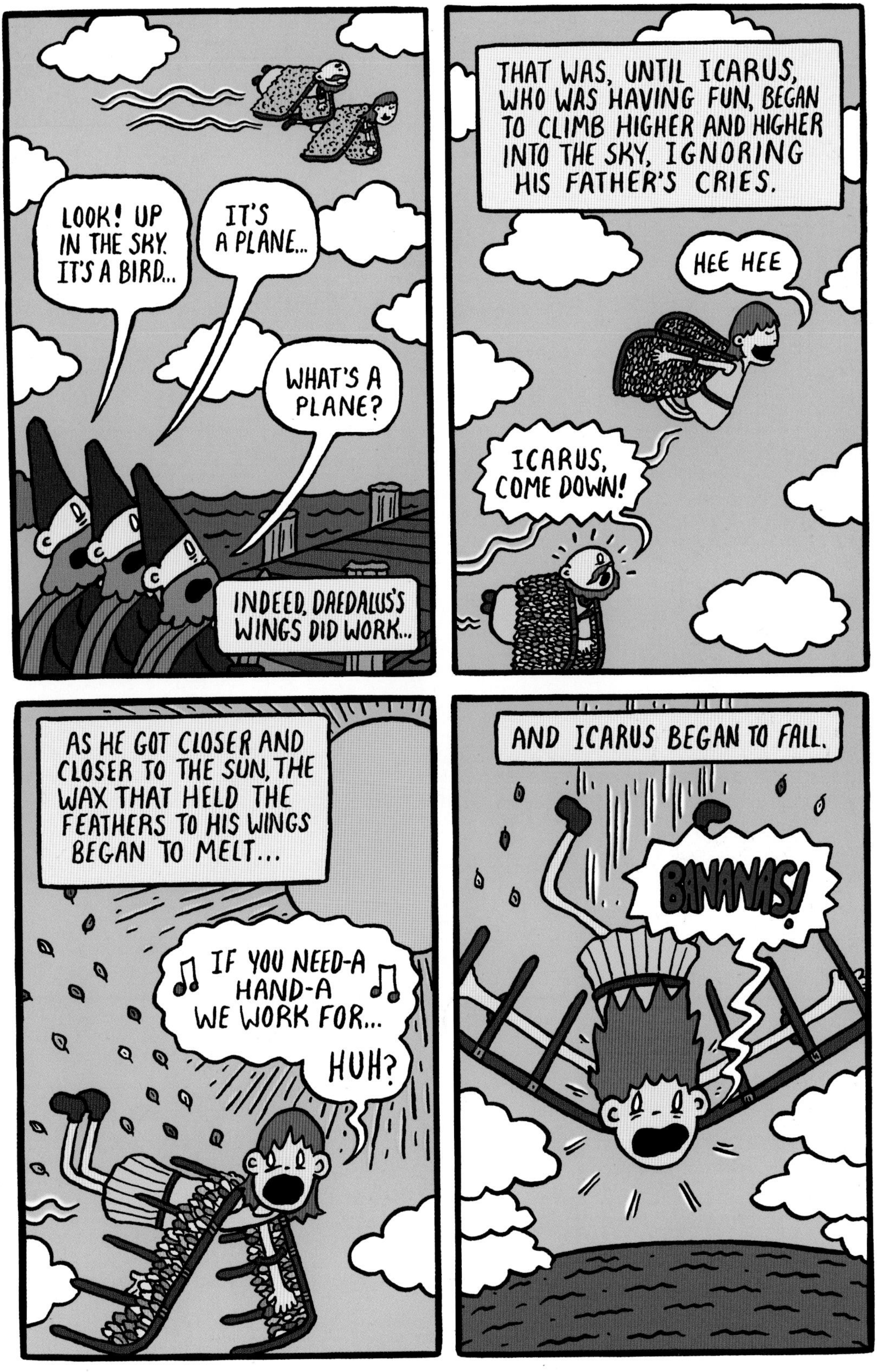
LOOK! UP IN THE SKY. IT'S A BIRD...
IT'S A PLANE...
WHAT'S A PLANE?
INDEED, DAEDALUS'S WINGS DID WORK...
THAT WAS, UNTIL ICARUS, WHO WAS HAVING FUN, BEGAN TO CLIMB HIGHER AND HIGHER INTO THE SKY, IGNORING HIS FATHER'S CRIES.
HEE HEE
ICARUS, COME DOWN!
AS HE GOT CLOSER AND CLOSER TO THE SUN, THE WAX THAT HELD THE FEATHERS TO HIS WINGS BEGAN TO MELT...
IF YOU NEED-A HAND-A WE WORK FOR...
HUH?
AND ICARUS BEGAN TO FALL.
BANANAS!

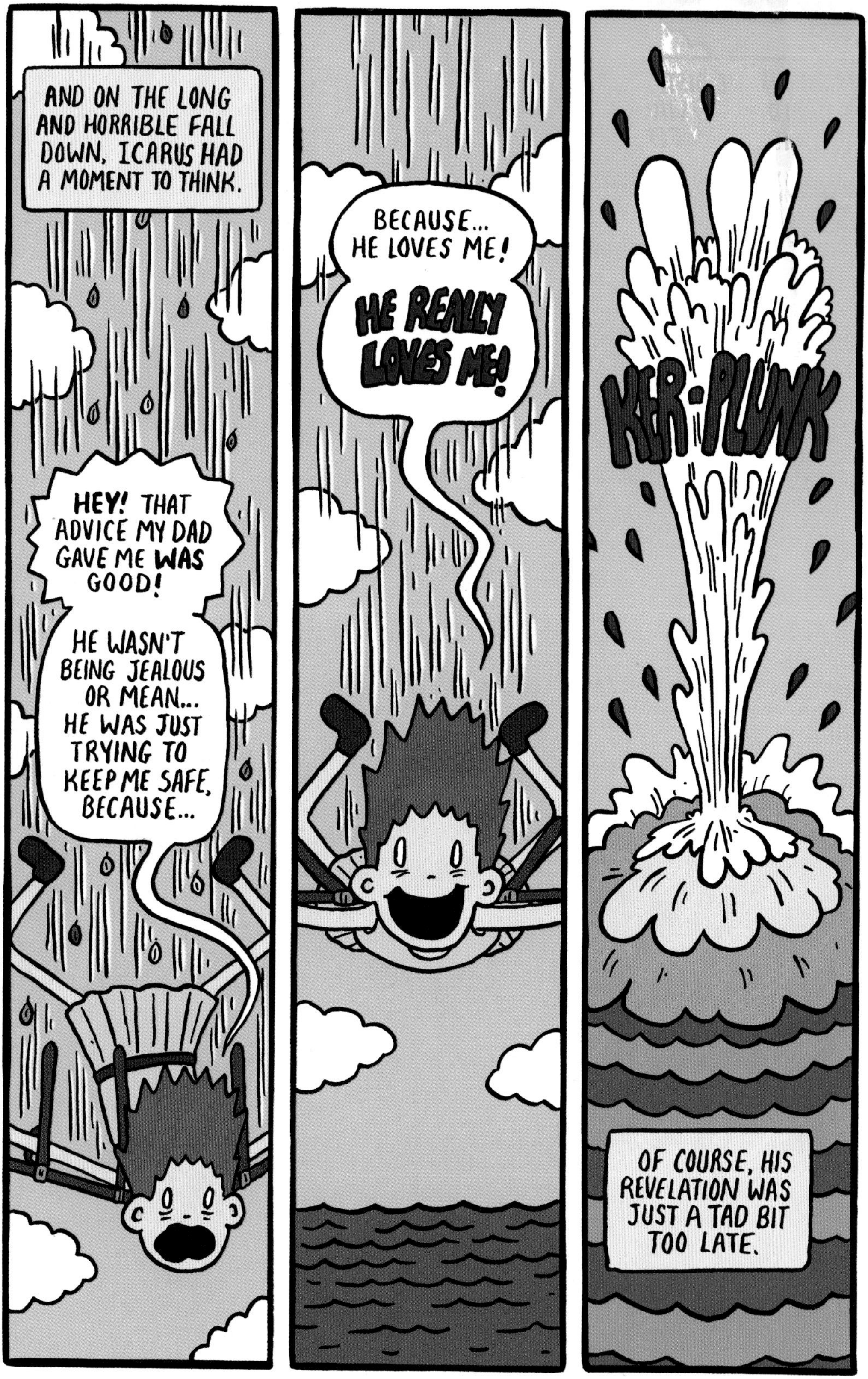
AND ON THE LONG AND HORRIBLE FALL DOWN, ICARUS HAD A MOMENT TO THINK.
HEY! THAT ADVICE MY DAD GAVE ME WAS GOOD!
HE WASN'T BEING JEALOUS OR MEAN... HE WAS JUST TRYING TO KEEP ME SAFE, BECAUSE...
BECAUSE... HE LOVES ME!
HE REALLY LOVES ME!
KER-PLUNK
OF COURSE, HIS REVELATION WAS JUST A TAD BIT TOO LATE.

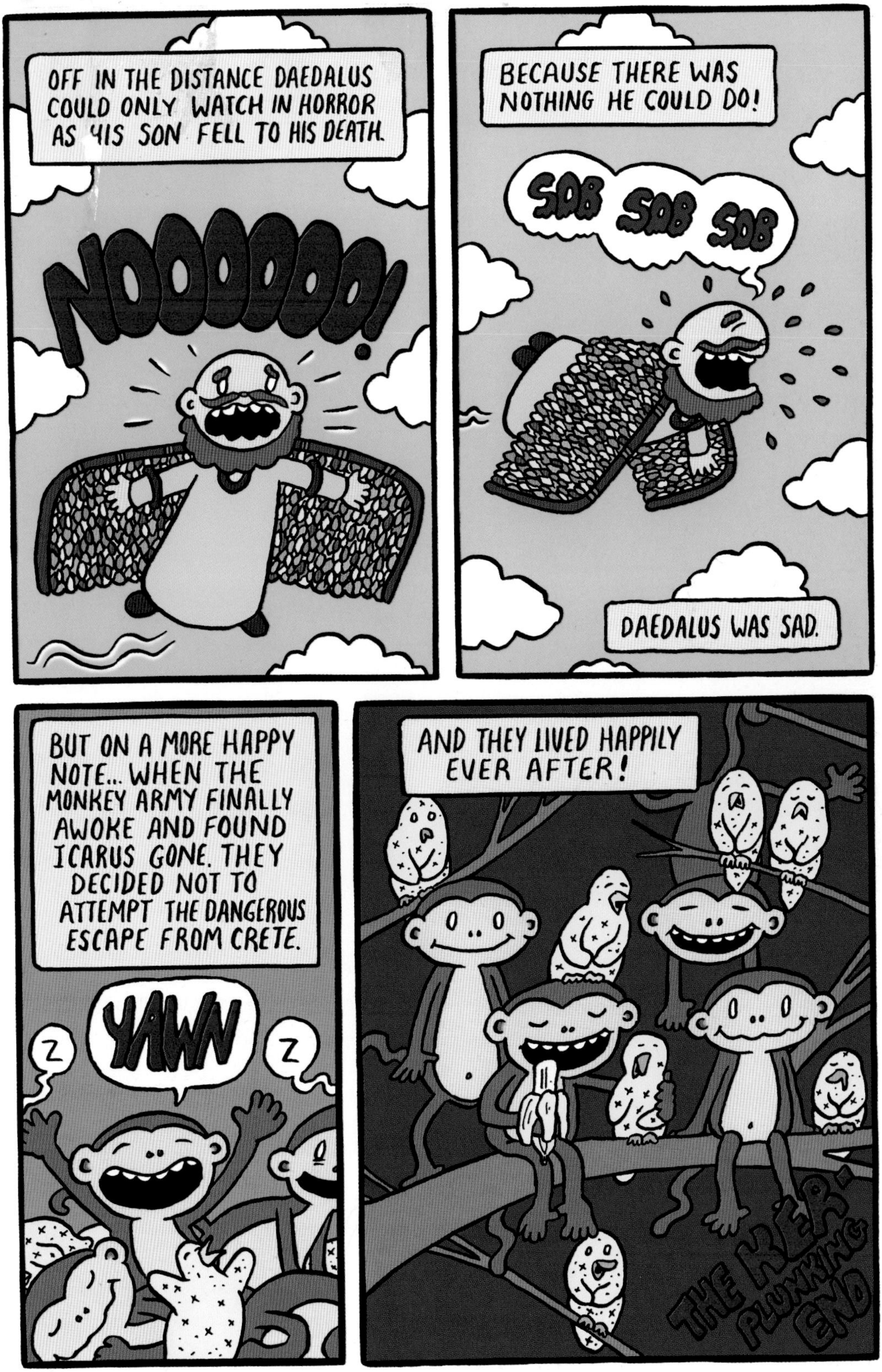
OFF IN THE DISTANCE DAEDALUS COULD ONLY WATCH IN HORROR AS HIS SON FELL TO HIS DEATH.
NOOOOOO!
BECAUSE THERE WAS NOTHING HE COULD DO!
SOB SOB SOB
DAEDALUS WAS SAD.
BUT ON A MORE HAPPY NOTE... WHEN THE MONKEY ARMY FINALLY AWOKE AND FOUND ICARUS GONE. THEY DECIDED NOT TO ATTEMPT THE DANGEROUS ESCAPE FROM CRETE.
Z
YAWN
Z
AND THEY LIVED HAPPILY EVER AFTER!
THE KER-PLUNKING END

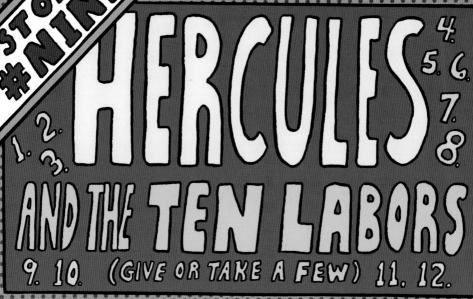

STORY #NINE

HERCULES

4. 5. 6. 7. 8.
1. 2. 3.

AND THE TEN LABORS

9. 10. (GIVE OR TAKE A FEW) 11. 12.

STARRING

HERCULES AND HIS HUGE MUSCLES

ZEUS AND HERA

PLUS HERCULES' COUSIN — KING EURYSTHEUS AND HIS TINY MUSCLES

PLEASE ENJOY ➡

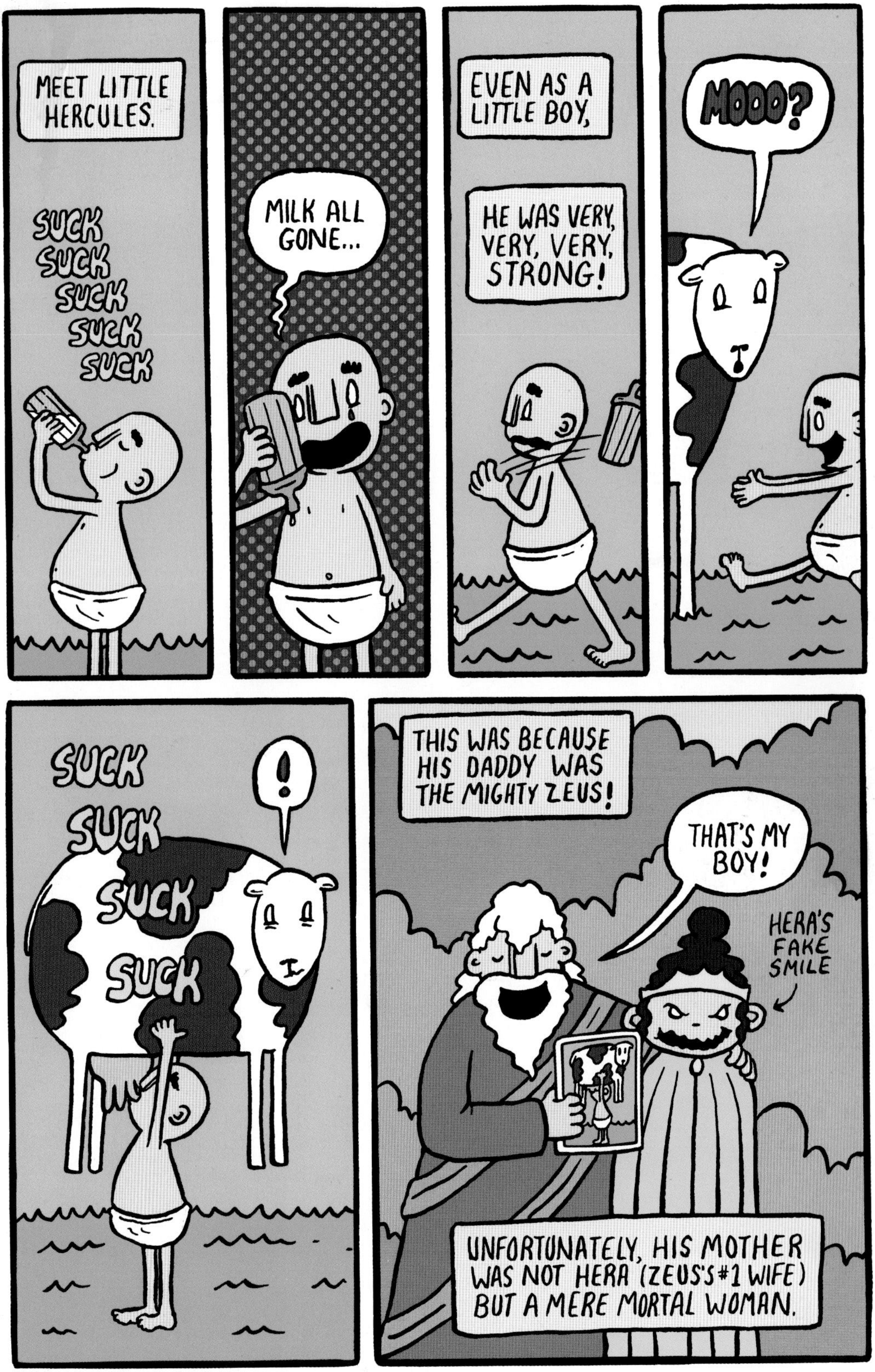
MEET LITTLE HERCULES.
SUCK SUCK SUCK SUCK SUCK
MILK ALL GONE...
EVEN AS A LITTLE BOY,
HE WAS VERY, VERY, VERY, STRONG!
MOOO?
SUCK SUCK SUCK SUCK
!
THIS WAS BECAUSE HIS DADDY WAS THE MIGHTY ZEUS!
THAT'S MY BOY!
HERA'S FAKE SMILE
UNFORTUNATELY, HIS MOTHER WAS NOT HERA (ZEUS'S #1 WIFE) BUT A MERE MORTAL WOMAN.

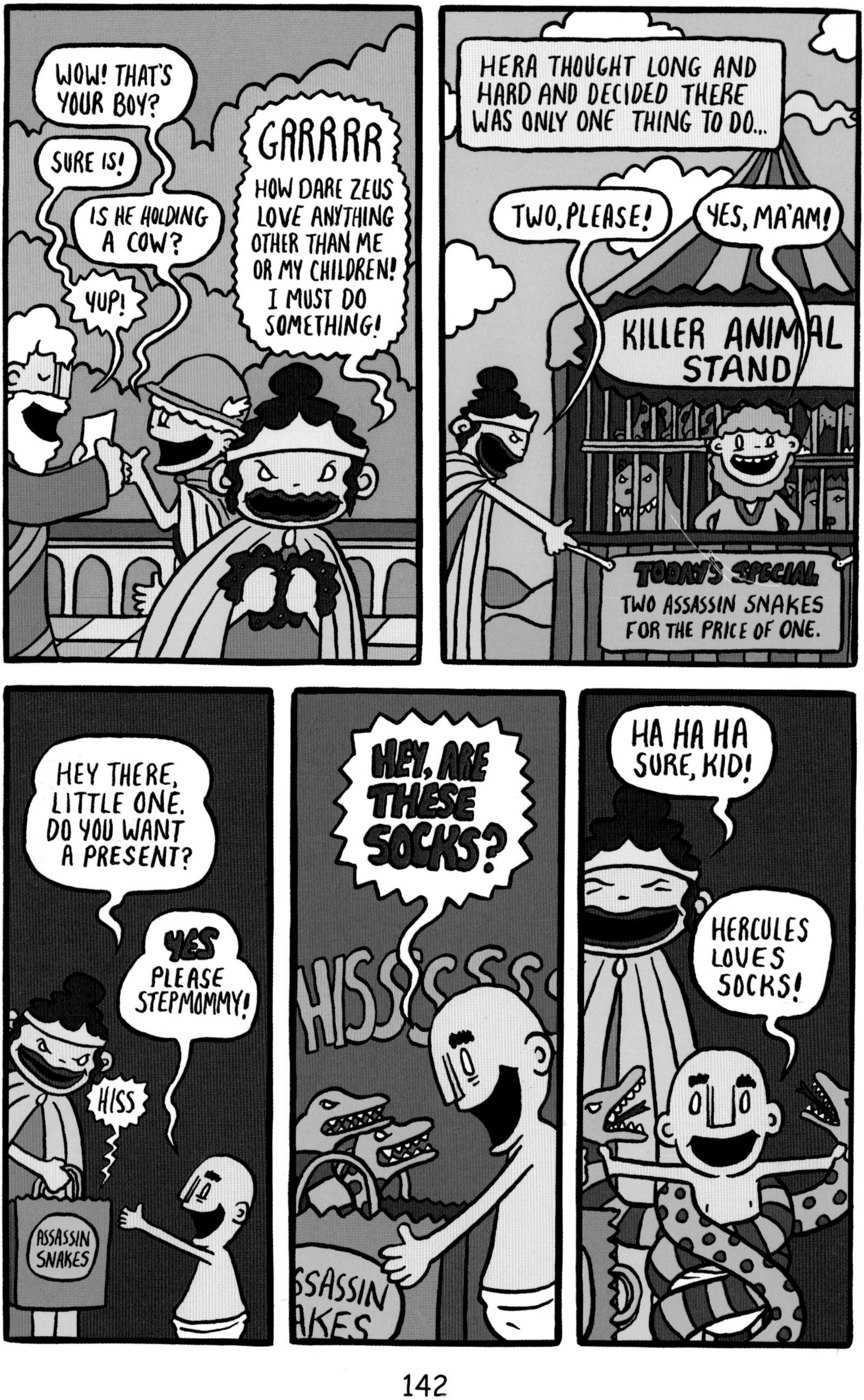
WOW! THAT'S YOUR BOY?
SURE IS!
IS HE HOLDING A COW?
YUP!
GRRRRR
HOW DARE ZEUS LOVE ANYTHING OTHER THAN ME OR MY CHILDREN! I MUST DO SOMETHING!
HERA THOUGHT LONG AND HARD AND DECIDED THERE WAS ONLY ONE THING TO DO...
TWO, PLEASE!
YES, MA'AM!
KILLER ANIMAL STAND
TODAY'S SPECIAL
TWO ASSASSIN SNAKES FOR THE PRICE OF ONE.
HEY THERE, LITTLE ONE. DO YOU WANT A PRESENT?
YES PLEASE STEPMOMMY!
HISS
ASSASSIN SNAKES
HEY, ARE THESE SOCKS?
HISSSSSS
HA HA HA SURE, KID!
HERCULES LOVES SOCKS!

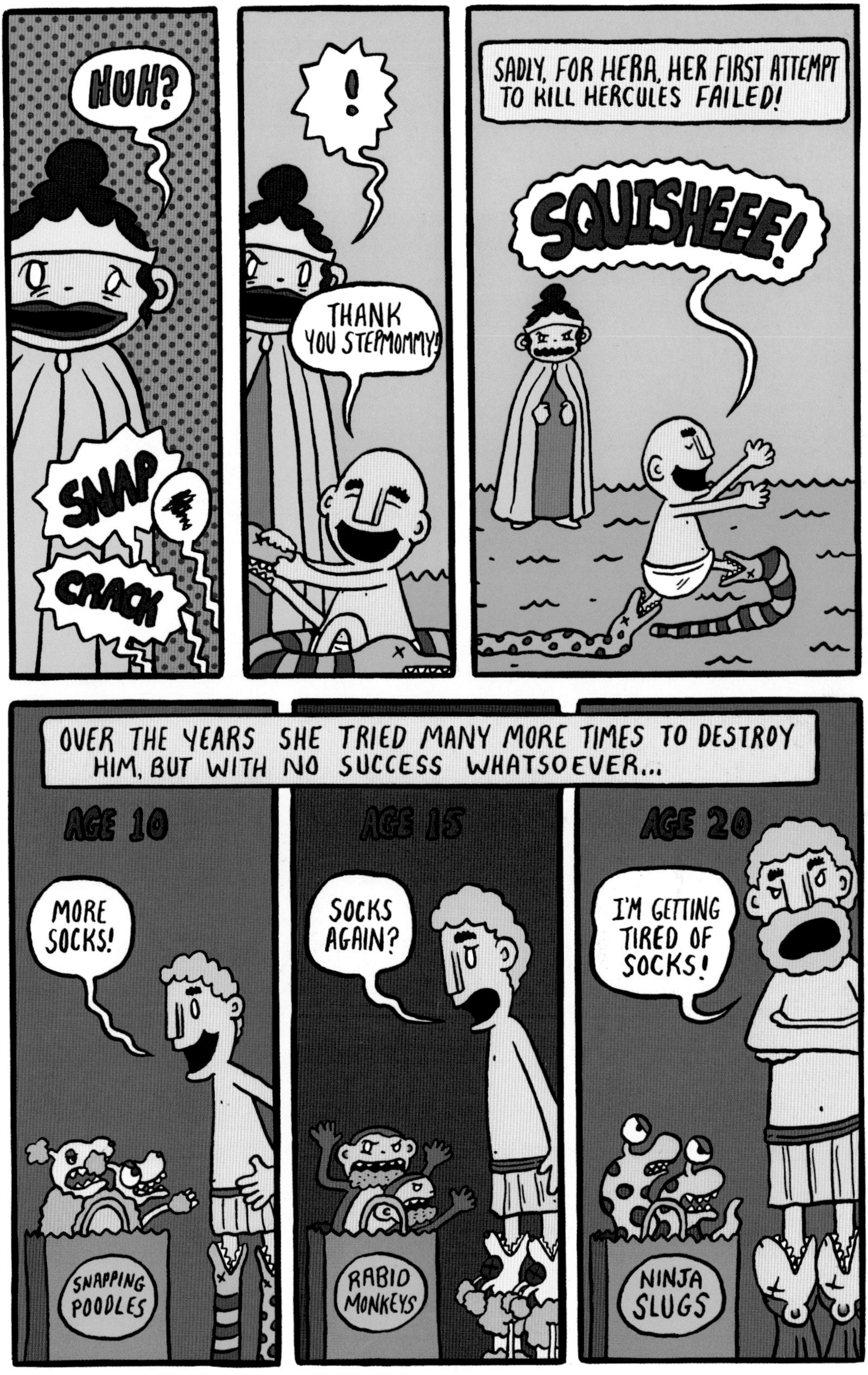
HUH?
SNAP
CRACK
!
THANK YOU STEPMOMMY!
SADLY, FOR HERA, HER FIRST ATTEMPT TO KILL HERCULES FAILED!
SQUISHEEE!
OVER THE YEARS SHE TRIED MANY MORE TIMES TO DESTROY HIM, BUT WITH NO SUCCESS WHATSOEVER...
AGE 10
MORE SOCKS!
SNAPPING POODLES
AGE 15
SOCKS AGAIN?
RABID MONKEYS
AGE 20
I'M GETTING TIRED OF SOCKS!
NINJA SLUGS

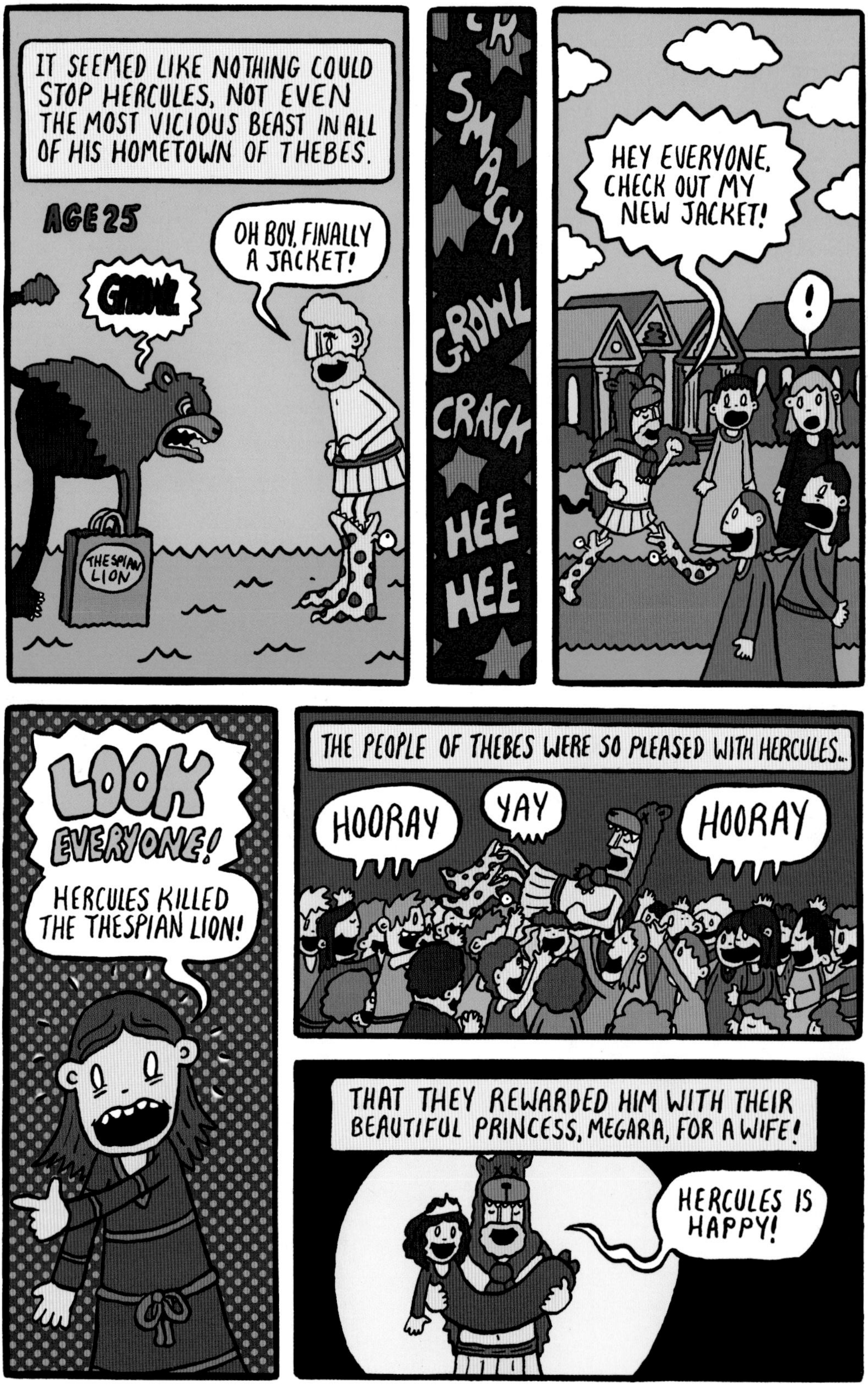
IT SEEMED LIKE NOTHING COULD STOP HERCULES, NOT EVEN THE MOST VICIOUS BEAST IN ALL OF HIS HOMETOWN OF THEBES.
AGE 25
GROWL
OH BOY, FINALLY A JACKET!
THESPIAN LION
SMACK
GROWL
CRACK
HEE
HEE
HEY EVERYONE, CHECK OUT MY NEW JACKET!
!
LOOK EVERYONE!
HERCULES KILLED THE THESPIAN LION!
THE PEOPLE OF THEBES WERE SO PLEASED WITH HERCULES...
HOORAY
YAY
HOORAY
THAT THEY REWARDED HIM WITH THEIR BEAUTIFUL PRINCESS, MEGARA, FOR A WIFE!
HERCULES IS HAPPY!

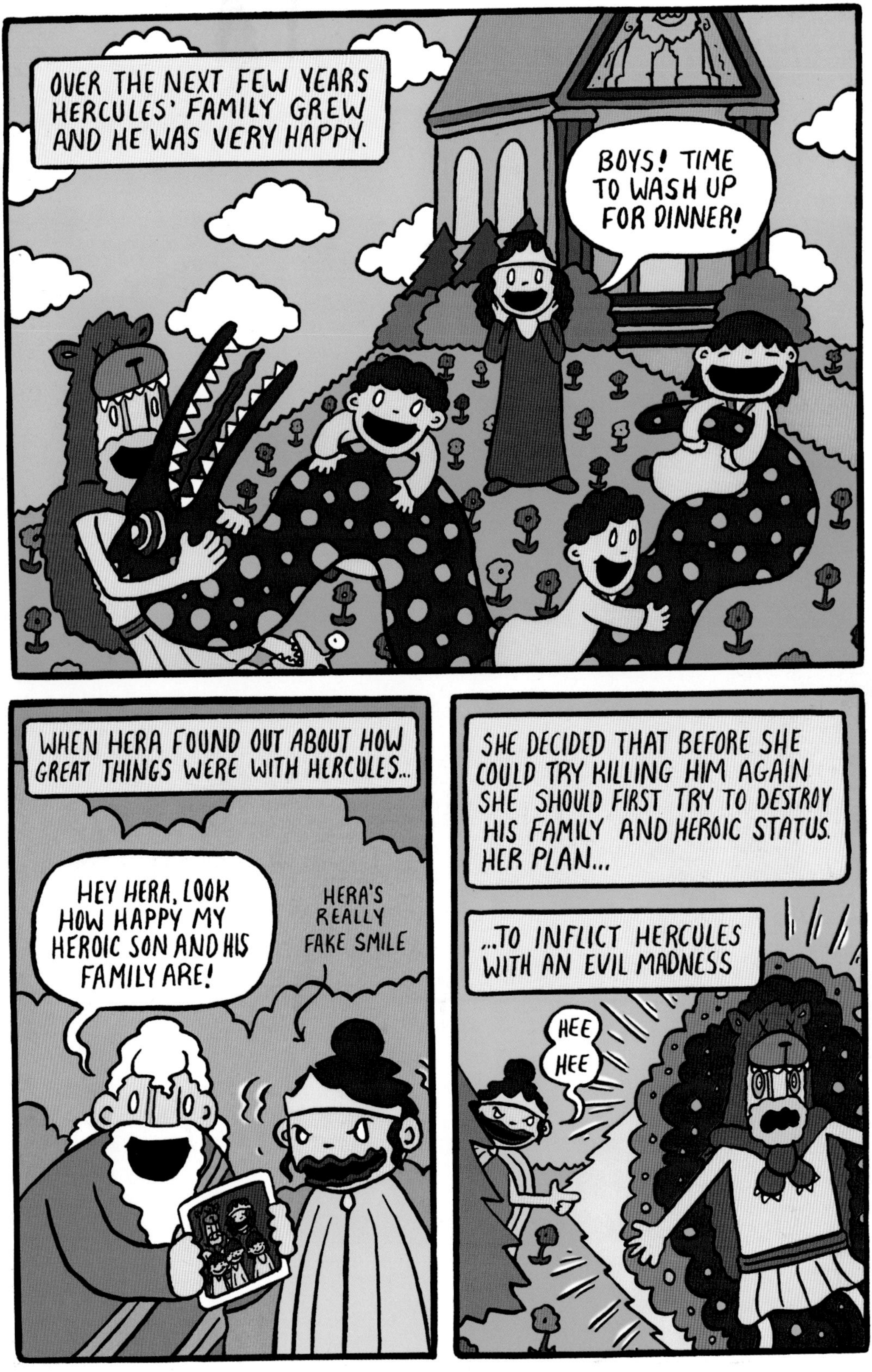
OVER THE NEXT FEW YEARS HERCULES' FAMILY GREW AND HE WAS VERY HAPPY.
BOYS! TIME TO WASH UP FOR DINNER!
WHEN HERA FOUND OUT ABOUT HOW GREAT THINGS WERE WITH HERCULES...
HEY HERA, LOOK HOW HAPPY MY HEROIC SON AND HIS FAMILY ARE!
HERA'S REALLY FAKE SMILE
SHE DECIDED THAT BEFORE SHE COULD TRY KILLING HIM AGAIN SHE SHOULD FIRST TRY TO DESTROY HIS FAMILY AND HEROIC STATUS. HER PLAN...
...TO INFLICT HERCULES WITH AN EVIL MADNESS
HEE HEE

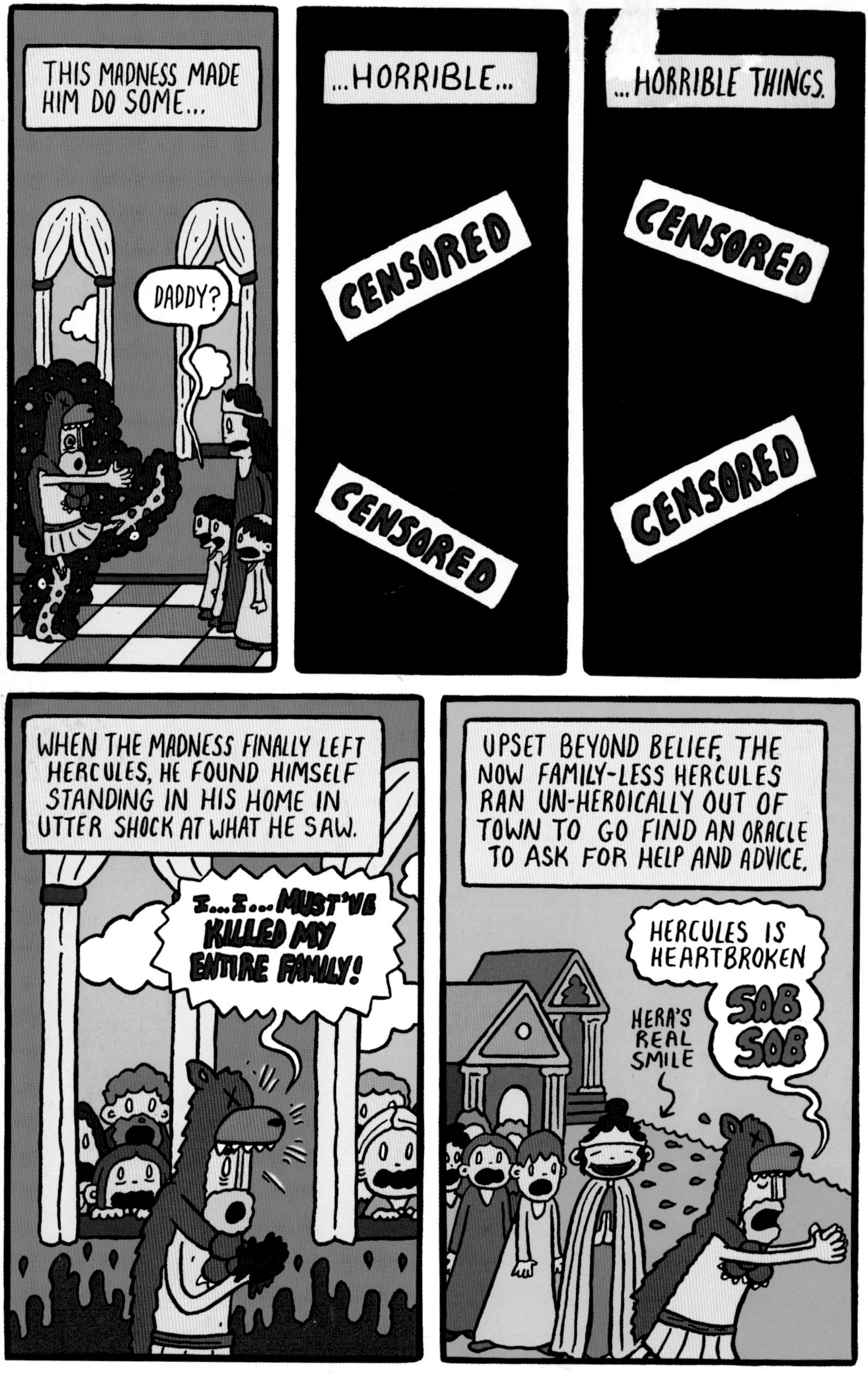
THIS MADNESS MADE HIM DO SOME...
DADDY?
...HORRIBLE...
CENSORED
CENSORED
...HORRIBLE THINGS.
CENSORED
CENSORED
WHEN THE MADNESS FINALLY LEFT HERCULES, HE FOUND HIMSELF STANDING IN HIS HOME IN UTTER SHOCK AT WHAT HE SAW.
I... I... MUST'VE KILLED MY ENTIRE FAMILY!
UPSET BEYOND BELIEF, THE NOW FAMILY-LESS HERCULES RAN UN-HEROICALLY OUT OF TOWN TO GO FIND AN ORACLE TO ASK FOR HELP AND ADVICE.
HERCULES IS HEARTBROKEN
SOB SOB
HERA'S REAL SMILE

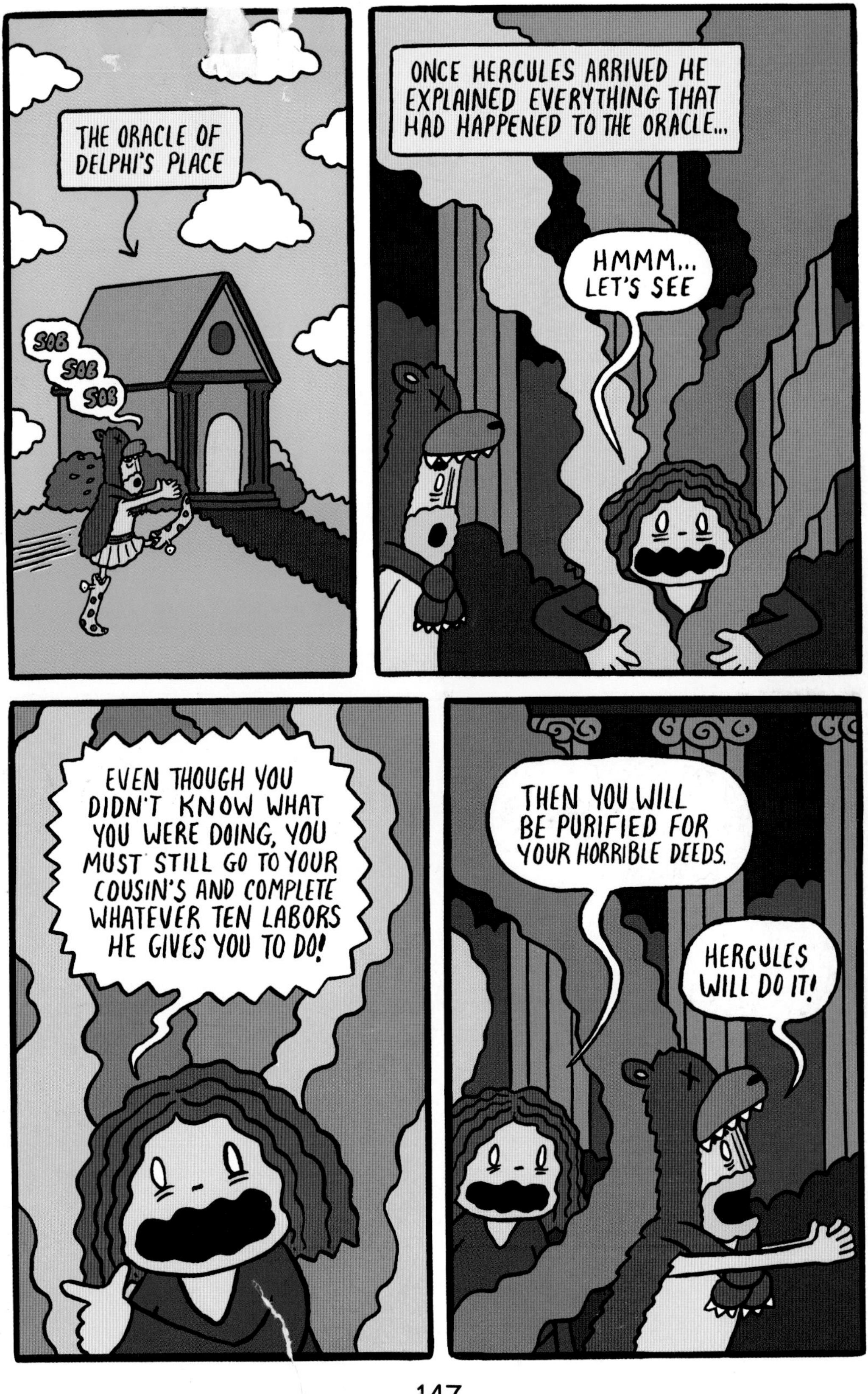
THE ORACLE OF DELPHI'S PLACE
SOB
SOB
SOB
ONCE HERCULES ARRIVED HE EXPLAINED EVERYTHING THAT HAD HAPPENED TO THE ORACLE...
HMMM... LET'S SEE
EVEN THOUGH YOU DIDN'T KNOW WHAT YOU WERE DOING, YOU MUST STILL GO TO YOUR COUSIN'S AND COMPLETE WHATEVER TEN LABORS HE GIVES YOU TO DO!
THEN YOU WILL BE PURIFIED FOR YOUR HORRIBLE DEEDS.
HERCULES WILL DO IT!

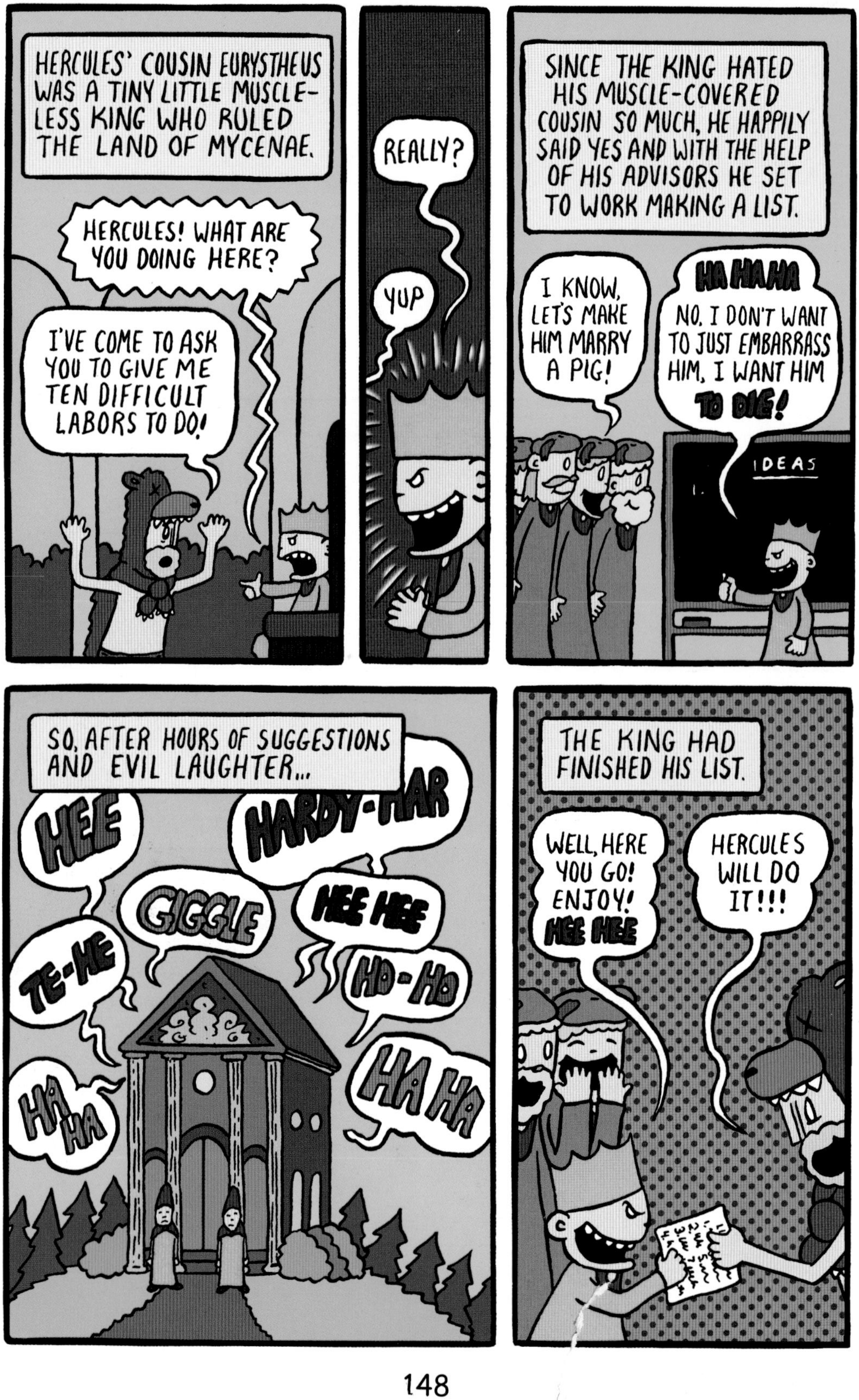
HERCULES' COUSIN EURYSTHEUS WAS A TINY LITTLE MUSCLE-LESS KING WHO RULED THE LAND OF MYCENAE.
HERCULES! WHAT ARE YOU DOING HERE?
I'VE COME TO ASK YOU TO GIVE ME TEN DIFFICULT LABORS TO DO!
REALLY?
YUP
SINCE THE KING HATED HIS MUSCLE-COVERED COUSIN SO MUCH, HE HAPPILY SAID YES AND WITH THE HELP OF HIS ADVISORS HE SET TO WORK MAKING A LIST.
I KNOW, LET'S MAKE HIM MARRY A PIG!
HA HA HA
NO, I DON'T WANT TO JUST EMBARRASS HIM, I WANT HIM TO DIE!
IDEAS
SO, AFTER HOURS OF SUGGESTIONS AND EVIL LAUGHTER...
HEE
HARDY-HAR
GIGGLE
HEE HEE
TE-HE
HO-HO
HA HA
HA HA
THE KING HAD FINISHED HIS LIST.
WELL, HERE YOU GO! ENJOY! HEE HEE
HERCULES WILL DO IT!!!

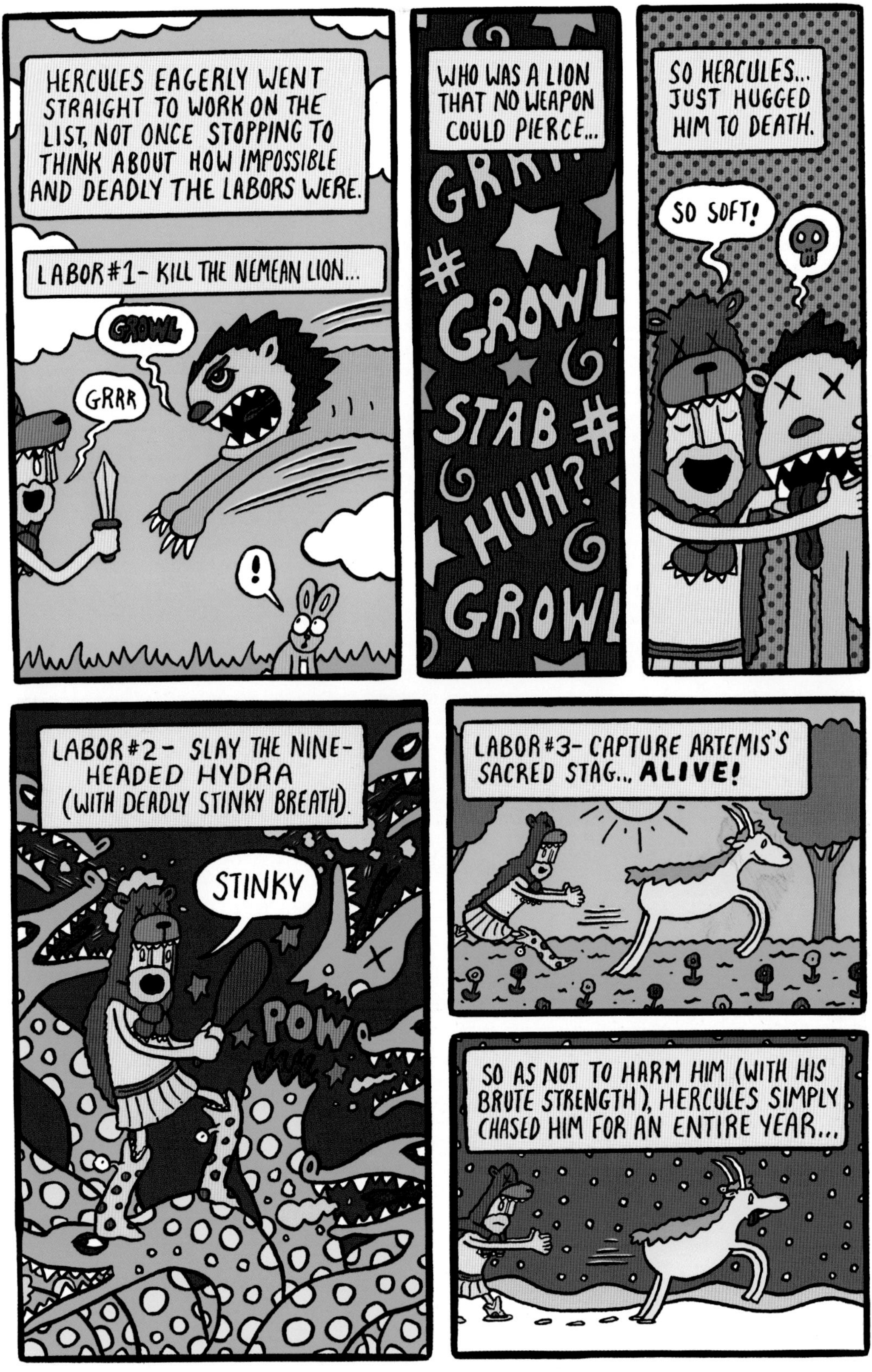
HERCULES EAGERLY WENT STRAIGHT TO WORK ON THE LIST, NOT ONCE STOPPING TO THINK ABOUT HOW IMPOSSIBLE AND DEADLY THE LABORS WERE.
LABOR #1- KILL THE NEMEAN LION...
GROWL
GRRR
!
WHO WAS A LION THAT NO WEAPON COULD PIERCE...
GRRR
#
GROWL
STAB
#
HUH?
GROWL
SO HERCULES... JUST HUGGED HIM TO DEATH.
SO SOFT!
LABOR #2- SLAY THE NINE-HEADED HYDRA (WITH DEADLY STINKY BREATH).
STINKY
POW
LABOR #3- CAPTURE ARTEMIS'S SACRED STAG... **ALIVE!**
SO AS NOT TO HARM HIM (WITH HIS BRUTE STRENGTH), HERCULES SIMPLY CHASED HIM FOR AN ENTIRE YEAR...

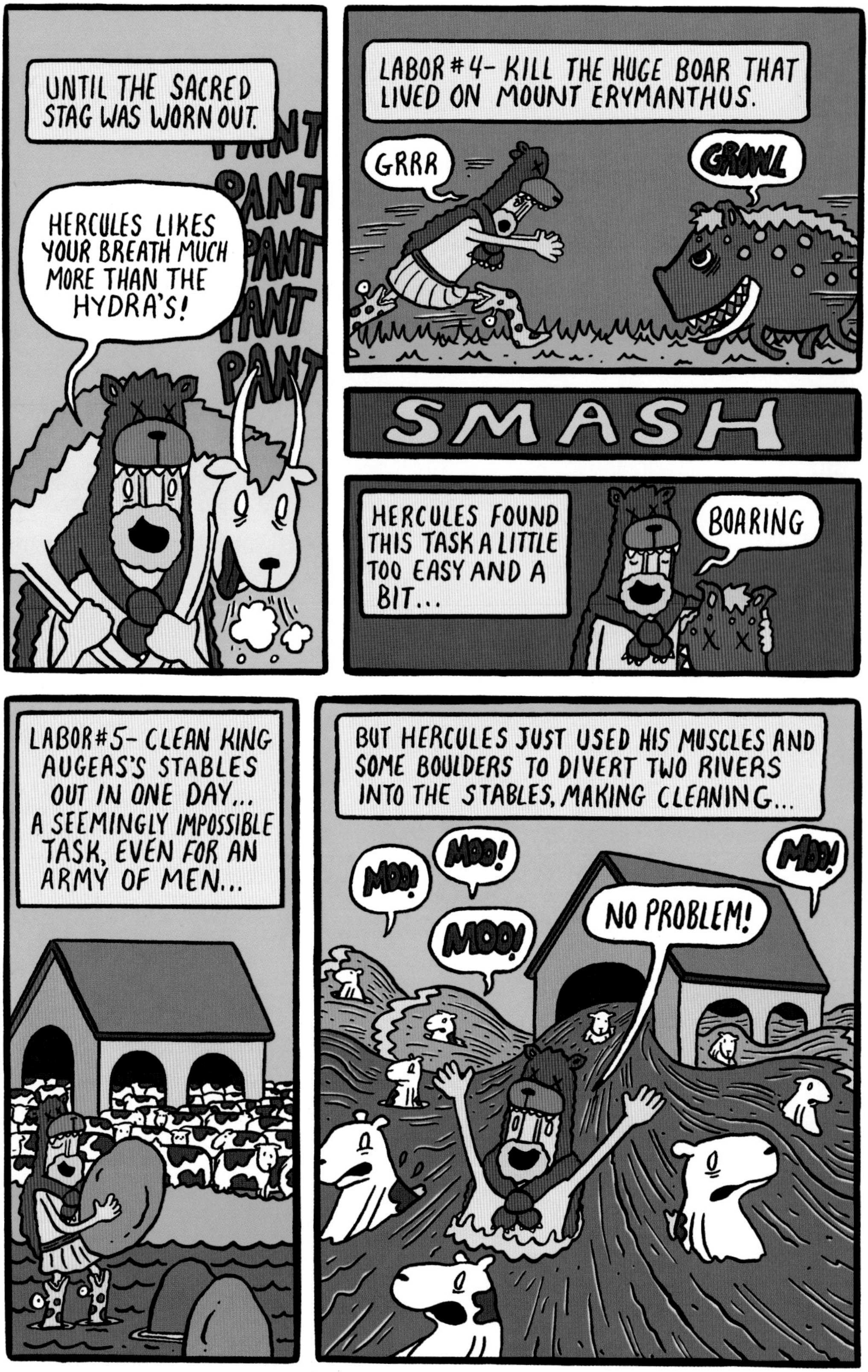
UNTIL THE SACRED STAG WAS WORN OUT.
PANT
PANT
PANT
PANT
HERCULES LIKES YOUR BREATH MUCH MORE THAN THE HYDRA'S!
LABOR #4- KILL THE HUGE BOAR THAT LIVED ON MOUNT ERYMANTHUS.
GRRR
GROWL
SMASH
HERCULES FOUND THIS TASK A LITTLE TOO EASY AND A BIT...
BOARING
LABOR#5- CLEAN KING AUGEAS'S STABLES OUT IN ONE DAY... A SEEMINGLY IMPOSSIBLE TASK, EVEN FOR AN ARMY OF MEN...
BUT HERCULES JUST USED HIS MUSCLES AND SOME BOULDERS TO DIVERT TWO RIVERS INTO THE STABLES, MAKING CLEANING...
MOO!
MOO!
MOO!
MOO!
NO PROBLEM!

LABOR #6- SAVE THE TOWN OF STYMPHALUS FROM THE THOUSANDS UPON THOUSANDS OF DANGEROUS STYMPHALIAN BIRDS.

SQUAWK

HERCULES *IS* GOING TO NEED MORE ARROWS!

SQ SQUAW SQUAR SQUAWK S SQUA SQUAWK SQUAW SQUAWK SQUAW

ALL DONE!

LABOR #7- CAPTURE A HUGE WILD AND CRAZY BULL FROM CRETE!

HERC-A-DOODLE-DOO I GOT YOU!

LABOR #8- DEFEAT THE EVIL KING DIOMEDES OF THRACE AND RETRIEVE HIS MAN-EATING HORSES.

ARRR

CRASH BOOM WHAM POW

HERCULES HOPES YOU GUYS ARE HUNGRY!

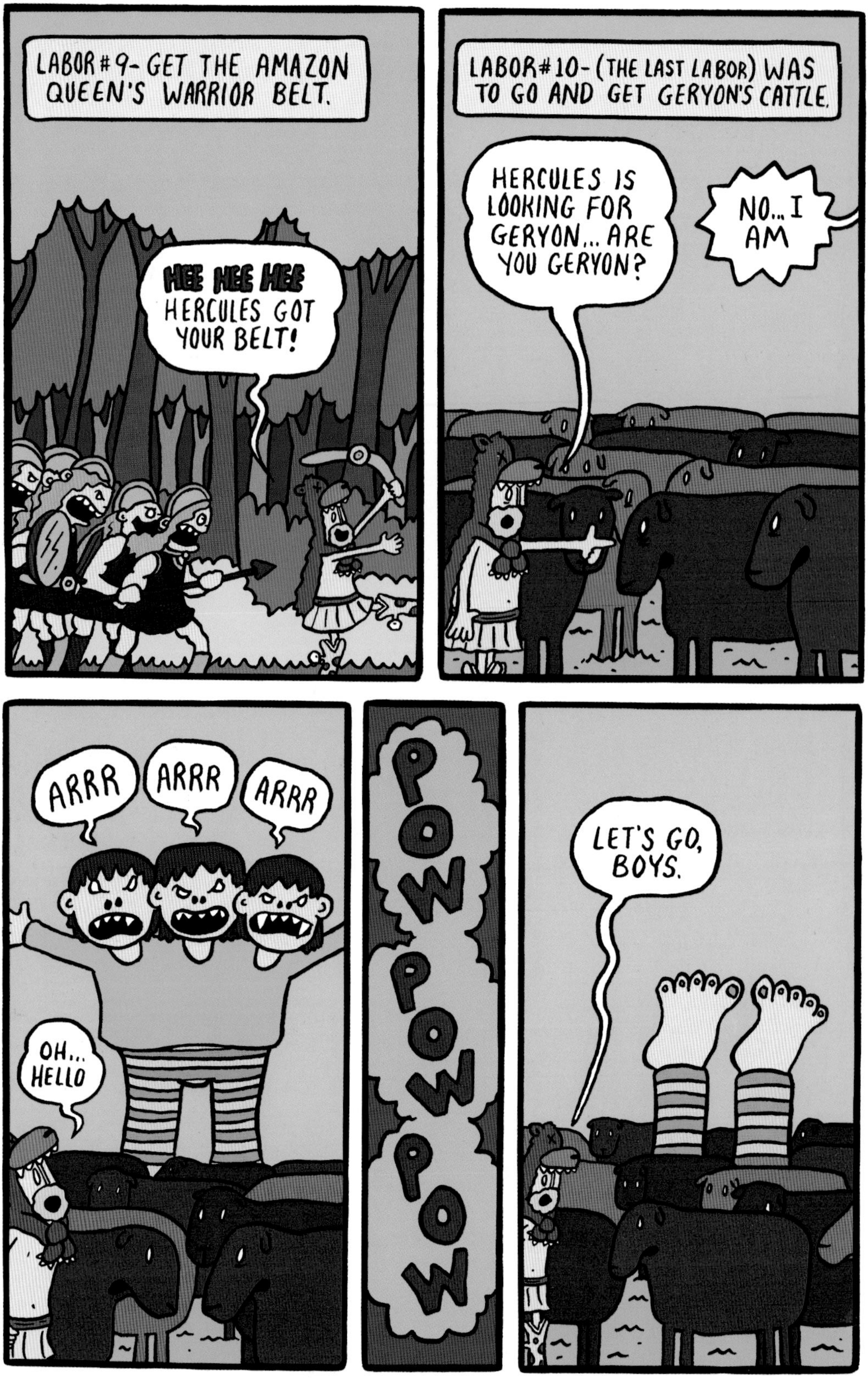
LABOR # 9- GET THE AMAZON QUEEN'S WARRIOR BELT.
HEE HEE HEE HERCULES GOT YOUR BELT!
LABOR#10- (THE LAST LABOR) WAS TO GO AND GET GERYON'S CATTLE.
HERCULES IS LOOKING FOR GERYON... ARE YOU GERYON?
NO... I AM
ARRR
ARRR
ARRR
OH... HELLO
POW POW POW POW
LET'S GO, BOYS.

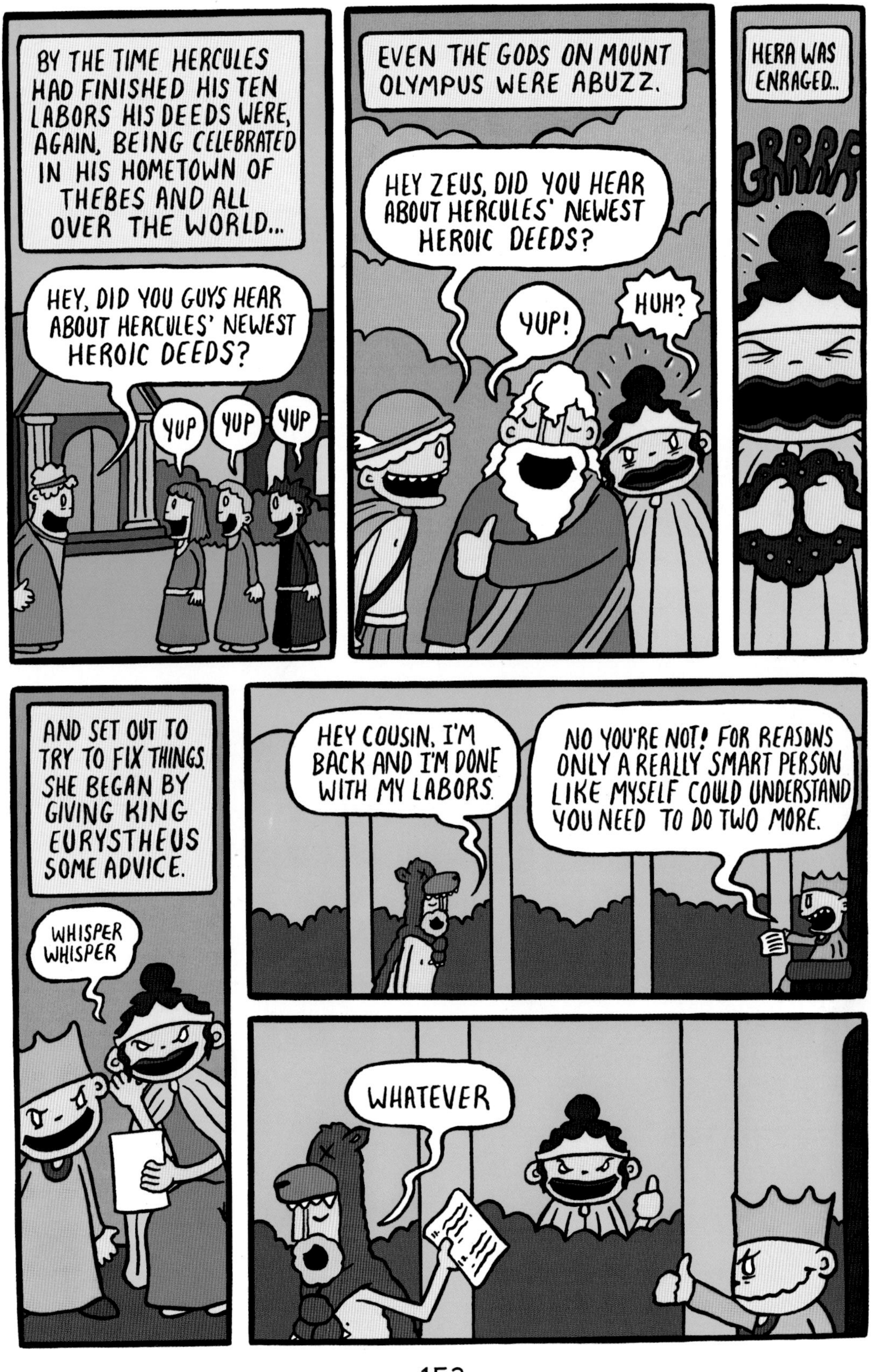

BY THE TIME HERCULES HAD FINISHED HIS TEN LABORS HIS DEEDS WERE, AGAIN, BEING CELEBRATED IN HIS HOMETOWN OF THEBES AND ALL OVER THE WORLD...
HEY, DID YOU GUYS HEAR ABOUT HERCULES' NEWEST HEROIC DEEDS?
YUP
YUP
YUP
EVEN THE GODS ON MOUNT OLYMPUS WERE ABUZZ.
HEY ZEUS, DID YOU HEAR ABOUT HERCULES' NEWEST HEROIC DEEDS?
YUP!
HUH?
HERA WAS ENRAGED...
GRRRR
AND SET OUT TO TRY TO FIX THINGS. SHE BEGAN BY GIVING KING EURYSTHEUS SOME ADVICE.
WHISPER WHISPER
HEY COUSIN, I'M BACK AND I'M DONE WITH MY LABORS.
NO YOU'RE NOT! FOR REASONS ONLY A REALLY SMART PERSON LIKE MYSELF COULD UNDERSTAND YOU NEED TO DO TWO MORE.
WHATEVER

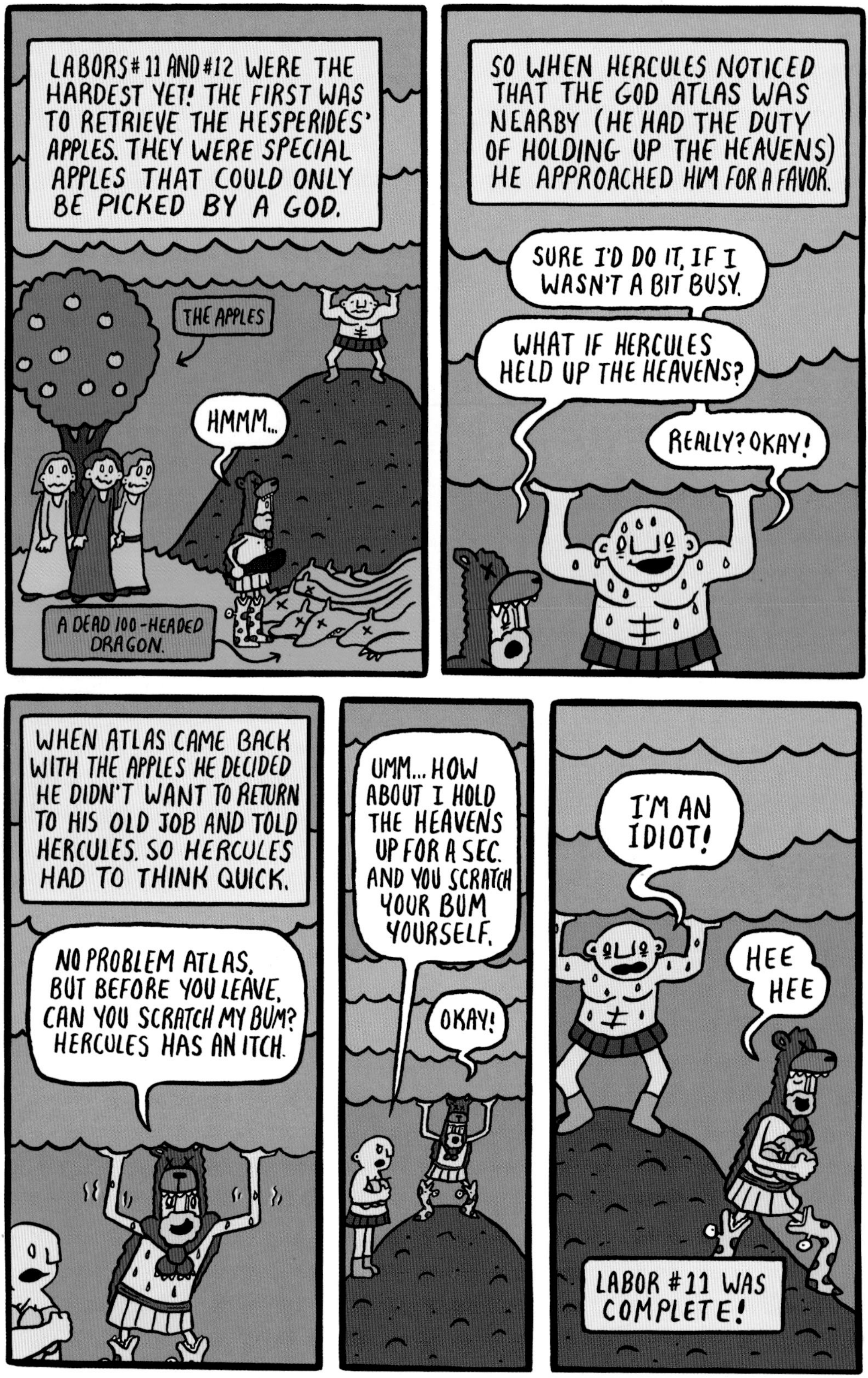
LABORS #11 AND #12 WERE THE HARDEST YET! THE FIRST WAS TO RETRIEVE THE HESPERIDES' APPLES. THEY WERE SPECIAL APPLES THAT COULD ONLY BE PICKED BY A GOD.
THE APPLES
HMMM...
A DEAD 100-HEADED DRAGON.
SO WHEN HERCULES NOTICED THAT THE GOD ATLAS WAS NEARBY (HE HAD THE DUTY OF HOLDING UP THE HEAVENS) HE APPROACHED HIM FOR A FAVOR.
SURE I'D DO IT, IF I WASN'T A BIT BUSY.
WHAT IF HERCULES HELD UP THE HEAVENS?
REALLY? OKAY!
WHEN ATLAS CAME BACK WITH THE APPLES HE DECIDED HE DIDN'T WANT TO RETURN TO HIS OLD JOB AND TOLD HERCULES. SO HERCULES HAD TO THINK QUICK.
NO PROBLEM ATLAS, BUT BEFORE YOU LEAVE, CAN YOU SCRATCH MY BUM? HERCULES HAS AN ITCH.
UMM... HOW ABOUT I HOLD THE HEAVENS UP FOR A SEC. AND YOU SCRATCH YOUR BUM YOURSELF.
OKAY!
I'M AN IDIOT!
HEE HEE
LABOR #11 WAS COMPLETE!

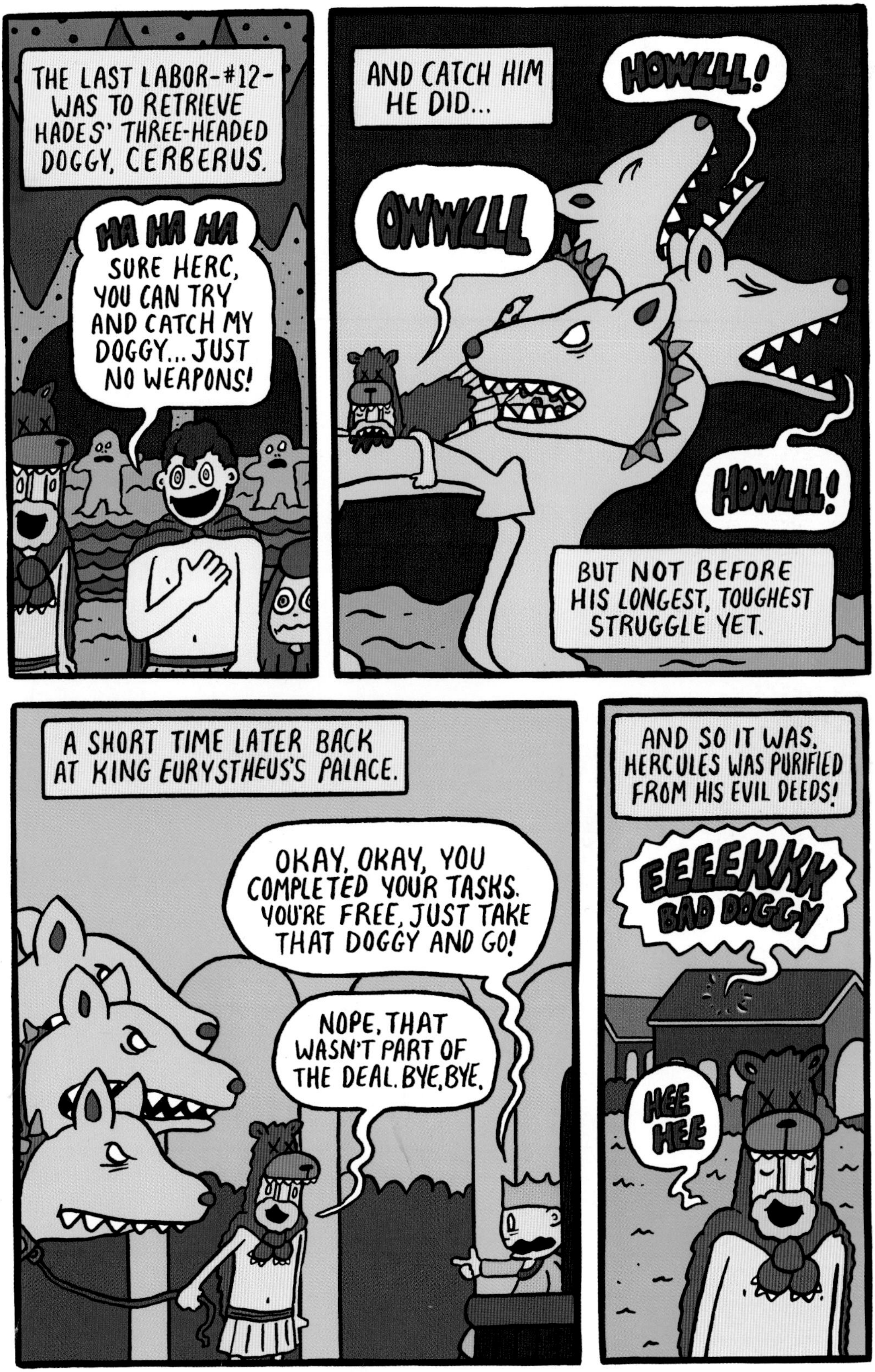
THE LAST LABOR-#12- WAS TO RETRIEVE HADES' THREE-HEADED DOGGY, CERBERUS.
HA HA HA SURE HERC, YOU CAN TRY AND CATCH MY DOGGY... JUST NO WEAPONS!
AND CATCH HIM HE DID...
HOWLLL!
OWWLLL
HOWLLL!
BUT NOT BEFORE HIS LONGEST, TOUGHEST STRUGGLE YET.
A SHORT TIME LATER BACK AT KING EURYSTHEUS'S PALACE.
OKAY, OKAY, YOU COMPLETED YOUR TASKS. YOU'RE FREE, JUST TAKE THAT DOGGY AND GO!
NOPE, THAT WASN'T PART OF THE DEAL. BYE, BYE.
AND SO IT WAS. HERCULES WAS PURIFIED FROM HIS EVIL DEEDS!
EEEEKKK BAD DOGGY
HEE HEE

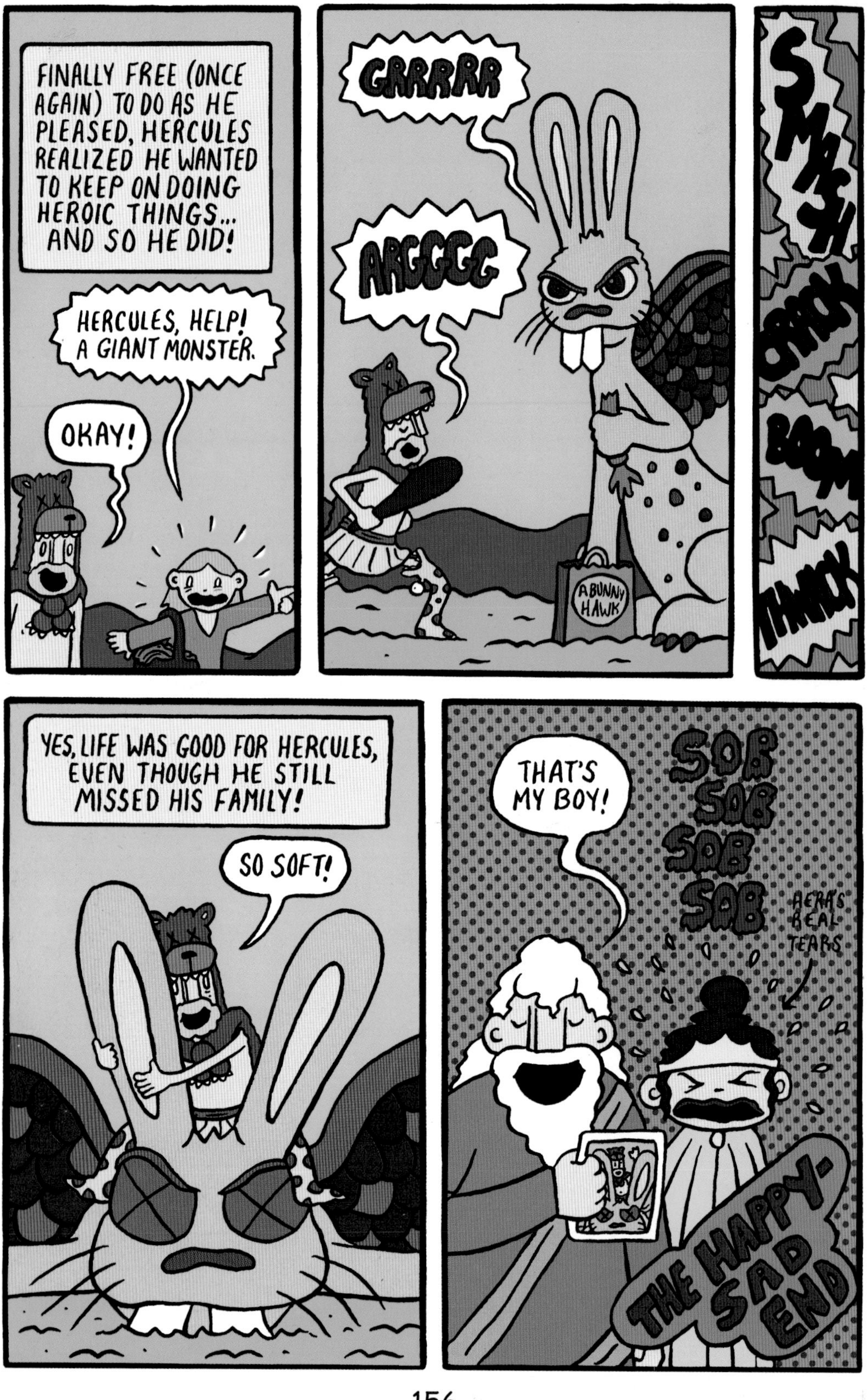

FINALLY FREE (ONCE AGAIN) TO DO AS HE PLEASED, HERCULES REALIZED HE WANTED TO KEEP ON DOING HEROIC THINGS... AND SO HE DID!
HERCULES, HELP! A GIANT MONSTER.
OKAY!
GRRRRR
ARGGGG
A BUNNY HAWK
SMASH
BOOM
THWACK
YES, LIFE WAS GOOD FOR HERCULES, EVEN THOUGH HE STILL MISSED HIS FAMILY!
SO SOFT!
THAT'S MY BOY!
SOB SOB SOB SOB
HERA'S REAL TEARS
THE HAPPY-SAD END

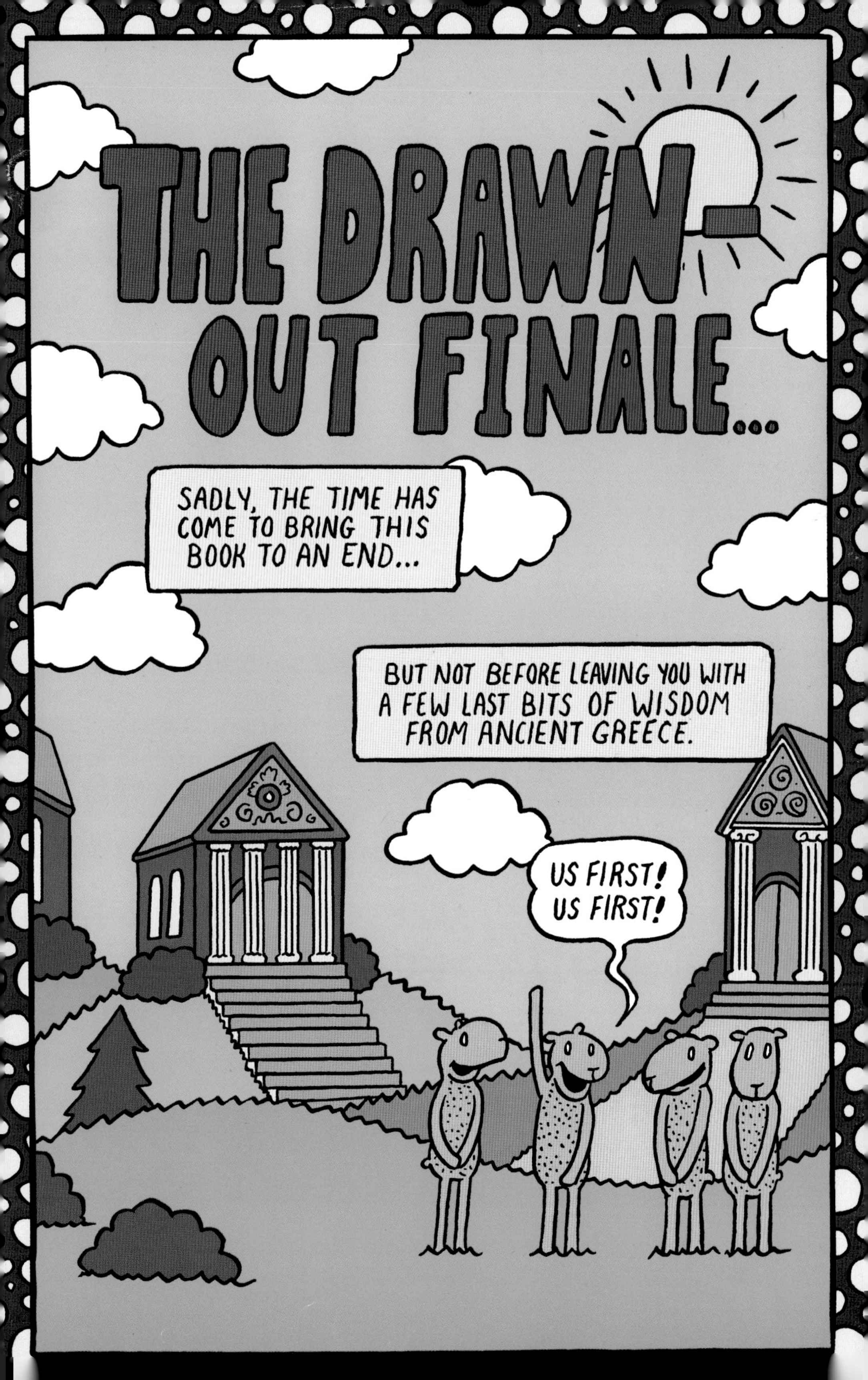
THE DRAWN-OUT FINALE...
SADLY, THE TIME HAS COME TO BRING THIS BOOK TO AN END...
BUT NOT BEFORE LEAVING YOU WITH A FEW LAST BITS OF WISDOM FROM ANCIENT GREECE.
US FIRST! US FIRST!

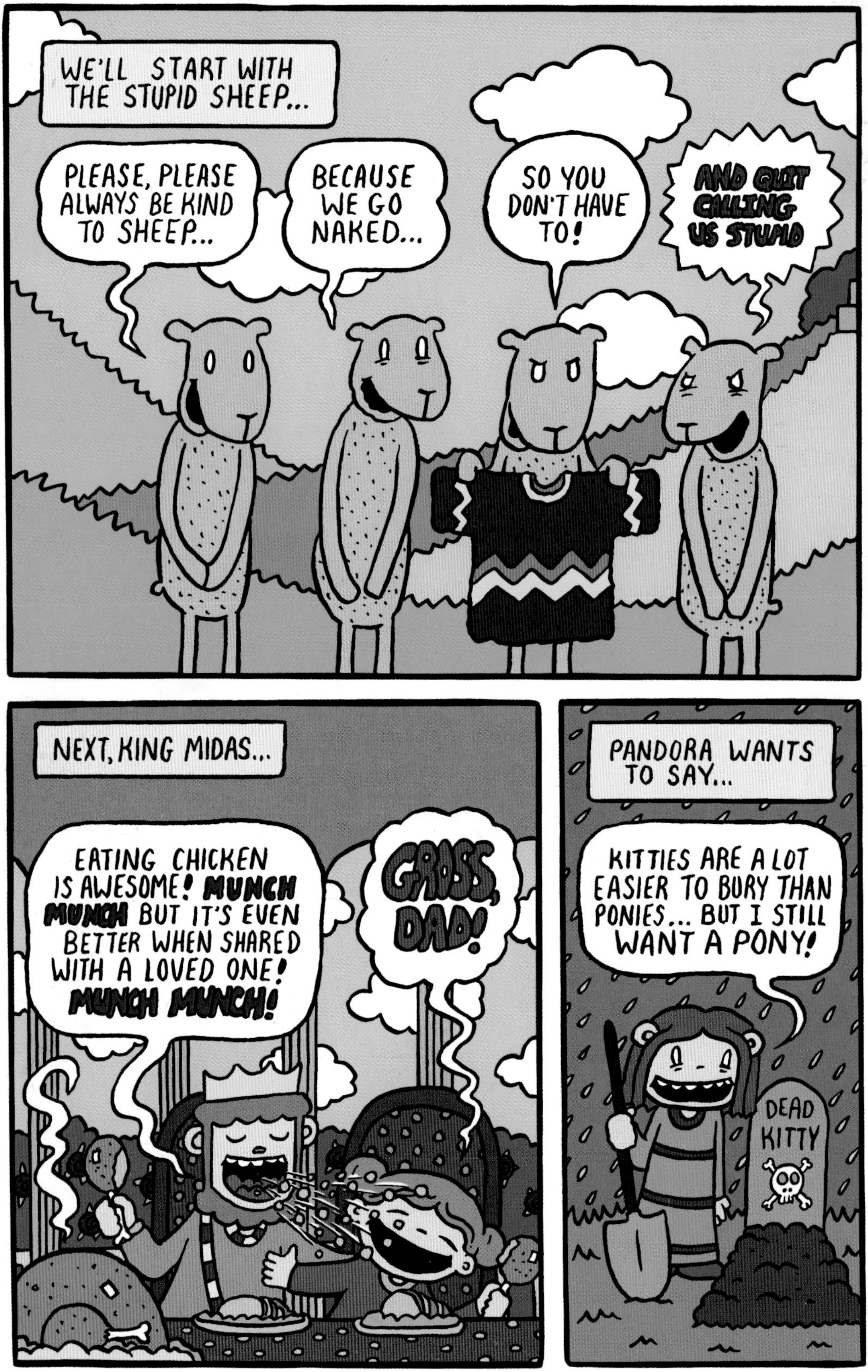
WE'LL START WITH THE STUPID SHEEP...
PLEASE, PLEASE ALWAYS BE KIND TO SHEEP...
BECAUSE WE GO NAKED...
SO YOU DON'T HAVE TO!
AND QUIT CALLING US STUPID
NEXT, KING MIDAS...
EATING CHICKEN IS AWESOME! MUNCH MUNCH BUT IT'S EVEN BETTER WHEN SHARED WITH A LOVED ONE! MUNCH MUNCH!
GROSS, DAD!
PANDORA WANTS TO SAY...
KITTIES ARE A LOT EASIER TO BURY THAN PONIES... BUT I STILL WANT A PONY!
DEAD KITTY

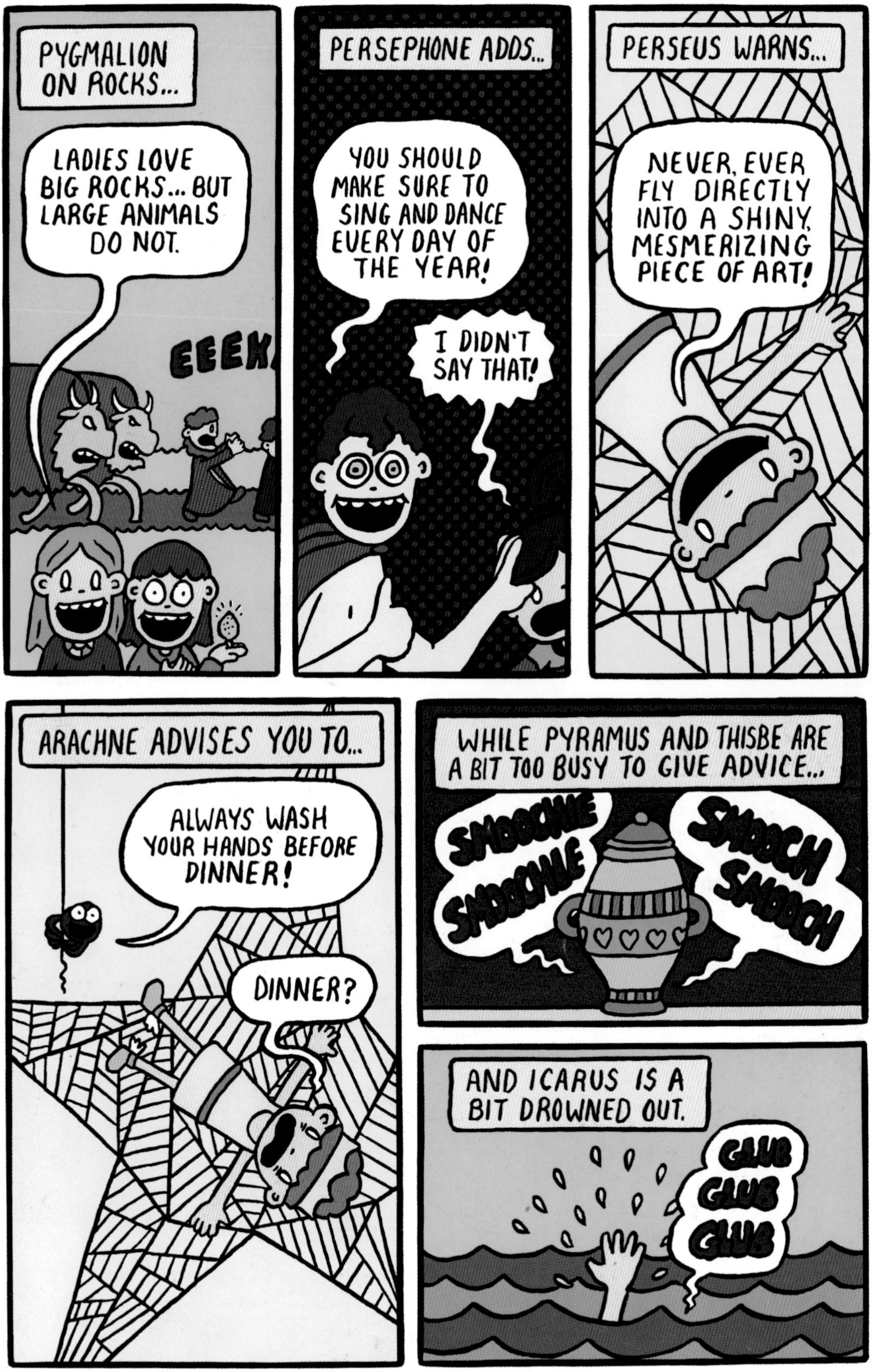
PYGMALION ON ROCKS...
LADIES LOVE BIG ROCKS... BUT LARGE ANIMALS DO NOT.
EEEK
PERSEPHONE ADDS...
YOU SHOULD MAKE SURE TO SING AND DANCE EVERY DAY OF THE YEAR!
I DIDN'T SAY THAT!
PERSEUS WARNS...
NEVER, EVER FLY DIRECTLY INTO A SHINY, MESMERIZING PIECE OF ART!
ARACHNE ADVISES YOU TO...
ALWAYS WASH YOUR HANDS BEFORE DINNER!
DINNER?
WHILE PYRAMUS AND THISBE ARE A BIT TOO BUSY TO GIVE ADVICE...
SMOOCHIE SMOOCHIE
SMOOCH SMOOCH
AND ICARUS IS A BIT DROWNED OUT.
GLUB GLUB GLUB

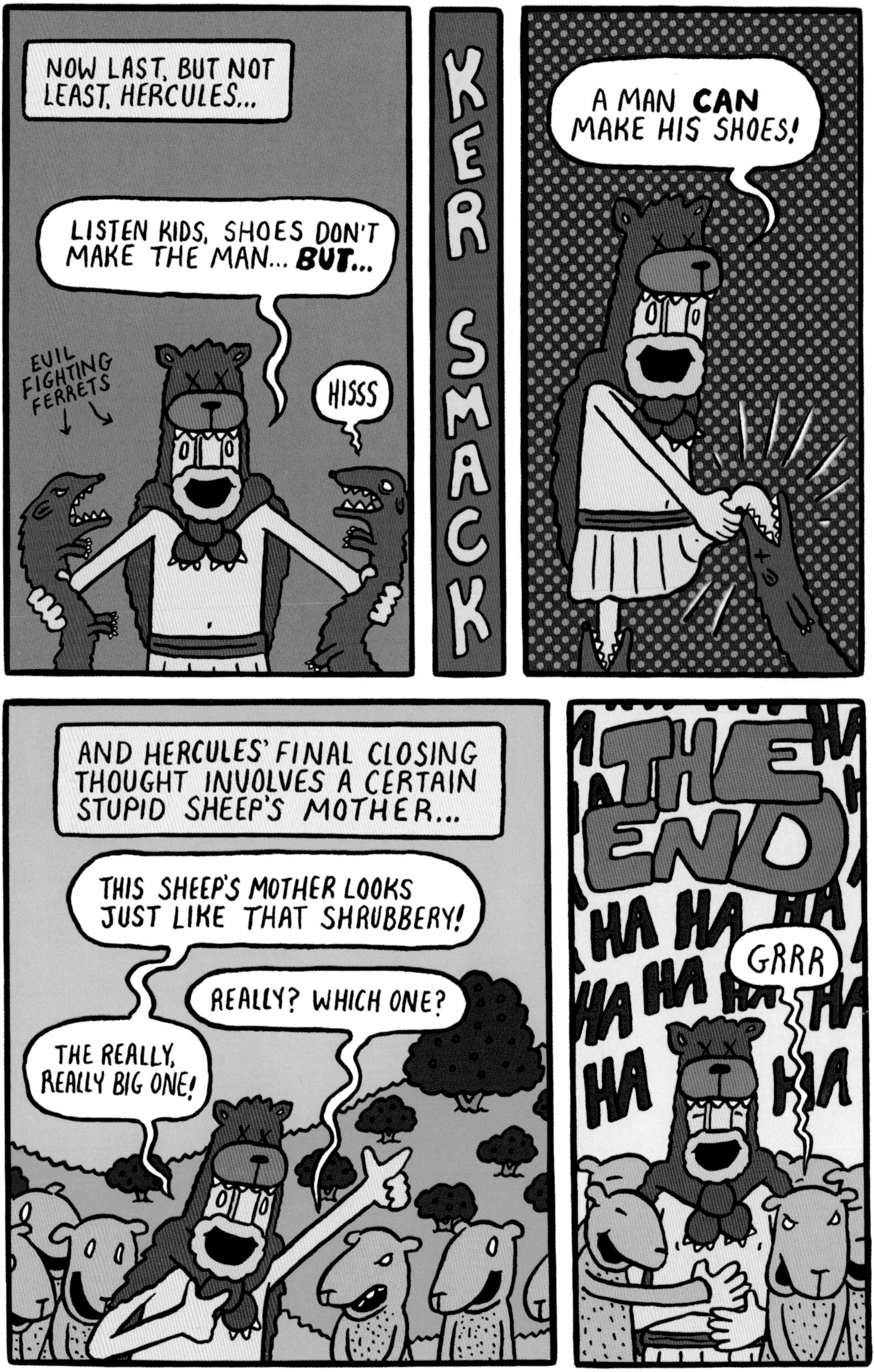
NOW LAST, BUT NOT LEAST, HERCULES...
LISTEN KIDS, SHOES DON'T MAKE THE MAN... **BUT...**
EVIL FIGHTING FERRETS
HISSS
KER SMACK
A MAN **CAN** MAKE HIS SHOES!
AND HERCULES' FINAL CLOSING THOUGHT INVOLVES A CERTAIN STUPID SHEEP'S MOTHER...
THIS SHEEP'S MOTHER LOOKS JUST LIKE THAT SHRUBBERY!
REALLY? WHICH ONE?
THE REALLY, REALLY BIG ONE!
THE END
HA HA HA
HA HA
HA
GRRR